IAN GRAHAM   MARC A HUTCHINS

WWW.WHOISSTELLAR.COM

Copyright © 2020 by Ian M Graham & Marc A Hutchins

Stellar logos & illustrations by Wes Talbott

Chapter illustrations by Stahlie Calvin
Additional artwork by Robert Williams
Cover design by Marc A Hutchins
Book design by Polgarus Studios

ISBN-13: 978-1-7360357-1-9   ISBN 10: 1-7360357-1-9

Published in the United States by Avendale Entertainment

FIRST PAPERBACK EDITION – NOVEMBER 2020

TO OUR DAUGHTERS –

HANNAH, SARA, KINLEY, RACHAEL, SARAH, REBECKA,
ANNAH, TALAH, AND HANNAH

– WHO SAYS GIRLS CAN"T FIGHT?

- MARC & IAN

CHAPTER 1

The shrill screech of a stray cat startled fifteen-year-old Patrick Newell. He turned as it hissed in the darkness of the alley, casting an eye over the gloomy urbanity behind him as he tried to remind himself why he'd chosen this shortcut. He stuffed his hands in his pockets and shrugged his coat higher onto his shoulders as though it could hide him. *Let's just get this over with.*

He walked on. Exiting the alley, he looked from side to side at the multistory brick tenements with their arched windows and steel fire escapes. To calm his nerves, he entertained memories of walking the same streets with his parents years earlier–shops–theaters–ethnic restaurants. But the city had changed over the years. It had become more dangerous and the businesses had fled.

He chose a direction. The in-window heating units in many of the apartments hummed as he made his way down the sidewalk, pulling his quilted coat even closer as a biting wind carried the musty smell of recent rains and the odor of the few remaining take out joints. Steam rose from grates in the concrete and the street lights flickered causing his shadow to appear and disappear in random places.

"Hey, mister. Gimme a dollar."

A shaggy blond-haired man wearing a grungy tank top and sagging red jeans stood from a crate near the mouth of an alley.

"C'mon. How 'bout it? Just one dollar."

Patrick crossed the street and glanced back to be sure the man hadn't followed him. The bum stood with his hand out but hadn't moved far.

"What are ya, hard o' hearing? You don't speak English?"

Patrick ignored him and walked on intently. *Just two more blocks.* A street light flickered and a cast shadow retreated. He looked to the rooftop above him. *Hmm. Nothing.* He quickened his pace. The southeast side wasn't a place to linger.

"Hey. Didn't you hear the man?"

Patrick stopped in his tracks. A man wearing a yellow #43 basketball jersey and black board shorts stood in the center of the sidewalk, blocking his path.

"I–I don't want any trouble."

"Oh, that's okay. We don't want any trouble either. We just need a little money."

"Yeah. Just some spare change." A third guy in a leather jacket and durag stepped out of the alley behind the guy in the jersey.

"Sorry." Patrick turned to go back the way he'd come. "I don't have any–any money."

"Aww. That's too bad." The shaggy blond-haired man had

crossed the street and now stood blocking the way he'd come.

Patrick swallowed hard and took a tentative step into the street, backing away from the three thugs as they closed in. Panic rose through him, making his bones feel as though they were vibrating. *Ugh. Some shortcut, Patrick. Way to go.*

"Aren't you a little young to be out so late? Maybe we should walk you back to your mommy."

Patrick turned and ran.

"Get him!"

He kicked a soda can as he crossed the street and entered an alleyway. The can rattled across the coarse concrete and ricocheted off a brick wall. He felt it crunch beneath his shoe as he pounded over the pavement, his blood pumping so fast he could hear it.

"Get back here!"

Trash cans filled beyond the brim lined each side of the alley. Patrick turned and pulled one over, spilling used takeout containers that stunk of grease and plastic drawstring bags torn open by cats and rats.

He turned a corner and powered toward a stack of pallets and used tires leaning against a fence that divided an alley. Behind him, he heard the trash can clatter as it was kicked aside. He turned and looked. The thugs cleared the corner and stopped.

"Oh, you made us run. Now you're really gonna pay."

Patrick backed toward the dead end. Could he climb the pallets and step over the fence? The thugs were older and bigger. With a good head start, he'd be able to get away. He bolted to the side and jumped onto a two-high stack of tires, gripping the pallets above and pulling himself up. The uneven column of roughly-hewn boards wobbled beneath his weight. He stuck his arms out like a surfer to keep his balance and tried to turn toward the fence, but the slightest change sent the pallets forward. He leaned back to even the distribution of his weight and froze. What did he do now? He couldn't jump. A fall from this height would mean broken bones, not a clean getaway.

"Ohhh look at this. We got a monkey."

One of the thugs stepped onto the tires and reached for his foot.

"Let go!"

Patrick pulled away, feeling the cold air on his sweaty foot as his shoe came loose in the thug's hand. He spotted a fire escape. The ladder was a good ten feet from the ground, but he was already at least eight feet up. He jumped and grabbed it, nearly letting go as his weight pulled the spring-loaded ladder toward the ground. *Clank!* He regained his hold as it hit the ground, and scrambled up, reaching the first-floor landing and hoping he'd hear the ladder retreating to its upward position. Instead, he heard the sound of footsteps on the rungs below. The thugs were climbing after him.

He got to his feet and ran to the staircase, grimacing as he felt the sharp angles of the ribbed steel beneath his socked foot. He climbed the stairs and rounded the next landing. He peeked over the railing. Even with his movement slowed by pain and uneven footing he was a good ways ahead of the thugs, the closest of which had only just cleared the ladder. He pushed himself harder, his lungs on fire and his breath coming in gasps. He reached the fourth landing and looked up. *One more to go.* He turned onto the last staircase and pulled himself up by the railings as heavy footsteps on the metal landings below continued.

Patrick looked over the edge of the building onto the roof as he pulled himself up and hopped over. Industrial-sized air conditioning units dotted the roof. He dodged around one, trying to hide from view as he looked for an exit. The thugs wouldn't dare follow him inside, would they? Inside he could draw attention to himself and other people would hear him. Inside he would be safe. He zigzagged around the units until he spotted a single doorway under a slanted roof at the opposite end. He took a relieved breath and ran to it, pushing the lever down and pulling at the same time. The latch didn't budge.

"No no no! C'mon!"

He tried it again and again, but it was locked from the inside. He turned and placed his back against the door.

"Uh oh." The jersey-wearing thug reached the edge of the roof and hopped up. "Look who's outta places to run."

Patrick looked from side to side at the nearby buildings. It was at least a fifteen-foot jump. Even with both shoes on and a sprinting start, he'd never jumped that far. He'd fall to his death for certain.

The last two thugs climbed over the edge of the roof and the three spread out, coming at him from different angles.

"What do you want? I don't have any money. I'm just–just a kid."

"We don't want your money anymore. Now we just want to hurt you."

Patrick ran to one side. It wasn't a planned run or even a conscious decision; it was just panic. Maybe he was faster. Maybe he could make it back to the fire escape and — he felt a powerful shove and his feet came out from under him. The world around him spun and he landed hard against the edge of the roof, his shoulder and neck taking the brunt of the impact.

"Ohhh yeah! That's what I'm talking about." The hoods laughed and slapped hands.

Patrick closed his eyes, pain ricocheting around his skull. He groaned and writhed, willing it to stop.

"Now we're havin' fun. Now we—"

"Don't you *men* have something better to do?"

The clear and authoritative voice registered unique in Patrick's ears. There was a pleasantry about it among the throaty growls of the thugs. A girl? When had a girl arrived on the roof? He opened one eye and then the other, looking about.

"What have we here boys?"

The thugs turned, their attention focused on something behind them. Patrick followed their gaze until his eyes settled on–he blinked. A petite, distinctly female shape stood next to the fire escape. He stared. Instead of a face, there was a dark hole created by a hood. And instead of the normal contours of a human body, he saw sharp angles created by some sort of armor. *Who*—

"Looks like two for one tonight."

"Why don't you boys run along before you hurt yourselves."

"Funny. You're the one who's gonna be hurtin'."

The thugs advanced and the shape moved, dodging a punch and countering the attack with a knee to the stomach and a chop to the neck. The shaggy blond thug collapsed and the shape returned to a neutral stance. She turned with the other thugs as they tried to surround her, her movements graceful and careful.

The jersey-wearing thug charged, attempting to grab her around the neck, but she ducked away and delivered a kick to the back of his knee, a kick to his side, and finally a kick to his face. Patrick watched in awe as the force of the attack spun the thug to the ground.

The shape returned again to a neutral stance. "Your turn, slick."

The leather jacket thug reached into his coat. "You're dead now!" With a mechanical click, he popped open a lever knife and charged, slashing and jabbing. The shape ducked and weaved, countering each attempt with smooth and evasive technique. When they reached the edge of the roof, she grabbed him at the wrist and punched a pressure point under his arm. He tried to move away from the pain, but she twisted his arm behind him, forcing him to drop the blade. She let go and he stumbled away. Pickingup the knife, shetossed it over the side of the roof. Patrick heard it clang repeatedly as it bounced down the fire escape.

The thug removed his leather jacket and bounced on the balls of his feet, raising his fists. He advanced with a right cross. The shape ducked and turned, grabbing his arm as she backed into him and dropped her weight, throwing him over her shoulder. He landed in a heap against the edge of the roof, his legs over his head, and a painful grimace on his face.

The shape straightened and looked at the fallen thugs. Two writhed painfully and one was out cold.

Patrick lifted himself into a sitting position against the edge of the roof as she approached.

She stopped a few feet from him. "Are you alright?"

He'd forgotten his pain. His mind was focused on her. Now that she was still and standing closer he could make out bits of dark red and a symbol that looked like a star. "You… you…"

CHAPTER 2

"… saved me."

Macy Davis smiled as she looked over Patrick Newell's shoulder. He was doing it again. He was daydreaming as he used a red ink pen to shade in a drawing of his crown creation; Stellar, a hooded crime-fighter who happened to be a girl—or a woman. Macy wasn't sure which.

A shadow fell over the desk and Macy tensed. "Hardly, Mr. Newell," a sandpaper-like voice said. Patrick shot upright in his seat. Macy cringed. "But I will most certainly fail you if you don't put away that silly drawing and pay attention."

"Yes, Spade—Mrs. Spader." Patrick closed his notebook and shoved it into a backpack at his feet, glancing in Macy's direction as he did.

Macy's heart leapt and her smile widened.

"And the same goes for you, Miss Davis. I know he's cute and probably even charming, but it won't matter in ten years' time when you're both unemployed because you're uneducated. So, wipe the puppy dog grin off your face and put your tongue back in your mouth."

A derisive snicker passed through the ninth grade science class as the teacher returned to the front of the classroom. Macy retreated into her seat, feeling like an ant beneath a magnifying glass.

"Now, as I was saying, your test tomorrow will be the final examination in our overview of Geology and will include questions on the dynamical, structural, physiological, and historical elements and the rock structures each produced. Spend your evening studying them and you'll do fine. Spend your evening doodling or canoodling and you won't."

Another snicker passed through the room and Macy felt even smaller. She glanced at Patrick, careful not to move anything but her eyes. His head was down and he was picking at a notch on his empty desk with the red ink pen.

A silent moment passed. Macy was afraid to even think about what was coming next. Wait, what time was—the bell rang and the sound of chairs scraping against tiled floors filled the room. Wishing to avoid the sideways glances and cocky sneers, Macy waited as most of the class filed past.

"Well, that was mortifying."

Macy looked up apologetically as her best friend, Keri Cartwright, arrived at her desk. "Tell me about it." She gathered her things and stood, watching as Patrick did the same and quickly left the room. She followed him out with her eyes, sighed, and shouldered her backpack as she walked with Keri toward the door of the dim basement classroom. They passed stacks of disused chairs and custodial equipment and climbed the stairway to the much better-lit ground floor. Macy turned for the exit.

"Uhh, this way." Keri motioned to a bathroom marked with a pink, dress-wearing silhouette that looked like something that would be found in an elementary school.

"Again?"

Macy looked down the hallway in the opposite direction as students filed toward the exit. If they hurried, they could make it onto the bus and have their choice of seats. If they waited they'd have to sit near the front and endure the childish pranks and guffaws of two dozen junior high schoolers.

"C'mon." Keri was off.

Macy sighed and followed, passing the pink silhouette as a few other girls exited, their sideways glances and small smiles saying they'd seen or just been told about what had happened in Spader's classroom. Nothing traveled faster at Alum Ridge High School than news of a freshman's embarrassment.

"Ugh." Keri fussed with her face in the mirror. "The lack of any natural light for half the day murders my skin tone."

Macy stood nearer to the entrance. She cared what she looked like, but not as much as Keri. To her, fashion was seventh-tenths comfort and three-tenths appearance. She stepped over to get a look at herself in the mirror. Who was she kidding? It was all about comfort. As hard as she tried to be more like Keri and the other girls around school, she just wasn't.

Her face was rounder than she would have liked and her chestnut brown hair was naturally straight. But not silky, smooth straight, just plain straight–boring straight. And her Alum Ridge Rangers t-shirt, faded jeans, and flip flops only added to the atrocity. She looked down. She hadn't even painted her toenails for a month—at least. The turquoise paint that had matched so perfectly with the sundress she had worn on the first day of school and had sworn was going to be the mark of a new her for high school was now as chipped and faded as the paint on the bathroom wall.

She frowned and looked back at Keri. Keri's black hair was short—probably mimicking a pop star or actress Macy hadn't even heard of yet—and had an on-purpose kind of chaos to it that accented her angular face and set off her big brown eyes. Her blouse, which was almost certainly homemade, was a soft pearl color that popped against her coffee-colored skin and had a small bow tied around her midsection to accentuate her slender waistline. Her designer jeans followed the natural curves of her legs in just such a way that the slight flare at the bottom punctuated her perfect size sevens and their matching, recent paint job.

Keri glanced away from her reflection to Macy's. "Oh, girl." She turned and gave a pouting face. "Why don't you just talk to him already? You've only known him since what—the first grade?"

"Kindergarten."

Keri turned back to the mirror. "Well, if that's not grounds for a relationship I don't know what is."

Macy groaned to herself. This is why she had kept her feelings a secret for the better part of six months. But Keri was right and she knew it. She had been torturing herself since the last semester of eighth grade when she had somewhat suddenly realized she found Patrick Newell attractive. His slightly oblivious smile, his brown eyes, and sandy blond hair had struck her in a way that had previously been reserved for Tylar Marsden, a dreamy, strapping English martial artist and actor she was sure to never meet.

"I know. But I freeze up and stutter like an idiot when I try. And you know I've tried."

Keri grinned as she put away her makeup. "If stuttering 'H—hi—Pa—Patrick' in the hallway as he passed by a few times counts as trying, sure. But if The Spade calling you out has one upside, it's that he now knows you were watching him."

"Oh, yeah. Great. Just what I need–to be thought of as some creepy stalker chick."

Keri held her hands up like a zombie and mimicked an Igor voice as they exited the bathroom. "H—hi—Pa—Patrick."

"Jerk." Macy elbowed her playfully. "Let's see you do better. Oh, that's right. I forgot. No one at Alum Ridge seems to be good enough for you."

"I'm waiting for the right man to come along."

"Ohhh a man, huh? I'm pretty sure that's illegal–for him."

"Shut up."

They entered the now-empty hall and made their way toward the next. Like most of the public schools built in the first half of the last century, the original interior of Alum Ridge was pretty unimaginative–three squares stacked on top of each other. Each floor had four hallways that surrounded a larger room such as the cafeteria, the library, and the old no longer used gymnasium in the basement. But the building had been added onto in decades past and now more hallways jutted this way and that. Macy wasn't sure she'd even seen the entire campus in the month she'd been there. They turned a corner into a hallway that was brimming with students desperately trying to squeeze between each other to get to the mass of lockers embedded two high down both sides.

"Those bathroom breaks really cut into my escape plan."

Keri flashed Macy a look as they waded into the melee. Every locker was taken. Some students kneeled, dodging elbows and feet as they leaned into their bottom units and others reached over them and tried with little success to flick their combinations on the antiquated padlocks that Macy was pretty sure had been recycled for every freshman class in the last fifty years. They stopped about halfway down when they arrived at their lockers, both top units and right next to each other by some odd stroke of luck.

Macy looked at the frenzy surrounding the two units. "Forget it. I'll just carry my books home."

"I know, right?"

They moved on, ducking, squeezing, weaving, and worming their way to the next hall.

"Excuse me. Pardon me. Sorry. Get out of the way. Thank you."

They reached the end of the hall and turned into the next, which would lead them through the atrium and past the main office to a side exit where the buses were waiting. This hall was less crowded and just maybe they had enough time to still get a good seat on the—a hollow, metallic slam echoed through the hallway behind them.

Keri startled and Macy stopped in her tracks as the sound faded and an eerie calm passed over the freshman hall. Macy looked at Keri and frowned. She knew the sound of a student being pushed against a locker. It was a common occurrence. She turned back into the hall as students shifted their attention to an alcove under the second-floor staircase. Leaning past a taller student, she could see three boys the size of living room armoires in letterman jackets cornering a smaller, skinnier student with glasses and a shock of dark, unkempt hair.

"It's tax day. Whaddaya got for us, Friddle?"

"Leave him alone." A heavyset, but muscular student with a blond afro, a pasty complexion, and a Property of Alum Ridge t-shirt stepped forward. "Please." His voice quivered.

The lettermen didn't even look at him. The closest one reached out and shoved him, his back hitting the lockers behind him and the slam echoing through the hall. "Stay out of this, 'bino."

The student backed down and looked apologetically at his friend.

Keri rolled her eyes. "Don't they ever get tired of—"

"Nope. Hold this."

Macy allowed her backpack to slide from her shoulder.

"Wait. Not agai—"

Macy moved forward as she felt Keri catch the backpack. "Hey." She arrived at the mouth of the alcove. "Leave him alone."

"What is with you people today?" The lead letterman turned around as the others kept the smaller student pinned against the locker. When he saw who had addressed him, his face fell. They'd been down this road before.

Macy crossed her arms. She knew the lettermen well. Zeke, Luke, and Trevor had been causing the same kind of trouble since elementary school and she'd called them out on it several times. Each time the same memory of three fifth grade tough guys with moussed hair walking around at recess aping 'I'm my brother's keeper' over and over passed through her mind and each time she fought a smile. They hadn't changed much.

The group's leader, Zeke, stepped forward. "Are you talking to us?"

Macy stood her ground. "Yeah. I'm talking to you. Just like I was last time. Do we really need to repeat this whole scene or can you guys just take a hint and get lost? Again."

Zeke laughed and turned to his friends. "You guys believe this? She still hasn't learned her lesson."

Macy lifted an eyebrow. "And what lesson would that be? I seem to recall you three cretins slinking back to the locker room last time. Too afraid to hit a girl?"

"Let Friddle go." Zeke turned back to her. "We'll catch up with him tomorrow."

The lettermen let go of the boy and he righted his glasses, grabbed his backpack, and hurried out of the alcove with his blond afroed buddy.

Zeke stepped up, his grin widening. "Well, alright, babe. You wanted our attention. You got it. I'm free to talk about our date now."

"Like I would ever." Macy uncrossed her arms and stared at Zeke. She had literally kicked his butt in the fifth grade. Back then that was all it had taken to send him and his buddies running. But they'd gotten bigger and bolder since. Would they actually fight her this time or would they back down when they realized she was serious?

Was she serious? Doubt crept into her mind. She had two black belts—one in Shotokan Ryu and the other in Budo Taijutsu—and had always been the kind of person who stood up for others. In her experience bullies were cowards. Few if any of them would actually stand and fight when confronted. Were Zeke, Luke, and Trevor the exception? Would fighting Zeke be different from the padded sparring she'd done in martial arts classes since she was six?

Zeke raised his fists.

A chorus of disapproving grumbles came from the hallway behind Macy. Though the world had largely left chivalry behind, Zeke had overstepped an invisible boundary. He and his cronies could beat up on smaller and younger boys, but girls had always been spared. Instead, girls got lewd comments, suggestive gestures, and vile rumors spread about them. Macy wasn't sure who had it worse.

Zeke kept his fists up, his cronies egging him on.

"Get her."

"Hit her."

"Do it."

"*Don't* do it."

The last voice came from behind Macy and was deeper, older, and more forceful than the others. Zeke looked past her and lowered his fists, melting back into his buddies as he did. Deputy Newell—the School Resource Officer—had arrived.

"Macy. Keri. I heard someone fall or something. Everything okay down here, girls?"

Macy turned to see a serious-looking man in a brown and tan uniform standing in the hallway entrance. His hair was graying, but his face was familiar. There was a definite family resemblance. Macy's frown disappeared. "Oh, sure, Deputy Newell. Just another annoying encounter of the jerk kind."

"C'mon, Macy," Keri said. "We're gonna miss the bus."

Macy realized Keri had moved up next to her and was still holding her backpack. "Yeah. Okay." She could feel Keri's eyes on her as they made their way out of the alcove and down the main hallway, passing glass display cases with sporadic trophies and team photos.

"So, what was that?"

"What was what?"

"Uhh–did I just imagine that whole low budget action flick back there?"

Macy frowned.

"I mean seriously, Mace. What's up with you this year? You're taking on these idiots all the time now. You're never going to stop them from beating up on everyone. It's just part of what our society calls 'high school.'" Keri made air quotes with her fingers and rolled her eyes.

Macy sighed. "I know. But doesn't it make you mad? People around here are having enough problems without them making things harder. Don't you wish someone could stop them?"

"Of course I do. But it's just one of those things. There's been bullies since–I don't know–since David took on Goliath or something."

"Yeah. Well, I don't know why the administration puts up with it. That makes me madder than anything."

"It's called selective hearing."

"Must affect the eyes, too."

"Sure does. Zeke and his lackeys are Alum Ridge's first chance at a winning football season since—well, since they opened the school.

Coach Rigby isn't about to let a slew of wedgies and bruises get in the way of that."

"Yeah. Well, you see what I mean about the administration. Newell didn't even bother to investigate what was happening. But he knew. They all know what Zeke and his goons get up to."

"How was he supposed to know anything was wrong with the way you were acting? Oh, sure, Deputy Newell." Keri fake swooned. "Looking forward to the wedding, dad."

"Shut up." Macy elbowed her.

"Well, it's true. That's your future father-in-law. If you ever get up the nerve to actually speak to his son anyways."

"Can we change the subject, please? We've been over this."

"Why? You don't seem to have a problem being your usual action figure self around everyone else. Why's Patrick so different?"

"I don't know. He's like—like my kryptonite or something."

"Yeah. Well—"

"Nice blouse by the way."

"You likes?" Keri turned and modeled the pearl-colored chiffon-like sleeveless. "It's 100% Cartwright & Co."

"Yeah." Macy had no idea how Keri did it. Besides makeup, gossip, and a tabloid magazine called ReNOWn, Keri's passion was designing her own fashions. Since the seventh grade, she had imagined, sketched, and sewn at least three dozen garments that looked as though they could compete with anything on the shelves at the mall. "When are you going to make me something?"

They arrived at a row of red-framed glass doors that marked the side entrance. Keri turned back as they filed through and the stale air of the aged building changed into heavy diesel fumes from the row of waiting buses. "When you go out with Patrick. I'll line it with lead."

Macy rolled her eyes. "Lead repelled X-Ray vision. Not kryptonite."

"Whatever."

CHAPTER 3

Macy climbed aboard the bus and made eye contact with the driver. "Hi, John."

"Heya, Macy. Keri." The middle-aged, Santa-looking man smiled cheerily.

Macy topped the steps and looked to the back. Every seat was full. She sighed and fell into a seat two back from the driver that was occupied only by a skinny boy with coke bottle glasses. She scooted as far over as she could without touching him. Keri sat next to her, barely able to fit on what was left of the seat. *Ahhh-choo!* The boy sneezed without covering his face. Macy cringed as he wiped his nose on his sleeve and looked at her apologetically.

"Sowwy. I'm not feering bery good today."

Macy turned away. Just what she needed; a cold from an uncouth sixth grader. She watched as John looked into his rearview mirror, closed the door, and shifted the bus into gear. Seconds later, they were rolling away from the school, fifth or sixth in a long line of buses that would leave the parking lot and disperse in various directions throughout the Greater Avendale suburb of Port Saint Dominic, the third-largest city in the American Midwest.

Macy kept her face turned away from her sniffling neighbor as the bus rounded the back of the school and made for the exit closest to her neighborhood. She watched through the window as they passed the cluster of imposing, penitentiary-like buildings. Like most of the schools in the burgeoning suburbs of Port Saint Dominic, the student body had outgrown Alum Ridge by nearly two to one. Already the campus had been added onto so many times Macy wasn't sure what was originally there and what wasn't and still to meet the ever-increasing demand, classes were being held in trailers adjacent to the main building and in carefully cordoned off areas of the labyrinth-like basement that had once been used for storage in the industrial era school.

They approached the rear entrance and every head in the bus looked up and out. Just outside of the wrought iron gates that blocked access to the parking area at night was a large wreath and a picture of a blonde girl with braces. Surrounding the wreath and placed along the brick knee wall that bordered the entire property were candles, smaller wreaths, posters, drawings, cards, and stuffed animals that had been left by family, friends, and other well-wishers. The students craned their necks as the bus passed the site, which seemed to grow every day. The memorial was dedicated to Brittany Crumb, a sophomore at Alum Ridge who had gone missing two weeks earlier and who had last been seen standing on the sidewalk just outside of the rear gates.

Keri made eye contact with Macy and frowned. "They still haven't found her, have they?"

Though Brittany was older than they were and had started Alum Ridge a year sooner, they still knew her from Junior High. Brittany was the kind of person who knew everyone and had never met a stranger. She had been a staple on the student committees in charge of organizing school social events and had been an active member of the Color Guard for both the junior and high schools. On the day of freshman orientation, it had been Brittany leading the charge with her infectious smile and a bright pink *Failure is Not an Option* t-shirt.

"Not yet. I heard her parents are having another press conference tonight."

"I can't imagine what's going through their minds right now."

"Me neither."

The bus turned a corner and the memorial disappeared from sight. But the somber mood the memorial had struck in the gathered students stayed with the bus. With the exception of a few of the less mature sixth and seventh graders for whom the emotions of the moment were still lost, every person sat straight, staring at the seat ahead of them or mindlessly fidgeting with their bags or phones.

Brittany's disappearance was a not-so-subtle lesson for many of them about the harsh realities of the world. For Macy, Brittany's disappearance had meant a loss of freedom. Since the news had broken her parents had refused to allow her to walk the six and a half blocks between the Alum Ridge property and their home in Greater Avendale, which she had been allowed to do since beginning junior high. She felt selfish and small for even thinking about it. Being forced to ride the bus to and from school would probably seem like a dream come true to Brittany compared to whatever she was dealing with. Wherever she was.

The bus turned another corner and came to a stop. John lit the stop signs and opened the door. Several students filed out and headed for the craftsman-style homes Greater Avendale was known for. Macy watched as they quickly disappeared into their houses where the windows were closed, the blinds were drawn, and there were no signs of life outside. Not even the leaves that had begun to fall from the maple trees that lined each side of the street had been raked and bagged as normal.

Like most of the suburbs of PSD, Greater Avendale was dealing with the side effects from and the occasional overflow of a crime wave that had been affecting the downtown and urban areas south and east of the city for months. While neither of those areas had been particularly safe to begin with, the emergence of a new street drug called Spaz had exacerbated already existing problems and in recent weeks the situation seemed to be spreading. A rise in burglaries had been reported in every major suburb and intrusive measures such as police checkpoints, increased patrols, and traffic stops that had once been mostly absent in the suburbs had become a staple of daily life. Even at school, efforts such as drug-sniffing dogs and routine locker searches had become far more common than they had been even a semester before.

Macy didn't know anyone who had come into contact with Spaz and hadn't heard of anyone at Alum Ridge who had been found with it, but she had seen news broadcasts of the effect the drug had on those who took it and the results sounded terrifying. Reports of users running into oncoming traffic and jumping off buildings had accompanied grainy videos of people acting erratic and highly aggressive. Rumors had also surfaced about long term use causing physical deformities similar to those of methamphetamine, but Macy wasn't sure if that was real or just imaginations taking hold and spreading the way rumors did. But ultimately it didn't matter if it was true. The mere possibility seemed to have entire neighborhoods frightened to the point of ignoring seasonal, curb appeal-increasing chores.

Keri moved across the aisle now that a seat was open and Macy scooted further away from Typhoid Tommy as John continued along his route. With the amount of students on the bus and the curvilinear pattern of the neighborhood, Macy's ten-minute walk to school was a forty-minute ride. She placed her head against the back of the seat in front of her and stared at the clock on her smartphone as the bus rumbled on and the diesel fumes threw Tommy into a coughing fit.

Thirty-nine and a half minutes later, the brakes squealed and the bus rolled to a stop outside of a bungalow-style house with a wraparound front porch and blue siding. Macy stood, elated beyond words at the prospect of putting substantial distance between herself and her dread disease-carrying seatmate. Her phone beeped. She looked at the screen and then to Keri. "Mom wants to know if you're coming to dinner?"

Keri raised her eyebrows. "And miss eating alone with my mother's housekeeper again?" She stood and shouldered her bag, following Macy off the bus.

Macy frowned. "Sorry about your mom working—again."

Keri shrugged. "It's not your fault she's a workaholic who barely takes time to feed herself let alone her teenage daughter. Bye, John."

"You girls be careful now."

They descended the steps and rounded the front end of the bus. Macy looked up and down her street as they crossed the road. The expanding crime problem had had an effect here as well. Despite the clear skies and balmy-for-October temperature none of her neighbors were outside. The sidewalks were empty and even the park at the end of the road looked disused and abandoned. She stepped onto the curb as she noticed an unoccupied white van parked along the street two doors down. Had the elderly folks who lived there hired a contractor for something?

"So, what's on the menu?"

Macy turned her attention back to Keri. "Dad's bringing home Leonardo's."

"Oh, yum. Your family always knows how to eat."

"Pepperoni and cheese–two of the five basic food groups."

"Oh, totally."

Macy forgot about the work van and climbed the front steps as she removed her keys from her backpack. "Grab that."

Keri lifted the lid on the mailbox beside the door and removed the stack of catalogs, bills, and credit card offers as Macy pushed the door open and entered the foyer. She let her backpack slide from her shoulder and held the door for Keri.

"Your house always smells so–lived in."

Macy made a face. "Thanks. I think."

"No, no. It's good. Like people actually live—"

The door slammed shut behind them.

"Arghh!"

Keri screamed and dropped the mail.

Macy turned, bringing her backpack around in front of her as the end of a broom handle glanced off the hardcover books inside. She smiled. "Cheater."

A broad man with a graying mustache and receding hairline wearing a forest green Henley and suspenders grinned back. "It's not cheating. It's called the element of surprise." He readied the broom again and fell back into a fighting stance. "Afternoon, Miss Cartwright."

Keri removed her hand from her heart and allowed herself to breathe. "Hello, Colonel Scary."

"That's Major General–Retired."

Keri scooped up the mail and moved onto the stairwell, taking a seat halfway up. "That's what I meant." She raised her hand to her temple in a mock salute. "Sir."

Macy's smile widened. She kicked her flip flops off and kept her backpack in front of her as she lowered herself into a defensive stance. It was always fun and games when Grandad came to visit.

"On guard!" Grandad attacked, jabbing the end of the broom at different parts of her body.

Macy moved the backpack up and down in several fluid motions, blocking each attack. "You're supposed to say 'On Guard' before you attack."

"I did."

"Yeah. A microsecond before."

"Well, how much of a warning were you expecting? Because that's even less than you're likely to get in the real world. Ha!" He lunged, extending the broom with one hand like a sword.

Macy stepped aside and hung her backpack on the end of it, making it too heavy to hold up and out.

Grandad tensed his arm and tried to avoid being pulled off balance. "Nice one."

"I'm just getting started." Macy gripped the would-be staff and pulled it toward her as she faked a front kick to the abdomen. "I win."

Grandad released the broom and pretended to double over and be thrown against the wall. "Not so fast." He stumbled for a moment, but recovered and raised his fists. "It would take more than a foot to the gut to stop a truly determined attacker. Remember, Macy, adrenaline is a powerful thing."

She dropped the broom and backpack. "Yes, sir." She gave him a quick salute and raised her fists.

Her grandfather had been a career military man and teaching her to roughhouse as a younger child and then to seriously defend herself as a young woman was his chief way of relating to her. Her parents hadn't seemed too sure about it at first, but she'd taken to it with such a willingness that they'd had a hard time arguing. Two black belts and a host of completion certificates that covered most of a wall in her room were the result.

Grandad threw a punch.

Macy knocked it aside and returned to her defense, keeping her hands in front of her face as she'd been taught.

Grandad jabbed at her.

She blocked and threw a counter strike at his solar plexus. The punch connected.

"Ugh." Grandad kept his fists up but stumbled back.

The front door opened and an older version of Macy in a navy blue pants suit pushed her way in, her arms full of grocery bags.

Macy kept her fists up and her eyes on grandad. "Hi, mom."

"Hi, everyone. Easy on the furniture, please." Becky Davis pushed the door closed with her foot and moved past them, her demeanor harried as though the workday hadn't ended yet.

Grandad laughed and lowered his fists. "Come here, sweetheart." He opened his arms.

Macy grinned. "Giving up?"

"Me? Never. But your mom gets nervous."

"Nice try." Macy leaned into his embrace. "Quitter."

Grandad had begun visiting more since he'd retired but always showed up at unexpected times. Unlike many retirees who hit the road when they were done punching the clock, Grandad had spent his career traveling the world and preferred the solitude of the lakeside cabin he'd owned since Macy could remember.

"It's good to see you, kiddo." He patted her back several times before letting go. "Always good to see you. And your mom." He picked up the broom and moved after Macy's mom. "Becky, let me help you with those."

Keri descended the steps. "Never a dull moment in your house is there?"

"Oh, there are plenty. Just not when Grandad comes for a surprise inspect—urr—visit."

"I heard that." Grandad called from the kitchen.

"I know you did." Macy led the way into the kitchen where her mom was putting away the groceries as Grandad handed them to her from the bags.

"How was school, Macy?"

"Fine." Macy placed her backpack beneath her chair at the kitchen island as she always did and climbed onto one of the stools.

"Hi, Keri. How was your day, dear?"

"Just fine, Mrs. Davis. Thanks for inviting me to dinner."

"You're most welcome. Macy's dad should be here any moment with—"

"Evening, Davises." The back door opened and a man in thin-rimmed glasses and a white polo shirt entered carrying a pizza box. William Davis glanced between Keri and Grandad. "And not so Davises."

Macy watched as everyone ducked around each other in the cramped kitchen. Late afternoons at the Davis house were always full of activity. Her mom and dad insisted that her homework be left until after dinner and that the family greet each other upon their individual arrivals. Then her parents would change clothes and they'd all have a conversation over their evening meal. Macy didn't know any other families that did the same and she'd resisted at times, but her parents had always had the final word. She'd rather eat and at least pretend to care about things like office banter, new real estate developments, and whatever it was her father did—some kind of research and development she'd never understood for a laboratory called Radiant Technologies—than be grounded.

"Alright, everyone. Wash up and dig in." Her dad carried the pizza into the dining room and her mom followed with paper plates and napkins.

Macy slid off the stool and brought up the rear as the group entered a dining room with an oval table made of dark mahogany and a matching hutch. They never ate dinner in the dining room. Macy wasn't even sure why they had it. The central island in the kitchen had always doubled as a table, but she guessed tonight was different. Tonight Grandad and Keri were present and that meant it was something special—and that there probably wasn't enough room for everyone around the island.

Chairs scraped against the hardwood flooring and soon everyone was seated and reaching for a slice. At first, everyone just chewed and made awkward glances at each other as they attempted to keep grease from dribbling down their chins. Leonardo's was a local legend known for New York-style slices the size of rolled-up newspapers when folded and eaten the way pizza was intended.

Macy's mom swallowed and wiped her chin. "So, dad, how was the trip in?"

"Uneventful until I reached the city limits. This place is going to the birds."

Her mom smiled politely. She was used to Grandad's no-holds-barred nature. "Well, the city's certainly been having its problems lately. It's causing some disruptions at work. We've had six deals fall through this week alone."

"Having its problems? The way I hear it you're dealing with a full-on crimewave because of this—this—drug—this—"

"Spaz." Macy smiled but instantly regretted it as her parents each looked at her. She took a quick bite and busied herself chewing.

"Yeah. That's it. They've got the police working double time to catch the crooks spreading this stuff around and it still sounds like they're losing."

"Oh, it's just the media blowing things out of proportion, dad, like they always do. I'm sure the police are getting closer every day to finding those responsible."

"Yeah." Macy's dad finished a bite. "These things are cyclical. Every city goes through it at times. It's just what happens when you have more than a million people living in the same concentrated area. Not everyone is going to play by the rules all the time. And the news just fans the flames and emboldens those already inclined to cause trouble. It makes the whole situation seem that much worse."

Macy thought about what her parents were saying. Maybe they were right. While the news of the crimewave had certainly seemed to have an effect on their neighborhood, perhaps people were just overreacting. It wasn't like there were roving gangs of drug-addicted people marching through the streets.

"Anyways," Macy's dad continued, "PSD has always been among the safest cities in the country statistically speaking. We wouldn't have chosen to raise our daughter here if it wasn't."

"Well, not always, Billy, but yeah. For the last few decades anyway."

Macy's dad made a face at Grandad calling him Billy. His name was William and he'd never used a shorter version such as Bill or Billy.

"Right, dad. Ancient history." Macy's mom finished another bite and looked at Keri. "It's always nice to have you, Keri. How's your mom doing?"

Grandad grumbled at the change of subjects.

Macy bit into her slice of pizza as Keri responded, but wasn't hearing what she said. She'd witnessed the same kind of awkward exchange before between her parents and grandfather and had heard them make vague references to a time in PSD when things had apparently been pretty bad. But when she'd asked what they were talking about their answers were never satisfying. Had there been another crimewave in the past? Had it been worse than the current one? She didn't know. History really wasn't her subject and if it had ever been mentioned elsewhere she hadn't been paying attention.

"So, Macy, how was school?" Her dad took another bite, but stopped chewing and made a face. "And don't give me the standard 'fine.' We want to know the details."

Macy blushed having been caught off guard. She hated being the center of attention. She thought about her day. What had happened at school today that was any different than any other day? Didn't her parents get tired of hearing about the same boring routine? She shrugged. "No tests or anything. Just classes and stuff. I have homework in science and math."

Keri grinned. "Macy took on a bully today."

"A bully?" Macy's dad stopped chewing for a moment and waited.

Macy panicked and gave a nervous laugh. "Heh. Yeah. I did."

"What do you mean by a bully and what do you mean by take on?"

"It was really no big deal, Mr. Davis." Keri smiled. "There's this guy named Zeke and he and his two buddies are the school bullies. They were about to give Josh Friddle a hard time and Macy stepped in."

Grandad gave a victorious nod. "Good for you, Macy."

But Macy could tell her dad wasn't nearly as happy about the news.

"Stepped in how, Macy? I don't want any fighting going on."

"Oh, no, dad. No fighting. I just told them to—to back off, you know. And they did."

"For cryin' out loud, Billy. It sounds like she did an admirable thing and you're looking at her like she just shot your puppy."

"Now, Lee, I'm not saying that standing up for others isn't admirable. I'm just saying there are ways to handle these kinds of things. And fighting isn't one of them. Did you report this bully to the office, Macy?"

"Oh, of course. Deputy Newell came by shortly afterward."

"Good. That's who needs to deal with bullies. Not you."

Grandad grumbled something under his breath.

Macy bit into a piece of Leonardo's chewy crust and hoped the matter would die there. She cut her eyes at Keri. What was she thinking? She swallowed the last of the crust. "Thanks for picking up pizza, dad."

"You're welcome, Macy."

"We need to work on our homework. May we be excused?"

"Of course." Her dad looked at his watch. "I suppose it's time for me to get ready to hit the pavement again, too. The grocery store shelves aren't going to stock themselves."

Macy's mom frowned at the mention of her husband's second job. He'd taken it a few months earlier, but Macy wasn't sure exactly why. She stood from the table and moved into the kitchen with Keri following. Placing her plate in the trash can, she held the lid as Keri did the same.

Keri made a face. "Are you mad?"

"Nope." Macy let the lid close on her hand and grabbed her backpack from under the kitchen island. They headed for the stairs. "You don't have much experience with parents, do you?"

Keri cringed. "Sorry. I guess I imagined your dad being proud of you. Mine took off before I was out of diapers or so my mom says."

Macy led the way as they climbed the stairs and entered her room. She closed the door and flopped onto the bed.

Keri gave an awkward shrug. "I mean dads are supposed to be proud of you, right?"

"Yeah." Macy punched the pillow to fluff it up then stared up at the poster of Tylar Marsden on her ceiling. "Dads are proud when you ride your bike for the first time without training wheels or bring home an A in science. Not when you go fist to fist with someone double your size in a place with a zero-tolerance policy."

Keri sank into the swivel chair in front of Macy's vanity that doubled as her computer desk. "Heh. Yeah. Zero tolerance for anyone not on the football team."

"Ugh. Don't get me started."

CHAPTER 4

Macy stepped off the bus behind Keri and looked at the collection of white pickup trucks and panel vans gathered along the curb in front of the school–an abnormal sight that had sparked much curiosity as the students dismounted the buses.

"Accu-sec Systems?" Keri lifted an eyebrow as she read the logo on the work vehicles.

Macy shrugged and continued to follow the throng of adolescents toward the side entrance of the three-story brick building. Like most mornings when the temperature was warm enough to allow it, the multiple sets of doors leading into the main hallway were propped open and everything appeared to be normal inside. Well, not quite. Deputy Newell was in his usual spot just outside the office door, but today there was another uniformed man standing with him—an older man whose uniform was white and brown instead of tan and brown. Macy studied him for a moment. She'd never seen him around the school before and if she wasn't mistaken it looked as though Newell was the tiniest bit afraid.

"Macy. Keri."

Macy quickly looked away from the man and made eye contact with Newell. "Good morning, Deputy Newell." She turned her attention back to the hallway in front of her. Besides the presence of the additional lawman, everything seemed normal. There was no sign of anyone working on anything. She exchanged looks with Keri as they continued on into the main atrium.

Macy stopped in her tracks as she looked at the main entrance. There—working just inside the arched doorways—were a crew of men in navy blue work shirts that bore the same logo as the vehicles outside. She studied the scene as some of the men drilled holes in the tiled floor and others ran wires through some conduit to a new electrical box that had been installed along the wall.

"C'mon."

Macy felt Keri tugging on her sleeve. "Wait. What are they doing?"

The front doors opened and two more men in the same navy blue work shirts pushed in a cart loaded with tall, slender boxes marked Accu-sec 10x Walkthrough Metal Detector.

"Metal detectors? They're installing metal detectors?"

Some other students who had stopped to look as well glanced at each other uncomfortably.

Macy thought she knew what was on each of their minds. Were these new devices going to be installed at every entrance? And, if so, did the presence of the additional lawman mean that soon every time anyone entered the school they would be scanned like in an airport?

She exchanged worried looks with some of the others. The measure seemed a bit much. Not only had there been no known violations of the school weapons policy this year, but she was pretty sure drugs like Spaz couldn't be found with metal detectors. What was next? Full body x-ray units?

"C'mon. We're gonna be late for class."

Macy relented as the last of the arriving students filed past them. She followed Keri, though the unease she felt at being scanned by a machine every time she arrived at school didn't stay with the work crew at the main entrance. It followed her towards the freshman hall.

"Ugh. Late again." Keri rolled her eyes as they turned the corner to see the hallway full of students struggling to get to their individual lockers.

But Macy's attention had fallen elsewhere. Directly across from the hallway entrance Patrick Newell was standing on a step ladder, trying to hold up a poster, and struggling to tape it in place all at the same time as the two friends he was always with–Josh Friddle and a boy everyone knew as Striker–held other posters and watched.

Keri nudged her on the shoulder. "A perfect chance. Looks like he could use a hand and those two he's with are dumbfounded as usual."

Macy felt her insides tighten. Keri was right. It would be the perfect time to step forward, offer a helping hand, and exchange more than the goofy grins and stuttered greetings she'd managed to date. But she couldn't. No–there was no way she'd be able to do anything but stutter and look like a jerk. Her insides tightened more and the hallway felt like it was closing in on her. "Let's just get to cla—" She turned and her face bounced off something soft, but solid.

"Excuse me."

Macy snapped out of her fearful trance and realized she now stood face to face with the white-shirted lawman. "Sor—sorry, sir." She took three giant steps back.

The man didn't smile or say anything, he just straightened his shirt and frowned.

"Sheriff Burke. Dad."

Macy froze at the sound of Patrick's voice behind her.

"Good morning, boys and girls." Deputy Newell stood next to the white-shirted lawman.

"Yes, indeed. Good morning." Principle Decker stepped out from behind the two men. She was a dark-haired woman in a pants suit and turtleneck who had a face so stern it could give a grizzly bear the willies. With her as always was her mousey assistant, Ms. Pollard, who followed her closer than her own shadow. "What are you kids up to?"

Macy could feel Patrick standing just off her shoulder. Clearly the close proximity had led the adults to believe they were together. "Oh—uhh—we're no—"

"We're putting up posters," Keri said as Macy felt her step up and grab her by the arm.

Patrick held out the poster he had been trying to hang. "We found these just sitting in the library unfinished."

Macy studied it. It was a piece of white poster board with *Halloween Dance* stenciled on it in multiple colors and a jack-o-lantern face in the O. Around the outside edges someone had hand-drawn various spooky characters along with comic book heroes and villains, though Macy didn't recognize any of them except one; Stellar—Patrick's prized creation—occupied the top right corner with her fists up and her body turned into a fighting stance.

"Unfinished?" Principle Decker took hold of the poster and looked it over. "Why would they still be unfinished? The dance is in two weeks." She looked back at Newell and Ms. Pollard. "Who's in charge of the Events Committee this year?"

Newell gave a small shrug and shook his head. Ms. Pollard seemed to retreat behind a clipboard she always carried.

Patrick cleared his throat. "Brittany, ma'am."

Decker stopped and stared vacantly at the floor, her mouth curling into a frown. "I see."

Newell and Sheriff Burke shared her reaction as each realized the reason why the posters hadn't been finished and hung as planned.

Decker straightened up and handed the poster back. "Well, good work. It's always nice to see students stepping up to make our school a better place. If you need a hall pass and permission to finish before homeroom see Mrs. Beakman in the office." She held out a hand to Newell and Burke and the three started down the hall with Ms. Pollard close behind.

"Sheriff Burke." Patrick stepped around Macy as the adults turned back to face them. "How is the investigation going? Have you found anything. . . useful?"

The sheriff glanced at Deputy Newell and cleared his throat. "The. . . uhh. . . the investigation is ongoing of course and as such I'm afraid I can't talk about it. But I did receive your tip, Rick. Great job in coming forward. Keep it up." He looked at Decker. "Shall we?"

Decker turned and led the way down the hall, the gathered students silently clearing the way like the waves of the Red Sea as Moses passed.

For a moment, Macy forgot her nerves and stood looking at Patrick as he watched the sheriff walking away with a look that could only mean disappointment.

"Hey. Did ya hear that, Patrick?" Striker—Patrick's blond afroed buddy—punched him on the shoulder proudly. "The sheriff said great job."

Patrick rolled his eyes. "Yeah, right. He couldn't even remember my name."

Josh Friddle shook his head at Striker's apparent thickness. "Sorry, Patrick. I'm sure he took your report seriously. He's probably gotten a lot of reports and just can't remember them all."

"Yeah." Patrick turned back to the step ladder and climbed the first rung as he straightened the poster.

Macy watched silently. What did Patrick know about Brittany's disappearance that he felt the sheriff should be taking so seriously? She wanted to reach out–to ask him about it and offer him some comfort. She started forward, but as she did her nerves came rushing back. *What am I doing?* She stopped herself mid-stride and turned back to Keri. "Time for homeroom."

Six and a half hours later, Macy was still replaying the hallway incident in her head as she did her best to pay attention in Mrs. Spader's fourth-period science class. She watched as the old woman strode regally across the front of the room before stopping to write something on the chalkboard. Seriously, who used a chalkboard anymore? The classrooms upstairs had all been updated with newer, easier to read Active Boards.

Technological updates were one of the things most students looked forward to about high school, but Macy had been looking forward to getting rid of Mrs. Spader. She'd only been stuck in her miserable science class since starting junior high and by some awful stroke of luck Spader had been transferred up a grade each year.

Apparently Spader–known to the entire Alum Ridge student body as The Spade–had refused to move into the modern age when she'd been transferred again and had taken up residence in a basement storage room made classroom that had been passed over by any kind of technological update.

Macy glanced around the room. While the location had changed the decor hadn't. To go with the last century chalkboard were worn out and badly creased posters that didn't match the modern science curriculum, a model skeleton Macy thought may have been Mr. Spader at some point, and foam solar system balls hung from the drop ceiling with bent paper clips.

She returned her attention to the front of the room. The Spade was mumbling about something and doing her best to squeeze the last bit of life from a sliver of white chalk. Macy placed her head on her desk. She was pretty sure this was how the dinosaurs died out; sheer boredom.

As usual, she was seated catty-corner from Patrick who was having just as much trouble focusing on the lesson as she was. She watched as he continuously stole glances at the front of the room to be sure he hadn't been seen as he scribbled something in one of his notebooks.

"Mr. Newell!"

Patrick shot upright. "Yes, ma'am. Just taking notes, ma'am."

Macy sat up and felt shock register on her own face as she looked back to the front of the room expecting to see a sour, beady-eyed face staring back at them. But The Spade was still turned toward the board and had her head cocked toward the teacher's manual cradled in one arm.

"Kindly come to the board and tell us what three surfaces on earth absorb sunlight."

Patrick swallowed hard. "I—uhh—yes, ma'am." He stood from his desk, stealthily sliding his notebook with him. As he dropped it into his unzipped backpack, Macy noticed a page slide out. She held her breath as it hit the floor and glided into the walkway between their desks. Had Patrick seen it? He started walking toward the front of the room like a death row inmate who had just learned his last-minute stay from the governor wasn't going to happen. Nope. He hadn't seen it. She looked at the page. She could tell there was something drawn on it, but it had landed upside down so she couldn't see what.

Patrick arrived at the front of the room and a laser-eyed Spade held out the same sliver of chalk she'd been milking for the last ten minutes. Her face, like a spider who just noticed a fly caught in its web, said she knew she had him dead to rights. He hadn't been paying any attention to the lesson.

"The—the surfaces—th—that absorb sun—sunlight?"

"Yes, Mr. Newell. The three surfaces that absorb sunlight. And I want them listed in order from the most amount absorbed to the least."

Patrick took the chalk and turned to face the board.

The class snickered.

"Well, there—there's la—land, right?" He looked at the numbers The Spade had written on the board, silently debating with himself about where land belonged.

"Choker." A boy coughed.

The Spade's head turned on a swivel. "You're next, Mr. Diesbach."

Macy smiled as the boy's face turned white and his mouth hung open.

Patrick marked land onto the board beside the number one. "Then. . . then there's water." He was beginning to sound more confident. He placed water beside the number two and moved onto the number three spot.

The Spade turned toward the class. Pop quizzing her students was a favorite tactic she deployed with enough regularity that everyone present should have known better than to get caught off guard. But Macy could sympathize with Patrick. She found The Spade's teaching methods to be so horribly boring that she routinely caught herself daydreaming. Luckily, the old woman was an easy tester. If you could read and retain any information at all you could pass her straightforward examinations.

Macy glanced between Patrick and The Spade. The Spade paced across the front of the room between her desk and the rows of desks her students sat in. Patrick's hand hovered just behind the number three as he tried to decide what other surface absorbed sunlight. *Ice.* Macy wished she were telepathic. *It's ice.*

"Trees," Patrick said confidently and began writing it beside the number three.

Macy frowned. This wasn't going to end well.

The Spade stopped pacing midway across the room and stared straight ahead like a Terminator robot acquiring a target.

Macy cringed and waited for the inevitable verbal eruption that would tear the young Mr. Newell to proverbial shreds. The room was silent—as if every living creature within earshot also knew what was about to transpire and had determined that deathly silence was the only way to avoid being caught in the line of fire. A moment passed. And then two. Even the block walls seemed to wait with anticipation.

"No, Mr. Newell." The world breathed at last. Instead of the soul-destroying, dry-witted one-liners she was known for, The Spade turned on her heel to face the aisle next to the desk Patrick had been sitting at. "Not trees."

Macy glanced at Patrick. His face was ashen as if he'd just watched as death fluttered by and had spared him. Or had it? Macy remembered the loose page and moved her eyes to the floor where it lay. Had The Spade seen it? Macy dared a glance. Nope. The old woman's beady eyes were focused on the rear wall of the room as if she were trying to decide what to do next. Macy tensed and slowly stuck a foot out from under her desk. She placed her heel silently on the edge of the paper and slid it from view.

"Not trees, Mr. Newell." The Spade started forward. "While it's true that trees do absorb sunlight they are not a surface. They are a plant. I can see why you'd be confused, though. Trees are commonly used to make paper." She bent down and picked up the notebook sticking out of Patrick's backpack. "And paper is used to make notebooks—like the one you were focused on when you should have been paying attention in class." She turned on her heel again and held up the notebook as she walked back to the front of the classroom.

Patrick's face went from ashen to ghost white.

"Shall we see what's so interesting?"

Macy's eyes went wide. She wouldn't. Not even The Spade was that cold-hearted.

"Page one." She flipped open the notebook. "Char-Ax." She turned the notebook out so the class could see the drawing of a flame-engulfed man with an evil smile and a flaming battle-ax. "Real name; Jacopo Carbonelli, nationality; Italian-American, height; six feet, weight; one hundred and eighty-six pounds, hair; ginger, eyes; green when powers are dormant and red when in use."

Macy couldn't imagine how Patrick was feeling, but she was furious—like she'd tear the notebook from The Spade's hands if she were standing closer. She'd never been able to tolerate bullies no matter how old they were. And what was this if not bullying? Sure she'd warned Patrick a few times about paying attention, but was this kind of public humiliation really necessary? Let his lack of attention show in his test scores or maybe assign him detention. But not this. This was ensuring everyone in the class would poke fun at him for weeks or even months.

"Carbonelli was born in Brooklyn, New York in 1976 to a shopkeeper and his wife. He quickly rose through the ranks of the mob by running favors for the neighborhood bosses—"

"Stop!" Patrick charged away from the board and grabbed the notebook from a shocked Spade. "Just stop!" He continued down the aisle to his desk where he scooped up his backpack as he flew past.

"Well, I do believe I've made my point." The Spade stared after him. "Your turn, Mr. Diesbach, as promised. The last of the three sunlight absorbing surfaces on the board. Now."

Macy watched as Patrick shouldered his backpack and disappeared around a corner. It would be another ten minutes until the bell rang. Where would he go? Being in the hall without a pass would only get him in more trouble.

She turned her attention back to the front of the room as the mop-haired boy who had dared to speak out earlier sauntered to the front of the room. If he was smart, he'd spent the intervening minutes looking back over the lesson.

"Ice, Mrs. Spader. The third surface that absorbs sunlight is ice."

"Saints be praised, Mr. Diesbach." The Spade placed a hand on her heart as Diesbach stood proudly at the front of the room wearing an ear-to-ear grin. "You do know how to spell it, right?"

Diesbach blushed and turned toward the board with the tiny sliver of chalk in his hand.

Macy looked away from the spectacle and remembered the loose page from Patrick's notebook she'd rescued. It was still on the floor under her foot. She slid it back to where it was within her reach and bent down innocuously, scooping the page up and quickly returning to an upright position while looking to make sure she hadn't been noticed. She set the page on her desk, smoothed away dirt from the tiled floor, and stared at the hand-drawn image.

Stellar. She studied the red and blue armored heroine. This picture was different from the others she'd seen Patrick working on. This was some sort of concept sketch that featured both the front and back of the costume as well as closeups of the mask around a human head—the head of Stellar's secret identity, she presumed.

The bell rang and the class stood simultaneously. Chairs scraped across the tiled floor and backpacks unzipped and zipped. Macy frowned as she folded the drawing and stuck it between the pages of her science book. *Is this Patrick's ideal woman? If so, I don't stand a chance.*

CHAPTER 5

The brakes screeched as the bus came to a stop outside of Macy's house. She stood and looked toward the back where Keri was seated. Because of Keri's end of day makeup routine, there hadn't been any room for them to sit together by the time they'd both boarded. But that was okay. Macy was still a little put out about the stunt Keri had pulled in the hallway that morning.

"You still mad?" Keri asked as they descended the steps.

Macy pursed her lips. "A little."

"I really am sorry. I just want to see you make a move and be happy. And it did work out okay."

"Yeah. I guess."

"Well, what do you think Patrick is more focused on right now?

His brush encounter with you this morning or that fiasco in The Spade's class? If I were him, you'd be the highlight of my day."

Keri had a point. Even if she wasn't as dashing and beautiful as Stellar she was far and away better than The Spade. And she did need to do something—eventually—or she'd just continue being miserable about it.

"You coming in?"

"Yeah. I need your help with whatever that was that The Spade was going over in science."

"Meteorology?"

"Yeah. I thought meteorology is what killed the dinosaurs, but now I find out it's got something to do with the weather." Keri shrugged.

Macy laughed. "A changing environment is what killed the dinosaurs. But meteorology has always been about the weather."

"Who knew."

"Uhh everyone but you and ReNOWn."

"Ouch. Bite me."

They crossed the slightly overgrown lawn to the wraparound front porch and climbed the stairs to the front door. Macy lifted the lid on the mailbox and pulled out the bills and junk mail.

"Ughhh. . ."

She snapped her head toward the porch swing in the corner. "Grandad?" She dropped the mail and her backpack and rushed over. Her grandfather was lying beneath the swing with an·empty medication bottle in his hand—the former contents spread across the wooden floor. "Grandad?" She touched him on the shoulder.

"Ughhh. . ."

"Give me your phone!" Keri rushed over and knelt beside Macy. "I'll call an ambulance!"

"It's in my back—"

"Heeya!" Grandad sat up and pushed Keri away, grabbing Macy by the collar and tugging her to her feet as he stood.

Macy struggled, but before she could think of a proper defense she was pinned against the porch railing.

"Always expect an attack, Macy, even from the unlikeliest of places."

Macy struggled in his grip as he grinned triumphantly.

"The first thing they taught me in the Army was—"

"—not to talk too much?" Macy raised her foot and pushed her heel down his shin.

"Ow!"

His grip loosened and she knocked his arms aside, giving herself the space to maneuver free and put some distance between them. She grinned and raised her fists. "You're gonna pay for that."

Grandad smiled and helped Keri to her feet. "Sorry about that, my dear."

Keri raised her eyebrows and moved back to the front door. "I'll just wait inside."

Macy pushed open the door, looking at Keri as she stepped across the threshold.

"Looks like you lost that round," Keri said from her perch halfway up the steps.

Macy brushed loose grass from her tousled hair and looked down at the green stains on the knees of her jeans. "Maybe just a little."

"Have you ever thought about using the back door?"

"And miss all that fun?" She pulled off her shoes and slid them against the foyer wall beneath a shoe rack. "He means well. He just wants me to be ready." She picked up her backpack and climbed the stairs behind Keri.

"For what—a roving band of ninjas?"

Macy shrugged. "For life, I guess."

"Well, most people I know haven't had to fight their way through hordes of Viking invaders." Keri gave a small shrug. "Hordes of Christmas shoppers maybe."

"Heh. Right." Macy headed for the hallway bathroom as Keri entered her room. "I'm gonna change."

Macy left the bathroom still rubbing her hair dry with a towel. Midway through changing her dirty clothes from the unexpected battle, she'd decided a shower was in order. She pushed her bedroom door open and tossed the wet towel into the white wicker hamper.

"I didn't know you drew."

Macy collapsed onto her bed. "I don't. What're you talking about?" She fluffed her pillow under her head, looked over at Keri, and stopped. Her science book sat open on her desk and Keri was holding up Patrick's hand-drawn page. Macy's mind raced. "I— uhh—"

"—have something to tell me?"

"It fell out of his notebook when he got called to the board, I swear. I didn't want The Spade to take it so I—"

"—covered for him like any woman would her man?"

Macy smiled sheepishly. "Yeah. That."

Keri turned the page in her hands and studied it. "Stellar," she said in a mock tough guy voice as she made a fist. "Doesn't look as threatening as whatever that thing was that The Spade read aloud."

"Stellar's his hero–or the hero–of his–whatever you call it–his world." Macy made air quotes with her fingers. What would you call Patrick's creations? Did he have some kind of overarching plan for them or were they all just sort of random figments of his imagination?

"Weird," Keri said absent-mindedly as she continued to study the drawing.

"As near as I can tell Stellar's like this young female heroine who takes on all of the bad creations he draws and keeps in that notebook." Macy sighed. "I don't know about taking on supervillains, but it sure would be nice to take on some regular ones." She unconsciously lowered her voice to just above a whisper. "And to have so much of his attention."

Keri looked up. "What was that?"

"Nothing." Macy regretted the words immediately.

"Oh my god." Keri smiled. "You're jealous of Patrick's made-up comic book girl? That is—that's insanely cute."

"No. It's pathetic is what it is."

Keri ceded the point with a small shrug. "She does look like you, though. Sort of."

"She does not. She's—well, she's pretty and—and mysterious. I'm just. . . just me."

"You're too hard on yourself." Keri turned the picture so Macy could see it. "Okay. So, she does have every brick in place, but she's also a comic book character or whatever so she's like this idealized version of a real person or something. Think about who she'd be in real life. By the looks of this drawing she'd be tall, have a sturdy build, she'd be someone who could be athletic, but not necessarily the captain of the cheerleader squad because all of these secret identity types are always the person you'd least expect–trust me I know–I've watched The KB for years. She'd have dark–almost auburn-ish–hair and big round blue eyes." Keri put the drawing down, held up her hands in a picture frame shape, and closed one eye as if she were looking through a viewfinder at Macy. "Bingo. Nailed it."

Macy waved her off. "You're crazy."

"Maybe, but I have an idea."

Macy rolled her eyes. "I'm afraid to even ask."

"Be her. Be Stellar."

"What? That's insane. You've gone insane–officially."

"Well, you're always wanting me to make you something. And this? This wouldn't be that hard. I made three costumes for whatever that cosplay thing was they did a while back at the PSD Comic-Con." Keri rubbed her index finger and thumb together and lifted an eyebrow. "Those people aren't afraid to plunk some coin down. Anyways, it'd be made mostly of printed and textured spandex and the armor would be some kind of sturdy material stretched over and glued to sports pads. And since you're besties with the queen fashionista of Alum Ridge High…" she snapped her fingers. "…easy."

"Yeah. I've been wanting you to make me something I can wear–as in actual clothes. Not a superhero suit."

"But you can wear it–to the Halloween dance."

"No. Oh no. No way. Seriously–have you ever seen me dance?"

"Umm, that would be a no."

"There's a reason for that."

"But think about it. The Halloween dance. Patrick and Stellar." Keri pointed at Macy. "Stars of the show."

"Now I know you're nuts. That's insane."

"Why? It's a costumed affair, isn't it?"

"Let me get this right–you're going to make a Stellar costume and I'm going to wear it to the dance and then what–Patrick's going to be so surprised that he falls madly in love and we live happily ever after?"

Keri shrugged. "Something like that, yeah. But of course I'm open to any better ideas." She placed a hand to her ear. "What's that sound? Oh, crickets. Right."

"Shut up. And nice try, but I don't think dressing up as a superhero is the way to his heart. You think Patrick was embarrassed this afternoon? Wait until everyone at school gets a load of this. And

I'd get to stand there and be embarrassed with him."

Keri shrugged. "Just an idea."

"Well, file it under B for boneheaded."

"Fine then." Keri let go of the drawing and watched as it sailed toward the floor.

Macy sat up and caught it before it could land. She studied it for a moment. Stellar definitely looked awesome. Most girl heroes were lame–mere sex symbols to keep pubescent male imaginations turning pages. But Stellar looked different. She looked like she was ready for a serious battle. Macy unconsciously squared her shoulders to match the drawing.

"Second thoughts?"

Macy snapped herself back to reality. "No."

"Ugh! Ugh! Ugh!" Macy threw a series of jabs and crosses at the black heavy bag suspended from the ceiling beam in her basement and finished with a left hook. "Ugh!"

She kept her fists up and bounced on her toes as she focused on breathing steadily. She worked out a minimum of three times a week, but her workouts normally consisted of a few miles on the treadmill and at least three reps of weights on whatever muscle group she was focused on that day. But tonight's workout was different. Tonight was all about stress relief and taking out her frustration on inanimate objects.

As hard as she'd tried to focus on something else, all that kept going through her mind was the close encounter in the hallway that morning, the debacle in The Spade's classroom that afternoon, Keri's ideas on making things better, and how she could have handled all three much better than she had.

"Ugh! Ugh!" She threw another jab and cross combo and then leaned in and drove her knee into the front of the bag. "Heeya!" The bag bounced upward, temporarily relieving the tension on the chain and causing the bag to come crashing back down.

"Easy, Macy. Those joists support the kitchen floor you know."

Macy exited her fighting stance and caught the swinging bag with a grunt as her mother walked in carrying a full laundry basket. "Sorry."

"Grandad has you pretty worked up with all this fighting stuff, doesn't he?"

Macy shook her head. "No. It's not him, mom." She gave a small shrug. "I actually like it when Grandad's around." She watched as her mother basically ignored what she'd just said. Both of her parents had been incredibly uneasy about her being taught to fight and had always steered so far clear of the subject that their reactions bordered on downright weird.

Her mom set the laundry basket down on the washing machine and turned. "Then what, dear? I'm not used to seeing you this worked up."

Macy pulled off her MMA style gloves and took a seat on the nearby weight bench. She sat for a moment with her eyes on the matted floor until she felt her mother take a seat next to her. "Sorry, mom. I've just been having a hard time lately."

"Oh, Macy. High school can be like that, sweetheart."

Macy felt her mother's arm slide around her back and her hands on her shoulders trying to console her. She looked up into her mother's eyes. There was no question which side of the gene pool she'd gotten her looks from. Just like her daughter, Becky Davis was tall, had an athletic build, and a full head of straight chestnut brown hair.

"It's not school. Well, not really anyways. There's this boy—" She felt her mother tense. "—his name's Patrick."

"Oh, I see. And what's going on with Patrick?"

Macy smiled sheepishly and felt her cheeks flush. "Nothing like that, mom."

Her mom tried to hide it, but Macy could feel her exhale in relief. She nearly laughed. "No. It's that I really like him, but he just doesn't seem to know–or care–that I exist. Do you think a boy would like me?"

"Oh, of course, honey. You're smart. You're beautiful. You're tough. You're—you're—"

"Intimidating?"

"Not the word I was looking for, but yeah. I suppose boys at your age are sometimes intimidated by. . . certain girls."

Macy watched as her mom turned her eyes to the floor and seemed to consider her next words carefully.

"But being tough—being you—isn't a bad thing. A boy might see you as a bit of a romantic challenge right now, but as you get a little older being tough and even a little intimidating will just make you all the more interesting to the right kind of guy. Trust me. We're cut from the same cloth."

"Really? So dad was intimidated by you?"

Her mom smiled at some distant memory. "Yeah. I think so. He barely said anything on our first date. But neither did I. I think we were both a little intimidated by each other, really. And I think that's where most good, long-lasting relationships begin."

"So, if Patrick's intimidated by me and I'm intimidated by him then we've got a good shot?"

"You've really got me curious about this boy. Anyone I know?"

Macy looked at the floor and smiled shyly. "You've never met him. He—he's an artist. He and his friends are into comic books."

"Comic books?"

"Not like little kids. He creates his own characters."

"Really? Like what?"

"Well, he created this girl hero named Stellar."

"That's a cool name. Does she have any superpowers? Can she fly or something?"

"No. I don't think so. I think she's just a crime fighter. A beautiful, tough, crime-fighting heroine."

"Sounds like you two have a lot in common."

"Heh. Yeah. That's what Keri said—right before I called her a bonehead."

"Ouch."

"Yeah. Not my finest moment. I've had a few of those lately."

Her mom patted her on the knee and stood. "I know it's tough, but it will work out. You just need to have more confidence in yourself and not be in a hurry. Good things take time to develop. And you might want to apologize to Keri."

"Thanks, mom."

Becky Davis smiled and turned to face the heavy bag. To Macy's surprise, she dropped into a fighting stance and frowned. "Heeya!" She drove her fist into the bag and followed up with an elbow attack. "Ugh!"

Macy sat stunned for a second. "Whoa, mom. Nice one."

Becky Davis stood upright and returned to her normal, relaxed posture. "Now you see why your father was intimidated." She winked and returned to the washing machine and the full laundry basket.

Macy stood and stopped the still swinging bag with one hand as she stepped around it to look in the mirror on the opposite wall. She glanced over her shoulder to make sure her mom wasn't paying attention and pulled the folded Stellar drawing from her pocket. She studied it for a moment and then glanced into the mirror again. Her mom was busy pulling dirty clothes from the basket and stuffing them into the open washing machine. Macy drew in a deep breath and squared her shoulders so that she was in roughly the same stance as Stellar in the drawing. She held the pose for a moment until a goofy grin won her over and she relaxed again. Maybe–just maybe– Keri had a point about the Halloween dance.

CHAPTER 6

"Oh my God," Macy watched as Keri turned on her heel to face their two other friends, Taylor and Emma, as the four of them walked past a clothing store window. "Isn't that dress amazing?"

Taylor and Emma, two girls from the cheerleader squad who were more Keri's friends than they were hers, teetered forward with the same excitement as Keri.

Macy hung back. The seersucker strapless dress they were looking at was okay, but not really her style. In fact clothes shopping, in general, wasn't her style. Her idea of clothes shopping was looking through her closet once a year, deciding what was too worn out to salvage, and logging in to Amazon to have a reasonable replacement shipped directly to her house. The few dresses she did own were generally more conservative than whatever was popular and only got worn a few times a year at events like Easter Sunday, graduations, and Christmas. Even the church she attended with her parents was more of an informal affair.

She stuck her hands in the back pockets of her jeans and waited as Keri added up what she'd already spent in the last five stores they'd visited and clearly decided there was room on her mom's credit card for at least one more. Followed by Taylor and Emma, she headed for the store entrance.

"You coming?"

Macy started forward but stopped as a flashing neon light a few stores down caught her attention. She studied the sign for a moment and realized it was a neon outline of a superhero emblem and that the store was a comic shop.

"Actually," she said, walking as far as the entrance and touching Keri on the shoulder just before she disappeared inside, "I think I'm going to walk on ahead. There's a pet store near Belk I want to go in."

Keri smiled. "Okay. We'll meet you there as soon as we're done here."

"Great."

Macy watched as Keri caught up with Taylor and Emma who had already found the dress on the rack and were holding up various sizes. As soon as she was sure their attention was no longer on her, she walked in the opposite direction of the pet store with her eye on the comic shop.

As she arrived she took a closer look at the signage in the windows. In addition to the bright neon emblem, there were large posters of suited men with their fists up, their eyes or hands glowing with some sort of offensive energy, and their gazes fixed on whatever threat was in front of them. She recognized a few of them from recent television shows and movies, but most of them were unfamiliar.

She got a little closer and looked through the narrow entrance. The inside of the store was mostly dark, but she could make out rows of bookshelves with brightly colored titles turned face out. She kept her hands in her back pockets and wandered in casually. As she crossed the threshold, a long *WHOOSH* sounded as though some hero or another had just taken flight.

"Hey. Welcome to Bozongo's Backlog of Books. Home of yesterday's, today's, and tomorrow's most awesome heroes. Are you here for Justicon #6–or maybe a copy of the new Goreclax anthology written by Steven Ambright and drawn by Will Troclar?"

Macy looked at the bespectacled clerk and gave a shy shrug. "No. Just looking around."

"Oh. Well, let me know if you need any help then—I guess." He stared for a moment as though he wasn't used to customers who didn't have an intended purchase in mind, but then returned his attention to his smartphone when the sound of a ninja star erupted from it.

Macy gave a small nod and wandered down the middle row. On either side of her were black particle board shelves stocked with what she assumed were the latest titles three deep. She raised an eyebrow as she looked at some of the images on the front covers. Some looked shockingly violent and definitely weren't like the comics she remembered her boy cousins reading when they'd been her age. She moved on and began to ignore the male heroes, purposely looking for anything with a female on it instead. The pickings were sparse, to say the least, but she finally noticed a cover featuring a woman–a scantily clad woman holding some sort of broadsword and dressed as though she were a medieval warrior facing down what appeared to be villainous monks. Was that what the average comic book reader thought of women? She hoped not, but she knew–as most people did—that it was definitely a male-dominated medium.

She picked up the book and began to flip through it. "Tharella?" She had to stifle a laugh. This poor woman wasn't only expected to fight off hordes of medieval zombie monks, but she was expected to do it half-naked. She set the book down and turned to the comics on the other side of the row.

There, in the middle of more fist throwing males, was another book with a woman on the cover, and this time she seemed fairly realistic-looking—at least as far as superheroes go. Macy picked up the book and studied it for a moment. Unlike Tharella—that poor woman—Sentury, whose name Macy guessed was a cool take off on the terms century and sentry, wore a dark red robe and an Islamic-looking headscarf that concealed her facial features with the exception of a set of piercing blue eyes. In her hands, she held a bronze scepter with a glowing blue jewel affixed to the end that matched the exact color of her eyes—surely not a coincidence.

Macy was intrigued. The only skin she could see on the woman was her feet on which she wore sandals—not the best footwear for fighting villains, but then there had always been something freeing about not having your feet wrapped up in shoes or boots. Macy could sympathize with the choice.

"Ohhh you found Sentury. Awesome." Macy looked to see the clerk walking in her direction carrying a cardboard box. He passed her and headed for the back of the store. "That's gonna be an awesome mini-series now that she's broken free of the bond that Jakhor had her in. She's been his slave for years."

Macy was suddenly less enthusiastic. What was it with comic book fans and bondage? And Jakhor? Seriously? Macy flipped open the book certain that there was going to be some whoring alright and she wasn't disappointed. The first page appeared to be a dream sequence of the kind of life Sentury had led before her apparent freedom. Chains, skimpy outfits, suggestive positions–yup–just like she thought. But hey, she was free now–that had to count for something, right?

"She's not out of the woods yet," the clerk said, returning from what Macy assumed was a storage room. "Jakhor's just unleashed the Hounds of Hilradus to drag her back to the abyss where he's been keeping her. That's where the mini-series starts." He gave a thumbs-up as he passed her. "Personally, I think she'll be enslaved again by the end because she's an important weapon in Jakhor's planned attack on the Justizone. No way the writer's will risk her staying free and not being around for that."

Macy closed the book and was about to set it back on the shelf when a familiar *WHOOSH* sounded. She looked toward the door and felt her heart drop into her stomach.

"Hey, Patrick," the clerk said. "Here for the new—"

"Macy?"

Macy felt her airway tighten. "He—hey." She managed a half-smile and shy wave.

"I didn't know you were into comics."

"I—uhh—well, it's a recent interest." She stuck the Sentury book back on the shelf. "Sort of."

"That's awesome." Patrick made his way down the middle row. "Who's your favorite?"

Macy was stuck. She couldn't bolt past him and out the door without looking like a complete psycho and the only thing behind her was the entrance to the storage room. She'd have to talk to him. She'd have to answer his question. Who was her favorite? She didn't have a favorite–at least not that was sold in this store. Her favorite was Stellar, which had to be his favorite, too, right? But she couldn't tell him that.

"I... well, they don't have her here. I just finished looking. I like—uhh—old comics and like stuff from other countries." Macy felt her head nodding and her face smiling, but couldn't believe the words that were coming out of her own mouth. "Like France–I've been taking French and am really into French superheroes at the moment."

"Huh. Well, alright. I always thought comics were more of an American thing, but I guess you learn something new every day."

"Yup. Sure do. Hey–by the way–where were you this week? You weren't in class." Macy felt her heart leap. That was the first normal thing she'd managed to get out of her mouth. Hopefully it was the beginning of a new trend.

Patrick shrugged and examined the floor. "Oh—I—uhh—I took a few days off."

Macy bit her tongue. Had she screwed up? She knew why he hadn't been in class–or at least thought she knew. She wouldn't have wanted to show up at school after the debacle with The Spade either. She tried to look sympathetic. "I don't blame you. She really wasn't fair to you. I mean–really–who *can* pay attention in that class?"

Patrick smiled. "I know, right?"

Macy smiled back. This wasn't going so bad, was it? It didn't seem like it. "Will you be back on Monday?"

"Yeah. My dad says I have to. I can't miss any more days in case I'm sick or in case something else comes up."

Macy nodded. "Yeah–only ten days a semester allowed."

"Yup. So, French superheroes? I didn't know there were any."

Macy tensed. Did they really have to revisit that? She swept her eyes over the nearby shelves, but wasn't really seeing any of the books there. "Yeah. Like I said–recent interest. I'm not sure there are a lot of them, but Mrs. Flor told us about one and the story sounded really cool." She looked back and was horrified to see Patrick looking at her expectantly. "I—uhh—she was a female private eye of some kind. It's historical. She investigated odd things like monks who never died and living Gargoyles at Notre Dame. But I can't remember her name so I just stopped in here out of curiosity."

"Sounds like a French Sherlock Holmes."

"Yeah. Sort of."

"Sounds cool."

"Does it really–or am I just out on the fringe–again?" She chastised herself. Was she really asking for his approval? Would he respect her if she sounded like a begging puppy desperate for attention?

A broad smile filled Patrick's face and he gave a short laugh. "No. It sounds great."

Macy relaxed.

Patrick continued. "I mean–it's different, but different is good. I like different."

"You do?"

"Yeah. I do."

Macy felt her cheeks flush. This was going a lot better than she'd ever imagined it would. "So, do you have plans for the Halloween dance?" Suddenly, she couldn't breathe. She couldn't believe the words that had just escaped her mouth. She stood deathly still as the world around her began moving in slow motion.

Patrick looked stunned. He opened his mouth to say something, but no words came out.

Oh no. He was going to turn her down, wasn't he? But had she really even asked him? Was asking if he had plans the same as—

"Yeah. Sort of."

Macy's heart sank.

"I made plans with Striker and Josh that night. The entire school will be open so we're going to use the computers in the library to— to—"

Macy did her best to smile. "Yes?"

Patrick shrugged shyly. "Well, we've started our own investigation into Brittany Crumb's disappearance."

"Oh. Okay." She'd nearly forgotten about the incident in the hall and Patrick's brief conversation with the sheriff. "Yeah. I—uhh—well, I hear ya." She chuckled, but inside she felt like her dreams were falling apart in front of her.

"Now I'm the one who sounds like I'm on the fringe, right?"

"No. No. Heck, no. It's just—well—I mean I'm not going to the dance either, you know? It's not really my thing. I just thought—you know—for the sake of conversation."

"Yeah."

An awkward silence began. Macy felt like she was dying inside. Had she really just told him she wasn't interested in going to the dance? She had. Her head was starting to hurt. How could she let this opportunity slip away? He wasn't going. That's how. Easy as that. But she couldn't leave it at that. She had to say something else.

"So… your own investigation, huh?"

Not what she'd been hoping for, but they were words.

"Yeah." Patrick looked down like he was examining his shoelaces. "I guess it sounds kind of stupid, but I really don't think the police are looking at it right."

"Really? Why?"

Patrick shifted his feet and seemed to be trying to decide whether or not he should say anymore. "Brittany texted me the morning she disappeared. She wanted to meet me and for me to help her talk to my dad about—" he shrugged. "—about something. But I never got to find out what. And the police haven't even talked to me about it—other than that brush off in the hallway at school."

"Wow. That's—uh—that's—"

"Macy?"

Macy looked past Patrick. Standing in the entrance of the shop and looking both confused and a little angry was Keri.

"Macy where have you been? We've walked all over looking for you."

"Ohhh. Sorry. I—I was—here."

"I've sent you like six texts. We have to meet Taylor's mom like now!"

Macy pulled her phone out of her pocket and looked. Holy crap! Keri was right. They were supposed to have met Taylor's mom outside of the food court ten minutes ago. With the heightened crime problem still affecting the suburbs, everyone's parents except for Keri's mom, who had been unavailable for comment as usual, had insisted they not go unescorted. All three sets of parents were probably freaking out right now.

"I have to go. Sorry."

"Oh, sure. Yeah. See ya at school."

"Yeah. Definitely."

She stepped around him and bolted into the cooler, brighter, and far more open area outside of the comic shop and began making her way towards the food court with Keri two steps behind.

"Was that who I think it was?"

"Ugh. Yes. And I totally just screwed it all up."

"OMG, Macy. Tell me everything."

The late-model Nissan Quest that Taylor's mom drove pulled into the concrete driveway beside Macy's house. Macy opened the side door of the minivan and stepped out, holding the door as Keri got out with an armload of shopping bags.

As usual, Keri's mom was working through the weekend and care for her only at-home child had been left to a loose-knit combination of friends' parents and the full-time housekeeper who occupied the carriage house behind the turn of the century Victorian-styled residence that sat in the center of Greater Avendale and that Mrs. Cartwright called home–when she was there.

"Byeee."

"See ya Monday."

"Okay bye." Macy pulled the door closed and watched as the van backed out onto the street. Thanks to the modern miracle that was text messaging Taylor's mom had informed the other parents that they'd be running just a tad behind and had avoided anyone being angry at Macy's tardiness.

But, if Macy was being honest, parental anger hadn't really been at the forefront of her thoughts on the drive home. Yet another debacle involving Patrick Newell had been–and still was. She watched absentmindedly as the minivan turned the corner and disappeared from sight.

"Okay. So, tell me everything."

Macy looked back as Keri switched her load from one arm to the other. She shrugged. "Nothing to tell really."

Keri gave her a look.

"Okay. Okay. So, there's something to tell, but it's not good."

Macy took a deep breath and proceeded to catch Keri up on everything that had happened after she'd left them at the dress shop as they entered the house and made their way to her bedroom.

"Oh, Mace." Keri set down the multitude of shopping bags and came in for a hug.

"I could shoot myself right now, but I was just so nervous." Macy placed her head on Keri's shoulder in a half-mocking display of being pitiful beyond words. "I kept rambling on like a total idiot."

"I'm sure it wasn't as bad as all that and at least you talked to him. That's something to build on, right?"

Macy shrugged again. "I guess."

Keri drew back and looked Macy in the eye. "It is. I'm serious. And I bet he was just as nervous as you were. I bet if you came right out and asked him to the dance he'd change his plans in a heartbeat."

"Yeah, right." Macy let go of Keri and plopped onto the bed. "He's way more interested in Brittany than he is in me."

"In Brittany?"

"Yeah. He and his friends have started their own investigation into her disappearance. That's what they're doing the night of the dance–using the computers in the school library for," Macy shrugged, "for something."

"Huh. Okay."

"I know, right? Patrick said she texted him the morning she disappeared and he seems to think that whatever she wanted will help lead to what happened to her."

"Huh. Isn't that what we have cops for? Sounds like the next step up from that goofy comic club he used to be in." Keri made a face and changed her voice to sound like the narrator of a Saturday morning cartoon show. "The Secret Decoder Ring Gang–traveling the world in a beat-up Oldsmobile looking for evidence of paranormal activity." She stifled a laugh and then pretended to be smoking something.

Macy laughed. "Stop. You're making him sound really pathetic." She continued to laugh as Keri kept up the smoking routine by sucking her cheeks in and crossing her eyes. She held it for a few seconds but then gave in to a fit of laughter.

After several seconds, Macy managed to catch her breath and stop herself. "I feel bad—" She fought another laugh. "I feel bad talking about him like this. He seemed really—I don't know—intense about it."

"Man," Keri kept up the cartoon voice, "this stuff's intense."

Macy laughed again, this time falling back on the bed and

covering her face with her hands. It felt good to laugh–to lose herself in a moment. Suddenly, she became aware of the complete basket case she had been for weeks now. Was a boy really worth doing this to herself? She took several deep breaths and wiped tears of laughter from her eyes. Slowly, the moment passed and Keri took a seat in the swivel chair.

"I'm telling you, Mace. You were almost there."

Macy sat up. "But almost doesn't count for much."

"True, but I'm telling you, Mace–if you show up as Stellar, admit that she's your real favorite superhero, and tell him why there's no way he could say no. He'd be nuts."

Macy put her head in her hands again as her feelings of inadequacy returned. An awkward silence passed as she sat there trying not to slip back into feeling sorry for herself.

"I made you something."

Macy looked up.

Keri raised her eyebrows and turned herself back and forth in the swivel chair.

Macy cringed. "What did you make me?"

Keri smiled as she stood and made her way to the shopping bags she'd brought home from the mall. "I just picked it up from the alterations shop over in Oaklawn this morning. The stitching around the shoulders was a little more than I could do on my own." She rooted around in the largest of the bags and pulled out a package wrapped in brown paper. She tossed it on the bed and returned to the swivel chair.

Macy eyed it for a long moment.

"Well, go ahead. It's not going to bite you."

Macy cleared her throat and took hold of the package. Even through the thick brown paper she could tell the item inside was some sort of garment by how soft and flexible it was. What had Keri done? Did she dare hope that it was only a blouse or—she dug into the paper with her fingernails and pulled it aside. "You didn't." She set the opened package down and sat looking at a folded bluish-gray garment with a zippered front and what looked like some kind of under armor that had been covered in dark red material. On the shoulders, she could clearly see the six-pointed star emblem of Stellar.

Keri cringed. "I know I shouldn't have and I know I'm risking making you angry at me–again–but I just want you to be happy. I hate seeing you beat yourself up over a guy–especially a guy you can have so easily. When he sees you in this," she snapped her fingers. "Done deal."

Macy pointed at the garment. "He won't see me in this."

"C'mon. It'll be fun and he'll love it."

"If you're so sure why don't you wear it."

"Well, I would–for Cordell Lachlan. In fact, I'd wear nothing at all for—"

"I get it. Thanks."

"So, try it on. Please?"

Macy felt a mix of emotions, but mostly incredulity at the fact that Keri had actually managed to make what looked like a real-life superhero costume. The garment in front of her was no second rate Halloween costume-looking fake. It looked more like a high dollar prop from a movie.

"C'mon. Please?"

Macy took a deep breath and thought about the times this past week that she'd tried out the Stellar pose in the mirror in both her bathroom and the basement gym. Both times she'd ended up laughing at herself, but she had at least been considering Keri's idea. "Alright. But I'm not guaranteeing anything."

Keri clapped and bounced up and down causing the swivel chair to make a pumping sound.

"Wait on the stairs. There's no way I'm risking Grandad seeing me in this."

"Ugh." Macy pulled the last zipper closed and did her best to stretch. The bottom layer of spandex had felt just fine, but the armor that went over the top of it and felt like it was made out of some kind of leather or vinyl was stiff and hard to move in. She moved her arms up and down causing the armor to squeak. It was definitely tight, but with some wear and tear it would eventually be a perfect fit. She took a long look in the mirror and frowned. She looked ridiculous–like a novice windsurfer in a new wetsuit–with her bare hands and feet sticking out of the partial costume. But if Keri could make this much of the outfit she could certainly come up with the gloves, boots, mask, and hood needed to finish off the look. "Okay. Get in here."

Macy took a deep breath and struck the Stellar pose. She fought the urge to grin and laugh and did her best to hold the neutral, but ready for anything, pose as the doorknob turned and Keri entered, closing the door behind her.

"Nice." Keri raised her eyebrows and nodded at her own handiwork. "I think it works. How does it feel?"

Macy rotated her shoulders and the costume squeaked. "Tight."

Keri adjusted the shoulder pads and pulled on the armor. "Well, it's new. It's going to be for a while. But what do you think overall?"

Macy let go of the pose and turned back and forth in the mirror. "You definitely have a bright future in Hollywood as a costume designer if nothing else."

"So, you'll wear it to the dance, right?"

Macy felt her insides sink. She stared blankly at Keri for a moment. The costume was second to none and she could only imagine the hours of work that had gone into its creation. Could she really tell Keri no after all of that–especially when she'd been considering the idea herself? She took a deep breath and opened her mouth. Slowly, she felt sound come out. "Yeeeah. I'll wear it to the dance."

Keri beamed as she clapped her hands and bounced on the balls of her feet.

Macy did her best to smile, but inside she felt like she'd just lived through an earthquake. She'd either made a good decision and things would work out like Keri was saying or she'd agreed to the thing that would complete her embarrassment in front of Patrick Newell and make her a cautionary legend in the halls of Alum Ridge High forever.

CHAPTER 7

Dance night had come far quicker than Macy had wanted. All week she'd been doing whatever she could to not focus on the dance and Keri's featherbrained scheme. But now, as she rode in the backseat of her mother's Ford Freestyle towards the Alum Ridge property, she realized that may not have been the best strategy. Instead of slowing things down it had actually made things seem to go that much faster.

She adjusted herself in the seat as they exited the Greater Avendale neighborhood. The Stellar armor squeaked under the overcoat she was wearing as she moved. When the headlights of her mother's crossover SUV illuminated the brick knee wall and wrought iron fence combination that surrounded the school property she felt her insides tighten and her airway restrict.

How had she let this happen? She'd known from the moment she agreed that she didn't really want to do it, but Keri's enthusiasm had silenced her. And the work Keri had continued to put into the costume had kept her quiet. Each day, instead of coming over to Macy's house as she normally did several nights a week, Keri had stayed on the bus to her own stop. And each morning–after what was probably a sleepless night–Macy had a text containing a picture of another completed piece. The mask, the gloves, the boots–by last night it was all done.

The SUV turned into the back entrance of the school and drove past a line of dormant buses. Keri's smile got wider as they got closer to the front door and Macy's insides got tighter. Luckily she hadn't eaten much in the last twelve hours or else it may have been forced from her stomach onto the floorboard.

"Alright, girls." Becky Davis braked and came to a stop at the curb. "I'll pick you up here at nine o'clock. No later, okay?"

"Yes, ma'am." Macy managed to squeak out.

"Thank you, Mrs. Davis."

Becky Davis lowered the driver's side window and waved to Deputy Newell.

"We'll keep them all on the straight and narrow, Mrs. Davis," Newell said from his perch next to the arched doorway. "You and Mr. Davis enjoy a dinner to yourselves for a change."

"Thank you, Deputy."

"Yes, ma'am. Happy to do it."

Macy pushed the door open and slid off the seat, looking up at the main entrance of the school. Like many buildings of its era, it was an imposing sight. She'd been driving past the building for most of her life and it had always reminded her of the U.S. Supreme Court with a clock tower atop it. It dawned on her that she had never actually used the main entrance–only the side entrance where the buses were always gathered. The three-story brick and mortar structure seemed to loom ever larger in front of her and she could already hear the bass pounding from speakers in the gym—or was that her heart rate increasing to an absurd level?

"C'mon."

She felt Keri slide out behind her. She'd worked out most of the kinks in the costume and managed to loosen it up some during her workouts, but she still wasn't entirely used to moving around in it. She straightened her overcoat and staggered forward. Her head felt like it was buzzing and things seemed to move in slow motion as she stumbled toward Newell and the front door.

"Evening, girls. What are you two supposed to be—the—"

"The Blues Sisters." Keri pulled a fedora hat from the bag she was carrying.

Macy did her best to smile, but couldn't manage any words.

"You girls have fun." Newell wrote something in a notepad he was holding.

Inside, only the hallways that led to the gym were lit. The others were dark and had a single chair holding up a yellow Do Not Enter ribbon across the entrance. But that didn't impede access to the library, the first floor of which was located just off the main atrium. Macy stared at the two sets of french doors that led to where thousands of books and dozens of computer terminals were housed on two floors. There was a faint trace of light inside, but no signs of movement as she was dragged past. Did this mean Patrick's plans to use the library were off? Oh, Lord—what if he wasn't even here? What if he'd stayed home when he found out the rest of the school would be closed?

"In here."

Macy was pulled into the first girl's bathroom they passed. The bathrooms nearest the entrance were the most recently remodeled as they were the ones likely to be used by visitors. Instead of the middle of the last century mustard-colored tile of the other facilities, this bathroom was mostly white with gray accents and had the latest in hands-free washing and paperless drying technology.

"Alright." Keri set down the fedora hat on one of the sinks and the bag she was carrying on another. "You didn't get a chance to try on the mask so I made it as adjustable as I could. It should work. Are you ready?"

Macy swallowed hard and pulled off her trench coat. "Yeah."

"Hey. You're her–you're Stellar. You're a hero to the unprotected masses–a crime fighter extraordinaire–you're. . . whatever else he made her."

"Heh. Yeah."

"My point is you've got this. He's going to be completely surprised."

"Oh, I'm sure of that." Macy tried to shake off the buzzing in her head. She'd come this far and there was no going back now. Even if this turned into the most embarrassing moment of her life it had become one of those moments she'd always wonder about if she chickened out. "Alright. Suit me up."

Keri pulled a padded glove/arm guard combo from her bag. Again, Macy was amazed at the lengths Keri had gone to with the costume. Seemingly printed onto the piece were the same dark lines as in the drawing–the same detail that made the costume look almost mechanical in some ways. She stuck her hand into the glove as Keri held it and watched as Keri secured the Velcro straps of the arm guard.

She flexed her hand in the glove. It wasn't that much different than the MMA-style gloves she wore when she was using her heavy bag at home. The material was a little thinner and instead of padding there seemed to be some sort of a plate inserted into the backhand and arm guard portions.

"What's in that?"

"Sheet metal."

"Sheet metal?"

"Yeah. Like the kind they use for air conditioning ducts. It's easy to cut and should bend a bit with your movements giving you more flexibility."

"Huh. That's awesome."

Keri pulled out the remaining pieces and set to work strapping them into place. From the looks of them, Macy thought she could probably do it herself, but Keri was intent on checking the fit of each one and making sure they were adjusted perfectly.

"Alright. Time for the last one." Keri reached into the bag and pulled out the mask. "What do you think?"

What did she think? Macy was awed just as she had been at the rest of the costume. Keri had texted her a picture of the mask when it was done, but the picture just hadn't done the piece justice. Shaped like a bluish-gray variation of the Phantom of the Opera mask, the piece had a fully adjustable strap and some sort of rubber sewn into the eye holes to keep the skin of the person wearing the mask from being too visible. Macy smiled. "Awesome job."

"Okay." Keri set the mask back down. "Close your eyes. We're going for uber-realistic here." She pulled a container of black eyeshadow from one of her pockets. "Hold still."

Macy obeyed and stood with her eyes shut as Keri liberally painted the velvety powder onto her eyelids and the surrounding areas.

"Okay. All set."

Macy opened her eyes and blinked to get used to the deliberate over application. In the mirror, she looked like she was going for a new goth look.

"That step alone takes this from Halloween costume to jumping directly out of a comic book."

Macy felt her nerves begin to tingle again as Keri picked up the mask, loosened the strap, and placed it over her head.

"Hold that."

Macy placed a hand on the mask to hold it in place as Keri moved around behind her and tightened the strap.

"Ow."

"Too tight?"

"A bit."

"How about that?"

"Better."

"Good."

Keri started pulling and pushing on the hood attached to the chest portion of the costume. "I ran two pieces of PVC-coated building wire into the grooves of the hood. That should allow us to shape it how we want and to hold it there." She pushed and pulled some more and finally lifted the hood into position.

Macy watched in the mirror. "How's it going to stay up?"

"Easy. It's actually made of two pieces of material sewn together and I left four holes."

"Holes?"

"Yup." Keri pulled four heavy duty-looking hair barrettes from her pocket and reached past Macy's face into the hood. One by one, she fastened Macy's hair and the hood together with the barrettes.

"Nice. Thought of everything, didn't you?"

"I think so. Except what you're going to say to Patrick when you walk in. I left that part to you."

Macy swallowed hard and stood there looking at herself in the mirror. It was hard to believe she was even looking at the same person who had barely stumbled and stuttered her way through the chance meeting at the mall less than a week before. Standing there in the darkened bathroom with only the whites of her eyes showing beneath the material and makeup had an oddly empowering effect.

"Are you ready?"

"As I'll ever be."

Macy moved to the doorway of the bathroom.

Keri passed her into the hallway, placed her fedora on, and grinned back at her with excited anticipation. "See you out there." She headed off in the direction of the gym.

Macy took a deep breath and stepped into the lit hallway for the first time. She stood still for a long moment and let her eyes adjust. When they had, she looked in the direction of the library. What if Deputy Newell saw her as she passed the main entrance? Was Patrick even in the library? Was he even here at all? She did her best to tuck away her uneasy feelings, which seemed oddly easier in the Stellar costume, and started off in the direction of the gym. She'd use one of the second-floor entrances to the library and could make her way around through the back halls.

She turned into the freshman hall and passed the rows of lockers. She'd passed through this hallway a dozen times a week for almost two months now, but it was suddenly as if she was seeing it with new eyes–empowered eyes. Inside the Stellar costume she didn't feel threatened. She felt like a threat. Even the way she walked felt different–less harried and more confident–like she was ready for anything. But was she ready for what she'd come here to do? She took another deep breath.

All week she'd known she would need to say something and that something should likely be prepared in advance and well-practiced. But she'd been unable to think of exactly what. She'd tried again and again to write something down, but each effort had begun and ended with *Hi, Patrick* and wound up in a crinkled ball on her bedroom floor. How exactly did you go about saying *'Hi. I'm so in love with you I had my best friend design a superhero costume based on a drawing I stole from you so I could come here tonight and impress you'* without sounding like an insane person?

A series of bright, multi-colored flashes drew her attention. At the end of the freshman hall, she looked at the entrance of the gym a stone's throw away. The student party planning committee with the aid of the maintenance crew had turned the relatively modern gymnasium into a dance hall that would rival any of the nightspots in the famed downtown club district. Through the opened doors, Macy could see sparkling disco balls hanging low over the makeshift dance floor, streaming tinsel covering the stowed bleachers, and a handful of students milling around. The event was only just beginning to get going and more people would be showing up continuously over the next hour or so.

She glanced over her shoulder at the empty freshman hall and then kept her eyes on the gym as she lifted one leg after another over the Do Not Enter ribbon, moving from the light into the dark as she did. There were teacher and parent chaperones present as well as a few of Newell's security staff, but she had yet to see any of them with the exception of Newell himself. Still, the quicker she moved away from the areas expecting heavy foot traffic the better her chances of going unnoticed would be.

She stayed close to the wall as she made her way down the back hallway. Stealthily, she passed the Freshman foreign language rooms where she took French with Mrs. Flor and the two science labs that were shared by both Freshman and Sophomore classes. The doors to the rooms were all closed and likely locked for the weekend, but a single light had been left on above the teacher's desk as was dictated by some sort of school board policy that Macy didn't entirely understand or really even care about.

"Hey!"

Macy flattened herself against the wall and looked back in the direction she'd come.

"Wait up!"

A student in what appeared to be a pirate outfit turned the corner out of the Freshman hall and headed for the gym followed closely by another who was trying to keep up. Macy watched them until they disappeared through the gym doors and then let out a sigh of relief. Whether it was paranoia playing tricks on her mind or a pubescent deepening of the boy's voice, she could have sworn it had been Deputy Newell calling out.

She picked up her pace and made it to the far corner of the school. She glanced down the empty hallway containing the entrance to the cafeteria and more freshman classrooms. There was still no one in sight. She followed the hallway to where the second-floor staircase switchbacked upwards and looked up the steps through the steel-framed windows. She could see a faint trace of the moon beginning to rise above the treeline at the edge of the Alum Ridge property. The rays of light exposed flecks of dust in the air that sparkled as they floated across the empty mid-floor landing.

Macy willed herself to put one foot in front of the other until she was on the landing looking at another set of french doors with the word library stenciled above them in black paint. On each door, below the windows, was a poster of a popular celebrity holding their favorite book and the word READ in bright red letters above their heads. Even in the dim light, she recognized the face of Cordell Lachlan, but she had no idea who his female counterpart on the opposite door was–probably some bombshell from one of the umpteenth remakes currently clogging the airwaves and cinemas if she had to guess.

She lifted her eyes from the posters to the windows. There was a light on inside, but did that mean someone was in there or only that one had been left on per policy? She listened intently for any noises coming from inside. Nothing. But would there be? Libraries were quiet places and whatever research Patrick and his friends were doing probably wouldn't involve making a lot of noise. Plus the library was two stories and filled with eight-foot high bookshelves that divided both floors into cavern-like sections with computer terminals scattered throughout. Patrick might not even be on this side of the building.

She moved to the base of the next set of stairs and stood there with the reinforced toes of the Stellar boots touching the bottom step. The buzzing in her head returned as she began to think again about what she was going to say. How was she going to—an idea hit her. How would Stellar handle this? Maybe she had been approaching this entire thing from the wrong point of view. Maybe instead of approaching this as Macy Davis in a Stellar costume she should be approaching it like Stellar. After all, Stellar was a drawing–a character–a figment of Patrick's imagination. Had he even gone so far as to give her an identity beyond that of a typical do good crime fighter? If she had to guess, probably not. And that meant the only real life Stellar had was *her* life–the heart that beat in her chest–the heart that was currently pounding a hundred miles an hour with no sign of slowing in sight. She was Stellar.

She rotated her shoulders and stretched in the still not quite broken-in costume, doing her best to psych herself up for what she was about to do. "Hi, Patrick." She said the words just above a whisper as she willed herself once again to place one foot in front of the other. No, that didn't sound right. That didn't sound like a hero. She squared her shoulders as she climbed a few more steps and tried again. "Hello, Patrick." That was it. That sounded confident. That sounded like a hero would sound. She placed her foot onto the second-floor landing and cleared the hallway of anything that shouldn't be there. She was alone.

Watching through the windows as she crossed the hallway to the library entrance, she looked for any sign of movement inside. Still nothing. She pulled open the door a few inches and listened. A shadow moved on a far wall and a croaky voice spoke. Macy smiled.

"I'm telling you guys if she were here she'd totally have handled this already."

"But she's not, doofus. She's a comic book character."

Macy recognized the voices of Patrick's two friends, Josh Friddle and a boy everyone called Striker for some reason she wasn't quite clear about. If they were present, so was Patrick.

"Yeah, but I'm just saying—"

"What you're just saying is ridiculous. Stellar's not here. She's not real."

"But if she was I'd—"

"You'd what?"

"That's not what I meant to—"

"You'd ask her out like you did Beth Tramer?"

"No!"

"See you wouldn't even talk to her. You'd faint."

"Would not!"

Macy's smile widened. She'd overheard these two talking before and they always seemed to be arguing like an old married couple. She wasn't exactly sure why Patrick hung around them, but she guessed that sometimes your friends picked you instead of the other way around. Josh and Striker had been by Patrick's side since elementary school and that kind of loyalty was hard to find–even if they were annoying and immature.

"Would you guys quit? You're giving me a headache. I swear I should have done this alone."

There it was–the voice Macy had been waiting for.

"Sorry to interrupt your work, Sherlock."

"Seriously, guys–if we're going to get anything done tonight we need to concentrate. Now you said you could get into the Sheriff's computer with my dad's InvestiMate login, right?"

"Yeah."

"Well, here it is. I scrolled all the way back to when he started at Alum Ridge and I found the email containing the login they assigned him."

"Heh. Your dad's gonna kill you if he finds out you hacked his email."

"I didn't hack it. He keeps the password written on the backside of a business card in his shirt pocket. And he's not going to find out–that's why we're using the computer here."

"Please don't tell me his password is password."

"Shut up and get to work."

Macy stepped away and allowed the door to close quietly. She squared her shoulders again. This was it–even with Patrick's goofball friends present she had to go for it. She'd open the door, walk in, and say *'Hello, Patrick'* dramatically. After that, she wasn't sure. Maybe she'd pull off the mask and admit the real reason why she was in the comic book shop and who her real favorite hero was. She imagined them all having a good laugh about it and her and Patrick going down to the gym to join Keri. This would be awkward, but worth it. Hopefully. She took a deep breath and reached for the door handle, but stopped just short of grabbing it as a shadow appeared across the hallway next to the library entrance.

She placed her back against the wall again and stood perfectly still as the silhouetted head and torso floated on the wall in the rays of moonlight coming through the windows. Who was it? Newell or another security guard making rounds? No. The person wasn't moving. They were just standing there. Macy waited. Moments that felt like minutes passed and the shadow stayed put, the person looking this way and that, but not moving from a stationary position.

The sound of a doorknob being turned echoed through the hall. "Woo hoo hoo!" a male voice said just above a whisper. "Ya boys ready for this?" Two more shadows arrived and a round of silent high fives were exchanged.

"Yeah."

"Let's do it."

Macy rolled her eyes. Pranksters. *Great. Just great.* The last thing she needed was to be seen by some idiots trying to let crickets loose in a classroom drop ceiling, remove wheels from a teacher's swivel chair or attack freshmen with toilet paper and Super Soakers. Maybe she could slip away and wait until they moved on. She stepped away from the wall intent on heading back down the stairs.

"Just remember," one of the boys whispered. "They said the Newell nerd was the one getting too close to things. They don't care about the other two. He's the primary target."

"Right."

"Got it. But we can still beat the other two, right?"

Macy stopped in her tracks. *Newell nerd? Too close to things? Primary target?* On second thought, this didn't sound like a group of pranksters at all.

CHAPTER 8

Macy moved back to her place along the wall and listened.

"How do they know this kid's getting too close anyway?"

"Hureeh?" one of the boys scoffed. "How should I know how they know? They just do. They said we need to hurt him–make sure he quits asking–or else."

Hureeh? Macy recognized the unintelligible sound as the same one Zeke made whenever he was poking fun at someone for asking a question. Were the flunkies in the hallway the bullies she'd been taking on since the fifth grade? It sounded like it and it sounded like they were intent on doing Patrick harm.

"Let's get these dorks."

Macy's cheeks flushed and she felt rage rise inside her. She did her best to fight it back, but her nostrils flared beneath the Stellar mask and her breaths came in short, powerful puffs. These guys weren't going to get away with this anymore. She stepped into the center of the hallway and stood in a neutral position with her arms at her sides. The entire student body of both the Alum Ridge junior high and high schools had put up with these boys causing trouble and putting their hands on people for years. The time for someone to do something about it had long since passed and from the sound of it, their wedgies, locker stuffing, and tax collections were about to graduate to full-on beatings. *Not on my watch. Not anymore.*

The boys' shadows moved forward, growing long as they reached the corner and disappearing against the tiled floor. The first boy to come into sight was undoubtedly Zeke. Macy knew him by his side to side, gorilla-like swagger. A few paces behind him were Luke and Trevor. The three of them were dressed in matching black jumpsuits featuring white bones and their heads were covered in white hoods. Their faces had been painted to look like skulls.

"That's far enough." The words echoed in Macy's head. There wasn't a disapproving hall full of students or a School Resource Officer nearby to give these goons pause this time. This could be it—this could be the fight they'd all been spiraling towards for years. The hairs on the back of Macy's neck stood and a chill ran down her spine.

Zeke lifted his head, taking notice of Macy for the first time. "Heh. What?"

"I said that's far enough."

"I heard what you said." Zeke motioned and Luke and Trevor moved out from behind him. "What I'm wondering is how you're going to back it up? What are you supposed to be—Tharella?"

Macy scoffed at the thought of the half-naked zombie killer she'd seen in the comic shop. What about her current outfit looked anything like that icon of the modern male mentality? "Tharella couldn't take down a five-year-old for jaywalking in that outfit, big boy. But if you want to see how I handle things by all means keep coming. And the name's Stellar."

"Ohhh ho! Let's do this, babe." Zeke pounded his fist into his hand and started forward.

Each time Macy had faced these three before they'd backed down, but the look in Zeke's eyes said that wasn't going to be the case this time. Whoever had charged them with hurting Patrick must have been someone they weren't willing to disappoint. But oddly enough, Macy's anxiety had disappeared. Mostly, she figured she'd finally just had enough of these guys and their threatening Patrick had pushed her over the edge. But the effect of the Stellar costume wasn't lost on her. Inside it, she still felt far more empowered than she had ever felt staring these guys down in a t-shirt and jeans.

Zeke bounced on his toes and raised his fists as he reached her position. "Heeya!" He threw a meaty fist at her head. Macy stepped aside and raised her arm in a circular motion, blocking his attack at the elbow. Zeke stumbled and she got a whiff of his body odor as he fell past her, his momentum carrying him off balance. He turned and bounced on his toes again, throwing another punch at her head. She ducked this time, allowing the punch to sail over her head as she stood and drove a knee into his exposed midsection. The sound of Zeke's painful gasp and the air rushing from his lungs filled the empty hallway. He collapsed onto his knees, his forehead on the floor, and his breaths fogging the tiles.

"An amateur mistake, slick. You're not used to someone fighting back, are you?"

Zeke continued to gasp for air but choked out a command. "Get... her..."

Macy returned to a ready stance as Luke and Trevor started forward.

But their movements were even less experienced than Zeke's. They raised their fists and bobbed forward and back again, afraid to commit to an attack. After years of training and sparring, she'd seen this many times in neophytes. "Oh, c'mon, guys. This is just pathetic."

Trevor advanced, throwing the same overextended jab attack as Zeke. Macy didn't even bother to block him. She stepped back, causing the punch to miss and fired an ax kick up and into his face. The force of the kick drove his feet from under him and he landed on his back. "Ugh! My nose!"

Macy returned again to a ready stance. A pair of arms wrapped her in a bear hug from behind.

"Got ya now!"

Macy struggled for a moment, but quickly remembered one of her most favorite moves. She raised her foot and drove it downwards, allowing her heel to scrape Luke's shin as she stomped on his foot.

"Ow!"

His arms loosened and Macy drove an elbow into his ribs, breaking his grip entirely. Free of the bear hug, she turned to face her attacker. Luke was gripping his lower ribcage and wincing, but slowly raised his fists. Macy turned and delivered a spinning back kick to his midsection, knocking him into the concrete wall behind him. He slid to a sitting position and slumped sideways with a painful grimace.

"It's gonna take more than that, babe."

Macy turned. Zeke had gotten back to his feet and despite still looking winded from his first defeat, raised his fists to try again. Macy moved toward him in a neutral stance. In front of the library doors, they met and began to circle one another.

"Heeya!" Zeke lifted his leg, using his height advantage to aim for a stomping kick. Again, Macy stepped aside and the attack missed. Zeke's foot stomped the floor instead of her and he put his arms out to keep his balance.

"Heeya!" He came at her again, turning and throwing a left hook. She stepped back and felt only the breeze as his meaty arm flew past, his momentum turning him away from her. She threw a front kick at the small of his back, knocking him forward just as the library door opened and a wide-eyed Striker narrowly missed the bully as he stumbled past.

"Whoa!"

Macy straightened up and strode past the awed boy into the library where Zeke was picking himself up after crashing into a pushcart full of books. In her peripheral vision she could see Patrick and Josh Friddle turn their attention away from a computer and freeze in shock.

"That's it! I'm not playing anymore." Zeke picked up a metal folding chair and held it like a baseball bat. "Yah!" He swung it like he was going for a home run in the bottom of the ninth. Macy dropped into a full split and as the attack sailed over her head she drove her fist into Zeke's exposed groin. She was done playing, too. She jumped back to her feet as he dropped the chair and doubled over in pain. She drove her foot forward in a powerful kick, her heel connecting with Zeke's exposed ribs. The bully stumbled backward into another cart full of books and landed with his legs over one shoulder. This time he didn't appear to be coming back for more.

Macy straightened up and looked to the computer stations. There, with a face that could only be read as utter and complete shock, Patrick Newell looked back at her, his eyes blinking in apparent disbelief.

"Hello, Patrick."

Macy held his gaze. Would he recognize her by her eyes or was he only seeing Stellar? What did she do now?

Patrick stood slowly, his eyes not leaving hers. "Uhh—umm—hi." He reached into his backpack and fumbled around before withdrawing a notebook that Macy recognized as the one that contained his drawings.

"Dude–this is so going viral."

Macy glanced away from Patrick to see Striker holding a smartphone up–not good. But what was behind him was even worse– a flashlight beam danced around the hallway–really not good. This was getting out of control fast. *Time to go.*

"What's going on up here?"

Too late. Deputy Newell stepped through the door, his eyes moving about the room until they landed on the fallen Zeke and his costumed conqueror standing over him.

"Whoa there." Newell stopped in his tracks. He glanced at Zeke and back again. "Did you do all of this? Who are you? Take off the mask." His hand reached instinctively for a taser on his duty belt. "Now."

Macy turned to face him completely. What did she do? Did she obey his commands and try to explain the situation? How would her father react to the news that she'd been in a fight? He'd be furious. She couldn't get caught. But she had been already, hadn't she?

"Alright now, young lady. I don't want to have to use this, but you need to take off the mask and come with me. We have a zero-tolerance policy about fighting in this school."

"Zero tolerance, huh?" Macy pointed to Zeke and to the hallway beyond. "What about them?" She could hardly believe the words coming out of her mouth, but she really had had enough of the double standard she'd observed for years. A chance at victory in a football game wasn't worth much if you had to sacrifice your integrity to get it.

"I'll deal with them later. Now I'm not going to ask you—hey!"

Macy bolted toward the door, keeping her eyes on Newell as he withdrew the taser from his belt and raised it. Could she make it?

Nope. She jumped at the wall and used it to redirect her momentum, launching into a spinning kick and catching the taser in Newell's hand a second before he pulled the trigger. The taser clattered away and the force of the kick caused him to stumble. Macy landed, barely able to believe the preposterous technique had worked. She took off running.

"Hey! Get back here!"

She bolted past Striker and through the library door into the hallway. She'd just attacked a police officer. How was she going to get out of this? She powered away from the library doors and around a corner, nearly hitting the far wall in her haste.

"Hey! Stop!"

She could hear the sound of heavy rubber soles behind her. She kept going, passing darkened classroom after darkened classroom as she made her way toward the stairwell in the far corner.

"This is Newell! I'm in pursuit of a suspect in a multiparty fight near the library! I need assistance!"

Macy reached the stairwell and placed her hands on the railing, leaping over it. The lower stairs rushed at her faster than she'd expected. She tried to bend her knees and absorb the impact, but the uneven surface caused her to stumble as she landed. She fell face-first onto the ground floor.

"Roger that, sir. On our way."

Macy stumbled to her feet as she saw the beam of Newell's flashlight illuminate the mid-floor landing above her. She glanced between the two routes she could take. Did she go for the front door where she could sprint across the main parking lot and make it off the property or did she go for one of the back doors where there would be more places to hide? Flashlight beams bounced around the hallways in the distance. Newell's backup was coming. Macy bolted toward the gym and the back door through the Freshman hallway.

"Suspect is a lone female approximately five foot six and wearing a red and gray—"

Macy turned the corner and powered toward the gym entrance, her lungs feeling like they were on fire as she pushed herself as hard as she could. Ahead she could see flashing disco lights and hear the pounding bass from the gym. Would anyone inside notice her? Did it matter? She flew past the gym entrance and dodged toward a side door, turning to hit the latch with her backside. Her momentum caused her to slide on the smooth metal and carried her into the beam between the doors, her shoulder taking the brunt of the impact. The sound of the metal latch disengaging echoed through the hallway despite the sound of the bass from the gym. The door flew open and banged against the brick exterior. Macy took a painful breath, her shoulder beginning to throb as she pushed off and finally felt the cool October air that signalled her freedom.

Outside, she tore across a concrete sidewalk beneath a metal breezeway. Beyond the breezeway was an expansive parking lot used by students who were old enough to drive. She stopped and looked at her options. Sidewalks led to darkened courtyards and rows of trailers set up as temporary classrooms but would mean more running. And Newell couldn't be far behind.

She glanced up–the breezeway. That was it. That was her best option. She backed up and got a running start. At the end of it, she jumped and grabbed a support pole, allowing her momentum to swing her out and around. She grabbed the roof of the breezeway with one foot and used it to pull herself up and onto it. She rolled onto her back and lay flat, her shoulder throbbing from the continued abuse.

The door below banged open and flashlight beams illuminated the walkway and the parking lot beyond. Macy did her best to slow down her breathing, but to little avail after the long sprint from the library. She stared at the clear night sky and willed herself to be absolutely still.

Newell cursed. "This is 101 at Alum Ridge High School. We've lost sight of a suspect in a fight at the B wing exit. We're going to need an APB to all Avendale units for a lone female approximately five foot six and heading away from the school. Suspect may be wearing a red and gray—a—a—" Newell stopped and Macy could practically feel his frustration and disbelief, "a red and gray superhero costume. Over."

"Umm copy that, 101," a female voice crackled over a radio, "I'll put the call out. Over."

The flashlight beams below her were lowered one by one until only one remained. It made a long sweep over the parking lot again and disappeared as sets of boots clunked away toward the B wing door. The hinges on the rear door squealed as it was opened and it banged closed again a moment later. Newell had given up his search. She was alone in the darkness now. She breathed in and out steadily, no longer afraid of being heard.

An APB? Macy had watched enough cop shows to know that meant All Points Bulletin and that Newell had just notified every Sheriff's Deputy in the Greater Avendale suburb to be on the lookout for her. How was she going to get away from the school now? Even if she ditched the Stellar costume there was no way to change the fact that she would be a lone female, about five foot six, and heading away from the school. She'd be seen for sure as she tried to cover the six and a half blocks between the school and her house. And even if by some miracle she made it she'd have to explain why she wasn't where she was supposed to be when her mom came to pick her up. She tried to fight off a feeling of panic. She needed to stay calm. She needed to figure out a plan. She had to figure out a plan.

CHAPTER 9

The unmistakable odor of diesel fumes invaded her nostrils as Macy stepped onto the front porch of her house and looked at the long yellow bus waiting in the street. *Nothing like a long walk to freedom, huh?* It was the first freedom she'd had since not being where she was supposed to be when her mother had come to pick her up from the dance.

The look on her mom's face and the wrenching feeling in Macy's gut as her mother had arrived home was still raw in her mind. *'In the dark? By yourself?'* Her mother's shrill words echoed through her head as she moved toward her waiting ride. *'What were you thinking?'* And of course, Macy hadn't been able to say what she'd been thinking, why she'd left the school, or that she'd ducked half a dozen Sheriff's

Deputies on the way. Instead, she'd stood there like a deer in a set of headlights and shrugged her shoulders–a response that only drew forth further anger and had elicited flaring nostrils, an I'd-beat-you-if-I-could stare, a forcefully pointed index finger, and a walk of shame to her room.

But that was over now. Well, mostly. Her parents had grounded her to her room and from her phone and other electronics for the weekend and to the house for the rest of the week, but at least they were back to talking to her without acting like she'd called the neighbors' new baby ugly to their faces. The morning exchanges around the kitchen island had been something approaching normal and her mother had even issued her standard *'Have a good day, dear'* in her usual cheery tone as Macy had choked down a bagel and shouldered her backpack.

"Mornin', Macy."

"Hi, John."

John's normal jovial demeanor was noticeably absent as she passed him and made her way towards the back of the bus where she could see Keri waiting. She passed seats filled with her gloomy and tired-looking schoolmates. *Wow. Is it a Monday or what?* She slung her backpack off her shoulder and around, allowing it to land at her feet as she plopped down into the seat next to Keri. "Hey."

Keri lifted an eyebrow and gave her a sympathetic look. "Hey."

An uncomfortable silence began as the bus rumbled away from her house. When John was almost at their next stop and Macy couldn't take it anymore, she turned to Keri. "So, yeah. My parents grounded me from my phone, my computer, my tablet, my television, and even my MP3 player, which hasn't been used in at least a year, and then refused to let me leave my room until this morning. My mom's been bringing a tray to my door as though it were the last meal for the condemned and I'm pretty sure I can cancel any social plans I may have had between now and Christmas." She gave a sarcastic smirk. "How was your weekend?"

"Heh. Better than yours, I guess. But only just."

"What happened?"

"To me? Nothing. It's what's going to happen."

Macy cringed and a familiar wrenching feeling returned. "To you?"

"To everyone who attends Alum Ridge for sure and possibly everyone who attends a public school in the district."

Macy's face sank. "It's that bad?"

"Oh, yeah."

Macy put her head down and slowly banged it against the back of the seat in front of her. "And here I was hoping it was just my parents who were treating this like it was some kind of last straw or something."

"I wish. I think everyone's parents are treating this like it was the last straw."

Macy banged her head on the seat one more time and slowly looked over. "Well, don't keep me in suspense. What do I have to look forward to?"

Keri raised her eyebrows and shrugged as her eyes darted around the bus. Macy frowned. She knew exactly what the gesture meant: saying any more than they already had would mean risking the revelation that they knew more about what had happened at the dance than they should. Macy gave a small nod and closed her eyes as she allowed her head to fall back against the seat again. The rest of the ride would probably be in silence and she wasn't sure if she could stand it. She hadn't had anyone besides Bun Bun, a well-loved stuffed bunny that normally occupied a permanent spot on her bookshelf, as company all weekend. And despite his natural curiosity and dry wit, conversations with Bun Bun just weren't as much fun as they had been when she was five. She felt her phone buzz in her pocket. She looked back at Keri.

Keri had her phone out and was giving her a knowing stare. Macy reached for the device in her pocket and swiped the screen. *Genius.* She'd nearly forgotten she was once again plugged in. She skipped through a long list of notifications that had appeared when she'd turned the phone on for the first time in over 48 hours and went straight to Keri's message.

> *You went full crime-fighter Friday night. Way to impress Patrick, but not exactly what I had in mind. What happened!?!?*

Macy pursed her lips and twiddled her thumbs over the glowing screen for a moment as she thought about her response. There wasn't really much she could say. What happened had happened.

> *Zeke and his goons happened. That's what.*

She pressed send and listened as Keri's phone vibrated. Moments later, Keri responded.

> *Duh. I saw that much.*
> *The whole city has.*
> *Zeke's a bully. What else is new?*

Macy stared at her screen for a long moment. How could the whole city have seen—it hit her like a folding chair in a wrestling match; one of Patrick's guffawing buddies had recorded part of her fight with Zeke on his phone. She looked up at Keri, her eyes pleading. Keri gave her a *duh* nod and turned back to her phone.

Macy put her head back down and stared at her screen as three little dots appeared beneath Keri's last message. The wrenching Macy had been feeling in her gut now felt more like someone had closed a pair of Channel Locks around an intestine. She could hardly breathe. In the rush of emotions and the hours of introspection that had come and gone since the dance, she'd completely forgotten about the video. But apparently, no one else had. Her phone buzzed.

You didn't know about the video?

Macy pounded out a response and hit the blue arrow.

I saw him with his phone but forgot about it in my rush to get away. And grounded from everything, remember?

Keri's phone clicked repeatedly as her thumbs blazed across the keyboard.

OMG r u kidding? Everyone has seen it.

Macy felt like crying as she typed.

Everyone?

EVERYONE! It's even on the news.

Macy felt like she'd just survived a bombing in a movie and was now stumbling around looking for fellow survivors. If the video had been on the news, then Keri's assessment of everyone having seen it couldn't be far from reality. Even her grandfather in his self-imposed exile from what he called *dezinformatsiya*–whatever that meant– watched the local news. Her phone vibrated.

U ok?

The bus slowed as it neared the end of the Greater Avendale neighborhood and Macy saw the Alum Ridge property for the first time since she'd jumped the fence on her way home after the dance. *Okay? Of course, I'm not okay.* For the umpteenth time in the last few weeks, it felt like her world was ending.

The air brake on the bus hissed and the students stood as John pulled the handle and the doors slid open. Macy was slower to rise. She hadn't imagined that everyone in the building would be discussing the exact details of Stellar's fight. When all the students before her had gone and she couldn't delay the inevitable any longer she slogged after them as they moved off the bus like a line of ants.

On the sidewalk, dozens of lines from a row of buses converged into a mass of bodies moving toward the side entrance, their individual voices joining into a din of conversations that made hearing much of anything impossible. But Macy wasn't trying to hear what they were saying. In her head, she was still second-guessing herself so loudly it drowned out all but her inner dialogue. Would theories about the masked girl's identity abound? She couldn't imagine them not. Had she made some kind of easy mistake that would tip the authorities or some other careful observer off as to who she was? *Ugh!* Her head felt like it was about to explode.

"So," Keri leaned in close. Macy startled. "Rumor has it that Zeke, Luke, and Trevor are all out for the season. Taylor and Emma were at practice Saturday morning and they said Rigby's furious."

Macy allowed the information to sink in for a moment. She hadn't realized she'd done that much damage, but she hadn't exactly been holding back either. "Serves them right." She thought about what she was about to say and leaned in closer, lowering her voice to just above a whisper. "They were about to do the same to Patrick–or worse, from the sound of it."

Now it was Keri's turn to let it sink in and from the look on her face, she was doing just that. "To Patrick? Why?"

"Umm as if they needed a reason other than just being their usual charming selves?" Macy felt a familiar rage well up inside of her at the thought of the scene outside the library. She took a deep breath and checked it off as she looked around to be sure no one else was listening. "Well, how's this? It turns out that Zeke knows something about what happened to Brittany so he and his two Neanderthals were there to shut Patrick up because he's been asking too many questions."

Keri's eyes went wide. "Are you serious?"

"As a heart attack. I overheard them with my own two ears."

Keri stopped walking as they reached the entrance and moved to one side to avoid the incoming stream of students as she took in what she'd just been told. Macy stood next to her waiting. She'd had a lot of time to think about what had happened Friday night and the more she thought about it the more she felt her actions had ultimately been right–despite the damages wrought upon the rest of her life as a result. Not that being right would shield her from any of the associated punishments, but at least she didn't feel like she'd overreacted on top of everything else. She had saved Patrick and his friends from getting beaten on–or rather Stellar had saved them–and she was glad for it. Even in all of her self-doubt and second-guessing she had managed to find a small glimmer of pride–for what good it did.

Keri made eye contact again. "So, let me make sure I have this straight. After I left you you wandered around the school looking for Patrick, found him, and at the same time found Zeke plotting to shut him up?"

"Yup."

"And of course you intervened."

"Well, yeah. What else was I supposed to do–just let them beat on Patrick and his friends while I ran away and pretended not to know?"

Keri shrugged and looked at the floor.

"That's not all either. Before I confronted them, Zeke talked about someone else–someone who told him to do what he was about to do."

Keri looked up, her eyes revealing her state of mind was something approaching totally freaked out. "Oh my god, Macy. You've got to tell someone. Did Zeke say a name?"

Macy shook her head. "No. He just said *'they'*."

Keri turned away again. "Okay. Alright. We can handle this. We can." She seemed to be talking to herself now as much as she was talking to anyone. "What is it my mom always says? We can't change what's been done so what's important is what we do going forward? Yeah. That's it. That's right. I think. We need to focus. Just focus."

Macy noticed the herd of students entering the school was beginning to thin. "C'mon." She tugged Keri into the building by the arm.

Keri shook her head repeatedly as Macy walked a step or two behind her towards the freshman hall. What was she thinking? Macy didn't usually spend much time on what was going through her friend's head, but right now Keri looked really spooked and spooked could lead to costly mistakes. They passed the main atrium where a team of blue-shirted Accu-sec employees were putting the finishing touches on the newly installed metal detectors.

"Hold up a sec." Macy slowed her pace and watched for a moment. The sight of the uniformed men had jarred something loose in her head.

"What is it?" Keri turned on one heel with a question on her face.

Macy looked back toward the side entrance. She scanned both sides of the hall before finally settling on exactly what wasn't right about the scene. In the rush of emotions and situations running through her head as she'd entered she'd failed to notice that unlike every other morning at Alum Ridge High, Deputy Newell wasn't positioned in front of the office door watching as the students entered. *Huh.* Visions of her improvised kick striking him on the wrist and knocking his taser away flashed through her mind. Had she broken his wrist? Would an injury like that keep him off duty for a while? She felt her stomach sink. Newell had never been anything other than decent to her. He hadn't deserved to be attacked and injured and for cryin' out loud he was Patrick's father.

Macy felt her face flush with anger as she started moving again. "Nothing. It was nothing." She caught up with Keri and they waded into the throng of students in the freshman hall. "Excuse me. Pardon me. Move please." Instead of struggling for just enough space to slide some books from their lockers as they would have been doing on any other morning most of the freshman body were huddled over smartphone screens in the middle of the hall. Their eyes darted between each other and a continuous course of *'whoa!'* drowned out nearly every other noise as they stared at the screens.

"Apparently not *everyone* has seen it," Macy said, her lips practically to Keri's ear.

Keri shrugged. "When Ad and Amanda are talking about it *everyone* has seen it. Trust me."

"Ad and Amanda aren't the news. They're a lame-o morning radio show focused on celebrity gossip, crude jokes, and poking fun at people who—"

"—mostly deserve it. And you know they're serious sometimes. The theme last week was how much homework is too much and this week it's violence at school." Keri leaned in. "Thanks to you."

Macy rolled her eyes. "Oh, joy. I'll be riveted to my grandfather's clock radio in the morning."

"Anyways. . . what's it matter? They're seeing it now."

Macy decided to let the matter drop. She turned the combination on her locker without having to muscle past anyone for the first time since school had started, unzipped her backpack, and placed her third and fourth period books inside. "I'll probably regret this later on when I have to try to get them back out before class."

Keri stuffed her books into the next locker over. "No doubt."

"Dude!"

Macy startled.

"C'mon! That kick was nothing. I can do that kick right now."

"Then do it. Let's see it."

"Yeah, Seth. Do it!"

A chorus of *Do It!* began a short distance down the hall and a red-headed boy who was nearly a head shorter than most of his classmates stepped out of the fray–Seth McCauley, the ninth grade's most annoying student.

"Oh, Seth's about to break another bone. This I have to see." Keri closed her locker and leaned out to watch. Macy did so as well, though she had no interest in whatever hijinks Seth was about to be up to. The boy was in ninth grade, but looked like he was in fifth grade, talked like he was in third grade, and acted like he was in kindergarten. The chorus of *Do It!* continued and the boy aimed himself at a nearby wall as he stepped back into what passed for a ready stance in Hollywood. Macy shook her head. This wasn't going to end well.

"Do it!"

"C'mon!"

"On three! One! Two! Th—"

"That's enough!"

Macy tensed at the adult voice behind her. She knew exactly who it was. She turned cautiously. Newell stood only feet away, his usual tan and brown uniform as crisp and clean as ever, but with an added flash of black–an immobilizing wrist brace secured around the lower part of his arm.

"Save it for YouTube, son."

The gathering dispersed and within a second the freshman hall was back to normal. Students grabbed for books, dropped them as they were pushed aside by others, and backpacks being zipped and unzipped sounded like a cacophony of broken xylophones. Macy set out to take advantage of the momentary confusion and made her way toward the end of the hall.

"Not so fast, Miss Davis."

Macy stopped in her tracks, her face twisting into a painful grimace. *Miss Davis?* Newell had only ever called her by her first name. Last names were reserved for those who were in trouble or who were about to be. "Yes, sir?"

Newell stepped closer to her as nearby freshmen did their best to gather their belongings and leave the area as fast as they could. Even Keri rushed past. "See you in fourth."

An uncomfortable silence overtook the hallway as Macy watched Keri disappear around the corner.

Newell cleared his throat. "Maybe you'd like to explain to me why I have you arriving at the Halloween Dance shortly after seven o'clock on Friday, but have no exit time or comments in my notes?"

Macy studied him as he stood looking at a notepad she recognized as the same one he'd been writing in as she and Keri had arrived at the dance. She looked at his wrist and swallowed hard. "Exit time?"

Newell frowned and crossed his arms so that the brace was less visible. "Yes. I'm sure you've heard there was a little mishap on the second floor Friday night."

"Oh, yeah. That. Who hasn't?"

Newell gave a quick smirk. "Well, I'm sure you're also aware there was a lockdown as a result?"

Macy fought a cringe. "Yup. Heard about that, too—on the bus."

"After the building was cleared of any threats, my officers and I personally talked with each student before they were allowed to leave. Of the three hundred and eighty-six who arrived, I have nine who were unaccounted for by the time the last student left the gym. You're one of them. Why?"

Macy's mind was all over the place. What should she say? How should she say it? Would he believe anything she said? "I—umm—I—left early?"

"Is that a question or an answer?"

"An answer. . ." Macy couldn't believe the squeak that had just come out in place of her voice. There was no way he was going to believe her. She was the worst liar in the history of lying.

Macy watched as he wrote something in his notebook and closed it with a frown.

"Thank you, Miss Davis."

She watched as he climbed the second-floor steps and disappeared. She stood alone in the Freshman hall barely able to believe the turn of events since she'd left the house hardly half an hour earlier. The bell rang. *Ugh!* She hurried toward her homeroom. Now, on top of everything else, she was late.

CHAPTER 10

Macy stared at the front of the classroom, mindlessly using her ink pen like a toothpick as her math teacher, Mr. Haier, finished his Algebra lesson. Like the rest of the day before it, math class had dragged on at an unbelievably slow pace. All she really wanted to do was go home, fall into her bed, and take a long nap. But she had science next and the bus ride home before that was even remotely possible.

"Right then." Mr. Haier stroked his tightly cropped beard as he finished writing something out on the Active Board and glanced at the class. "As I've just shown you to solve this system of equations, your first goal is to cancel out the variables by adding equations together. I want you to practice using the equations on page forty-three of your textbook for your homework tonight."

Normally Macy was attentive enough in class and took good notes, but all she'd managed to accomplish this period was the date at the top of a blank sheet of paper. The bell rang. Chairs scraped and students stood begrudgingly as though they had been awoken abruptly. Macy could tell the rest of the student body was looking forward to their fourth block classes just as much as she was.

But if fourth block had one upside it was that she'd be with Keri again. Both the high and junior high schools in the Greater Avendale district divided student schedules into A days and B days to allow for all the classes that were necessary to pass the ever-increasing state standards. And today being an A day, meant Macy hadn't seen Keri since they'd walked into the building together hours earlier.

Macy closed her notebook and stood as she placed it into her backpack. But before she could begin making her way to the door, an ear-piercing ring sounded over the school-wide intercom and someone fumbling with a microphone could be heard.

"Is it on?"

"Yes, ma'am."

Principal Decker cleared her throat. "Attention, students. In light of recent events at our school, the district superintendents and I feel it necessary to address all of you in order to quell the various rumors and misinformation that has begun to spread. So as of now, all fourth block classes are canceled and you are to report to the gymnasium at once. Thank you."

A chorus of *yes!* sounded as the mood in the classroom shifted at once. Macy sat quietly. While she was as relieved as anyone to escape another period with The Spade, she wondered what *rumors and misinformation* Decker was talking about. *Recent events* could only mean the fight at the dance and the resulting lockdown, so clearly, the two were connected. She thought back over the day. Surprisingly, the theories and ideas about what had happened hadn't been nearly as wild as she'd expected. All everyone really wanted to know was who the girl in the mask was. The events on the video seemed to speak for themselves.

Macy shouldered her backpack and headed for the door after nearly everyone had gone. When she wasn't following Keri's charge for the bathroom mirror she always hung back a bit. That was a habit she'd learned from Grandad and the idea made sense to her. Better to see or hear what was coming and be marginally prepared than to be caught completely off guard. She exited the room a full ten feet behind the last student and followed the mass toward the gym. If being a freshman had one advantage it was the close proximity of the gym. She and Keri would have their choice of seats before the upper grades could make their way downstairs and from further regions of the school.

Macy watched from her perch in the upper corner of the bleachers where she had a bird's eye view of the proceedings. The assembly had quickly become standing room only as she had known it would. That was what happened when you had two thousand and some people trying to cram into a building designed–or rather redesigned–for fifteen hundred.

In a cordoned-off area of the gym with half a dozen chairs and a podium Principal Decker and her usual entourage of vice principals and assistants observed the gathering student body like hawks staring hungrily at passing field mice. Surrounding the small section and preventing anyone from sitting too close–as if anyone would dare– were four of the school's eight security guards and a yellow caution ribbon held up with chairs. On the wall behind them a gigantic mural of Randy the Ranger–Alum Ridge's Wild West lawman mascot– looked down over the gathering.

"So, he just left and didn't give you detention or anything?" Keri asked.

Macy shifted positions on the metal bleacher. She'd had a few moments as the gym continued to fill with students to catch Keri up on what had happened in the Freshman hall. "Yeah. Something tells me I haven't heard the last of it, though. Unfortunately."

Keri nodded her agreement and was about to say something when Decker stepped to the podium, adjusted her turtleneck, and cleared her throat. The gym fell eerily silent as she gripped each side of the podium and stared out at the gathered student body as though they were all about to get a spanking.

"Thank you for gathering in a timely and orderly fashion this afternoon. As all of you undoubtedly know, our Halloween dance was interrupted by violence. And of course, many of you have seen the video that recorded those events in part. Now I have heard all of the theories and speculation going on today and I want to caution you. What you have seen shows only the smallest part of what actually occurred. What you have not seen—what you could not have seen—is the circumstances that lead up to that event. With the help of our security staff and our beloved School Resource Officer, Deputy Newell, we have concluded a preliminary investigation and I want to share the results with you."

Macy leaned forward, placing her elbows on her knees and her chin in her hands. Since Decker had begun to speak it felt as though the temperature in the room had dropped ten degrees.

"After interviewing eyewitnesses it is our sincere belief that the hooded woman seen in the video was not a student at Alum Ridge High, but was here taking advantage of the Halloween costumes worn by the faculty and student body to accomplish some purpose which may now never be known thanks to three brave students; Zeke Pennington, Luke Bartlett, and Trevor Wright."

Macy felt her mouth drop as Decker and those seated behind her in the cordoned-off area began to applaud. Slowly, as if they were as shocked as Macy, the student body followed their lead until the entire assembly was clapping. A few whistles erupted and someone near the front row threw a football jersey into the air before Decker held up her hands and the room quieted again.

"These three–as the primary eyewitnesses to Friday night's violence–provided detailed accounts of their encounter with the masked woman and their statements have been provided to the Greater Avendale Sheriff's Office who will be handling the matter going forward."

Decker continued to speak, but Macy wasn't hearing her. Her face felt hot, her teeth were clenched, and her stomach was twisted into such a knot she wasn't sure it would ever come undone. How could the administration have it so wrong? Of course, she knew how they'd gotten it wrong–because they wanted to get it wrong. They wanted to believe what Zeke, Luke, and Trevor were selling, so they had. Furthermore, they wanted everyone else to believe it, too. And to that end, they'd called the assembly to begin the process of burying what had really happened in the minds of the student body once and for all. The next step would be a recorded message from Decker that would go out to each and every parent through the school system-wide automated phone thingy and then a warm and friendly email. Slowly but surely, the matter would die as the official version of the events made the rounds and was accepted by people far too busy to dig any deeper. But people needed to dig deeper. Zeke, Luke, and Trevor were connected to Brittany Crumb's disappearance and the administration was unwittingly helping them to cover it up.

"You okay?"

Macy frowned. She was anything but okay. She shook her head. "Why do I feel like we're the only ones here willing to face reality?"

Someone in the row ahead of her glanced back at them and Macy stopped talking. She still needed to be careful, though she felt like throwing caution to the wind. What would really happen if she did come forward and tell her side of things? Would it change anything? Would the sheriff take what she'd overheard seriously or would she be treated like Patrick and dismissed out of hand? She didn't know for sure how the sheriff would respond, but she felt like she knew how the administration would. Their entire focus would be on 'violence in school' and she'd be expelled while they ignored the punishments visited daily upon students by the likes of Zeke, Luke, and Trevor. It wasn't worth it. She turned attention back to Decker.

". . .and that's why violence will never be tolerated at Alum Ridge. Thank you."

The applause was light and mostly led by the faculty as Decker turned away from the podium. Macy rolled her eyes. The gathered students stood and stretched as Decker and her entourage made their way toward the exit. Macy watched them walk. What was the term Grandad used for what they'd just done? *Grandstanding.* That's what he'd called it–among other more colorful adjectives.

"Let's go." Keri tugged on her sleeve.

Macy shouldered her bag and followed Keri as students filed off the bleachers. On the floor of the gym, the lines from the steps combined into a huge mass all vying to get out of a single entrance. Macy stood quietly behind them happy to let them elbow each other and squirm for position. What were they accomplishing? Any chance of getting a good seat on the bus home had vanished with the presence of the entire student body on the main floor of the school.

"Mr. Fickel. Detention."

Macy raised herself up on her toes and looked over the dozens of heads in front of her. At the entrance to the gym Principal Decker and Deputy Newell stood on either side watching as students moved through. Her stomach tightened as she watched Decker hand a pink slip to a student.

"Mr. Jones. You, too. Detention."

Macy drew in a deep breath. Why were detention slips being handed out? Had the students done something during the assembly to warrant the punishment? Macy could only hope so. But as the mass in front her thinned and more slips were handed out it was clear that those who had left the dance early were Decker's target. Macy continued to step toward the door as student after student filed out.

"Ugh!" Something slammed into her and she stumbled, tripping over her own feet and struggling to stay upright. When she found her balance she turned to face what had hit her, her fists unconsciously rising to protect her face.

"S—so—sorry."

Macy stared at the pimpled face of the blond-haired boy known as Striker.

"We—we—were—"

"Acting like kindergartners." Keri broke in. "Why don't you dweebs watch what you're doing?"

Macy lowered her fists. "It's fine. It's no—" She stopped mid-sentence as she noticed Patrick standing a few feet behind Striker and Josh Friddle. Her heart skipped. Patrick's face was red and he was clearly embarrassed by his friends' behavior, but as he saw Macy looking at him his mouth curled into a small smile.

"Hi."

Macy smiled back. "Hi."

"Miss Davis. Detention."

The shrill voice jarred Macy back into the real world. A pink slip was thrust at her by a slender hand with a silver signet ring on the index finger. Some sort of insignia caught her eye, but she couldn't make out exactly what it was. A crown maybe?

"Detention? Wh—when? Why?" The words slipped out unconsciously as her attention was momentarily fixed on the ring.

"Why? Because you left a school function without permission. When? Now and for the rest of the week. Your parents have already been notified."

Macy let out a resigned breath, took the pink slip, and looked at Keri. "I guess I'll see you tomorrow."

"Yup. Looks like Ramen Noodles alone in my studio for me tonight."

As if the day hadn't been bad enough already, detention had seen Macy and a dozen other students cleaning graffiti from an outside wall of Alum Ridge. She'd never noticed how much 'tagging' had come to cover the more obscure walls in between buildings where overnight patrols couldn't readily see. Under the supervision of Deputy Newell, they'd managed to clean off about half a wall and had the dirt, grime, and wet to show for it. It would take her the rest of the night to clean the filth from under her fingernails.

Macy was miserable as she slogged last in line up a set of rusted metal steps and back toward a rear door marked D WING. She'd probably seen the door a dozen times since school started, but had never really noticed it and had certainly never seen it opened. It led to what could only be described as an alley and looked like something she would expect to see on a social media page featuring photographs of the narrow passageways often associated with ancient European cities. Only a sliver of daylight could be seen between the looming buildings and from the dried leaves and other drainages along the concrete walkway it was clear the alley had been the product of the many remodels and additions rather than a purposeful creation.

Macy stepped over a soaked pile of leaves. "Ugh." The edge of her Birkenstock caught and muck squished between her toes. "Ohh–

eww." As if she wasn't filthy enough. She looked ahead as she tried to kick the sludge free. None of the students in front of her stopped or acknowledged her plight. Within seconds she was alone in the alleyway, the slam of the D WING door echoing as it shut. *Ugh. Where's a patch of grass when you need it?* She kicked again and her Birkenstock flew from her foot, ricocheted off the brick wall, and landed on a metal drainage grate clogged with more filth. *Wonderful.*

She let her backpack slip from her shoulders, fished her gym towel out, wiped her foot and the edge of her jeans off, and hopped to the drainage grate to grab her wayward shoe. She wiped it as clean as she could, replaced it on her foot, and picked up her backpack as she continued toward the D WING door.

When she reached the door, she shouldered her backpack again and pulled at the handle. The door swung open with surprising ease and not so much as a squeak from the hinges. She smiled. Either the door had been recently maintained or else it wasn't used enough to experience any wear because every other door in the building sounded like a cacophony of dying cats. She stepped into the school and was blinded by the stark difference in the light.

"Hey!"

Macy startled.

"Someone wants to see you."

Macy opened her eyes in a squint and looked to the end of the hall. Zeke, Luke, and Trevor had approached someone at the corner meeting of two hallways. She took a step back into the doorway to avoid being noticed. The attention of those three was the last thing she needed this afternoon—even if they weren't physically in their prime thanks to the beating she'd delivered.

"She wants you down there. Now."

Macy studied the scene for a moment. Who were they talking to?

"C'mon already."

Deputy Newell appeared from around the corner and Macy felt shock register on her face. Her heart leapt into her throat as Zeke pulled Newell into the hallway by his shirt and pushed him towards the D WING door.

"Move it."

Macy ducked back into the alley and did her best to let the door close without slamming. She looked this way and that for someplace to hide, but faced only brick walls and the metal staircase she'd climbed moments before. She made for the staircase, took the steps two at a time, and retreated beneath the apparatus as the D WING door slammed above. She laid her bag at her feet and flattened herself against the brick wall. What were three bullies doing addressing the School Resource Officer as though he was beneath them? She shook her head. Those three had really grown bold since starting high school.

"It's this way."

"I've forgotten more about this school than you've ever known, Pennington."

"Whatever." Zeke guffawed. "Hey–you smell bacon, Trev?"

"Yeah. Oink!"

Macy rolled her eyes. Those three couldn't even come up with an original joke–most likely because an original thought had never passed through their brains.

Newell appeared on the landing, the metal soundingunder his heavy duty boots. While he was walking on his own, it was clear he was still being forced along by Zeke. What was wrong with this picture? How could Newell be at the mercy of those three and where could they be going at this time of day in such an out of the way part of the school?

The four made their way down the steps above Macy, their weight causing the metal apparatus to shift back and forth and rain bits of dirt and brick dust. She held her breath. When they reached the bottom and turned a corner she considered her options. Did she bolt back up the steps and into the school? Surely her mother was waiting for her at the front entrance by now. She frowned. *Mom'll have to wait. I need to know.* She grabbed her bag and moved to the corner, daring a peek.

Yards ahead, the four walked in a single file line before disappearing around another corner. Macy moved down the walkway towards them, her back still pressed against the wall as though it would hide her if they turned back. She stopped at the corner and listened as Zeke whispered something and his two lackeys snickered.

A door squealed open. "Hmph… Newell… Good. Your boy's become a problem… one we tried to remedy Friday night, but failed to for obvious reasons."

"Hey! We didn't know—"

"Shut up."

"P—Patrick? They were there for Patrick?"

Macy recognized Zeke's voice and Newell's, though she'd never heard him stutter, but the other voice was new. There was an unnatural deepness to it–like the person was drawing in more air than normal and then forcing the words out. Was it a man or a woman? Macy couldn't tell.

Newell continued. "He and his friends were using the computers in the library to—"

"—to access the Sheriff's Department files on the Brittany Crumb investigation. They logged in with your InvestiMate credentials. Hmph… luckily they were interrupted before they could discover there's little to nothing in those files."

"Oh, Patrick."

Newell's voice was filled with dread. At the sound, Macy felt her insides shrink.

The deep voice continued. "As it is, the failure had a fortuitous side effect… hmph… we now know there is a much more dangerous threat out there. The Alderwoman has decreed that this masked woman be identified and found forthwith. Anyone who could know anything about her is to be spoken to at once and made to understand that the truth is of the utmost importance… to them."

Hinges squealed and a door slammed shut.

"Wait!"

Macy heard a fist pound on a door.

"What about my son? Keep your hands off my son!"

Hinges squealed again and Macy was sure she heard Newell take at least two sizable steps backward.

"Hmph… your son's fate," said the deep voice, "will depend on your ability to keep his attention focused where it should be from now on."

The door slammed shut again.

The middle door of the main entrance closed behind Macy with a *thunk* after Newell made eye contact with her mother and waved. Macy breathed a sigh of relief as she heard the door lock behind her. She'd booked it away from the meeting with the deep voice and back up the steps without being seen. Inside, she'd come from a bathroom as Newell passed by and had made up a believable excuse about trying to clean herself off from the detention chores. She was certain he'd bought it–his mind so clearly occupied with other things.

She tried to push away the dozens of questions circling her brain as she moved down the concrete steps and climbed into the front seat of the Ford Freestyle. She made brief eye contact with her mother. "Hey." She wasn't at all sure what to expect. Would her mom be angry at her being the last out by quite a long time? Would both her parents be angry at her for getting detention or had they been expecting it as a natural response to what she'd done? Her mother pulled away from the curb without saying a word.

Macy watched through the window as they rounded the crowd of buildings that made up Alum Ridge. Where on the campus had she just been? The odd architecture of the multiple additions and the looming rooftops of the original building made it impossible to tell.

Becky Davis was approaching the rear gates before she spoke. "So, I guess the principal thought about as much as I did of your little stunt after the dance, huh?"

Macy shrugged. "I don't know why everyone's making such a big deal out of it. I just didn't feel like waiting around for hours while the administration tried to figure out what happened. It was a fight. It happens all the time and each time they act completely mystified as though it's never happened before."

"Everyone's making a big deal out of it young lady because you left the safety of a building without adult supervision when there was a—a—"

"A what? A girl in a costume on the loose? News flash: we were all wearing costumes. It was a Halloween dance."

"Don't get smart with me, Macy. I wasn't talking about the girl in the mask."

"Everyone keeps acting like she's bad for taking on those three creeps. Well, those three have been beating on half the student body for years and no one's said a word. All I saw is someone finally standing up to them."

"That's beside the point. Don't try to change the subject. The bottom line is that what you did was dangerous. I wish it weren't the case but it is. It's the cold, hard reality this city is dealing with right now. One girl's already lost her—her—she's been taken. Do you want to be next?"

Macy opened her mouth to retort back, but instead, she sat

stammering for words. "Lost her—her what?" That wasn't what she'd wanted to say and she was embarrassed by the innocent-sounding squeak, but it was the only sound she'd been able to form. She knew what her mother had been about to say; Brittany Crumb had lost her life. The thought hit her like a sucker punch. The deep-voiced creep back there had engineered her murder just as it had threatened to engineer Patrick's.

Macy thought she saw her mother's eyes moisten as she drew in a collecting breath and spoke softly. "I—we—we don't know anything for sure yet."

Macy was sure, but she played along. "But being missing for over a month isn't a good sign, is it?"

"No. No, it isn't."

Macy looked at the weathered photo in the center of the ad hoc memorial as the Ford Freestyle passed through the rear gates. The idea of Brittany having been murdered shouldn't have felt like a surprise, but then Macy was beginning to realize she'd been naive about a good many things before this afternoon. To put it in her mother's words that was the cold, hard reality PSD was dealing with.

The rest of the ride home was in silence. When her mother pulled to a stop in the driveway, Macy got out and shouldered her backpack without a word. She kicked off her Birkenstocks in the foyer like she always did as she entered the house and slogged up the stairs towards her room.

"Dinner's in half an hour."

"I'm not hungry."

CHAPTER 11

A few hours passed and Macy's appetite hadn't returned. Seemingly aware of the effect the conversation on the way home had had on her, neither her mother nor father had bothered her when she'd spent the usual family dinner time in her room alone. When she'd finally emerged and headed for the basement gym, her mother gave her a sympathetic smile.

Instead of taking in calories, Macy felt like burning them and hopefully burning away the anger she felt in the process. "Ugh!" She threw an elbow and followed up with a quick series of uppercuts before backing away and raising her fists again. The black heavy bag rocked back and forth from the impacts. In place of the heavy bag Macy usually pictured the smug faces of Zeke, Luke, and Trevor, but tonight there was a new face — Newell. How could Patrick's father be involved in the murder of a student? How could a person charged with upholding the law break it as bad as it could be broken? And then there was this Deep Voice character… she felt like Zeke had said a name, but couldn't for the life of her remember what it was.

Macy felt nothing short of violent. She drew in a deep breath and exhaled as she launched another flurry of attacks with her hands and feet.

"You're hitting with the ball of your foot again."

Macy glanced at the doorway of the basement. Grandad was leaning against the doorframe, the exposed light bulbs in the ceiling reflecting off his balding head.

"Not in the mood for a critique." Macy let loose again, landing a one-two punch combination and a front kick.

"The only significant pain you're going to cause doing that is your own." Grandad left the doorway. "Kick me." He stopped about leg length from her and stood in a neutral stance.

Macy blew her hair away from her face and turned to him, raising her fists and squaring off. She bounced momentarily on the balls of her feet.

"There." Grandad pointed. "That's what the balls of your feet are for. Not kicking."

Macy ignored him, drew in a quick breath, twisted her hips, and launched her foot at his midsection. Grandad stepped aside and caught her foot in his hand, stopping her forward motion instantly as he stepped forward himself and twisted her foot at the ankle. Macy fell, catching herself with her hands, the sound of her palms striking the gym mat echoing through the room.

"You see?" Grandad held her foot aloft making it impossible for her to stand or even sit up. "If you insist on landing your kicks on the ball of your foot you're leaving yourself wide open to an experienced attacker." He clasped his hand across the bottom of her foot just below her toes. "There's no power there. Sure it'll hurt if you hit your target in the face or some other sensitive area, but that's not the most effective way to use a kick. It looks good in the movies, but it's practically useless in reality. Now pull your toes back toward you."

"Arghh!" Macy jerked her foot away and rolled into a standing position. She wasn't in the mood for lessons. *Can't you hear?*

"Hey now."

Macy looked at Grandad. He stared back at her, his dark eyes caught between shock and maybe a little anger at her treatment of him, but it quickly melted into an understanding only he seemed to have for her at times. She exhaled and took a seat on the weight bench. "I'm sorry."

Grandad shook his head. "What's eating you, kiddo?" He crossed the mat and took a seat next to her.

While Macy knew she could talk to either of her parents whenever she needed to most of the time she felt like they were too concerned with keeping her on the straight and narrow to really take the time to understand how she was feeling and give her advice. But that had never been the case with Grandad. Grandad always seemed to have an uncommon clarity in his thinking that made sense to her. But did she dare tell him about what had happened–what had *really* happened–at school? Would his understanding go that far or would he feel the need to tell her mom and dad? She shrugged and exhaled, trying to breathe out her frustration.

"Hey." Grandad held up a finger as though he'd just had an idea." You know what this calls for, don't ya?"

Macy lifted an eyebrow.

He smiled ear to ear. "Ice-cadix!"

"Ice. . . cadix?" Macy's mouth slowly stretched into a smile. She hadn't heard his goofy term for ice cream in a long while. Memories of summers at the lake and of Grandad with far more hair making funny faces at a younger, pig-tailed her as she licked an ice cream cone flashed through her mind. "Alright, if you're buying."

"Yeah. I'm buying."

The suspension on the old red pickup truck Grandad had driven ever since Macy could remember squeaked as he turned from the smooth pavement of a four-lane throughway onto the rough asphalt of a parking lot belonging to a brick strip mall. Like the scarcely maintained lot, the strip mall itself was faded and stained and characteristic of the area they had entered. Unlike Greater Avendale, which was a newer and more residential suburb of PSD, Oaklawn was an older, more commercially oriented neighborhood and it showed. But it was still safe for the most part and it was home to many beloved local establishments such as The Starlite Drive-In and Iggy's Ice Cream.

Grandad shifted the truck into park. "Ready?"

Macy nodded and opened the passenger side door. They hadn't said much on the fifteen-minute trip between her house and Iggy's, but she was already feeling better. Hanging out with Grandad always had that effect on her as his world-weary yet open-minded outlook agreed with her far more than just about anyone else she spent time with. She hopped down, adjusted her coat to cover the fact that she was still wearing tight-fitting workout clothes, and met Grandad at the door.

A metal bell affixed to the doorframe jingled as they entered. The air had a slight chill to it like any ice cream shop and smelled of freshly baked waffle cones. Two girls Macy's age looked up from their phones and did their best to look happy as they made their way from a booth to their places behind the counter. "Welcome to Iggy's."

"Hey, they have hot dogs, Mace. Feel like some dinner before we stuff our faces with ice-cadix?"

"Sure. An all-beef brat with everything on it. And some fries."

Macy turned and looked the place over as Grandad pulled out his wallet and began placing their order. A row of arcade and pinball games from years gone by occupied one wall and red and white booths occupied the other. Hung haphazardly above the booths on nearly every inch of wall space were photos of at least three generations of area rec teams—some of them so old the color had long since faded leaving the faces and team names blurry.

Grandad stepped up next to her with a tray of hot dogs and french fries. "I'd venture a guess that your father's picture is up there somewhere."

"And maybe yours, too, judging by the age of some of these."

"Nah. They didn't have rec teams when I was young. We chased rolled stones and played hide and seek from dinosaurs for fun."

Macy laughed.

Grandad set the tray down at a booth and took a seat. "C'mon. Eat. You've got to be starving."

Macy slid into the booth and grabbed one of the dogs. She was hungrier than she'd realized and everything about the contents of the tray smelled fantastic. Chili, cheese, onions—what wasn't to love? She bit and chewed steadily for several minutes and watched silently as Grandad did the same. When she'd downed most of her dog, Grandad finished his bite, wiped his mouth, and made eye contact for the first time.

"So, why don't you tell me what's eating you, kiddo?"

Macy swallowed the last bit of her dog and gave a small shrug. She'd known this question was coming, but she was still at a loss as to how to answer it. "I—uh—I don't know. There's been a lot going on at school and—and, well, there's this boy—"

"Ohhh." Grandad smiled. "I see."

Macy blushed and proceeded to wade slowly into her feelings for Patrick while carefully skirting around the events that had transpired at the dance and since, which she just wasn't quite sure how to bring up–or if she should. But she could see she wasn't fooling Grandad. From the way she'd picked her way around the story it was obvious, he knew there was something he wasn't being told. She took a deep breath. "And—"

The bell above the door jingled and Macy looked to see a scruffy white man in a black flat bill hat enter. He held the door as two others came in behind him; a black man in a purple button-down shirt that was hanging open to reveal a white tank top and the another white guy in a grungy t-shirt that read I Pee In Pools on the front.

"Umm… you guys were asked to stay out of here, weren't you?" One of the girls behind the counter said.

Macy shifted in her seat so she could see the sales counter and Grandad stopped stroking his mustache, his eyes falling on the flat bill hat guy as he sauntered to the counter.

"You sayin' our money ain't any good in here, little girl?"

"No. That's not what she's saying." An older man wearing glasses and an Iggy's apron appeared from a back room behind the counter. "It's not your money that shouts swear words and cuts up, causing other customers to leave. It's you. So, *you're* no longer welcome."

"Oh ho… can you believe the set on this guy?" Flatbill glanced over his shoulder at his friends and they guffawed. "Tell you what, pops. Since our money ain't any good here anymore, how about we fix it so no one else's is either?" Purple Shirt and I Pee In Pools moved to either side of an arcade game and took hold of it. With a series of grunts, they pulled the game up onto its axis until it dropped face forward onto the floor with the sound of breaking wood and shattering glass.

"That's it," the spectacled man said, coming around the counter. "One of you call the police. Now guys, I'm the owner here and I've had enough of this. Businesses around here are having a hard enough time because of this Spaz epidemic and we don't need your kind coming in and making it worse." He reached the front of the counter and stared down Flatbill. "Now you're going to lea—"

Flatbill shoved the man abruptly. The man lost his balance and toppled backward into a display of potato chips, the sound of bags popping and crackling as both he and the rack hit the floor.

Grandad wiped his mouth with a napkin and stood from the booth. Macy followed suit and slid from her seat, lowering herself to her knees next to the downed owner who was still wrestling with the display rack and trying not to break open any more chip bags. Macy pushed the bags aside and helped him to his feet. "Are you okay?"

"You know, you boys should really treat other people's property with a little more respect. Maybe one day you'll have some of your own."

Macy turned to see Grandad position himself between the counter and the three thugs.

Flatbill scoffed. "How's this for respect, fogey?" He walked over to their table and shoved the tray containing their french fries onto the floor. "Are you feelin' respected yet, fogey? Hmm?"

Grandad frowned and nodded. "You see, Macy, this is what I'm always talking about. Ever since these boys have been fouling Pampers they've been handed everything on a silver platter — everything except discipline, humility, and common decency. Their entire generation, present company excluded," he motioned toward Macy, "have no respect for themselves or for anyone else. So, they go around picking fights with people who have been taught to be too timid to do anything about it. See what I mean?"

Macy nodded. She'd seen this kind of behavior in the likes of

Zeke, Luke, and Trevor for years and wasn't the least bit shocked that there were so-called adults who still acted the same way.

"Listen, fogey." Flatbill moved to square off with Grandad, the french fries squishing under his feet. "I'm gonna give you to the count of three to get back in your Bonneville and—"

"That's two more than I'm going to need, son."

Flatbill threw a right hook.

Grandad stepped back, allowing the punch to sail past his face before stepping forward and grabbing Flatbill by his exposed throat. The punk choked and his eyes bulged.

"Now look here, son. My name's Esley Abendt, but you can call me 'Lee.' All my friends do. I've lived seven decades, visited six continents, fought three wars, and raised two girls to know that bottom-feeding scum like you should be mopped up like the soon to be stains you are. You're obviously the kind of guy that starts trouble, but I'm the kind who finishes it. Now take your two playmates here and go back to your sandbox. You're out of your depth."

Flatbill's eyes rolled back in his head and drool started at his mouth. Grandad let him go with a shove and he collapsed onto the floor, gasping.

His lackeys advanced, kicking bags of potato chips out of the way as they moved.

Grandad raised his fists and blocked a punch from Purple Shirt, countering with a one-two combination that sent the man stumbling away.

I Pee In Pools moved around for a sucker punch.

Macy stepped between him and Grandad. "Not very sportsmanlike."

The man's eyes fixed on her and he raised his fists, his nostrils flaring.

Macy stared back, staying in a neutral stance. This guy wasn't any different than Zeke except that Zeke had smelled better. "Ugh. Do you ever bathe?"

He threw a straight punch.

Macy waited until he was committed, stepped aside, thrust her leg straight up, and dropped it into an ax kick, the heel of her foot striking the man's extended arm. The impact drove him toward the floor with a painful cry and she followed with a roundhouse kick to the side of his head, which sent him face-first into the base of the sales counter. He landed in a heap atop bags of potato chips.

Grandad chuckled as the goons got gingerly to their feet and hurried to the door only to stop dead in their tracks as blue lights flashed in the parking lot. "Now that's what we used to call an attitude adjustment." He patted Macy on the back. "Nice move there, kiddo." He mimicked the ax kick with his hand and then rotated his wrist around a bit as if it were sore. "I guess we got some 'splainin' to do to the boys in blue, huh?"

"Next time save something for us besides the paperwork, won't you?"

Macy gave a sideways smirk to the Oaklawn police officer as he slammed the rear door of his cruiser on Flatbill and his buddies. The owner and employees of Iggy's had explained everything and though the officers were initially uneasy with the idea of citizens taking matters into their own hands, they'd smiled and joked about it soon enough.

"Yeah, really," his partner said, getting into the driver's seat. "The captain's going to have a thing or two to say about this when he reads the report."

"You guys can have the next ones and the ones after that. Promise."

"Not me. I'm retiring after this one," Grandad said, still working his wrist. "I can't throw 'em like I used to."

The officers laughed as they closed the cruiser doors, shifted the vehicle into gear, and drove out of the lot.

"Thank you both again," Mr. Ignakowski, the spectacled owner of Iggy's, said. "Those punks would have done a lot more damage if we'd had to wait on the police. Ice cream for life, on me."

"That's not necessary," Grandad turned for his truck. "But thank you all the same. You all have a good rest of the evening."

Macy gave a small wave and retreated to the passenger side of the red truck.

"Well, that was one you can tell your kids about someday, huh?" Grandad said as Macy got in and shut the door.

"Uh-huh. You sure know how to show a girl a good time."

Grandad chuckled and reversed out of the parking spot, waving to the Iggy's staff as he made his way out of the lot and back onto the four-lane throughway that would take them back to Greater Avendale.

Macy was still feeling the effects of the adrenaline rush she'd experienced the moment it had been clear there was going to be a fight. Just as she had outside the library after her last fight, she was having trouble getting rid of a panicked feeling. But as the truck picked up speed and she watched the brick storefronts, corner takeout joints, and aging strip malls of Oaklawn become the tree-lined sidewalks, two-story homes, and quaint parks of Avendale, another feeling made a comeback–dread. Before they'd been interrupted, she'd been about to tell Grandad everything that had *really* happened and why it had her so bothered. He'd obviously known she wasn't telling him something, but did he remember or had the events of the evening shifted his focus so much that he'd forgotten? Did she bring it up again or let the matter die? The butterflies in her stomach began anew. She crossed her arms over her abdomen.

"So, I may be old, but I'm not blind," Granddad turned into their neighborhood. "—yet anyway."

Macy couldn't help but crack a smile.

"There's more to what's bothering you than you were letting on."

And there it was. She had to tell him something now. She inhaled, summoned as much courage as she could, and exhaled slowly. "I dressed up as a superhero to impress Patrick at the Halloween dance. While I was there looking for him I stumbled upon three bullies getting ready to hurt him for asking questions. I fought them, beat them, and may have broken the School Resource Officer's wrist while trying to run away." *Phew. That wasn't so bad.* She watched Grandad's face as he turned into their driveway. It seemed like it took forever for him to shift the truck into park.

"Alrighty. Let me see if I got all of that. You dressed up as a superhero to impress… Patrick, right? He's the one you like. Okay. And while you were dressed up you stumbled upon some bullies getting ready to hurt him for… asking questions? You fought. You won. You assaulted a police officer. Okay. Think I got it."

Macy cringed and cringed again at the words 'assaulted' and 'officer.' "And on top of that one of Patrick's friends–both of whom were also there–got a video of the whole thing and it's gone viral."

"Gone… viral?"

"One person sent it to another who sent it to another who sent it—"

"Gotcha."

"Yeah. And now it's all over the place and everyone wants to know who the girl in the costume was and the school administrators are freaking out about violence in school and everyone seems to have completely missed the fact that she was doing a good thing and stopping three morons who have been terrorizing the student body for years." She threw her arms up in a frustrated shrug. "And yeah… it's a mess."

"Hmm. Hmm. Hmm." Grandad stroked his mustache. "Indeed."

Macy pulled her phone from her pocket, brought up the video, and handed it to him.

He watched it in silence, still stroking his mustache. "Heh." He raised his eyebrows at her jump kick off the wall. Was he impressed? It kind of seemed that way. The video ended and he looked the phone over. "That's a pretty neat little trick there, isn't it?"

Macy laughed and took the phone. At times it was easy to forget Grandad was as old as he was and at other times it wasn't. But that was one of her favorite things about him. Surely, if she could tell anyone the truth, it was him. "So…?"

Grandad straightened himself in the truck seat, put his hand to his head, and gave her a salute. "Your secret identity's safe with me."

Macy glared at him mockingly before giving in to a smile. "Good. It better be." But the smile faded. There was still something she hadn't told him. She lowered her head and the mood in the truck became serious again. Grandad's goofy look disappeared.

"Before the fight began, I overheard something the bullies said. They said they'd been sent by someone else to hurt Patrick."

Grandad nodded. "…for asking questions."

"Yup."

"Questions about what?"

Macy caught Grandad up on the sheriff brushing Patrick off in the hallway, her encounter with Patrick in the comic book shop, he and his friends' private investigation into Brittany Crumb's disappearance, Newell's meeting with Deep Voice, and the mention of someone known as The Alderwoman–who, from the sound of it, was behind the whole thing–for some reason.

Grandad sat silently, staring at the steering wheel of his truck.

"Uh-huh. Exactly my reaction," Macy said. "And I don't have any idea what to do about it. I can't tell the police because at least one of them is involved — but probably more from the sound of it. I can't

tell the school admins or I'm as good as expelled if not arrested —
plus they'd never deal with it as they should anyway — and I can't
just let it go because whoever this Alderwoman is is looking for me
and might not fail next time. And… and… I don't know." She
shrugged again in frustration.

"Hey. Easy. Easy. It's okay." Grandad pulled her into a side hug.
"It's going to be okay."

She rested her head on his shoulder and they sat silently. She
glanced up at the lights on in the window of her house. They seemed
to loom. How was she ever going to explain this to her parents?

"Macy…" Grandad's voice was heavier than usual. "It's said that
there are two kinds of people in this world; sheep, and wolves, and
to a large degree, that's true. But there's a third kind, a rare kind,
seldom talked about and always misunderstood–the shepherds.
They're the ones on the outside of the fold protecting the flock…
making sure the wolves never even get close. That's me. And I'd bet
dollars to donuts that's you as well. As much as you want to at times
you can't turn a blind eye to what's coming. Protecting the flock is
hardwired into you. It's who you are… for better or worse."

Macy sat up and looked at her grandfather. His eyes were on the
steering wheel, but he wasn't looking at it. He was looking beyond
the wheel to some other time and place–a time and place where Macy
felt like the worst he had just mentioned was far more real than he'd
like it to be. "But what do I do with that?" she asked. "How do I—"

"You accept it, Macy. You realize it's who you are and you
embrace it along with the responsibilities it comes with. That's the
only way you'll ever be at peace with yourself."

"So, what do I do next?"

"What you mean is what do *we* do next."

CHAPTER 12

Keri raised her eyebrows. "So, the police showed up at your house?"

"Yeah," Macy said as they left the bus and entered the school. "The officer forgot to give Grandad back his ID so my parents found out about the whole thing. My mom had a fit." She raised her voice to a mimicking squeak. "Dad, it's not nineteen whatever anymore. You can't go around doing things like that–especially in front of Macy." She returned her pitch to normal, grinning. "It was great." She studied Keri for a moment. "What?"

"I don't know, Mace. Honestly, I'm kind of regretting this whole thing. I feel like–like you're just not you anymore." Keri motioned towards Macy's outfit. "You're not even dressed like you anymore. It's like wearing that costume flipped a switch in your head or something."

Macy gave a small shrug. She couldn't argue. The costume had certainly given her a charge of confidence she'd never experienced before and though the ensuing situation was definitely dangerous there was a certain thrill about it, too. And that's why she'd chosen to wear more flexible clothing. Trying to run from the meeting with Deep Voice in jeans and Birkenstocks hadn't been easy. Today, she'd opted for a hoodie, jogging pants, and sneakers instead. Next time she'd be ready.

"I think you need to get rid of it. Someplace where no one would—"

"No way." Macy was shocked at her own volume. She looked around and lowered her voice again. "I'm not getting rid of it now. Someone needs to find out what's going on."

"Yeah—like the police."

"Umm—have you been listening to anything I've said?"

"Duh. Oaklawn? Downtown? There's more than one police department around. And this isn't just some teenager's theory. This is an eyewitness. This is different."

"Is it, though? You don't think the first stop any other department is going to make to verify my story is the Avendale Sheriff? And if this Alderwoman can influence one department why can't she do it to another?"

Keri looked stuck for a comeback so Macy pressed on.

"Let's face it—someone needs to find out who that deep-voiced creep was and what they're doing and there's no one in a better position to do that than Stellar."

"Macy, are you kidding me? You can't wear that costume again. The police were looking all over the neighborhood for the person in that suit and now some—some criminal organization is, too? If they find you with it—or worse, in it—you could be arrested or—or expelled—or—"

Killed. The idea hit Macy like a slap in the face. Not because it was something she hadn't considered, but because she just now realized she couldn't quit being Stellar even if she wanted to. Whoever these people were they were looking for her… coming for her. Would they stop just because she did? She didn't think so. That meant that not only was she in danger, but everyone she knew and was close to was as well. Either she had to take the fight to them or they'd eventually bring it to her.

"So, no one will find it, and when we figure out how we're going to do this no one will see me."

"Oh, yeah, because I have so much faith in your ability to not be seen after what happened at the dance."

"Look–I'm not getting rid of it. And even Grandad's on board with that decision."

At least Macy was pretty sure he was on board. He really hadn't said. After their conversation in the truck, he'd seemed distant the rest of the night and had spent most of his time in the spare bedroom on the phone. And after the police had come knocking and her parents had found out about the fight at the ice cream parlor he'd abruptly packed his things and left, telling her not to do anything until he got back. But where was he going? How long was he going to be gone? Again, he hadn't said.

"Fine." Keri shrugged and turned to leave the bathroom. "I gotta get to class."

Macy watched her leave, a sinking feeling in the pit of her stomach stopping her from saying any more as Keri disappeared from view. She hadn't expected this reaction. She and Keri had been nigh inseparable since elementary school. Macy couldn't even remember the last time they'd had a fight. *Great.* Now she could count the people she had to help her through this on one finger — herself.

A schedule days were usually long days because those were the days Macy only had one class with Keri. Normally, B schedule days were a much-needed break, but this one had sucked royally. While they had sat in their usual places Keri hadn't had much to say and each time a class ended, she'd hurried off, leaving Macy behind.

To make matters worse, day two of detention had had her and a dozen others cleaning another part of the wall they'd started on yesterday, and again she was wet and nasty as a result.

She tried to understand Keri's point of view as she moved through the now empty hallways. Things certainly had moved at a fast pace since the moment she'd put on the Stellar costume. That she could understand. But she hadn't asked for any of it. Really, she hadn't even wanted to wear the costume originally. If anyone had the right to be angry it was her. It was her who had been grounded all weekend. It was her who would be in detention all week. It was her life spinning out of—Patrick appeared from the hallway ahead. Macy's heart leapt and she moved a step closer to the wall out of habit. With the dozen others from detention ahead of her, Patrick didn't notice her. His attention was focused on the door of Deputy Newell's office. Macy watched as he peered into the corner office.

"Hey, punk. Come in here."

Patrick entered the office and closed the door except for a crack.

Macy had a feeling she knew what this father and son pow-wow was about. She made her way to the wall just outside the office and stood listening.

"What's up?"

Newell cleared his throat. "So, I got a call from Sheriff Burke a bit ago. Did you and your friends use my InvestiMate login Friday night to try to access the files on Brittany Crumb?"

Macy frowned. Newell was lying. While she didn't know who Deep Voice was, she was pretty certain it hadn't been Sheriff Burke.

Zeke had referred to *her* not him. She waited for Patrick's answer. Would he lie, too?

"Yes, sir."

"Patrick," Newell sighed, "we've talked about this. I'm not a part of that investigation anymore. I reported my initial findings to the sheriff as I'm required to do and he took it from there."

"I know. I'm sorry."

"That's not going to cut it this time. Now I'm as worried about Brittany as anyone is—she's one of my kids just like the others who walk these halls every day. I feel responsible for all of them you know I do. But that doesn't mean I can go charging around doing my own investigations. There are laws and procedures and—and other things that have to be followed, Patrick. And I have to look after the other two thousand and some who are still here every day. That's my job. As frustrating as it can be to have to stand by and let other deputies handle actual crimes, that's the role I play."

Macy was taken aback by the sincerity in Newell's voice. The emotion was palpable. He was actually telling the truth.

"Of all people," Newell continued, "I expected you to understand that."

"I know and I do understand it. I really do. It's just that Zeke and those guys have been terrorizing people ever since I can remember. And you know that. They give Josh a hard time every day and they have people calling Striker an Albino. Whatever they were doing outside the library when Stellar—when that lady–found them couldn't have been good."

"Stellar? You've given her a name?"

There was a long silence before Patrick cleared his throat. "She's one of mine. I created her."

Another silent spell.

"I mean she's one of my characters."

Macy imagined Patrick holding up his notebook full of creations.

"Okay," Newell said. "And do you know who was in the costume?"

"No. But she's called Stellar."

"Stellar?"

"Yeah. Stellar."

A sense of dread rose in Macy's mind. Would Newell fish for an identity to give to Deep Voice? Patrick didn't know it was her in the costume, but Deep Voice making the connection between Stellar and Patrick would not only be bad for him but would put that creep at least one step closer to her. There couldn't be that many people who knew about Stellar and anyone searching would naturally start with those closest to her creator and work their way outward. But what kind of father would put his own son in that kind of danger?

"Okay. And who else knows about her?" Newell asked.

Macy tried to read the tone of his voice for a clue as to his intentions but came up empty.

"She was on some of the Halloween dance posters," Patrick answered, "but I haven't told anyone about her specifically. Just Striker and Josh."

"And do either of them know who was in the costume?"

"No. I asked them."

"Sounds like I need to have a conversation with Mr. Friddle and Mr. Austreicher. Someone has to know who was in that costume and if only the three of you knew about this 'Stellar' it stands to reason—"

"They don't know." Patrick's voice had become more forceful. "They'd have told me if they did."

Mr. Austreicher? Macy frowned curiously. She understood the Striker nickname now. In all the years she'd known Patrick and his friends she had never heard Striker called by any other name.

"Alright, son. Let me make sure I have this right. A character you created showed up in the flesh to take on bullies and the School

Resource Officer and the only three people in the world who have ever heard of her have no idea who was wearing the costume?"

"I'm not lying to you. Quit treating me like a suspect or something."

"But you weren't exactly going to tell me all of this, were you? You slipped up when you said her name."

Patrick sighed and Macy imagined him shrugging in frustration. That's what she did when her parents were grilling her about something.

Newell took a resigning breath. "Look, you're right. I'm sorry. It's hard to know where the cop ends and the dad begins. We've talked about this. I'm just trying to work my way through this. In my world, in a situation like this, either someone knows more than they're telling or more people know about your girl hero than you think. You did say she was on some of the posters, right? So, it's possible someone copied the outfit."

"Yeah. Maybe. But it was a really good copy and that costume can't be bought at a store. And one of my drawings is missing."

"Missing?"

"It was in my notebook the day The Spade—Mrs. Spader, I mean—got onto me in class. I put it in my backpack, but when I got home it wasn't there anymore."

The hairs on the back of Macy's neck rose as the feeling of dread deepened. There were even fewer people who would have been close enough to grab the drawing during science class than there were who could possibly know about Stellar and she was one of them.

"And you think whoever took it is the person wearing the costume?"

"I guess so."

"That doesn't do much to help us, son. I mean you could have dropped that drawing anywhere and anyone could have picked it up."

Macy breathed a sigh of relief.

"Yeah. I guess so. I don't know why it matters so much. I mean–I don't think she's the bad guy she's being made out to be."

Newell was silent for a long moment. Macy waited, the dread in her mind feeling like actual pressure on her brain.

"It matters a lot, Patrick." Newell sounded depressed. "You and I both know she's probably not the bad guy. But not–not everyone sees it that way—"

"You mean *wants* to see it that way."

"—and I need to be careful. I can't lose my job. We need it–now more than ever."

Macy couldn't see their faces, but she imagined a knowing look between father and son. Newell's soft-hearted approach to his son surprised her after finding out he knew more about Brittany Crumb than he should. But from the sound of it, his hands were just tied by whatever circumstances he and Patrick were referencing–not to mention the threat of Deep Voice.

Newell's chair squeaked as though he'd sat upright. "Listen, Patrick. I—uhh—this is going to be hard to understand, but I need you to forget about this Stellar. I need you to get rid of anything you have with her on it and I need you to stop talking about her to anyone and everyone. I can't explain why, son, but I need you to do this for me. You have to do this and you have to lay off the investigation. I—uhh—I can't lose you the way I lost your mom."

The feeling of dread in Macy's mind vanished and was replaced with sadness that manifested in her chest–like a heartache. Had Patrick's mom died? Divorced his dad? She didn't know.

Another period of silence passed. Macy imagined Patrick trying to figure out why he needed to do what his father had just asked him to do. It's life or death, she wanted to be able to say. Your dad is saving your life because if Deep Voice catches you as the creator of

Stellar, they'll never believe you weren't involved.

"What is it, son?"

"Nothing. If only life were like the comics, huh?"

"If only." Newell's office chair squeaked again and a hand grabbed the edge of the door. "Sorry to take off, but I've got to let the convicts out."

Macy darted away from the door.

"Hey!"

Patrick's voice was clear and surprised. Macy turned and positioned herself next to the far wall as though she'd been walking by. She stopped and looked at him with a smile, doing her best to appear natural. "Hey."

He seemed elated to see her and she realized she hadn't actually spoken to him since their encounter in the comic book shop.

"I'm working at Dom's again tonight," Newell said, exiting his office after Patrick and making his way down the hall toward the main atrium. "Mrs. Austreicher is expecting you for dinner and I'll see you when I get off, okay?"

Patrick gave a nod, his face shifting from elation to what looked like a mixture of fear and disappointment as he followed his father down the hall with his eyes.

Macy watched his face change again as he turned his attention back to her. Normally, she'd have been delighted to have such an effect, but the current circumstances were anything but normal.

"I–uhh–don't usually see you here this late."

Macy looked down at her wet, dirt-stained clothes. "Detention. I snuck out after the dance."

"Oh. Yeah. I heard about that, I think."

"I think everyone has by now… unfortunately."

Patrick shrugged. "Don't sweat it. If that's the worst thing you've ever done you—"

"What are you doing?"

"Uhh, what?"

"What are you doing? Right now. What are you doing?"

Patrick shrugged and motioned towards his dad's office. "Waiting on my ride. Dad's working security at—"

"Walk me to the car line. My mom's picking me up."

"Yeah okay. Let me grab my things."

Patrick ducked into the office and reappeared with his backpack. Macy tried hard to keep a grin off her face. She was amazed at her own boldness. It had taken her months to summon this much courage and while it wasn't a long walk between Newell's office and the main atrium it felt like a victory lap.

"So… uhh… you created her, huh?"

No! How could she have just said that? Now he'd know she'd been eavesdropping.

"Oh, you–uhh–you heard that, huh?" Patrick chuckled.

Macy shrugged. "Oh, no. Well, yeah, but–well, I was just walking and stopped because I didn't want to wait with—" she motioned to the others who had been in detention.

Patrick looked ahead at the small gathering. "Heard that. I mean yikes."

Macy laughed.

"Anyways, yeah. Stellar's mine." Patrick held up his notebook. "I have a few."

The first words that popped into Macy's head were *I know* but she kept them from popping out.

Patrick opened the notebook and flipped through the pages. Each page had a drawing of a hero or villain of some kind. Some Macy recognized from the comic book shop and others were clearly Patrick's own creations.

"Wow. Is that what you want to do–be a comic book artist?"

Patrick shrugged. "Yeah. My dad says it's a tough way to make a living, though."

Macy gave a small shrug. "I don't know a lot about it, I guess."

"Me neither. They don't exactly advertise comic book artist jobs on Instagram."

"Heh. Right."

They arrived at the main atrium where Newell stood at the entrance watching as the other kids left in waiting cars. Macy smiled when she saw only two cars left; her mother and someone she assumed was Mrs. Austreicher.

"Hurry it along, you two," Newell said, smiling.

Macy wasn't sure, but she thought she saw him flash a thumbs up to his son as they passed through the main doors.

She eyed the cars and the distance between them. It was a twenty-yard walk. Not long enough. She didn't want to leave and didn't want this conversation to end. It was going far better than the last time they'd spoken.

"Have you seen her again–since the other night, I mean? Do you have any idea who she might be?"

"No." Patrick looked nervous and glanced back toward the main door where his father had been standing. He lowered his voice. "Not since that night. And I don't have a clue who she could be. I mean why would anyone want to rip off my ideas for their Halloween costume? There are plenty of other more popular characters out there."

Macy thought about all the ways Stellar was different from the other female heroines she'd seen. For starters, she actually had on a complete outfit instead of a skimpy bathing suit-like appliance. But she didn't want to mention that. If she did, she'd risk tipping her hand too much.

"Maybe someone saw her on the dance posters and thought she was cool."

Patrick smiled. "Yeah. Maybe. But I don't know. I mean that costume was just like I imagined. And the way she looked at me? And the way she spoke? She seemed–I don't know–it was only a brief moment, but it was like she knew me and she was there for me. I guess. I mean that probably sounds really stupid."

"Sure did–I mean sure she did." Macy laughed, nervously. "If you created her, she'd have to know you, right?" She did a mental facepalm. *That* sounded stupid. What'd Stellar jump out of his imagination and into real life or something? *Idiot.* She was an idiot.

"Yeah. I guess." Patrick didn't seem to be paying attention. His eyes were fixed on the ground in front of him. "I've just never seen anyone actually fight like that. She's *exactly* how I imagined. And how could anyone know that from a drawing? It's like she hopped out of my head and came to the rescue."

Macy beamed at the idea of her Stellar being just like Patrick had imagined. "To the rescue? Is that what you think she was there for?"

Patrick shrugged. "I guess so. I mean I don't think she's the bad guy she's being made out to be, that's for sure. I think she came to help."

"I can remember those idiots she took down walking around in elementary school." She crossed her arms, made a mean face, and lowered her voice to mimic them"And I'm brother's keeper."

Patrick laughed.

Macy melted inside. This was actually fun.

"Dude!" a voice called. "Stop mackin' and let's go!"

Macy looked to see Striker half hanging out the rear window of his mom's four-door sedan.

Patrick turned three shades of red. "I gotta go." He walked toward the waiting car.

"Hey," Macy called. "For what it's worth I think you're right. I've seen that video at least a dozen times and there's no doubt she was there to help. I think she's a friend."

Patrick beamed and entered the back seat of the sedan, punching Striker on the arm.

"Ow! Dude!"

Macy smiled as she opened the door to her mother's Ford Freestyle. She'd accomplished a lot in the last several minutes personally. But there were a lot more serious things that needed to be done. Soon it would be Stellar's turn again.

CHAPTER 13

Soon hadn't turned out to mean what Macy had thought. Instead of Grandad returning after a day or two and helping her decide what they needed to do next he hadn't returned at all. Halloween night had come and gone and then the first few weeks of November, but still no Grandad. Now the calendar was bearing down on Thanksgiving and Macy had decided she couldn't wait any longer. Someone needed to find out what Deep Voice had been doing at Alum Ridge and apparently that someone was her–by herself–as usual.

Macy stepped onto the brick knee wall, gripped the wrought iron fence, and pulled herself over, landing with a soft thud on the wet grass of the Alum Ridge property. The Stellar costume groaned at the joints as she crouched, the material still wearing in since she'd only worn it once. She froze at the sound of a car passing nearby, its tires splashing through a puddle. Headlights washed over a section of the fence and she waited. Police patrols had been stepped up in the area in general and she was sure special attention was being paid to the school. The headlights faded and the vehicle moved on into the Greater Avendale neighborhoods. If it had been a patrol they'd get back around to the school soon enough.

She stood and headed for the glut of buildings that looked even more like a prison at night than they did during the day. The yellow gleam of the twenty-four-hour lights spaced along the exterior walls and throughout the parking lot cut through a mist leftover from a passing evening rain and gave the property an eerie glow.

She'd spent the last few weeks trying to make sure she knew the inside of the school like the back of her hand but wasn't sure if she could identify the exact place she'd overheard the meeting with Deep Voice without access to the inside and the D WING door to help orient her. But she needed to see the spot. Was there something going on there she needed to know or had Deep Voice only been there to threaten Newell? She had tried brainstorming the possibilities, but nothing seemed anymore plausible than anything else. This was an eyes-on kind of mission.

She ducked between a row of trailers set up as overflow classrooms and surveyed the cluster of buildings from the narrow space between them. The exterior of Alum Ridge was a mess of sidewalks that cut through courtyards, in between buildings, and led to dead ends, but somewhere there had to be a way to access the roof. Her plan was to find a ladder, locate the main atrium, and then use her knowledge of the interior to follow the roof to the D WING and thus the meeting site.

Seeing no signs of an overnight watch, she left the narrow passage and moved along a brick exterior wall, stopping and looking at her surroundings at every corner and sticking to the shadows as much as possible. Moving rapidly in short bursts seemed like the surest way not to attract any unwanted attention. At the fifth or sixth dead-end, she abandoned the search for a ladder and jumped to grab the lowest branch of a silver maple tree planted along the side of the building. *Why didn't I think of this earlier?* With all the courtyards full of trees she could have been on the roof awhile ago. Climbing from branch to branch, she made her way to the edge of the roof and pulled herself up.

She surveyed the roofline. This wasn't going to be as easy as she thought. Like the sidewalks that snaked around the property, the roof was a labyrinth. Multi-story climbs, jumps, and drops stood between her and anything remotely recognizable. *What now?*

The sound of grinding gears and the high pitched beep of a backup warning sounded from somewhere on the other side of the building. She listened intently. *Is someone here?* Trucks didn't back themselves up, so yes.

She moved toward the sound doing her best to minimize the crunch of the gravel roofing underfoot as she dodged around air conditioning units, ductwork, and exhaust fans and climbed ladders, pipes, and antennas. When she reached the opposite edge she crouched low and looked over. A tractor-trailer had backed in along a loading dock. She watched as the driver left the truck and made his way onto the dock. From the roof, she couldn't see beneath the metal awning so she moved to the far side where the awning ended and waited until she heard the driver open the rear doors of the truck and enter the school.

She climbed down and lowered herself onto the concrete dock, keeping her eyes moving between the back of the truck and the doorway into the school. She moved to the truck and looked inside.

Plastic crates filled with milk and other frozen food items filled the trailer. She'd never thought about what it took to feed two thousand and some kids every day, but a tractor-trailer load sounded about right. And she guessed that delivering at night was easier than waiting until daylight when the place would be mobbed with teenagers, teachers, and other staff. *Nothing to see here.*

"Oh, for heaven's sake—"

Macy ducked away as the driver returned, backing out of the doorway and doing his best to pull a cart that wasn't agreeing with him.

"Wheel's busted…" he mumbled, picking up crates and stacking them. "…hauling explosive chemicals and they give me a broken pushcart… idiots."

Wait… did he just say explosive chemicals? Macy watched as he pulled crate after crate out. Each one read Five State Dairy & Produce Co. in white letters against the black crate and was filled to the brim with milk cartons. Until one wasn't. She heard glass bottles and watched as the driver tensed up and carefully placed the crate between two others. He repeated the process of stacking a few crates and carefully securing one until the cart was full. Then he tightened a strap around the cart and pulled it back into the school, his movements methodical so as to not cause the crates to move abruptly.

Before the door could close, Macy slipped in and watched as the driver made his way down a darkened hallway. Despite her best efforts to see the entire school, she'd never seen this part. The only light came from some kind of wall-mounted auxiliary units spaced infrequently along the hall that caused as many shadows as they did light. She stuck to the shadows and followed the driver. He stopped outside of a walk-in refrigerator where he was met by a group of Asians.

Macy was sure they hadn't arrived with him as they had appeared from somewhere inside the school. They were all skinny, unkempt, and wearing white lab coats stained with colorful splotches. If she didn't know better, she'd swear they'd been dying Easter eggs. Each had on a pair of leather work gloves and they stood eyeing the crates.

The driver started moving the milk crates into the refrigerator and stopped each time he got to one of the secured crates. Each time one of the gloved Asians took it cautiously and moved off into the school.

What was in the crates that they were being so careful? More than once Macy heard a glass bottle cling against another and watched as the person carrying the crate drew in a sharp breath and tensed.

The driver made several trips back to the truck and brought in dozens of crates. Inside of each cartload were four or five crates filled with the glass bottles. When he'd finished unloading and the Asians had taken the last of the other crates, he waited alone looking this way and that.

Macy watched from the shadow of a commercial ice chest created by the dim, wall-mounted lights.

"C'mon already," the driver mumbled. "… got your stuff here again now where is she…"

She? Macy heard footsteps on the tiled floor. The driver perked up and a moment later a lean figure in a black, almost robe-like coat and circular rimmed hat appeared from the same direction as the Asians. Macy couldn't make out a face. It was either covered or the shadow of the hat and the dim lighting conspired to conceal it. The figure regarded the driver for a long moment, its chest rising and falling almost constantly.

"Hmph…" it sucked in a ragged breath that Macy recognized immediately. "…your payment as promised."

Deep Voice. Macy's mind raced.

The figure held out an envelope and the driver snatched it greedily, ripping it open and catching what appeared to be a tablet as it fell out. He struggled with the device for a moment. When the screen finally lit up he took a deep breath and pressed a button. "Baby?"

"Da—daddy?"

The driver's face glowed in the light of the screen and Macy was sure she saw tears. "Oh, God. Baby. My baby." He touched the screen.

"Daddy?"

"Yeah, baby. I'm here. Daddy's here. Are you okay? Why can't she see me?"

"Because it's dark. Always dark."

"Oh, God. Baby listen… daddy's here. I'm gonna get you out of there. You're gonna get out of this. You're going to be okay. I promise."

"Oh–okay."

The confused voice coming from the device was Brittany Crumb. Even through the tears and distress, Macy was sure of it. She stood frozen. *What do I do?* Did she confront Deep Voice and demand her release? No. What if she wasn't actually here, but being kept elsewhere? Any direct encounters could cause her captors to harm her.

"No, wait!" The screen went dark. "Bring her back. Bring her back now."

"You have what you asked for. Every night your services are provided as requested you'll receive a call from her. Hmph… but stop doing your job or show that device to anyone and you'll never see her again. Am I understood?"

"Ye–yeah." The driver stowed the pushcart next to the refrigerator door and walked away, his head down and hugging the device like someone was going to take it away.

Macy flattened herself against the wall and watched as he passed. *Mr. Crumb…* she said to herself as she followed him with her eyes until he was out of sight. *How did you find yourself and your daughter at the mercy of this creep?* The meeting she'd just witnessed reminded her of the meeting with Newell. She'd never imagined a trained law enforcement officer stuttering and stammering in fear either. Deep Voice was manipulating these people into doing what they were told by threatening their children.

Macy heard footsteps and peeked out from behind the ice chest just as Deep Voice moved back into the school. She left her cover and followed, staying a solid distance behind and making sure her boots didn't sound against the tiled floor as they snaked through darkened hallways.In a far corner that Macy definitely didn't recognize Deep Voice came to a long hallway that ended at a freight elevator. The figure inserted a key and entered. The freight car rattled downward carrying its occupant out of sight.

What now? There was no way she could follow using the elevator. The noise would surely alert anyone nearby that there was an intruder and that was the last thing she wanted. *Stairs!* She rushed to the elevator. Where there was an elevator there had to be a staircase for emergency purposes. And there it was, a doorway marked "staircase" along the wall next to the elevator.

She pulled the door open and entered, allowing it to latch quietly before taking the steps two at a time in a hushed run desperate not to lose her target in the bowels of the school. After a flight of steps, she reached a metal door with a small window. She heard the freight elevator slam closed and watched as Deep Voice passed. She waited until she felt like enough distance had been created and pulled the door open just enough to slip through and avoid the hinges making noise. She leaned around, revealing a bit of the room beyond at a time until she was sure she wouldn't be seen.

The room beyond was a part of the school she knew she'd never seen, and she was pretty sure few others had as well. Was it even part of the school? Was it even a room? She wasn't sure. It looked more like a cave. Darkness concealed most of it, but she could tell it was cavernous and that the concrete floor was covered with a thick layer of dust that appeared to have been there for a long time. The ceiling was exposed steel H-beams supported by concrete columns that were painted green halfway up and spaced evenly throughout. Old lighting fixtures lined the ceiling, but only a few of them were lit—just enough to reveal a well-trodden path in the dust between the freight elevator and wherever Deep Voice was heading.

Macy moved into the shadows and made her way through the dust trying not to kick up any more than necessary. Deep Voice was forty or fifty yards ahead and approaching a wide opening, a bluish glow coming from the room beyond. She had compared Alum Ridge to a prison both metaphorically and physically many times, but she'd never realized just how well the analogy fit. *What is this place? And why is it located beneath a school?*

Deep Voice reached the opening and moved into the next room. "Hmph… hurry. Mix them now. It's imperative they be below forty degrees when mixed."

Macy reached the opening. The room beyond was less cavernous but still constructed of H-beams and concrete columns. Instead of using the overhead lights, blue iridescent lights had been strung low between the columns, and metal laboratory tables had been placed underneath. Each table had multiple workstations with white trays directly under the lights and masked workers who were carefully removing small cylindrical glass bottles from the milk crates, opening them and pouring rust-colored liquid onto a tray that already contained small anthills of green, orange, or purple powder. An audible hiss sounded each time liquid and powder met and the workers began mixing the substances together with gloved hands.

"Faster." Deep Voice paced back and forth at the head of the room and five men who could only be hired thugs circled the room watching. "This stage is the most critical."

Macy watched intently as the workers formed green, orange, and purple blobs of a dough-like substance by kneading the liquid and powder together over and over and—she jumped as a loud clang sounded.

"Oh, dude!"

Macy recognized the voice immediately–Striker. She caught a glimpse of the blond-afroed boy as he retreated back into the stairwell. She melted into the shadows as Deep Voice rushed to the opening and looked towards the basement door.

"Someone's here."

The thugs rushed to the opening behind Deep Voice who looked over her shoulder at the workers. They picked up their pace. "Get those separated and into the cooling bins at once." Her head snapped back to the stairwell. "Find out who it is and bring them to me. Now."

The five thugs moved out, a few of them entering the freight elevator and others taking the stairs.

Macy cursed under her breath. Where Striker was, Patrick was probably leading the way. How could he be so thick? Hadn't his father warned him to lay off? She drew up to her full height and stepped out of the shadows.

"Hmph…"

She stared at the darkly clad figure. The person's face was definitely covered by some sort of scarf or mask and their body style was slender beneath the robe-like coat. Deep Voice was definitely a female.

Deep Voice lifted a hand and pointed. "…you."

One of the overhead lights flickered and the light glinted off something, drawing Macy's attention to a ring. She stared at the silver signet ring and its insignia on Deep Voice's index finger. She'd seen one just like it on Principal Decker's hand.

"Heh. Me." Macy turned and delivered a back kick to Deep Voice's abdomen and took off in a run. She'd face her again soon if she had her way, but right now she needed to be sure Patrick and Striker weren't the latest teens to vanish without a trace. She bolted into the stairwell and started up just as the last of the thugs cleared the door into the hallways of the school. At the top of the steps, she heard the freight elevator open and stepped into the hallway, blocking the two thugs exiting the elevator. "End of the line, guys."

The first thug advanced, throwing a right cross. Macy stepped aside, bringing her leg around into a powerful spinning front kick that landed first at the thug's extended elbow and then at the side of his head, throwing him to the floor.

The second thug didn't hesitate. He moved in before his buddy hit the floor and delivered a stomping front kick, catching Macy behind the knee. The impact drove her to one knee, but she dropped into a back roll and hopped to her feet, her leg threatening to buckle under her own weight from the successful attack.

"Ope, now you're dancing prettier." The thug bounced on the balls of his feet and raised his fists. "Let's give that face a good seeing to." He advanced into a right-left jab combo.

Macy blocked each punch at the wrist, his fists bouncing off her forearm guards, but his momentum was driving her backward. This guy was an experienced fighter. She needed to create distance or else he'd have her cornered. She blocked a right jab and ducked aside, letting the left brush the top of her head as she rolled away. She bounced out of the roll and back onto her feet, her leg buckling a bit as she turned again to face the thug.

He took a deep breath and came at her again with his fists up.

She raised her hands as if to protect herself and stepped forward as if to go fist to fist causing him to commit to the attack. Instead of blocking him, she turned and dropped, extending her leg and sweeping it across the floor. She caught him behind the ankle and knocked his feet from under him, his head making a sickening crack as it hit the floor. *Ouch. He won't remember what day of the week it is when he gets up from that.* She took stock of her surroundings and moved off into the school.

Her knee throbbed and continued to give way as she moved in a hushed run through the hallways. There were a thousand places in Alum Ridge to hide. How was she going to find three thugs and two teenagers? It would be worse than looking for her mom in the grocery store.

She crossed through the first floor of the library and into the main atrium. She'd yet to see or hear anyone. Had Patrick and Striker left the building and made a run for it outside? It made sense that they would want to get away, but they'd be easier to spot outside. Hiding inside was a better strategy, but so was obeying your father's wishes and staying away. She considered the irony of that for a moment—what would her father say if he could see her now?

Her eyes fell on the door to the main office and an idea hit her. She was certain Deep Voice hadn't actually seen Striker, but had certainly seen her—and felt her. She'd made sure of that. Maybe just maybe she could convince the thugs she was the only one who'd been there. She crossed the office to the intercom system and picked up the mic.

"Attention, boys. This is Stellar—your favorite neighborhood crime fighter. It was me who found your little lab downstairs so if you're looking you'll find me in the main atrium. C'mon down."

She hung up the mic and left the office. Would it work? Perhaps if Patrick and Striker had managed to stay out of sight it would. She stood in the center of the atrium and listened. A door slammed somewhere. This was a bold plan. She could end up fighting three thugs at once and if they were anything like the last one who'd just given her a run for her money she could end up regretting it. But the atrium was wide open with plenty of space to move. If she kept her distance and used her surroundings as Grandad had taught her she could do it.

"Hey now." A thug wearing atank top stained with the orange chemicals from the lab descended the second-floor staircase. "Let's do this, chica." He raised his fists and bounced on the balls of his feet.

"What is it with you guys and the dancing routine?" Macy snarked. "Did you all go to the same ballet school or something? Seriously, it's like the Bad Lip Reading version of Street Fighter."

He advanced and she dropped, spinning around and sweeping his legs from under him. He hit the floor but took the impact with his shoulder instead of his head. She stayed low and threw a front kick to his face that connected with his nose.

"Aww! You—"

She kicked him again and he lay writhing. "No bad words now. You're in a school, remember?"

"Harghhh!"

Macy ducked and narrowly missed a piece of pipe aimed at her head. The pipe clanged as it hit the floor and skittered away. She jumped to her feet and turned. Another thug–this one with arms full of tattoos–twirled a second pipe in his hands like a pair of nunchucks.

The third and last thug appeared from a hallway to her right. He looked at the fallen thug bleeding profusely from his face and put his hands up. "No way. I'm done." He turned and left the way he came in a run.

"Now he's got the right idea. Why don't you follow his lead, huh, slick?"

"Argh!"

The tattooed thug swung the pipe at her head. She turned and grabbed it, pulling it out of his hands as he overextended himself and tumbled forward.

"I'm telling you," she said, flipping the pipe end to end, "you should vamoose."

The thug bent down and picked up the pipe he'd thrown. He advanced, swinging it as though it were a sword.

Macy blocked the attack with her own pipe and a loud clang echoed through the atrium. *Clang. Clang. Clang.* She matched him move for move, blocking each attack. "Ha! I know something you don't know!" She laughed and moved the pipe to her other hand. "I am not left-handed!" She struck him on the back of the hand causing him to drop his pipe as the tiny bones in the back of his hand shattered. She smiled. "How was that for a one-liner? Funny or not so much?"

The thug brought his hand to his torso, cradling it as he backed away. "You cocky little brat. If Zmija doesn't see to you soon enough, The Alderwoman will." The thug turned and ran.

"That's the second time someone's said that." She threw the pipe after him and it clanged down the hallway. "Maybe another chick will have a better chance since you got beaten by a girl!"

She watched as the thug fled. *Zmija.* That's the name Zeke had used for Deep Voice. But what did it mean?

A loud thud echoed through the hall as the fleeing thug burst out of the side entrance. A moment later a wailing siren started as the alarm sounded. *Time to leave.*

"Dude–the alarm."

Macy looked up and saw a pair of heads disappear behind the second-floor pony wall. She couldn't believe it. They were still here? A moment later she saw Patrick and Striker slip past the top of the stairs. She turned to leave but realized she couldn't–not while they were still around. Even though she'd taken care of the immediate danger there was still the chance they'd run into the police as they left. No one could know they were here. She took off for the side entrance betting she could get there before they did.

"You're really thick, aren't you?" Macy appeared from around a wall as Patrick and Striker exited the school.

Patrick's eyes went wide. "I—uhh—I—"

She pushed him against the wall "Your dad warned you to forget about me and lay off the investigation, but clearly you didn't listen. And on top of that, you brought loudmouth here with you." She flinched like she was going to come at Striker and he jumped back.

"I—uh—we weren't—we've been looking for you." Patrick stammered. "At–at night."

"So, you've been out here before? Great."

"How could I just–just forget?"

"You just have to." Sirens sounded in the distance. "We have to go. Now."

Macy grabbed Patrick by the shirt and pulled him away from the wall, pushing him down the sidewalk next to the school. Striker fell in behind him without encouragement and she brought up the rear, marshaling them towards the fence and the Greater Avendale neighborhoods where they all lived.

"I just wanted to find you," Patrick said, looking back. "I just wanted to help."

"You can help by doing what you were told. Now they know I was here and that I know about their little lab down there."

"What was that place anyway?" Striker said, his voice quivering.

Macy's demeanor softened a bit. "I don't know. Some kind of old bunker maybe."

"Beneath Alum Ridge?" Patrick said. "That's incredible."

"Don't go getting any ideas. Your little gumshoe gang is officially retired after tonight."

Striker held up his hands in surrender. "You don't have to tell me twice. This was his idea. I was supposed to be home raiding the fridge for leftover tacos right now."

Flashing blue and red lights lit up the walls of the school as they arrived at the fence. Macy glanced back to see two police cars enter the parking lot and begin using spotlights to survey the outside of the school. She reached for the fence and made to pull herself over.

"Wait–you can't–you can't just disappear." Patrick took hold of her shoulder armor, but then thought better of it and backed off. "You have to talk to me. You have to tell me who you are–and *how* you are."

Macy got down off the fence and faced him. His eyebrows were raised, his mouth was open, and moisture gathered in his eyes. He was about to cry. The emotion on his face was heartbreaking. What was it about Stellar that was so important to him?

"Did my mom send you?" He reached out again and touched the Stellar emblem on her shoulder armor. "Are you… real?"

She didn't know what to say. She still didn't know what had happened to his mom, but the feeling she was getting was that she had died. Did he really think she was some kind of angel or something? Oh, if only it were that simple and she could just vanish into the ether. No, she had to stay and deal with the situation she'd started when she first put on this getup. She had to find a way to save everyone on this Alderwoman's hit list–including herself.

Not knowing what else to do, she struck a mysterious tone. "Some things just are, Patrick. And this is one of them. Now get yourselves away from here before the cops see you." She climbed the fence and jumped over, landing on the other side and breaking into a run.

CHAPTER 14

Macy read the text message again as she left the bus.

Hey. Jess's @ 7pm? We need to talk.

She smiled. While it was short and to the point, it was the first real communication she'd gotten from Keri in weeks, and hopefully a sign the ice between them was beginning to melt. Keri still hadn't had much to say since their disagreement over whether to continue as Stellar or not and weeks had gone by with minimal conversation. They'd sat in their usual places during classes, but at lunch, Keri would sit with Taylor and Emma and ride with them in Taylor's big sister's car to and from school.

To say Macy felt alone and abandoned would be the understatement of the year. She felt terrible about the strain on their friendship and had tried to offer some kind of olive branch in the form of a few texts, but Keri just hadn't seemed interested. And Macy really didn't feel like an apology was in order. She had remained resolute in her decision to be Stellar and last night's foray into Alum Ridge had proven her correct—at least in her mind.

Even Macy's parents had noticed Keri's absence and had inquired and Macy hadn't known what to say. *We're just having a moment, right? Friends have disagreements sometimes and that's what this is, right?* They would get past it eventually, she'd hoped. But still, she'd spent no shortage of time thinking about it. In fact, the absence of both Grandad and her best friend was about all she'd been able to focus on when she wasn't trying to figure out who this Alderwoman was and what she was up to.

See you there. :)

She clicked her phone off as she entered the building. She had so many things to tell Keri. 7pm couldn't come soon enough.

"Here we are, sweetie." William Davis turned into an alley and stopped. "Text me when you're done, but I won't get off until at least ten. I'll come runnin' as soon as I can."

"Thanks, dad."

Macy got out and made her way down the sidewalk of what once had been downtown Avendale, but was now just a chic main street area located on the outskirts of Avendale University, an ever-expanding technical college that now boasted an on-campus student body that made up a tenth of the population of the entire Greater Avendale suburb.

Macy approached the aged wood-framed entrance of a two-story brownstone storefront and pulled open the door to Cup O' Jess. The aroma of the local hot spot's famous creole blended coffee washed over her like the warmth from a wood-burning fireplace as she stepped inside.

"Evening, Macy. Usual?"

"Yes, please."

"Half Sweet, Non-Fat Iced Mocha Latte with an extra shot!"

"Thank you." Macy wondered for the umpteenth time how Jessica Blencarn, the owner of the shop, managed to remember so many names and orders. She made her way to the back of the exposed brick shop and up a wrought iron staircase to the second-floor balcony where she always sat with Keri when they came to study.

Even though Macy was ten minutes early, Keri was already seated at a corner table against the wrought iron balustrade. As soon as Macy laid eyes on her she felt her insides drop. Something wasn't right. Keri was dressed in loose-fitting earth tones, wore a pair of Jackie O style sunglasses, and a far more liberal amount of makeup than even she normally wore. Was she still mad? Had she come only to deliver an in-person death blow to their friendship?

"Who's funeral is it?" Macy said, cracking a half-smile as she sat down.

Keri sniffed loudly as though she'd been crying and removed the sunglasses.

Macy felt her mouth hang open and her eyes widen. Beneath the glasses, Keri was sporting two black eyes, a lot of swelling, and a deep cut above one eyebrow.

"Pretty, huh? These are just the ones you can see."

Macy searched for words, but nothing came out. Her face felt flush and her hands began to tingle. *Who did this and where are they? They can try taking on a two-time black belt next.*

"Some guy called Dude with Zeke and Trevor looking on," Keri said as if she could read minds. "They cornered me as I left Taylor and Emma's practice yesterday afternoon and forced me under the bleachers beside the football field."

Macy teared up. "Did they…"

"What? Rape me?" Keri ran a finger around one of the water rings on the table. "No."

"Tell me the truth, Keri."

"I am. But they made it clear that would be next if they found out I was lying."

Macy placed her elbows on the table and her face into her hands. Was she responsible for this? Had The Alderwoman found out she was Stellar and sent goons after her best friend as a warning? She wiped away tears. "I… I don't know what to say. I mean… why? Did they—"

"The superhero cosplays I did for the Comic-Con last spring. They found them on my Instagram."

"And decided if anyone at Alum Ridge had made a superhero costume it was you."

Keri frowned and nodded. "But I didn't tell them a thing about you… or Stellar."

That was a relief, though Macy wasn't sure she'd have blamed her if she had. Keri could well have been killed. From the sound of it, this wasn't just a typical dust-up caused by Zeke and his lackeys. This was an attempt to gain information. And who was this Dude guy? He wasn't anyone she'd seen Zeke with before, which meant he must be one of the many thugs who seemed to be employed by this Zmija and The Alderwoman.

"So, they are looking at Alum Ridge students," Macy said as much to herself as to Keri. "Decker made it sound like they'd decided it wasn't a student at the rally a few weeks ago."

Keri looked confused. "What does Decker have to do with anything?"

Macy scoffed. "We have a lot of catching up to do."

"That's why I wanted to meet. I owe you an apology. You were right. They're not going to stop."

Now wasn't the time to say I told you so, but the words popped into Macy's head regardless. She'd rather have been dead wrong than for Keri to have been hurt, though.

"Oh, they're going to stop. I'm going to see to it."

A heavy silence followed. Macy wrestled with her thoughts. Part of her wanted to be angry–wanted to lash out about being all but ignored for weeks–about it taking a life-threatening situation before trusting your best friend. But the other part of her was just glad Keri was okay and that she was back–however it had come about. "So… we're good?"

Keri wiped away tears. "Girl, we're always good. Even if I forget it now and then. I'm so sorry I doubted you."

Macy shook her head. "Don't. It doesn't matter anymore." She shrugged. "And it's not like you didn't have a good reason. I'm as new to this whole hero thing as you are. Mistakes are bound to be made."

Keri nodded and blinked away more tears.

Macy looked over her shoulder to make sure there was no one close enough to be listening. Thankfully the second floor was mostly empty. Only two tables closer to the stairs were being used and both occupants had their attention on laptops and were wearing headphones. She turned back and proceeded to catch Keri up on Stellar's visit to Alum Ridge the previous night. Keri sat stunned as she listened to the blow by blow account.

"So… Decker?"

Macy shrugged. "I guess so, though she apparently calls herself

Zmija when she's all dressed up as The Phantom of the Opera or whatever."

"Zah what?"

"It's pronounced ZAH MEE AH. I Googled it. It means snake in about half a dozen Eastern European languages."

"Ugh. Creepy."

"I know, right?

"And you're sure it's Decker?"

"It has to be her I think. What are the chances of someone having the same ring on the same finger and knowing about a hidden bunker beneath Alum Ridge High School?"

"I'm going to go with pretty low."

"Mmm-hmm. And is it really that surprising? I mean the administration has been turning a blind eye forever and now we know why."

"Yeah. And that means they're behind what happened to me, doesn't it? That means this Dude guy was acting on orders."

Macy nodded. "I'm sorry."

"I was so naive. 'It's just what society calls high school.' I was such an idiot."

"Hey. Don't. You didn't have any control over what happened last night. And no one could have known how far this went. It's only by being in the right place at the right time twice now that I found out."

"Keri!" A barista shouted from downstairs. "Macy!"

Macy patted Keri's hands one more time and stood from the table. She returned a few minutes later with their lattes and an order of Jess's Famous Chocolate and Cheese Windmill Cookies.

Keri wore a thousand-yard stare. "I want a piece of these guys, Mace, even if I have to get it… some other way."

"Vicariously. They call it living vicariously. And I know a certain masked heroine who would be honored to issue a few beatings on your behalf."

Keri flashed a half-smile. "So, what do we do now?" She took a long sip of her usual Dark Blended Iced Mint Latte.

Macy finished a cookie. "I've typed Dr. Sara Decker into every search engine I can think of and the furthest reference to her I can find is the Avendale Journal story on her when she was announced as the new principal at Alum Ridge. That was three years ago."

"What's it say?"

"Only that she arrived from a school system in the Czech Republic after teaching and administering abroad for many years."

"Convenient."

"Right?"

"And you said she had some kind of insignia on her ring? I wonder what it means."

"I've probably pored over a thousand pages of crown signet rings and again–nothing."

Keri started tracing a finger along the water rings on the table again. "What's an Alderwoman? Sounds like the name of some kind of supervillain on The KB."

"I looked that up, too. That was about the only moderately useful thing I was able to find. Alderman–or alderwoman–is an ancient term from old European countries like England. Apparently, it's derived from elder man or wise man and in ancient times they oversaw 'shires.' Kind of like today's city councils or board of supervisors."

"So, someone in the government is behind this?"

Macy shrugged. "Maybe. I mean it's an old term that's been replaced by others like counselor and supervisor and such for decades if not centuries. It's only used now in a few places. Chicago was the only one I recognized. Some smaller towns around the US still use it and I think I read a few rural places in Canada."

"Okay. Hold on. So, the Czech Republic is an old European place, right? If Decker was there it makes sense she brought these terms back with her and is using them to conceal her real identity and to make herself sound more menacing or something."

"Yeah maybe. But when I overheard Zmija threatening Newell she talked about The Alderwoman in the third person–as if she was someone else–someone who was in charge of all of them. And last night one of the thugs I fought said something similar. It definitely sounds like we're talking about two separate people."

Keri shook her head. "Got me then."

"Me too. But I thought about this all night and most of the day and I don't think it matters so much who she is right now as it does what she's up to. What is that stuff they were making and what are they doing with it? And where are they holding Brittany?"

"You said it was dark where Brittany was, right? Sounds to me like this bunker is a good place to start."

"Yup. And that means Stellar's going back to the school. Only this time it will be during the day when they're less likely to be working down there."

CHAPTER 15

The weather being cold had its advantages, Macy thought as she let her backpack slide from her shoulder and land at her feet. She couldn't imagine having to put the Stellar costume on at school. Were there even any unused rooms she could have used for cover? She doubted it. Even the broom closets had secondary uses it seemed.

As usual, she'd ridden the bus to school and had stayed long enough to be checked off in homeroom as present, which was enough to make sure the automated attendance system wouldn't notify her parents. Now that second block was beginning she had ducked away. Hopefully, her parents wouldn't notice a couple of extra absences if they were only in certain classes. The bell would ring any second and the last of the few students still in the halls nearby would be gone.

She placed her hands in the oversized pockets of the plaid-lined car coat Keri had loaned her to cover what she was wearing underneath and stood waiting just around the corner from the long hallway that led to the freight elevator she'd seen.

After begging her father for a pass on her curfew, Macy had closed down Cup O' Jess with Keri looking for any information available on what it was that was located beneath Alum Ridge. It was a good idea to know what you were walking into, right? But local history, it turned out, was in short supply. Hours of searching and more caffeine than she cared to think about had turned up only two sources; the long-forgotten blog of a former history major at Avendale University and an article titled Ten Surprising Secrets From Port Saint Dominic that had contained as many affiliate links as it had actual words.

In a strange twist of fate, the article and the blog had actually worked together. What the article made vague references to the blog went into more detail about and both pointed to the bunker being a World War II-era bomb factory.

According to the blog PSD like every other local economy during World War II had shifted from producing normal goods and services to trying to outproduce the German Third Reich. Instead of auto parts, clothes, sporting goods, and other commercial product lines, factories had been transformed into streamlined war machines that produced tanks, airplanes, uniforms, rifles, and of course bombs.

Due to the sensitive nature of the manufacturing process, most bomb factories had been hurriedly constructed adjacent to existing rural facilities, and to contain any accidental explosions they were built into the ground like basements using thick concrete walls and columns.

The description had certainly sounded like what Macy had seen, but hadn't Alum Ridge always been a school? She wasn't sure. She knew the original building dated to the industrial era because she remembered her history teacher saying as much. But she wasn't even one hundred percent sure when that had been. She supposed that like everything else surrounding PSD the area now known as Greater Avendale had once been a rural community all to itself and had simply been assimilated as the city grew up and out.

The bell rang and jarred her thoughts back to the task at hand. She listened as voices died out and doors closed and then she turned into the hall facing the freight elevator. There were no classrooms down this hallway. It was just a long corridor that served a solitary purpose; access to the bunker–or factory–beneath. She grabbed her backpack and made for the stairs.

Inside the stairwell, she opened her bag, stashed her tennis shoes and Keri's coat, and took out Stellar's mask and boots. She put the finishing touches on by securing the hood as she made her way down the steps to the metal door and peered through the window. Just as it had been the other night the room beyond was dark. Not even the few overhead lights that had been on then were lit now. It looked just as she'd hoped it would–vacant.

She fished her phone and a small tactical flashlight out of her bag and then set the pack beside the door where it would stay until she returned. She set the phone to airplane mode to make sure it didn't make any noise and opened the camera feature. What good was sneaking into the bad guys' lab if you didn't get evidence to prove it existed? She raised the phone but struggled to hit the camera button while also holding the flashlight. She reached around for someplace to stow it, but the Stellar suit didn't have any pockets. *Ugh. Annoying.* She would have to remember to talk to Keri about–what was it called in the comic books–a utility belt? She moved the flashlight to her mouth and snapped a few photos of the steps and the door before pulling the door open.

She took the flashlight out of her mouth, clicked it on, and shined it into the room beyond, surprised at just how much light the little device gave off. The room was bigger than she'd realized. It extended past the freight elevator to a point where not even the thousand lumen whatever flashlight reached. But like the rest of the room, there was no sign of any recent use–only the trail in the dust leading toward the lab.

She followed the trail, moving the flashlight between her hands and her mouth, snapping photos, and sweeping the light around. From the looks of it, no one had been here since the other night. She saw her own path in the dust where she'd followed Zmija and a wide snow angel where she imagined Zmija had landed after her kick. She reached the lab entrance and stopped, shining the light around the room. Here everything had changed. The lights and tables were gone along with the trays and the powder. So much for evidence and proof. The place had been cleaned out. Whatever was being done here had been moved someplace else.

Macy couldn't say she was surprised–disappointed–but not surprised. Criminals didn't like witnesses and what else was she if not a witness? She entered the former lab, snapping photos as she went. This was the first real look she had gotten at it and judging by the black and white pictures she had seen of World War II bomb factories on the internet last night the place certainly fit the bill. Black stenciled letters had been placed at even intervals around the walls reading DO NOT HAMMER OR USE FORCE IN ANY OPERATION. Undoubtedly that was a warning to workers about the explosive nature of the materials they had been handling.

Her light fell over the rear wall of the room and an area of knocked away concrete drew her attention. She approached and shined the light into the area beyond. Steel lintels and two-by-fours had been used to support the concrete wall and what appeared to be a tunnel beyond. The narrow passageway extended beyond the beam of the flashlight, but she thought she could make out a wider opening in the distance. She took a few steps back and snapped several photos.

"नमस्कार?" *Hel*

Macy jumped and turned the light towards the sound. Had that been a voice? A doorway at the corner of the room stood illuminated.

"के त्यहाँ कोही छ?" *Is someone*

Macy was sure it was a voice this time, but she didn't recognize the language. She approached the doorway and pushed the windowless door open. The smell of human waste hit her and caused her eyes to water. After taking a moment to collect herself and to steel herself against the foul stench, she shined the light around what appeared to have been an office or storage room and at least a dozen pairs of eyes looked back at her. Her mouth fell open. Metal cages had been erected along each of the walls and two or three people sat in each one like dogs in a pound.

"हामीलाई सहयोग गर्नुहोस्!" They all cried out with a sudden rush of movement to the ca*ge doors.*

Macy entered the room, covering her nose and mouth with one hand as she shined the light around with the other. Judging by the white smocks and the purple, orange, and green stains these people were the workers she'd seen mixing the powdery substance. She shined the light over each of the people gathered there, in search of Brittany. Was she being kept in here as well? No. She didn't recognize any of them.

"हामीलाई सहयोग गर्नुहोस्!" The people rattled the ca*ge doors.*

"Okay. Okay." Macy held up a hand for them to stop their commotion. She didn't understand what they were saying, but the message was obvious; *get us out!* She moved to one of the cage doors and followed the edge of the door down with the light to find a heavy padlock. She took hold of it and pulled. Nothing. She had about as much of a chance of breaking it loose as she did of becoming prom queen. She shined the light at each of the doors to see them all padlocked the same.

"You… must… help… us…"

The English was broken, but understandable. She moved to the man who had spoken. He looked to have been a clean-cut Asian man before he was forced into this life–if it could be called a life. Who were these people? Slaves? Macy had heard about human trafficking but had never imagined it went on so close to home.

"You… will… help?"

"I'm trying." She took hold of the padlock on his cage door and pulled again. She moved the flashlight to her mouth, set her phone on top of the cage, and gripped the lock with both hands. She pulled with everything she could manage, but it didn't budge. "Key. I need a key." She pointed to the hole in the front of the lock.

The man shook his head. "No… they have."

Macy let go of the lock and removed the flashlight from her mouth. She shined it on the walls next to the entrance on the off chance that a key was hanging there, but there was nothing. She turned back and looked the man in the eye. "Was there ever a girl here with you?" She moved her hand over her head and pointed at her teeth. "She had blonde hair and braces."

The man shook his head again. "No."

"Are you sure? You've never seen a blonde girl here ever?"

"No."

"Okay." She gave him an apologetic look. She didn't want him to think she was only there for Brittany. She'd help them all if she could. "I'll be back. I'll come back with tools and get you out."

"No," a voice crackled through the air. "I don't think you will."

Macy turned at the clear and authoritative voice. The people in the cages shuddered and ducked away from the doors like whipped hounds. Macy forgot about taking pictures and shined the light at the entrance of the room expecting to see someone, but caught only a faint glow from the bigger room beyond. She exited, moving cautiously toward the source of the glow. It grew brighter as she drew closer to the center of the room.

"Ahh. There you are," the voice said as Macy stepped into the line of sight of a tablet device that had been strapped to one of the concrete columns at eye level. The vague shape of a woman's face filled the screen, but her features were kept carefully hidden by shadows. "I've been waiting for you."

Macy studied the face and considered the voice. There was something regal and old-world about the woman–something she recognized–but couldn't zero in on. "You're the… The Alderwoman."

"Hmm." The woman laughed derisively. "Yes. Quite. And you are Port Saint Dominic's newest masked crusader. Let me guess… The Starlet? The Beamstress? Luminesa Jr.?"

"It's Stellar."

"Ahh. Stellar." The Alderwoman laughed again. "How creative."

Macy fixated on a tiny red light on the column above the tablet– a motion-activated camera. The Alderwoman had known she would come back and had been waiting for her to arrive. But why? *I've walked right into a trap, haven't I?* The hair stood up on the back of her neck and she shined the light around in search of anyone else. The room was still empty.

"I wanted to give you enough time to look around. Not what you remember, hmm? I'm afraid your visit the other night dictated that I move this little operation elsewhere."

"You forgot your labor force."

"Yes. With the closure of this facility and some more recent acquisitions, I'm a bit overstaffed. But I'm sure they'll find the retirement plan adequate. And so will you. I've satisfied my curiosity."

Another red light blinked on near the top of the column and another one on the column next to it. Macy shined the flashlight up. More red lights followed until every column in the room had a light. *Explosives!* Macy's mind raced and her heart began to pound faster. Her eyes darted around the room after the flashlight beam.

"Goodbye… Stellar."

Macy ran for the closest exit; the tunnel carved into the rear wall. The ground rocked beneath her and a deafening roar sounded. Bits of dirt and rock pelted her as the tunnel caved in behind her. She pushed on, keeping the flashlight beam on the ground in front of her even as dust filled the air and blurred her vision. She'd seen an exit, she was sure of it, but would what was beyond it cave in to? The flashlight illuminated a steep drop in the floor and she jumped, flying out of the tunnel in a tsunami of dirt and debris.

Macy came to and blinked away dirt and dust. "Ugh…" Her head was pounding and her body throbbed. She removed a glove and wiped her eyes as clear as she could with her palm. Beneath the glove was the only part of her not covered in filth. She touched the right side of her forehead where it throbbed, but couldn't feel much through her mask. Had something hit her in the head? She couldn't remember, but with the amount of debris she felt on her and around her it seemed likely. But she was pretty sure she'd avoided serious injury. The pain she felt wasn't much more than she'd felt many times after being slammed into a rubber karate mat by a sparring partner.

Where had the flashlight and her phone landed? She looked around hoping it wasn't buried beneath a pile of rubble. Illuminated dust particles caught her eye and she followed the light back to its source. The flashlight was a few yards away and mostly covered, but at least some light was shining through. *That's a good sign, but what about my phone?*

Macy closed her eyes as she raised herself into a sitting position, knocking away bits of concrete and chunks of hard clay as she moved. She stood and beat the dust and dirt off her suit. She pulled her hood loose, pushed it back, and pulled off her mask before opening her eyes again. The last thing she needed was another eye or two full of dirt.

She stretched and went for the flashlight, picking it up and dusting it off. Now the brighter, unobstructed light revealed a sheer concrete wall in front of her. She shined the light up and followed with her eyes–she was in another tunnel–but this one had been constructed more professionally. Enormous concrete slabs had been stacked together and mortar had been spread between them to hold them in place, though from the looks of it, time and other elements were beginning to take their toll. Some of the blocks had shifted, others had deep cracks, and rebar stuck out randomly. How old was this tunnel? How far did it go? And most importantly, where was the exit?

Macy turned the light to the collapsed tunnel behind her and a feeling of dread hit her. The workers had still been locked in their cages. The Alderwoman had blown the support beams and caused the roof to collapse. Who were they? How many had there been? Did they have families? They had to be dead. No one could survive that kind of collapse. The thought took her breath away. And what about the school? Had the same support beams also supported the floors of the school above? Macy drew in a sharp breath and a sob escaped– *Keri!* She stood looking at the mangled steel lintels, broken two-by-fours, dirt, and other debris from the tunnel.

She blinked away tears and made her way to the far concrete wall, leaning against it to support herself. How much of the school had been supported by the bomb factory beneath? Were her friends and teachers dead, too? She slid down the concrete wall onto her backside and placed her head in her hands. Images of buried people struggling and crying out for help filled her mind. Some hero she had turned out to be.

She winced as her hand on her forehead brushed a tender spot just above her eye. She felt it with two fingers and discovered a small cut. She pulled her fingers away and saw only a bit of blood. *That's good–I guess.*

She sniffed heavily to clear her head and wiped her eyes again. She needed to know for sure what had happened above and that meant she had to find a way out of here–wherever here was. She stood and shined the flashlight at the pile of rubble, looking for any signs of her phone. *Not a thing–great.* She knew she'd had it in her hand as she'd left the workers and faced The Alderwoman–or had she? Had she remembered to pick the phone up from the top of the cage? Had she dropped it during her harried escape? She wasn't sure but either way meant the device could be anywhere underneath the pile. She kicked at a few of the pieces of timber and concrete, but none of them budged. Anything underneath was likely lost forever. *Great–just great.*

She gave up with a heavy sigh and shined the flashlight around, aiming it first in one direction and then the other. The tunnel extended beyond the beam both ways. She had a fifty percent chance of going the right direction. She watched the dust particles in the air for movement and walked in the opposite direction. She couldn't detect any breeze, but if there was one she reasoned that she was much heavier than dust particles, and moving opposite of them would lead her to the source and hopefully to an exit.

Condensation leaked from above and soft dirt squished beneath her feet as she walked. Sweeping the light in front of her she saw rats scatter away from trash bags and boxes. Clearly, someone knew this place existed if there was trash new enough for rats to still be interested. Who had built these tunnels and what had they been used for? And why had The Alderwoman's people made a new tunnel connecting the bomb factory? It was hard to imagine anyone using such a dark and dreary place as a means to transport anything, but then maybe that's why criminal activity was referred to as the underworld.

The light revealed something on the wall as she swept it to one side. Macy moved the light up and stopped. Emblazoned in purple paint was the same insignia she had seen on the signet rings worn by Zmija and Principal Decker. She studied the insignia. The paint wasn't new and judging by the amount of fading the marking had been there for many years. It was definitely supposed to be some kind of a crown and this time there were words beneath it.

"Priori Iustitia." It looked Latin, but Macy had no idea what it meant.

An uneasy feeling settled on her and she shined the light around. *Why do I feel like I'm being watched?* She replaced her mask and hood. Had she just broken the biggest superhero rule in the book by revealing her face? Boy was she really starting to suck at this.

She moved on. The tunnel turned widely a few times and made several inclines and declines. More crown insignias had been painted at random intervals as if someone was marking their territory and wooden steps and bridges had been constructed at points due to the washout caused by the leaking condensation. Occasionally another smaller tunnel jutted off the big one. At the mouth of one such opening, she stopped to inspect some broken down crates. She shined the light on the logos. *Blencarn Bros. Ltd. Brampton U.K. Handcrafted Northumbrian Gin.* The lack of sunlight in the tunnel had preserved the markings, but age and the moist air had brought the crates to the point of crumbling. Is that what these tunnels were; bootlegging tunnels? She remembered reading about the illegal movement and sale of alcohol during the Prohibition period in one of her history classes. That explained a lot. If these were bootlegging tunnels they could extend for miles throughout the city and whatever it was The Alderwoman was making could be transported anywhere without being seen.

Clink!

The movement of a glass bottle echoed and the hairs on Macy's neck stood. There was definitely someone or something around. She moved on, shining the light this way and that. What other choice did she have? Turning back wasn't any better than going ahead, was it?

A few hundred yards and a wide turn from the crates Macy spotted natural light ahead. She clicked off the flashlight as she moved closer. The tunnel ended and she emerged into a spacious room constructed with brick walls and cobblestone floors. Beams of sunlight shone through what appeared to be the gigantic windows of an empty building above and either age or shoddy construction had created wide gaps in the wooden floorboards, allowing rays of light to pass through and illuminate the room below. Other entrances dotted the room and beside each was a painted insignia. The one she had emerged from and the others along the same wall had the crown marking beside them in purple paint. On the wall across from her, the openings were marked with a different insignia painted in red. Far simpler in its construction than the crown insignia, this one appeared to be—what was it? A ninja mask maybe? No. There appeared to be pointy ears. The face of a raccoon? She wasn't sure, but it had almost certainly been painted by an amateur hand.

She looked between the two insignias, studying them. What did crowns and raccoons have in common? Were they the territorial markings of rival gangs? That seemed likely. Having grown up in the suburbs of PSD she was aware the city had the same problems most cities had with gangs, but she'd never seen symbols like this. As far as she knew the gangs in PSD were of the typical street variety, were named mostly after the neighborhoods they were associated with, and mostly operated in the more downtrodden areas south and east of downtown and in a particularly rundown area known as The Slip.

A metal door opened somewhere above.

"Okay…" a voice echoed, "…they're all here."

"Hmph… show them in."

Zmija! Macy ducked back into the shadows as a door slammed somewhere above. She looked around for a way up into the building and spotted a set of rickety steps just inside one of the crown marked entrances in the far corner of the room. She approached cautiously and made her way up, careful not to move too fast or distribute her weight unevenly in case the aged boards creaked. Luckily the room above had as many shadows as the room below and she settled into a spot just inside the doorway at the top of the steps.

The building was completely empty and multiple stories stretched upward to a water-stained roof where mildewed insulation hung from steel rafters. Time and the elements had rotted away the upper floors and left the building an open square framed in by brick walls and enormous industrial windows. In the center of the room, illuminated by shafts of light from the windows above, five men stood in a line behind Zmija. Macy didn't recognize any of them, but it was obvious from the way they were dressed that they were gangsters, some of them from the streets, and some of them from other, more organized, places.

A metal door sounded again and a man dressed in a trendy-looking winter coat, jeans, and work boots entered. He stood aside and began ushering others in. Two by two a trendy thug escorted a well-dressed man or woman in, their faces covered with thick, black bags. The last hooded man through the door wore what appeared to be a police uniform with a white shirt and blue striped pants, his gold badge catching the light and reflecting it off. The thugs lined the people up in front of Zmija and forced them to their knees, standing behind them like a row of executioners. In total there were nine thugs and nine… well, Macy guessed they were prisoners. They certainly didn't appear to be there willingly. The metal door banged shut and the trendy winter coat thug moved to stand near a side door like the sergeant-at-arms at the many dojos Macy had been in over the years, his arms crossed and a threatening sneer on his face.

Zmija motioned and the thugs pulled the hoods off. Sweaty faces blinked at the light. Macy studied each one but didn't recognize any of them. Their eyes settled on the group in front of them and they watched as Zmija paced.

"Greetings—"

"Skip the crap," the police uniformed man said. "Who are you? Why are we here?"

Zmija stopped in front of him. "Chief Williams… glad you could join us. Your role in this unfolding drama is the most important. As you can see, assembled here behind me are the heads of our fair city's most notorious gangs." Zmija moved to the first in the line of men. "Gregory Knapp, president of The Howlers Motorcycle Club…" Zmija moved on to the next in line. "Reverend Noir of The Southeast Sons & Daugh—"

"I said skip the crap. I know who they are. Now who are you and why are we here?"

Zmija stopped and looked at the thug behind the policeman. The thug brought his knee abruptly up and into the back of the policeman's head. A terrified gasp passed through the gathering as the policeman's head snapped forward and he fell face-first at Zmija's feet. The policeman groaned and the thug tugged him back to his knees by the collar of his shirt. His head lolled, but the thug grabbed him by the hair and held his head upright.

"Hmph… anyone else have anything to say?"

Two of the people on their knees sobbed, but none of them spoke.

"Good. You're here because you are the elected or appointed leaders of this city–the mayor, the city council, the chief of police, the district attorney–you're the chief influencers of law and order in Port Saint Dominic. But I'm here to inform you that the true leader of this city is back and is retaking her rightful place in Blackville House. From now on–just as she now controls the city's gangs–your orders, your legislations, your budgets, your decisions– will all be dictated to you by The Alderwoman."

"The… The Alderwoman?"

"Hmph. Yes, Mayor Bartlett. Long before your term, this city was controlled—"

"She's–she's been gone for twenty-five year–years."

"Not anymore. Weren't you listening?"

"Yes! I–I was!" The mayor ducked his head and held up his hands as if he were about to be struck.

"Good. And just in case any of you are thinking you'll agree now and do differently later I've arranged a demonstration… a warning if you will."

Zmija held out a hand, directing the room's attention to the side door where the trendy, winter coat thug stood. The thug pushed open the door and whistled. The sound of a freight door in a trailer being rolled open came from outside.

"Argh! Argh! Pfft! Argh!" The agitated screams echoed at first as though whatever was making them was inside the truck. Then they faded for a moment before growing louder again. "Argh! Pfft! Arghhhh! Arghhhhh!"

The trendy winter coat thug stumbled away as a shirtless man burst through the door, a thick, black bag covering his head and long steel rods attached to restraints at his wrists and neck. Four men were all but dragged in behind him, each one holding onto one of the rods and doing their best to control the enraged human.

Macy got a better look as he moved into the beam of light near Zmija. Bulbous blue veins bulged under pale skin and his muscles twitched as though he had electricity flowing through him. Zmija motioned and one of the men holding a restraint rod moved closer and pulled the hood off.

"Pfft! Argh! Argh! Pfft!"

Macy's eyes widened, her mouth dropped open, and her stomach knotted. Underneath the hood was Luke Bartlett, spittle flying from his mouth and his eyes bloodshot and bulging as he continued to scream. Macy's mind shot back to the night before. Keri said she'd been attacked by a guy called Dude with Zeke and Trevor looking on. She'd made no mention of Luke. Macy hadn't thought about it at the time, but Luke's absence was odd. And now it was explained. She never thought she'd see the day when she felt sorry for any of Zeke's crew, but standing there in the shadows, she did. Whatever Luke's sins, he didn't deserve to be turned into this. No one did.

The Mayor's face twisted up in terror. "No no no no! Luke! What have you done?"

"Hmph... a concentrated dose of Spaz." Zmija held up a syringe full of a neon orange substance. "I'm sure you've heard of it, Mr. Mayor."

The mayor's mouth seemed to go dry as he stared in horror.

"He'll come down from it in a day or two... if his heart doesn't burst before then."

The mayor sobbed.

"Hmph... should any of you renege on today's agreement your own children will receive similar treatment and be set loose in public where the only choice will be to kill them... before they kill others."

One of the gang members behind Zmija handed over a manila

envelope. Zmija took it and withdrew some pictures, flipping through them in such a way that made sure the gathered city leaders saw them. Fearful gasps followed each picture and Macy was certain they were photos of their kidnapped children. Just as The Alderwoman had taken Brittany Crumb to control her father, she'd taken the children of the city officials to control them.

"We will do whatever it takes. Will you?"

Zmija motioned to the metal door they had all arrived through and the thugs behind them replaced the black bags over their heads, yanked them to their feet, and led them away, the effects of their heinous attack still evident in the policeman's stumbling walk.

"Hey! There's someone down there." The trendy winter coat thug pointed to a space in the floorboards.

Macy turned and looked down the steps to see a shadow pass hurriedly across the room below.

"Release him."

Macy snapped her head back to Zmija. The thugs stood looking between each other.

"Release him now."

The thugs drew stun batons from their belts, held them at the ready, and released the rods holding Luke's restraints.

"Argh! Pfft! Argh!" Luke turned about looking for a direction to run. At each turn, he met an electric shock from his handlers until he was facing the steps. They prodded him again on the back and he was running.

Macy felt the knot in her stomach leap into her chest as the enraged letterman rushed for the steps she was on. *Time to go!* Macy stood and jumped down the steps three at a time, the aged wood threatening to crack from the impact. She blew through the doorway and caught sight of what she thought looked like the end of a red cloak as someone slipped into a red raccoon marked tunnel. Did she follow or did she head back to the—a pair of hands grasped her shoulders and something heavy hit her from behind. Before she knew it she was sliding face-first across the cobblestoned floor and could hear Luke's agitated screams above her. Meaty fists struck her repeatedly in the back and on the head, driving her face into the rocks under her.

"Get him back! Get him back!" An electric shock sounded and Luke's attack stopped. "Hold him!"

Macy tried to collect herself. She dragged herself into a sitting position and looked behind her. Luke's handlers had chased him down the steps, which he had apparently jumped down to catch her as fast as he had, and were doing their best to corral him into a corner. He lashed at them again and again like an animal.

"Here here, you Ragamuffin scum." The trendy winter coat thug approached from the stairwell, lifting a stun baton and pounding it into one hand threateningly. "Ope… whadda we have here? You're not one o' them, are you? Unless they're upgrading their outfits now."

Who? What? Macy had no idea what he was talking about. She stood gingerly.

The thug turned and looked back. Zmija stood at the mouth of the stairwell.

"Hmph… you're supposed to be dead. No matter… you will be shortly."

Macy stayed in a neutral stance. After Luke's attack, what felt like hours of walking through darkened tunnels, and taking a good hit jumping out of the collapsing factory, she wasn't sure how much fight she had left in her, but something told her she was about to find out.

Sharp pops continued to sound from the stun batons still being used to corral Luke. Could he not feel any pain?

"Hmph…" Zmija touched her abdomen, looked at Luke, and then back at Macy. "Let's see what kind of damage you can do when you don't have the element of surprise. Release him."

The men with the stun batons backed away and fanned out, covering the entrances so neither Macy nor Luke could escape. Luke ran at her. Macy turned and ran for the back wall, jumping and running up it as far as her momentum would take her before flipping off. She landed behind Luke who looked up and down the wall in confusion.

Macy used the time to create distance. Under normal circumstances, she'd have been more than happy to fight Luke again. But this was anything but normal. Luke turned to face her still spitting and screaming. She didn't want to hurt him—could she hurt him? He ran at her from across the room. She waited until he was closing in and launched a jumping side kick. The impact knocked him aside and she followed with a series of front kicks that drove him backward and pinned him against the wall. She kept up the flurry of attacks, but it was clear they were having no effect. All she was accomplishing was keeping him away and from the looks of it, she'd run out of energy long before he did.

"Ahh!"

An electric shock shot through her body and before she could recover Luke was on her, his movements erratic like an infuriated ape. She brought her arms up and tried to block him, but his hands flew in and out from unusual directions and each strike felt like being hit with a sledgehammer. She moved backward trying again to create distance, but he launched himself at her and wrapped her in a bear hug. Crushing pain shot through her body in up and down waves and her breath left her.

"Hmph… get him off."

Loud pops of electricity preceded Macy being thrown to the

ground, her head and back taking the brunt of the impact. She writhed painfully and tried to catch her breath. Something heavy pressed on her chest and she saw Zmija standing over her, a foot on her chest.

"Hmph… your time here is at an end. Finish her off and throw her down the chute for our scavenger friends to find."

Zmija walked away. Macy lifted herself into a sitting position, but the room spun around her and her vision blurred. She couldn't take another hit like that. She lifted herself first to one knee and then to her feet. Her head throbbed and her heart was beating so fast she could hear her blood pounding through her veins. She tried to steady herself but stumbled.

A meaty fist met the side of her face full force and the room spun again. Another fist hit her from the opposite side. She stumbled into a wall behind her. A sweeping kick to the back of her knees drove her down and she brought her arms up to cover from the flurry of attacks she knew had to be coming. Instead, she felt the heat and heard the pop of the stun batons. She jerked her arms back as electricity shot through them. They forced her to scoot into a corner and cover her head. This was it… she'd be joining the great beyond soon.

A shrill whistle sounded and a bright light exploded. "Leave her alone!"

Macy lifted her head to see the source of the voice. A lone figure stood beyond the men surrounding her, but she couldn't make out anything other than the general shape of a human body. The men turned away from her and another shrill whistle preceded a bright flash.

"Ahh!"

"My eyes!"

Macy heard a scuffle followed by painful gasps and more whistles. Bright flashes continued—some like camera flashes and others like small explosions. She placed her head in her hands as the sound of the thugs being beaten and falling came from nearby. Who was there? She tried to focus but just needed to close her eyes. She curled into a ball, desperate to protect herself from any more attacks and grateful for the darkness that was slowly taking her.

CHAPTER 16

Macy opened her eyes a bit and slowly began to focus. *Hmm.* A smile tugged at her lips. Muscles… a tight t-shirt revealing a washboard stomach… muscular legs in faded blue jeans stretched out in a perfect sidekick… *am I in heaven?* She tried lifting her head and pain shot down her spine all the way to her toes. *Nope—not in heaven.* She relaxed and blinked rapidly, her eyes focusing on the poster of Tylar Marsden on her bedroom ceiling. "Ugh…"

"Heyyyy," a soft voice said as a hand touched her shoulder.

"Mom?" Macy gingerly turned her head.

"Heyyy." Becky Davis placed a hand on Macy's forehead and brushed her hair aside. "How are you feeling?"

Macy grimaced as flashes of the fight with Luke flew through her head followed by even briefer flashes of defeated thugs, someone carrying her, and people standing over her. "I'm… okay. I think."

"Oh, honey." Her mom rubbed her head and smiled. "I'm going to get your dad."

"Okay." Macy watched her mom get up excitedly and leave the room. She took a deep breath as the door clicked closed and winced as pain ricocheted around her body again. It was less painful than last time, though, so that was a good thing, right?

She glanced around the room. Vases of flowers sat on just about every available surface and a group of balloons bobbed up and down and against each other making a rubbery sound. How long had she been here? And how had she gotten here? She vaguely remembered people standing over her talking to one another. "Ugh…" She sank back into her memory foam mattress. Did everyone know she'd been masquerading as a superhero? Did everyone know she'd had her head handed to her by the city's criminal elite? She tried to remember what had happened, but all that was clear was the beginning of the fight with Luke. After that things got fuzzy and she could only remember the briefest flashes of events.

Her mom returned, leaving the bedroom door open. Her passing made the balloons bump harder off one another. "He'll be right—"

"How long have I—"

"Been out?" Her mom sat down at the edge of the bed and put her hand back on Macy's forehead. "It's been about a week. The doctor had you on some pretty serious muscle relaxers so you've been sleeping almost around the clock."

A week? Macy furrowed her brow. How could it have been a week since she'd faced down a drugged and enraged Luke Bartlett? And what had happened in the meantime? She couldn't remember anything but the same brief moments and it was driving her nuts. She felt her fingertips go numb as panic welled inside her and made her cheeks flush.

"Honey, it's okay. Take it easy. The doctors said you took a pretty hard hit and that it's common to have some memory loss and even be a little confused for a while afterward."

Confused? I'm not confused. She'd fought for her life against The Alderwoman's thugocracy and she'd lost. The fact that she was even standing—or lying here talking to her mom was a miracle, wasn't it? She concentrated on the brief memory of the defeated thugs lying around her. Had she done it in some kind of blind rage? No. Someone had been supporting her–carrying her even–as she'd captured the glimpse. Someone had rescued her. Someone who'd used bright flashes of light to distract their opponents. She took a deep breath and willed the panicked feeling to leave as she closed her eyes and exhaled.

"There you go, dear. Just relax. It's all going to be okay."

Her mom was right. She couldn't beat herself up over not remembering something she'd barely been conscious enough to see. Instead, she shifted her focus to thinking backward. What had happened before the fight? Could she remember that? She saw Zmija pacing in front of the city leaders and remembered the rickety steps she'd taken to see the meeting and the basement room full of marked passageways. *Yeah…* She remembered it all.

She opened her eyes and made eye contact with her mom. "What happened at school?" Her cheeks flushed again and her stomach knotted. The answer that was already pinging around her head terrified her. Would she hear that Alum Ridge had collapsed and that there were fatalities throughout the building? She steeled herself as her mom shifted positions and pursed her lips.

"Oh, honey. Don't—"

"Hey." William Davis appeared in the doorway, beaming. "Good news, sweetie. I talked with the doctor earlier and he said you're done with the meds. The swelling's nearly gone and your injuries are healing so he doesn't see the need to refill the prescription." He walked in and held his arms out as though he was expecting a cheer.

"Oh, William. She's just woken up. Give her some time."

"Oh, yeah. Definitely." He took a seat in Macy's desk chair and smiled at her.

"I want to know, mom." Macy stared up into her mom's eyes trying to relay how serious she was. "I need to know."

"Know what?" her dad said. "What are we talking about?" He looked between his wife and daughter.

"She wants to know what happened at school."

"Oh, that's easy."

Macy saw her mom flash her dad an uncertain look. Her dad nodded confidently in return and faced Macy again.

"A sinkhole opened up near one of the newer additions and part of that building and the road adjacent to it collapsed." Her dad shrugged. "Everyone got out with only a few minor injuries, but the school's closed for at least a few weeks while county engineers investigate and determine whether or not it's safe to return to the rest of the buildings."

Macy exhaled, a refreshing, weight-lifted feeling after the last few minutes. "Only minor injuries?

Her mom nodded. "Yes. Only minor injuries, thankfully. You were the worst of them. You took a really good hit, they said."

"Wait. What?"

Her mom nodded again. "Yeah. I don't think anyone knows what hit you exactly, but you apparently were able to make it out of the building before…" She teared up and her dad moved to comfort her. "… before passing out."

Macy watched them embrace and watched her mother wipe away tears. She couldn't recall ever seeing her mother cry before–she was sure she had at some point–but couldn't remember when.

"Yeah," her dad said. "Someone found you next to a back entrance a few hours after it happened."

Now Macy was confused. *That's not true.* She hadn't been anywhere near the school when she'd passed out—if that's what you called being beaten to within an inch of your life and losing consciousness. And she'd been dressed as Stellar. Who had changed that and where was her costume? *Ugh.* She was back to feeling frustrated about not being able to remember.

"Anyways," her mom said, wiping her eyes. "There's someone downstairs who wants to see you when you're up for it."

Macy raised an eyebrow.

"Grandad."

"Grandad's back?" Macy made to sit up but only got halfway before stiffness and soreness stopped her. Lying in bed for a week and after a thorough beating no less would do that she imagined. But Grandad was back. That was awesome. Now she could kick his butt for disappearing for so long.

Macy took the stairs one at a time with her mom a few steps in front of her and holding her hands as if she were a toddler. Macy had insisted she could do it on her own but hadn't had the heart to argue when her mom pressed the issue. Her mom had escorted her to the bathroom, too, and only left her alone while she cleaned up a bit and changed pajamas. But the stairs were where she'd drawn the line. *'You're my only child,'* she'd said. *'I'm not letting you out of my sight until I know those drugs have worn off and your head is clear.'*

"Hey. There she is," Grandad said, leaving the armchair in the living room and moving into the foyer as Macy left the last step. "Looks like you called Sugar Willy Clemson a sissy." He put his fists up and made to throw a fake punch at her, but winced and stopped.

Macy smirked. "What's the matter? Getting old?"

Her smile vanished just as quick as the movement of the muscles in her face caused her pain. She did look like she'd called whoever that was a sissy. In the bathroom mirror, she'd been unable to count all the bruises; her face, her back, her arms, her legs. How could anyone believe she'd gotten them all escaping a building that was still mostly standing? She guessed it was believable if she'd been hit in the head and had been stumbling about, but mostly she was just glad her Stellar endeavors appeared to remain undiscovered—at least to her parents anyways. But what about this person who'd rescued her? There were a lot of pieces she needed to put together.

"Do you want to sit down," her dad asked. "Maybe relax and watch—"

"No. The doctor said no television or screens," her mom chimed in. "Remember?"

"Oh, yeah. Well, how about some dinner?"

"Or a light workout?" Grandad jabbed the air half-heartedly. "The best way to get better is to get back to work."

Macy felt crowded. The three adults in her life were all within arms reach and spitting out suggestions like hyper kindergartners. "I think I actually just want some fresh air."

"Oh, but, honey, it's so cold out."

"Nonsense," said Grandad. "It's nearly fifty degrees out there."

"A healthy meal will put you on the road to recovery faster than anything." Her dad smiled.

"Alone!" Macy held up her hands for everyone to be silent. "I want fresh air and to be alone for a while."

Macy sat rocking gently in the front porch swing under a heated blanket. It was warm for December. The sun was still out despite the late afternoon hour and there was no wind so she wasn't the only one enjoying the outdoors. A few neighbors down the street had taken the opportunity to hang Christmas decorations and their next-door neighbor's college-aged daughter, whom Macy guessed was home for Christmas break, waved as she jogged by with the family dog.

Macy continued to look up and down the street. In this part of Greater Avendale, it was as if people had finally decided to begin ignoring the claims in the media about a serious crimewave and had gone back to life as usual. You'd never know there had been a fully functioning drug factory underneath the local high school just a week before. *That is what that was, right?* She thought about the neon orange substance in Zmija's syringe and felt pretty sure of it. She couldn't ignore the obvious correlation between the bright colored powders in the lab and the color in the syringe. The Alderwoman was manufacturing the 'Spaz' that had had the city's police force working overtime and its citizens frightened for months. Only now she was in control of that police force if the chief wanted to see his child again. That meant things could only get worse, right? Then why did things seem so normal around her house?

She reached for her phone out of instinct. *Ugh! My phone.* She remembered losing it beneath the pile of rubble in the tunnels. How was she supposed to call Keri without a phone? Just as in the coffee shop on what seemed like last night she had a lot to tell her. She would have to fish through her desk, find one of her older ones, and reactivate it. Hopefully, her parents wouldn't notice the difference– or did it matter since they thought her injuries had happened because of a sinkhole?

The front door opened and Grandad peered out wearing his coat and a beanie. "Hey, kiddo." He looked back into the house as if he was trying to avoid being noticed by her parents. He came out and clicked the door closed quietly, grunting and grimacing as he took a seat on the swing next to her. Once he got comfortable he smiled. "You doing okay? I'm sorry. I guess we got a bit excited there. It's been kind of touch and go this week. The doctors all said you were going to be just fine, but—"

"Where were you?" Macy charged. She didn't care about his thoughts and feelings on her injuries at the moment and she didn't care about her volume. "You disappeared for weeks and just left me hanging."

Grandad frowned and looked down at the floorboards of the porch, his eyes studying the wood as if it held the answers. "I—I'm—"

"And now you're going to do that thing where you stare off into the past again and tell me nil about what you're thinking. I'm not stupid, you know?" She glared at him, narrowing her eyes and lowering her voice to just above a whisper. "I know there are things you haven't told me."

Grandad took a deep breath and seemed to stew for a moment. She was pretty sure she'd never spoken to him this way before. Honestly, she couldn't remember ever being this angry at him. Of all the people in her life over the years he'd been the most consistent. The world she figured always seemed kind of black and white to him. When everyone else was adding ifs, ands, and buts Grandad would strike at the heart of things without apology. She'd always liked that about him and she'd always liked that she took after him.

"I—uhh—I deserve your anger. I do." He pursed his lips, still not making eye contact with her. "I'm really sorry for my extended absence, Macy. It wasn't my intention to be gone so long."

He stayed looking down and she could see a certain sadness that she'd only seen once before on the night they first talked about her situation and about Stellar. His apology was sincere, she could tell, but that didn't excuse anything. She wanted to know why and she stayed staring at him silently to communicate that.

"I went to look into something–to answer some questions–and was delayed by some unforeseen circumstances." He looked away and absentmindedly placed a hand on his abdomen as though he was remembering some pain. "It was my intention to be back in a matter of days and for us to begin working together on a plan of some sort, but… but sometimes things don't go as planned."

"Stop. Just stop. I'm not going to sit here and just let you try to lie to me. You've never lied to me. Why are you starting now?" Tears came to her eyes, but she tried to choke them back. "I know you know something. I can see it in your eyes. I saw it in the truck after Iggy's and I see it now. I can see it in mom and dad's eyes, too, like when they lied to me upstairs about what happened at school or whenever someone starts talking about past crime problems in the city. I've seen it for years, but until recently I was just too preoccupied with other things to care. Well, newsflash–I've done a lot of growing up in the last few months and I care now."

Grandad held his hands up, pleading with her to lower her volume. "Alright. You're right." He shook his head and sighed. When he looked up after a few moments, he made eye contact and frowned. "I told them this would never work."

Macy stayed looking at him. He seemed resigned to a course of action he didn't like, but that he'd known was coming. He scanned the windows and front door of the house and then looked back at her. "We can't talk about this here. Your parents don't want me to talk about it and neither does anyone else."

"Then where? Let's go there. Now."

Grandad held up a hand to quiet her. "Soon. I promise."

Macy chewed her lip. She didn't like not trusting him and despite the recent past her gut still told her she should, but "soon" really wasn't her favorite word right now. "You'd better keep your word this time. No more… whatever this is."

Grandad nodded repeatedly. "I promise. Just give me a few days to work it out."

"Fine," she said as he stood, gingerly.

He started towards the door, but turned back, his eyes sad again. "Macy… I'm glad you're okay, sweetheart."

She followed him with her eyes as he reentered the house and clicked the door closed quietly again. She had so many questions running through her mind her head seemed as though it was swimming. She went back to watching the neighborhood around her but wasn't really seeing anything that was going on. What was it Grandad knew that no one wanted him to tell her? She'd noticed tense changes of the subject for years whenever a conversation turned towards crime or bullying and Grandad always seemed to be on one side of the issue while her parents were on the other. But what did that mean? There was only one thing it could mean; a past crimewave of the same kind or size as the one reported to be going on now and based on things Zmija and The Alderwoman had said it sounded as though she had been at the center of it. It sounded as though PSD had faced The Alderwoman before.

But she would just have to go on wondering about the details it seemed. She looked back at the front door and frowned, reasoning to herself that compartmentalization was the only way to deal with this. She needed to focus on other things and the most important thing she could think of was that Stellar seemed to need a new costume. She rose from the swing, pulled the plug on the heated blanket, and made her way to the front door to call Keri.

"Macy? Hey!"

Macy snapped her head toward the street and her heart leapt as Patrick crossed her front lawn. In a split second, her mind went from calm, confident, and resolved to OMG my hair's a mess and I haven't brushed my teeth in a week. She let go of the doorknob, pulled the blanket closer to hide her pajamas, and did her best to smile. "Hey."

Patrick stopped at the bottom of the steps. "I wanted to see how you were doing and–uhh–give you this." He held out a folded piece of paper and gave a small shrug. "I didn't get a chance to send flowers or anything."

He wanted to send me flowers? Macy melted a little inside as she crossed the porch to the top of the steps. She gripped the paper with two fingers afraid to let go of the blanket and reveal her bumblebee pajamas. But she was going to have to make a decision; bumblebee pajamas meet world or stand here pinching this paper like a bird and looking like a dork. Either avenue presented further embarrassment. Did the universe just have it in for her? She let go of the blanket and one side fell loose; her shoulder, chest, and back feeling the cool December air beneath the smiling faces of chubby bumblebees complete with little dotted lines showing their flight pattern. *Wonderful.*

She unfolded the paper and instantly forgot her misgivings. Stellar looked back at her. Her mind raced. In what appeared to be a hand-drawn comic book panel the hero stood looking triumphant against a backdrop of distant rooftops. The foggy landscape and wrought iron fence in the foreground coupled with the hue from the moon above reminded her of the last time she'd seen Patrick. Had he drawn the scene of them leaving Alum Ridge from memory? It seemed so. Did this mean he knew it had been her in the costume? She studied the card closely, pretending to be transfixed by the detail while she considered the possibility. A word bubble above Stellar read *you'll be back in fighting form before you know it* and below the picture, Patrick had written Feel Better Soon and signed his name like an autograph.

Macy smiled upon seeing the autograph. This wasn't a sneaky way of saying he knew she was Stellar. This was just his way of expressing how he felt. She looked back at him. "Wow."

Patrick blushed. "It's not a bouquet of flowers, but—"

Macy scoffed. "Oh, c'mon. Anyone can send flowers. But this… this is awesome." She folded it back and held it to her chest.

Patrick beamed.

Macy stepped down to meet him and took a seat on the steps. "So, you said you came to see how I was doing?"

"Ye—Yeah. Uhh–how are you?" Patrick smiled sheepishly and took a seat next to her.

Macy laughed. "Much better. Thank you. It's all such a blur, though."

"Yeah. The last few weeks have just been insane." He looked down at his shoelaces and studied them as though he wanted to say more, but didn't know if he should.

"Insane is a good word for it, yeah. Sounds like you've had it pretty bad, too. What's up?" For some reason that Macy couldn't explain, talking to Patrick felt easier today. A few weeks ago she'd have cringed at the idea of asking him *what's up* and almost certainly chickened out.

"Oh, I don't know." Patrick shrugged shyly. "I mean I didn't get hit in the head and lose consciousness or anything like that."

Macy felt her cheeks flush. She'd have to remember not to get hit in the head and go stumbling around the school again anytime soon. *As if.*

Patrick continued. "A few weeks ago my dad told me I had to forget about Stellar. He's always on my case about my drawing and writing, but he's never told me to forget about them before. He always says he just wants to make sure my expectations for the real world are set appropriately–that things like that are done more as hobbies than as jobs. I mean… I understand I guess, but this time was different. I don't know why, but he seemed so scared. I guess maybe it just has to do with my mom dying, but he's been so different lately."

Macy didn't know what to say. She'd overheard the conversation Patrick was talking about and knew something had happened to his mom, but hadn't known exactly what until now. She couldn't imagine having to live without one of her parents. While they could be annoying at times as she supposed all parents could, she shared a bond with them she wasn't even sure how to describe. How did you describe your relationship with someone you'd known and relied on since before you could remember? "I'm sorry. I didn't know about your mom."

Patrick frowned and shook his head. "We didn't make a big deal out of it. My dad's funny like that. She'd been sick for awhile–breast cancer. She died a week after school let out for the summer."

Macy didn't know Deputy Newell much beyond his role as the School Resource Officer, but not making a big deal out his wife's death sounded horrible. Maybe it was some kind of tough-guy cop routine, but whatever it was it sounded like his son needed to deal with it differently. "I really am sorry. I know it probably sounds hollow, but I do mean it. I can't imagine having to live without my mom."

"I don't even know why I'm telling you all of this. I really did come here to check on you. I enjoyed talking to you when we were leaving school that one day and for some reason, I feel like I can. I guess I feel like I know you. Somehow."

Macy smiled. "You can certainly get to."

Patrick smiled back. "I'd like that."

They stayed looking and smiling at each other for what felt like forever but was probably only a few seconds. Macy had imagined this for months now. Sandy-colored locks of brown-ish blond hair just barely out of his eyes, the way his cheeks dimpled when he smiled. He really was cute–and that was certainly a plus–but that's not what she found so interesting. There was a gentleness about him–a kind of quiet she just didn't see in most of the guys around school. He was a thinker more than a doer and she liked that. But was he really available for a relationship? His mom had passed away only months ago and from the sound of it, he hadn't been given much of an opportunity to grieve. He seemed to be struggling and from the looks of it, there really wasn't anyone around to help him. She couldn't imagine him trying to talk to his two buddies about such a thing. The two of them seemed dense to say the least. She let out a nervous laugh and turned away.

Patrick laughed, too. "Yeah. Anyways, I was concerned when I heard you were injured. And surprised. I didn't remember anyone having to go to the hospital that day. All the emails and calls my dad got afterward said everyone had made it out okay and there were only a few minor bumps and bruises."

"Huh." Macy thought back over the last week. She still couldn't remember much and the only memory she had beyond being rescued by whoever was of people standing over her. But had it been at a hospital? Had they been doctors and nurses? The memory was brief—only just a flash really—but the background around the people didn't seem like a hospital. In fact, it seemed like her bedroom. Behind the people, she was pretty sure she could see the out of focus poster of Tylar Marsden on her ceiling. *That's odd.* But it could have been after the hospital… or it could have been an hour before she'd awoken. She just didn't know. She shrugged. "It's nothing that won't heal up in a week or so."

She opened the handmade card again and looked at Stellar, desperate to move the conversation away from her and her injuries. "So, tell me more about her."

Patrick turned red. "Oh, I don't—I don't know what to say. What do you want to know?"

"C'mon," Macy nudged him with her elbow. "Give me your

synopsis… give me the Netflix blurb. Who is she? What's she all about?"

Patrick hesitated for a moment. "She's based on my mom. Well, in honor of my mom, really."

Macy's heart sank into her stomach.

"I haven't given her a secret identity or much of a story because I just don't know what to write. I mean I guess I was always focused on the fighting and the bad guys' evil plan and such. I've never tried to create a real person beyond that. Besides, it seems like her story is writing itself at this point."

Macy struggled for words. She'd never considered Stellar meaning so much to Patrick on such a personal level. Now she was beginning to understand his reluctance to follow his dad's advice and forget her. How could he forget her when she was created to honor someone so close to him? Stellar was his way of grieving.

She shrugged. "Girl hero saves guy creator from bullies in school library. Hey–I'd give it a shot."

"It's more than that now, though. I saw her again."

"You did? Like recently?" Macy raised her eyebrows and tried to look surprised.

"Yeah. Like ten days ago."

"How? Where?"

"After the dance, I figured she had to be at the school for a reason. She must have been there looking for something or someone so Striker and I watched the school from his house. He lives just around the corner from the back entrance so with a pair of binoculars we could see a lot. And I was right. It took her awhile–I guess maybe she was waiting for the heat to die down or something–but she came back just like I thought she would. We saw her jump the fence and we ran down and followed."

"That is… that's awesome. You actually followed her? Like in the movies?"

Patrick shrugged shyly. "I mean it wasn't all that. We'd lost her by the time we got down there and over the fence, but I might have an extra key that used to belong to my dad so we went in and managed to find her again."

She listened as he recounted the story right up to the moment where she'd jumped the fence and disappeared back into the massive neighborhoods of Greater Avendale. "So, she said there was some kind of lab under the school? That's crazy."

"You want to know what's even crazier? I think that's what caused the collapse–not a sinkhole. I think whoever was doing whatever down there tried to get rid of the evidence and now they're covering it up."

"Covering it up? You mean like people at the school knew about the lab and—"

"That's exactly what I mean."

"Whoa." Macy tried to act surprised again. An image of Zmija and of the ring on Principal Decker's finger flashed through her mind.

Patrick took a deep breath as though he was trying to calm himself. "Yeah… I told you. Insane, right? But it makes sense. Think about how quick the administration was to play down what happened at the dance. The assembly, the emails and phone calls to parents, the way they shaped the whole thing as an attack on innocent students when anyone who's spent more than a day at Alum Ridge knows better."

"Do you think maybe that's why your dad seemed so scared?" *Careful, Macy.* The words had come out before she'd had time to fully consider what she was saying. She needed to tread carefully or she'd reveal more than she should know.

"You mean like he's involved?" Patrick sounded insulted.

"No. No. I mean like what if someone was threatening him or

something? I mean Stellar was first seen at the school. Maybe he was trying to protect you since he knew you created her."

"Maybe. I did tell him about her right before he said that." Patrick stared pensively out at the yard as though it was an idea he hadn't considered. "Yeah. You might be right."

Macy shrugged. "Just a thought. I mean if they knew you created her they'd naturally think you knew who she was and—yeah. You know what I mean." She stopped there. She almost wished she could tell him who Stellar was. That's how this whole thing had gotten started. She hadn't intended to become a hero or a threat or anything. All she'd wanted was for the boy she liked to like her back. But that thinking seemed so small–so naive–now. Would he even believe her if she told him? It's not like she could show him the costume. It was gone.

"I need to see her," Patrick said, making a fist and a determined frown. "… talk to her. If there really is something criminal going on in our community we all have a responsibility to fight it. And I think that's what she's about. I think that's why she's here."

"Duh. Superhero." Macy grinned.

Patrick blushed and stared straight ahead with an "I walked right into that one" look.

"I'm sorry." Macy laughed. "I couldn't resist."

Patrick shook his head and chuckled, his face staying red.

A long moment passed and Macy studied his face. Did he still think Stellar had been sent by his mom? He'd seemed so sad the last time she'd talked to him. No… she wasn't getting that vibe now. Maybe their meeting at the school had proven to him just how real she was. "But, seriously, how are you going to do that?"

"I don't know exactly, but I have an idea. Before all of this–before she showed up in the library–Josh, Striker, and I were going to write, draw, and publish stories about Stellar online. We were working on a website and were going to launch it as soon as Josh was done coding everything. Heh. The funny thing is we had some videos planned, too–that was Striker's part, the cameraman–but that's taken a whole different direction than we planned. Obviously."

"Right." She was glad he'd explained Striker's role. Maybe she'd developed a bit of a dislike for him because of the boyishness he'd displayed of late, but she couldn't imagine him drawing or writing anything. Hulking around cameras and equipment, though? Sure. He seemed uniquely suited to that job.

"So, I'm going to contact her through the site. Instead of writing and selling stories, we're going to make it a news and information site–the only place online for real news about the world's only real superhero. We're launching it any day now."

"How do you know she'll see it?"

"Social media. We're going to upload the video from the library and other videos, too. We got one of her fighting in the school that night and I mean if something was dedicated to you or something you'd done you would want to see it, right?"

"Sure." Macy did a mental facepalm. At least she knew now why he and Striker hadn't left the school when they were being chased by thugs. They'd been hellbent on aiming a camera at Stellar again. Nothing like risking life and limb to ensure you had an audience. She felt annoyed.

"Right. So, I'm going to create a coded message in a post asking her to meet me."

"How do you know she reads codes?"

"I don't. But if she's half the detective I think she is–that she has to be–she'll recognize it."

"What if someone else does, too?"

Patrick shrugged. "I don't know. I'm still working it out. Maybe it'll be something only she'd know–something that wouldn't make any sense to anyone else."

"Ahh. Good idea."

Patrick shrugged again. "I guess."

The conversation lulled and they both sat there looking out over the front lawn for what felt like forever.

"Well, I should go. It's gonna be dark soon."

"O-okay." Macy stood. "It's been—"

"Yeah. It's been fun." He stood, beaming at her as he moved onto the front walk. He turned back. "By the way… cute bumblebees."

"Ugh." Macy grinned ear to ear, placing her head in her hands to conceal her reddening face.

"Sorry. Couldn't resist," he said, reaching the sidewalk.

"Hey," she called as he was almost to the neighbor's, "text me later or something." She stood there beaming, watching as he walked into the distance until a car passed and she remembered she was in her pajamas in public. She pulled her blanket tight and scurried for the front door.

CHAPTER 17

Headlights shone brightly through Macy's curtains and she looked to see a dark-colored, late-model SUV in the driveway. *Who is that?* She didn't recognize the vehicle, but after watching it for a moment her eyes adjusted and she could see Keri in the passenger seat talking to someone. Was it her mom? It sort of looked like it, but her mom drove some kind of a sedan, not an SUV. The passenger door opened and Keri got out, making her way to the front door. Macy shrugged and let the curtain fall closed. Hopping off her bed, she moved to the second-floor landing as the doorbell rang. "I got it." She came charging down the steps, her mouth curling into a smile as she saw Keri grinning at her through the tiny windows beside the front door.

"Oh my God," Keri practically bounced into the house and embraced her. "Oh, girl!"

"Ugh." Macy winced as Keri's hands found her many bruises.

Keri's eyes went wide and she backed off, putting her hands up. "Oh, sorry."

Macy smiled. "It's okay. I'm fine."

Keri did another excited bounce. "Tell me everything." She took Macy's hand and led her to the staircase. "Hi, Mr. and Mrs. Davis."

"Hi, Keri."

A few minutes later they were seated on Macy's bed and Macy had caught Keri up on everything from the moment she'd entered the bomb factory, to the flashes of events she remembered in the week since, and Patrick's unexpected visit earlier that afternoon.

"Okay. Wow." Keri examined the patterns on the bedspread as she took it all in. "I feel like I just entered the Twilight Zone or something. I mean… congrats on Patrick, but…" She shook her head and shrugged.

Macy knew what she meant. The news of Patrick's visit was exciting–she guessed–but even that was dwarfed by the account of what had happened in the basement of the abandoned building.

"So, Luke got 'spazzed' and that's why he wasn't with Zeke when… when they did this." Keri waved a hand over her face. Her injuries had almost completely healed except for a scab above her eyebrow and a tiny bit of bruising beneath both eyes.

"Yeah. Spazzed. That's a good one." Macy shook her head. "I've never seen anything like that in my life. It was like he wasn't even human anymore."

"How are you gonna fight something like that, Mace? Especially if they do it to multiple people next time."

Macy shrugged. "I don't know if I can." Flashes of being driven to the ground by the enraged Luke ricocheted around her head for what seemed like the hundredth time since she'd awoken. The idea of multiple spazzed-out teenagers coming at her completely unrestrained gave her pause. They'd tear her and anyone else who got near them limb from limb and the police really wouldn't have a choice but to take them down. The thought of kids her age that she probably knew if they went to Alum Ridge being shot like rabid animals made her mad. As if there wasn't already enough of that with all the mass shootings in recent years. But hopefully, it wouldn't come to pass.

"So, what now?"

Macy shook her head. "I don't know. Hopefully, the police chief and other city officials just do as they're told… for now anyways."

Keri frowned.

Macy looked at the door and lowered her voice. "Grandad knows something, but says he can't tell me what while anyone might hear."

"Knows something? That sounds…"

"Ominous? Yeah. I think this city has faced The Alderwoman before and I think people have been covering it up for a long time."

Keri furrowed her brow and shook her head. "I can't even."

"Me neither. Before Patrick showed up I'd decided the only way to deal with it all right now is to just put it out of my head for a while and focus on something else. It's not like I'm in the shape to do anything about it right now anyway. And there's another problem."

"Oh? More good news? Stop me if I get too excited."

"The costume's gone."

Keri locked eyes with her. "You mean whoever it was that rescued you took it and knows who you are?"

Macy nodded. "Yup. Looks like it."

"Oh, girl."

"I know. And I don't have a clue who it could have been."

"Whew. That's bad."

Macy frowned. It was bad. What if that person decided to use her identity against her in some way? No… something didn't feel right about that idea. Whoever it was had cared about her enough to save her life and had known her well enough to take her back to Alum Ridge. That couldn't be a long list, but who was on it?

"How did you hear about me being injured?" Macy thought about what Patrick had said about no one going to the hospital.

Keri shrugged. "After the school got done shaking like we'd just experienced a California earthquake and everyone was finally allowed to leave, I walked here. No one was home so I came back later that night after dinner. Of course, I was totally freaked out by then since I hadn't heard from you. Your grandad was back and your mom was really upset, but she told me what happened. I knew there was more to it obviously, but without any way to ask you I just–I just waited. I called a few times and your mom updated me. She said yesterday was your last day of meds so hopefully, you'd be awake more today. I decided to stop by again and check. Looks like she was right. Why?"

"I don't know. Just something Patrick said about no one going to the hospital after the collapse. And I really don't remember any doctors or nurses or hospital rooms."

"Sounds like there's a lot you don't remember, though."

"Yeah."

A long moment of silence passed before Keri took out her phone. "So, I guess my job is a new costume. Any special requests this time around?"

"Heh. A utility belt. Please."

"A utility belt? What's a utility belt?"

"You know… the belts the guys in the old superhero shows always wore–the ones they kept the shark repellent on?"

"Shark repellent? I don't think there are any sharks in the Ocran."

"Like the ones the police wear with all their things on it. But less bulky. More tactical."

Keri raised her eyebrows and started typing on her phone. "I'll see what I can do."

Macy went back to thinking about the list of potential rescuers. No one besides Keri and Grandad had known she was Stellar before she went into that factory–or so she'd thought. *But maybe that's all there needs to be.* Grandad had gone absent rather mysteriously and clearly knew more about The Alderwoman than he'd ever let on. She'd seen him take on punks before, but never so many and certainly not a drugged up super bully. But who else was there? She remembered the phone calls he'd spent the evening making before his lengthy disappearance. Who had been on the other end? Her talk with The Alderwoman popped into her head. *'You're Port Saint Dominic's newest masked crusader'* The Alderwoman had said and then proceeded to guess at her name mockingly. Newest crusader clearly meant there had been at least one other at some point and what were the names she'd mentioned? One, in particular, had stood out–Luminesa Jr. Did the mocking addition of junior mean that a hero named Luminesa had been the first masked crusader? Luminesa certainly didn't sound like a masculine name, but could that be who Grandad had called?

Keri looked up from her phone and raised an eyebrow. "I've seen that look before. What's on your mind?"

Macy told her.

"Well, you know it wasn't me. As much as I'd like to hand them all their heads, these hands were made for stitching, not punching. But do you really think your grandad has been hiding some sort of… superhero?"

Macy shrugged. "Who else is there? And that could be why I don't remember any hospitals or doctors. Maybe he just had this Luminesa bring me back here. Maybe I never was at Alum Ridge and he just made that up so my parents wouldn't know what had really happened." She looked around the room. "That doesn't explain how everyone knew to send me flowers and balloons, though."

Keri lowered her head and blushed. "I think I can explain that…" She raised a hand sheepishly. "Sorry."

Macy gave her a deadpan look. "Of course you can."

Another quiet moment passed and Macy stood from her bed, taking Patrick's card from the bedside table and unfolding it as she walked to the mirror above her vanity that doubled as her computer desk. Her parents had lied to her earlier as well it seemed. Maybe they knew more about it than they were letting on, too. She was doing a lousy job of putting it all out of her head. She took a piece of tape from the dispenser, flattened the card against the mirror, and taped it in place at eye level. For a long moment, she stared at the image. Stellar was still the same as she was when Macy had been peeking over Patrick's shoulder earlier in the year, but so much else had changed.

CHAPTER 18

William Davis started his aging Toyota Camry as Macy sat down into the passenger seat. She shivered, breathing out a visible stream. The balmy for December temperatures hadn't hung around overnight and the interior of the car felt even colder than the air outside.

"I guess I should have warmed the car up." Her dad chuckled as he twisted the dial for the heat causing even more cold air to blow from the vents. "Oh, sorry. That was cold, dawg." He grinned at her and flashed a mock gang sign.

Macy rolled her eyes but said nothing. She had wanted to ride with Keri this morning, but her mom had insisted her dad take her. The careful eye they had kept on her since she'd awoken was getting more than just a little annoying. How was she going to accomplish anything with them nearly puppy dogging her every step?

She watched as he disengaged the parking brake with a pop and shifted the car into gear. The vehicle whined slightly as it rolled to the end of the driveway. Her dad had gotten rid of his late-model Jeep Cherokee about the same time as he had started working a second job at a nearby grocery chain, but neither he nor her mom had explained why to Macy. She guessed the answer was obvious; times for the Davis family were tight just as they were for a lot of families in PSD. Was it the crimewave affecting the local economy? Macy hadn't considered that on top of all the other villainy The Alderwoman was capable of that she could also be the reason her dad needed a second job and a beater. The idea brought a frown to her face.

"Are you sure you want to do this? Last chance. You can run back to the warm house if you want."

"Yes," Macy said, though she was tempted to take him up on the offer. "We've been over this. I just want to put it behind me and the best way to do that is just to get on with life."

"Okay." Her dad pressed the accelerator and turned the car onto the road. "You know as worried as your mom is, you're probably right about this."

Macy loosened out of her perpetual shiver a few minutes later as warm air finally began to blow. Coupled with the sunlight coming directly through the windshield now that they were away from the shadows cast by the house there was a noticeable difference in temperature inside the car. They turned out of their neighborhood and Macy shifted positions so she could see the buildings of Alum Ridge in the distance. As they drew closer she could see construction vehicles and excavating equipment near the back.

"They said on the news last night preliminary inspections haven't found any serious structural damage to the school," her dad said, braking as they approached orange road signs. "Just some cracking in the brick and apparently the parking lot the food service staff uses and where deliveries are made is pretty shot."

"Huh." Macy studied the scene. From her vantage point on the road that ran above and along the backside of the school she couldn't see much, but it was obvious the attention was being focused on the back corner of one of the furthest additions from the front entrance. No wonder few had known the factory was there. It appeared to have been located under the ground beside the school more than underneath it. Just a forgotten remnant of a bygone era long buried under new roads and buildings.

She turned her attention to the road in front of them. Orange barricades had been placed around a half oval-shaped section of pavement that had cracked and pulled away. The section appeared to have dropped about a foot and a line that looked like a fissure from an earthquake extended down the hill and out of sight. Macy followed the fissure as far as she could as her dad obeyed the temporary traffic signal erected to manage travelers being diverted into one lane.

"Dad…" she said as he guided the car around the orange barriers and back into the right lane. "How do drugs like Spaz work? I mean I know about scheduled substances and such. We learned about that in STEM last year. But the news keeps saying this Spaz is a designer drug. What is that and how does it work?" She tensed and waited for his response. It was a totally random and hair-brained idea, but she had to start somewhere if she had any hope of learning how to handle the drug and anyone on it. Plus, this might create an opportunity to find out how much her parents really knew about her activities as Stellar.

"I—umm—" Her dad cleared his throat. "I'm not sure exactly how to answer that, honey."

Macy was reaching here and she knew it. Her dad had a scientific background and worked in a laboratory for a company called Radiant Technologies, but he wasn't a doctor or involved in medicine in any way. She sat silently looking at him with the best curious expression she could muster.

"Why do you ask?"

A question with a question. *Strike one.* Not what she was hoping for. She studied the dashboard trying to decide what to say next. "Uhh… just a boy at school. Everyone keeps saying he's on it, but I don't know if it's true or just a rumor. Never mind." *Ha. Reverse psychology.* Maybe he'd feel guilty about not conversing with her.

"Well, the signs of drug abuse are things like increased aggression and sudden changes in attitude or personality. Also physical changes like bloodshot eyes and weight loss. Stuff like that."

The ruse worked. Macy was quite pleased with herself, though the signs of drug abuse had been taught repeatedly since at least the third grade. "This guy's one of the school bullies so he's always been aggressive and had a bad attitude, but he doesn't have any of those other signs. That's why people say he's on Spaz instead of something else like cocaine or whatever."

Her dad pursed his lips. "From what I know of this 'Spaz' it works like a steroid on steroids basically. In small, controlled doses it's basically a physical performance enhancer that makes people better at things than they usually would be. Things like sports or fighting or…" he cleared his throat again. "… sex. Maybe that's why this boy is interested in it if he is on it."

Ground ball to right field. "So, that's why the news keeps calling it a party drug, right? Because it makes it so you can keep partying a lot longer than you normally would."

Her dad nodded.

"How does someone get off something like that once they're on it?"

"Oh, I don't know, sweetie. There are all kinds of counseling services and treatment centers. I think I've only ever known one person who had drug issues so it's just not something I have a lot of experience with."

Caught by the first baseman and out. Oh well. It was a valiant effort anyways. But she had come away with something that might be useful. If Spaz acted like a steroid then maybe counteracting it was similar. Could steroids be counteracted? She wasn't sure. At least it was a direction in which to start searching. She watched through the windshield as they entered the brick storefront-lined main street that separated the Greater Avendale neighborhoods from the commercial developments on the outskirts of Avendale University.

"Here we are." Her dad slowed the car and turned into a parking lot.

Macy looked at the Greater Avendale Public Library. Like many of the other buildings in the area that had been built mostly in the middle of the last century, the library looked like it was in bad need of an architectural update. Silver maple trees that had been saplings when the place was constructed had now grown into giants that stood perilously close to the brown brick facade and reached the metal parapets that accented the upper floors and roof.

"I'll be right here when you get done."

Macy raised her eyebrows in acknowledgment. She wasn't done asking questions and felt like just going for broke–just opening up on him and asking what he knew about her activities, how she was injured, and why they were lying to her. But if she did and they didn't know, she'd be opening up a can of worms she didn't even want to imagine, considering how they were already handling things. No, she thought better of it and got out of the aging Toyota. She'd have to come up with another plan or else wait on Grandad to tell all. She gave her dad a small wave as she crossed in front of the car, made her way up the sidewalk to the glass doors, and entered the tiny vestibule. She stopped to hold the door as she heard the distinct sound of someone on crutches nearby. *Click. Click. Click.* A moment later she smiled as the person rounded the corner, her eyes moving from the ground up to meet them. But her smile vanished instantly as she settled on the face of Luke Bartlett.

"Thanks," he breathed.

Macy stared, unaware that her mouth was hanging open. The bulging blue veins, twitching muscles, and foaming mouth were gone. In their place was a jaundiced skin tone, bruised knuckles, and bloodshot eyes.

"What?" he barked as he hobbled past her into the vestibule.

Macy was jarred back to reality and opened the next door for him. The stale aroma of old books filled the air and Luke hobbled in without another word. Despite the physical differences, he seemed like his usual charming self. Macy entered behind him, watching as he made his way across the faded commercial carpeting to a table occupied by other students in letterman jackets.

"Macy. Hey."

Macy turned to see Taylor and Emma arrive behind her.

"It's really something, isn't it?" Taylor said, brushing a lock of blonde hair off her shoulder as she looked past Macy to where Luke had taken a seat. "Rumor is he's been addicted to painkillers since the beating in the library and they've messed up his liver."

"Ugh." Macy made a face.

"Yup. My how the mighty have fallen. Keri here?"

"Don't think so," Macy said, falling in behind the two cheerleaders as they made their way past the circulation desk. Like the outside of the building, the inside was also in need of remodeling. Aged yellow carpet stretched around a mostly square room with wood-paneled walls and suspended metal staircases leading to upper floors. "She didn't say anything about any classes today."

"Shame. I brought her seersucker dress back."

Shame alright, Macy thought. Friendship with Keri was the only thing she had in common with Taylor and Emma and she always felt less than welcome whenever she was alone with them. But she followed them to the back of the library anyway. There, other kids she recognized from Alum Ridge were gathered around tables.

Since the school had been forced to close at least until after Christmas break the School Board had moved all two thousand and some students to a modified homebound schedule. Students would meet their homeroom teacher for a few hours once a week to receive assignments, ask questions, and hand in written work while the rest of their instruction happened online in chat sessions through the school system's customized interface. It was inconvenient for everyone all around–parents, teachers, and students–but the board had decided it was the only avenue available to avoid Alum Ridge being the one school in the district to fall behind state and federal standards.

Hands began to clap as Macy set down her backpack at the same table as Taylor and Emma. First, it was only one set of hands and Macy paid no attention. But then there was another and another after that. Before she knew it the entire gathering of students were on their feet and looking at her as they clapped. She glanced around the room awkwardly wishing she were anywhere else as her face turned a bright red.

She smiled, gave a small wave, and took a seat. Slowly, the applause died. Lawrence Diesbach, Josh Friddle, and some boy whose name she didn't know were already seated there and beamed at her. Josh flashed her a sideways grin and raised an eyebrow. *Ugh.* Was he hitting on her or acknowledging her newfound friendship with Patrick? She wasn't sure she wanted to know. She opened her notebook and did her best to ignore everyone else, which wasn't hard considering her mind was mostly still focused on Luke Bartlett and the effects the large dosage of Spaz had had on him.

Mr. Haier stood from a table near the center of the room and cleared his throat. "Alright, everyone. Let's get started. There are forty-six of you here today and we only have two hours to get things handed out and get any questions answered."

Macy absentmindedly placed the end of her pen in her mouth. The questions she had were ones Mr. Haier couldn't answer. Like what would an overdose of Spaz do to someone who wasn't in the same kind of physical shape as a high school football player? Surely not all of the children of the city officials were Brent "The Psycho Viking" DuBois reincarnated. If Spaz had made such a mess of Luke then a less physical being would barely be able to function at all. She recalled Zmija saying something about Luke's heart bursting. She didn't know a ton about anatomy and medicine, but she did know from an eighth-grade nursing class that burst was a common name for a rupture of the myocardium and was usually a side effect of a severe heart attack. Had Luke suffered such a heart attack? The idea made her feel sorry for him for the second time in as many weeks. He couldn't be more than seventeen and something like that could affect him for the rest of his life. If The Alderwoman would do something like that to someone loyal to her what would she do to someone showing descent? Macy could only imagine, but it wasn't pretty.

"Miss Davis," Mr. Haier said as he plopped down a stack of papers. "Excellent to see you're back in good health."

Macy flashed a quick smile and then glanced at Luke again. Staying focused enough to get schoolwork done was going to be impossible.

CHAPTER 19

Macy had slogged through a few days and gotten as much done as she could after Grandad announced he'd talked her parents into allowing him to take her away for the weekend. In just a few minutes they would be leaving for the cabin he'd owned and lived in on Lake Wasena since she could remember.

"You have your phone, right?"

"Yes, mom. And my charger and the phone numbers for the police, the Army, the Marines, the Coast Guard, and Her Majesty's Royal Air Force in case America runs out of reinforcements."

"Haha." Becky Davis kissed Macy's forehead and handed her the overnight bag she'd insisted on packing for her. "Be careful driving and call when you get there."

"Yup. We'll send a smoke signal."

Macy bounded down the walkway to Grandad's pickup and got in the passenger side. She was psyched about getting away for a few days. Ever since she'd awoken from her ordeal, her parents had been smothering her with attention and to say it was getting annoying was an understatement. She imagined it was a reasonable response to someone being injured and unconscious, but enough was enough already.

Grandad shifted the truck into gear and they reversed into the street. "Next year when we do this you can drive."

"Bet."

A few minutes later they circled onto an acceleration ramp. The truck rumbled as Grandad pressed his foot further onto the pedal and put Greater Avendale and the world Macy had spent much of the last fifteen years in behind them.

She had made this trip many times as a younger girl, but it had been at least five or six years. Grandad had received a promotion in his work for the U.S. Army that had taken him to Washington D.C. for the last handful of years of his career and summer trips to the lake had been one of the many things sacrificed.

They passed the grounds of Avendale Park—an enormous green boundary with its own lake between the suburbs and the city—and for the first time in recent memory, Macy could see the highrises of Downtown PSD.

She felt a quiet kind of exhilaration at the sight. Even though she'd visited many times, the city always felt like entering a new world. Nothing ever seemed the same. In the approaching darkness, an eerie glow rose from the light pollution at street level, giving each building a sort of murky halo. The one exception was the Nace Tower, a hulking highrise that stood far above the reach of anything at street level. Macy considered the impressive mass of concrete and steel. The halo of light surrounding it came instead from the enormous Nace Observatory atop the building, which, when opened as it was this evening, seemed like a giant eyeball casting its glare ever upward.

"So, I uhh told your parents a lie."

Macy broke her attention away from the skyline. "Oh?"

"We're not heading to Wasena. At least I don't think we are."

"Then where are we going?" Macy had expected the conversation to turn to Grandad's knowledge of the past at some point and if it hadn't, she'd planned to force the issue. She wanted answers. But couldn't those answers be given at his cabin while they sipped coffee?

"First, we're going to meet an old friend of mine. Then, depending on what he has to show us, we'll decide where we're heading."

"Oh, mysterious." Macy's curiosity was more than piqued. She knew almost nothing about Grandad's career in the army, but what he'd just described sounded like some sort of secret mission. And she was pumped for it.

Grandad took the first downtown exit. Were they going into the city? It seemed so. Macy looked through the windows as the open land and trees around them became hidden by concrete noise barriers and the two-lane highway became four. They passed under a sign that read PSD in the middle of an abstract logo that Macy had always thought looked like a sunflower.

Grandad grumbled. "Your parents don't want me to talk about this and neither does anyone else, but Port Saint Dominic was supposed to get a clean break for your generation, a new start free of past stigmas that haunted it for a long time. They even rebranded the city 'PSD' with that stupid department store-looking logo." He rolled his eyes. "The truth is this city has faced The Alderwoman before."

Of course, Macy wasn't a bit surprised, but this was the first time she'd ever heard someone speak plainly about it.

"It was a dark time—a scary time for a lot of people. The whole city and everywhere near it had a reputation for not being a very nice place to live or a safe place to do business. The Alderwoman's M.O. is to look for weaknesses she can profit on and then use the threat of physical violence or some other unpleasant reprisal to do so."

Macy thought about the kidnapped children. Talk about an unpleasant reprisal. Who wouldn't do whatever they were told when a loved one's life was on the line?

Grandad continued. "But The Alderwoman isn't just a local mob boss running protection rackets and buying officials' silence. She's an institution—a relentless system of greed, graft, and violence. For her and her people, it's all about power. She sets up and functions like a shadow government and once a system like that gains traction it attracts others who are willing to victimize people. Once that becomes the way things are done it has a way of corrupting everything. It just worms its way into every crevice and that's what happened here. Everyone from street sweepers to city officials' first priority was to find ways to supplement their paycheck in some dishonest fashion. It was like the freakin' USSR and The Alderwoman controlled and profited from all of it."

Macy had heard Grandad rail about the USSR many times. When she was younger she'd asked him about it and the answer he'd given her was that the USSR had been a union of nations tightly controlled by their government under a system called communism and that they had been the chief opposing force to America during something called the Cold War, a conflict Grandad had participated in as a part of the military. Macy didn't understand the intricacies of such a system since she'd never experienced one, but what Grandad had just described certainly sounded like what she had witnessed when the city officials were hauled before Zmija and told what was happening. The Alderwoman, it seemed, was laying the groundwork for her return. "So… what happened? How did PSD… how did we get rid of her?"

Grandad braked and flipped on his turn signal, checking his mirrors as he drifted into the far lane and onto an exit ramp marked Riverside–Penn Forest–Norwich. "It took a lot of years, Macy. A brave soul began challenging The Alderwoman and her henchman and with each success other decent, hardworking men and women joined the fight by beginning to stand up for themselves and their neighbors. At first, the politicians and officials, all under The Alderwoman's control, tried to stop it. But the people wouldn't have it. They began recalling them, running against them, and replacing them. Slowly, the tide turned and the good outnumbered the bad. The Alderwoman, her henchmen, and all their cronies in the government were arrested, tried, and sent to Ocran Holm."

"Ocran Holm? You mean that prison we pass on the way to the beach every summer," Macy had always thought the place looked haunted, "the one on the island in the middle of the river?"

"That's the one. A Category A supermax for the criminally insane–the worst of the worst. It's one of the few prisons of its kind still in use in this country thanks to the deinstitutionalization movement."

Macy couldn't help but shake her head and smile. Grandad's political and social critiques and rants were nothing new and would never change. Her thoughts turned to the brief exchange she'd had with The Alderwoman. She hadn't been able to see much on the tablet screen. There had been a white wall with a sashed window in the background, which had helped hide The Alderwoman's face by creating a well-lit background to contrast the dim foreground. Macy guessed it could have been a prison cell, but who would have allowed an inmate with such a reputation to make a video call? Had The Alderwoman escaped? If so, wouldn't a breakout from such a prison have been headline news? Of course, it would have. But then Grandad had just said her generation was given a 'clean break' and she hadn't known much of this until today. Did 'clean break' mean hiding the city's sordid past even to the point of not reporting a prison break? That seemed like a real stretch of the imagination.

And what of this 'brave soul' who had spearheaded the movement to take down the criminals? The brief memory of the person who'd rescued her, the bright flashes, and the defeated thugs crossed her mind as well as her thoughts about Grandad's lengthy absence and the phone calls he'd made before leaving. She needed to know more.

"This 'brave soul'…" She looked at Grandad and raised an eyebrow. "… Luminesa?"

Grandad furrowed his brow. "Yes…" He stayed left at a three-way fork, taking the exit for Riverside and coming around into a winding two-lane road that aimed them north along the banks of the Ocran River. "But how do you know that name?"

Macy stared out the window for a long moment. It was nearly dark now and the lights of the city reflected on the river. In the distance, tug boats pushed and pulled ships and barges into position at the Swarthmore Wilmont Shipworks, an enormous port on the east side of the river. She'd crossed a threshold of no return now. Instead of Grandad telling her about the distant past she'd have to tell him about much more recent events. "I–uh–I didn't wait for you to come back like you said. You'd been gone too long so I—so Stellar—paid a visit to Alum Ridge." She proceeded to tell him about everything from the moment she'd first jumped the fence to the last thing she remembered before falling unconscious in the basement full of passageways. "So, yeah… I wasn't anywhere near the school when all of this happened." She motioned to the bruises on her face. "But you already know that, don't you?"

Grandad frowned and removed his beanie, tossing it onto the dashboard. "I suspected as much, yes." At first, his expression looked angry, then amazed, then he finally just pursed his lips and nodded. "The fact that you could have been and almost were killed aside, what you're saying is impossible. When I left–when I was gone all those weeks–it's because I went to see if there was anything to what you'd said in the truck that night after Iggy's; that The Alderwoman was in charge of this Deep Voice character. But there was nothing. The Alderwoman is safely behind bars in Ocran Holm where she's been for twenty-some years now, and the mansion, the city house, and half a dozen other places associated with her and her underlings," he shook his head, "they're all in ruins."

"But—"

Grandad held up a finger. "But I believe you're telling it like you saw it. I believe you saw someone who's up to no good and I think I might know who it is." He touched his abdomen and frowned.

"Who?"

Grandad nodded in the direction of a parking area along the river. "That's what we're here to find out for sure." He turned the truck into a spot and shifted it into park.

Macy looked to see that they were at one of the many batteries located on the west side of the river away from the docks and other more industrial uses on the opposite side. She followed Grandad's lead and left the truck, moving her hair out of her face as the wind blew it to one side. They crossed a small grassed area between the parking spaces and the battery that contained one of the many statues of Saint Dominic of Caleruega, the city's namesake, and stopped next to a row of coin-operated binoculars.

From this vantage point, Macy had an incredible view. Leaning on the brushed nickel balustrade, she could see for miles to the north and south. In the dark, the city looked more lit up than it had on their journey in from Greater Avendale. Spotlights on top of the tallest buildings shined upward and many of the buildings were decked out in green, blue, red, and yellow exterior lighting making the riverside look like a summertime carnival.

Grandad leaned back against the balustrade next to her, his eyes on their surroundings, and keeping a lookout for something or someone.

"It's Zmija," Macy said.

Grandad raised an eyebrow.

"The Deep Voice character. She calls herself Zmija. It means—"

"Snake."

"Yeah, but how did you—"

"There are a lot of things you don't know about me, Macy." Grandad stewed for a moment. "As things ramped up against The Alderwoman last time and her influence on the government had lessened, an agent stepped forward, a high-value informer inside her organization who began feeding… feeding us details we could use to take her down forever."

"Us?" Macy studied his face for a moment. "You were there, weren't you?"

Grandad nodded. "You don't know a lot about my service in the military, Macy. No one does and there's a reason for that. I was an intelligence officer. At one point it was my job to run informers—to meet with spies in the field, take whatever information they had back to my commanders, and to send them after information valuable to the United States. I was what was known as a handler and I was good at it." He shrugged. "As such, when the new leadership taking hold in PSD during the battle with The Alderwoman reached out to the federal government for help because of the amount of corruption in the police force, the feds provided a resource to help set up and run this informant—me. And I did run her… all the way up to the moment the cell door slammed shut on The Alderwoman."

"Luminesa?"

Grandad shook his head. "No. Not Luminesa. This agent was known as Codename: Cold Knife. Her real name was Barbara Wraith and she was The Alderwoman's daughter. She'd grown tired of her mother's ways and wanted out of the organization. She offered information in exchange for a new identity and a new life and the new officials in charge of Port Saint Dominic were only too happy to give it to her if it meant taking down The Alderwoman once and for all."

"What happened to her?"

"I turned her over to the U.S. Marshals Service to set up the new identity and new life she wanted and I never saw her again… until a few weeks ago. After I visited Ocran Holm I tried the other properties to see if maybe someone had tried to take things up in The Alderwoman's absence, an underling maybe, but as I said there was nothing. As I was leaving the last property someone approached me. It was her… Barbara Wraith. I only saw her for a few seconds and then… then someone attacked me from behind. They left me for dead and that's where I was all that time. My body doesn't heal as fast as it used to, Macy. I should have seen them coming, but I'm an old man now even if I don't like to admit it."

Macy felt a wave of guilt. Something she'd said and done had nearly caused Grandad's death. She'd noticed the way he touched his stomach a few times now. *Was he stabbed?* What if he had been killed? This whole thing had become far more serious than she'd ever imagined. Part of her wished she'd just pulled her mask off in the library in front of Patrick and Deputy Newell and been done with the whole thing. Whatever the punishment was it wouldn't have been the death of anyone. *Or would it have?* She mulled the idea for a moment and another wave of guilt hit her. How could she think so selfishly? Because she'd made the decision she had she was the only one who knew about Brittany Crumb and the others who had been kidnapped. She was the only one who knew about The Alderwoman's plan to take control of the city again. How many would be killed if The Alderwoman returned undeterred? She stuffed her feelings as deep down inside as she could and forced herself to focus. Stellar had to continue on and so did she. "So… the daughter is trying to rebuild her mother's empire after helping to destroy it in the first place?"

Grandad shrugged. "That's the only thing I can think of, though I can't imagine why. Barbara was a sweetheart. She was a reader in a house full of book-burning Nazis. She wasn't the kind of person cut out for criminality at all, but she loved her mother and did as she was told until she just couldn't anymore."

Macy thought over what she'd told Grandad again as she watched a PSDPD patrol boat shoot up the river toward the Lafayette Dam, a concrete monstrosity that blocked the Ocran River just north of the city. There were a few details she'd neglected to mention because the story was just so big and she'd been so nervous she'd forgotten some of the finer points. Could any of them be a lead? "What is Blackville House? Zmija told the city officials The Alderwoman was retaking her rightful place at Blackville House."

"It's an old mansion on the northeast side of the river near the crest of the Panorama Heights. But I went there. It's a ruin now. The gates are rusted shut, the walls have more graffiti than an apartment building inside The Slip, and the entire property looks like it's been swallowed by kudzu. No one's taking up residence there without a minor miracle and a lot of renovation."

"Then how—"

"I think this Zmija meant The Alderwoman is retaking the city.

Last time she had control Blackville House was known as 'the lair of the real mayor' by a lot of people."

"I don't know then." Macy shrugged. "The only other thing I can think of is this crown insignia on a ring that Zmija wears. Principal Decker at school wears one just like it. That's where I first saw it, but they were painted throughout the tunnels, too. In the tunnels, there was an inscription beneath it. It sai—"

"Priori Iustitia. It means 'And from tradition, justice' in Latin. That's the insignia of The Blackville-Wraith Clan. The Alderwoman's name is Adelia Blackville-Wraith and that name signifies the union of two of the oldest crime families in Eastern Europe. You'll find that insignia on a lot of their properties and people. It's how they show ownership. Graffiti and tattoos are the most common, but if someone has a ring, well, that's a sign of leadership. You say your principal wears one?"

"Yeah. On her index finger just like Zmija. When I first saw Zmija's ring my gut told me they were the same person and when I tried to find information on her all that came up was one local article in The Avendale Journal. You said the Blackville-Wraiths are Eastern European?"

"Uh-huh."

"That's where the article said she came from. It said she'd been teaching and administering in the Czech Republic before taking the job at Alum Ridge."

"And what does your gut tell you now?"

Macy looked at her grandfather and he looked back with a knowing expression. "That they're the same person."

"Bingo." Grandad looked at his watch as a set of headlights washed over them. "Right on time."

Macy turned to see a large sedan come to a stop next to Grandad's truck. A man with a shaved head and a thick, graying beard who looked about Grandad's age got out and made his way towards them, pulling a dark-colored trench coat closer to his body as he walked.

"Marc." Grandad held out his right hand.

The man took it tightly and smiled. "Lee."

"It's been a long time. You're not as pretty as I remember."

"They say the memory's the second thing to go."

Grandad laughed and turned to Macy. "This is my granddaughter, Macy. Macy this is Marc Cameron, United States Deputy Marshal - Retired."

Macy almost couldn't believe it. "Turned her over to the U.S. Marshals, huh?" Grandad smiled and she gave him a look before turning to Cameron. "Nice to meet you, sir."

Macy suddenly felt completely out of her league. Even though she'd just learned for the first time what it was that Grandad had done for the Army, seeing him standing there with a man who had obviously had a long and distinguished career in law enforcement cast him in a whole different light than she'd seen before. Standing together, they both looked like hardened warriors.

"Nice to meet you, Macy," Cameron said. "I hear you're something of a protege to my old friend Lee here."

Macy smiled.

Cameron frowned. "I know we just met, but Lee's told me a bit about what you all are dealing with and I want you to make me a promise. I want you to promise me you'll pay attention to everything he tells you and shows you and take it as seriously as a train wreck. When it comes to HUMINT he's one of the best in the business."

Macy nodded. "Yes, sir." She didn't know exactly what HUMINT was, but she'd heard the term used in movies she'd watched starring Tylar Marsden and other action stars. Images of spies in foreign locales, secret meetings, lightning-fast fights, and narrow escapes flashed through her mind. Had Grandad really participated in those kinds of operations during his career? It seemed so.

"So, what'd you bring us?" Grandad looked at Cameron and motioned for Macy to come closer.

"I called in a lot of favors to get this." Cameron loosened his coat and pulled out a well-worn file folder with the Department of Justice and United States Marshals Service emblems on it. Stenciled in black letters was a long case number and on the tab near the top was a name. "Let's take a look at it in the car. If any of it goes missing they'll rescind my retirement and have me manning a game station in Alaska."

Grandad chuckled as they started toward the sedan.

Macy got into the backseat, resting her arms on the seats in front of her and looking over Grandad's shoulder as Cameron opened the file. Inside was a stack of lengthy reports, fingerprint sheets, and photographs. "That's her." She pointed to the photograph on top. "That's Principal Decker."

Grandad gave her a serious look. "You're sure?"

"I've seen her nearly every day since I've been at Alum Ridge. She's aged some, but it's her."

"Well, that's interesting because the name I know her by is Barbara Wraith."

Cameron nodded. "That's whose file this is–Barbara Jane Wraith. Now legally known as Jennifer Leigh Behr."

"Jennifer Leigh Behr?" Macy shook her head. "She goes by Dr. Sara Decker at Alum Ridge."

Cameron furrowed his brow. "Sure sounds like something funny is going on, but it's like I told you on the phone, Lee. The Marshals have never lost a witness. We have had some just up and walk away, but there's no evidence of that here." He flipped through some pages in the file. "She's been making her bi-weekly check-ins and the deputy assigned to her has visited her house quarterly now for years with nothing out of the ordinary to report."

Grandad nodded. "I think it's time to see what we can dig up then."

Cameron closed the file and handed it back to Macy. "Let me know as soon as you're done and I'll get that back to headquarters. Bi-weeklys have just been made so we have a week or ten days until anyone realizes it's missing. I wish you both the best of luck."

Macy got out of the truck and shouldered her overnight bag, looking at the rustic cabin Grandad called home for the first time in years. The place hadn't changed much—not that she had expected anything with him to have ever done so—and in the dark looked just a little bit abandoned.

Arriving at this house had always seemed strange to her because the driveway was in the back and the house faced the lake, which made sense, but just felt odd. Adding to that feeling was that the house was built into the side of a hill so not only did you arrive at the back, but you entered on the second floor.

She waited as Grandad unlocked the house and turned on the lights. After leaving Cameron, they had taken a long look at Barbara Wraith's file and had been surprised to learn they'd be heading to Lake Wasena after all. Barbara, it seemed, hadn't gone all that far away.

Grandad pushed the door open and stood aside for her to enter. "Mi casa su casa."

Macy flashed a quick smile and entered the L-shaped kitchen. Like the outside of the house, the inside hadn't changed. The same junkyard wood design ran throughout and encompassed the floors, cabinets, tables, and even the beds completing the rustic cabin in the woods look she was sure Grandad had created on purpose.

"I think I may have gotten a new couch since the last time you were here."

"You think?"

Grandad shrugged. "I can't remember the last time I bought a couch."

Macy gave him a look and set the Marshals file down on the countertop. It was a three-inch-thick volume that detailed everything from the moment Barbara Wraith had first made contact with PSD officials to what was known as the Administrative Resolution; the point in which the case she was involved in was concluded and her file was transferred to a field office for ongoing management. Macy had spent the drive from PSD reading over it and in the process had learned a lot about how The Alderwoman and her organization worked. But questions remained.

"So," she took a seat at the table in the center of the room, "this file doesn't make any mention of Luminesa. Zero."

Grandad grumbled and ran a hand over his goatee. "Yeah, it wouldn't." He set about the kitchen gathering some things. "Luminesa was considered a vigilante so anything she did had to be corroborated officially to be admissible in court. So, we were on pretty shaky ground from a legal standpoint. In the end, a federal task force armed with information provided by Barbara Wraith arrested The Alderwoman, the core leadership of her organization, and over a dozen city officials and charged them with a laundry list of financial crimes. They went up the proverbial river for every white-collar crime on the books and have stayed there thanks to a three-judge panel who sentenced them consecutively and without the possibility of parole."

Grandad turned the stove on and plopped a frozen pound of hamburger into a pan. "But what the trial, the convictions, the appeals, and that file don't mention are the myriad of violent crimes carried out on behalf of The Alderwoman. They say the memory gets a little fuzzy at my age, but I'm pretty sure I couldn't forget a single one of them if I tried. It was six hundred and three assaults and batteries, two hundred and twenty-nine aggravated assaults with deadly weapons, ninety-four forcible rapes, fifty-two vehicular homicides, and eighteen murders for hire. That's nine hundred and ninety-six lives and families forever altered and that's only the ones we know about—the ones where someone lived and actually had the cojones to file a police report. But my guess is the actual number is three or four times that."

Macy stared down at the file as she ran the numbers through her head again. "That's a lot of people who never saw any justice."

"Yes, it is, though there was some justice for some of them."

"Luminesa."

Grandad nodded. "And a loosely knit gang of civilians known as The Down n' Outers, men and women so tired of the desperate economic circumstances they were placed in by the criminals and the failing economy that they began taking the law into their own hands. Their brand of justice wasn't the most even-handed, but they got the job done at a time when the average joe really didn't have many advocates."

Macy thought about her dad needing a second job in recent months. Was that the start of the kind of hardships that led to people taking the law into their own hands? She'd considered the same idea earlier in the week and the more she heard the more it seemed like a fact—The Alderwoman was responsible for far more ill than what she and her minions physically caused. Macy closed her eyes and collected herself for a moment before turning her thoughts back to Luminesa. "Who was she?"

Grandad pursed his lips as he mashed the pound of hamburger with a spatula.

"Give me that." Macy stood and shooed him away from the stove. "You've got the heat on too high. You're going to burn it." She turned the heat down, moved the pan off the burner, and turned back to face him. "I deserve to know the truth and to know who saved my life."

Grandad took a beer from the refrigerator and popped it open. "Whoever rescued you certainly fits Luminesa's M.O. but I don't know who it was. I never knew who she was. It was safer that way for her and for everyone. As far as I know, whoever she was she gave up the Luminesa identity after Operation Rocksteady."

Macy opened her mouth. "…"

"And before you ask, Operation Rocksteady was the final battle with The Alderwoman. It was a concerted effort between federal law enforcement officers, Luminesa, and The Down n' Outers in which the latter two picked a huge fight with every known criminal element on The East Side to draw attention away from the pending arrest of The Alderwoman and her core minions. It worked like a charm. They never saw it coming and not a single shot was fired. But it wasn't without cost. Several Down n' Outers were killed in the massive riot and after that's when Luminesa disappeared. Forever."

"Forever," Macy said to herself as she studied the countertop.

"Make of that what you will I guess."

"But no one ever confirmed her death… or anything?"

Grandad shrugged. "How? We didn't know who she was."

Macy chewed on the information for a moment as she moved the pan back to the burner and began mashing up the hamburger with the spatula. "And what was mom and dad's involvement?"

Grandad looked at her for a long moment and then shook his head. "Nothing that I'm aware of. Your mom was away at college and I didn't know your dad back then. But I assume like most people in the suburbs he was on the sidelines the entire time. The worst effects the whole situation had on places like Greater Avendale was the drop in real estate values and an occasional rise in burglaries."

Macy wasn't sure what she had been expecting, but that definitely wasn't it. A sizzling sound and the smell of cooking meat rose from the stove. She flipped on the overhead fan. "But they lied to me. I could see it on their faces in my room just after I woke up."

"Look, kiddo. Your mom and dad like a lot of folks who remember the old days get nervous and jerky anytime something even remotely close to what happened last time comes up. They're scared and in your parents' case it's worse because they're terrified of you being more like me and running headlong into it." A smile played at his lips. "Not that you'd ever do a thing like that."

Macy stifled a laugh. "Never."

"C'mere." Grandad set down his beer and opened his arms.

Macy leaned sideways into him and made a guttural noise as he hugged and shook her.

"I've wanted to tell you for a long time. I never agreed with keeping it a secret and I really didn't agree with the lengths they went to do it."

"It's just frustrating because I can't remember. It's the same flashes over and over. Fallen thugs. Someone carrying me. People standing over me and talking. That's it. And none of it makes any sense. Whoever got me out of there must have also taken the Stellar costume and that means they know who I am. But they also knew me well enough to know to take me back to Alum Ridge."

Grandad frowned and shook his head. "As far as I know you were found at a back entrance of the school by some firemen and taken to the hospital. The school called your mom and she was on her way out the door when I showed up, so we rode together and met your dad there. You stayed a few days before they allowed us to move you home, but you were out of it the entire time, kiddo." He moved to the pantry, retrieved a box, and handed it to her with a smile. "You kept waking up randomly and asking for tacos."

Macy took the Old El Paso taco kit with a deadpan look. "Tacos? I wanted tacos?"

"And Leonardo's pizza once. But mostly tacos."

CHAPTER 20

Macy pulled a rain slicker tight as Grandad pushed the throttle forward on his Bayliner 160. The bow of the dark blue and white boat lifted off the water and the noise from the outboard motor increased as the craft bounded over the freezing gray waters of Lake Wasena.

Macy watched as Grandad's cabin shrank from view. The wind whipped her hair straight back and the cold air stung her face. Boating in December wasn't her idea of fun, but Grandad had insisted it would be faster and she knew from experience that he was right.

While Lake Wasena was located just north of PSD it was also one of the largest man-made lakes in the United States with a footprint of over two thousand square miles and hundreds of miles of shoreline. It was possible to leave PSD and drive for several hours before reaching your destination and they just didn't have that kind of time.

"This should be it," Grandad said nearly an hour later as he throttled down, looking between a map and the mouth of a narrow finger of water. "Craddock Creek Inlet." The outboard motor gurgled as he piloted the craft into the narrow passageway at a slow speed.

Macy surveyed the evergreen forest on both sides. There were no homes or docks or signs of anyone living nearby, only thick tree cover. "Secluded."

"As you'd expect from someone in hiding, I guess."

Macy nodded. "I guess."

"So, I've been thinking about this whole thing most of the night, Macy, and I think we should back off a bit."

Macy raised her eyebrows. Piloting a boat up to the home of a woman who had been in the Witness Protection Program for over twenty years and who had overseen you being attacked didn't sound like backing off.

"And by that I mean I think there's a smarter way to go about this. I appreciate everything you've done and uncovered as Stellar, but you and I can't fight an entire organization head-on by ourselves— even if it is mostly broken. And from the sound of it, there are still enough of them around to do some damage. I think we should build a case and hand it over to the Marshals Service—convince them there's something amiss here—and let them take it from there."

Macy frowned and watched as a cardinal took off from a downed tree limb at the edge of the water. The bright red bird retreated into the forest, its vibrant color keeping it visible far longer than any darker colored bird would have been. The scene struck her. As Stellar, she'd felt as though she'd almost been able to fly. The confidence the costume and the anonymity had given her had allowed her to push herself to feats she would have otherwise never known were possible. But now Grandad was talking about her giving it up and despite her feelings to the contrary, she couldn't entirely disagree with him. They had both nearly been killed in recent weeks.

"Whoa-ho. Holy Baba Yaga."

Macy followed Grandad's gaze. In a corner at the end of the navigable water was a rickety dock leading to a winding trail and a cedar-sided A-frame in bad need of exterior maintenance.

Grandad turned the boat and steered it toward the dock. Macy stepped out as it bumped against the aged structure and tied off the nylon dock line before turning again to get a better look at the house. This place wasn't anything like Grandad's. While she'd always thought of his house as a cabin because of its relatively small size, this place fit the bill far better. There was no covered boat slip or carpeted bar area and the path between the house and the dock looked like it had been worn in by use rather than constructed with any kind of purpose. If not for the satellite dish on the roof and the small clearing of trees above it the place would have looked abandoned.

"I guess the Marshals don't spring for the Hilton, huh?"

"Doesn't look like it, no." Grandad turned the boat off and climbed out. He studied the exterior of the house and the surrounding property for a moment. "Well, let's take a look."

They climbed the path, gripping tree trunks here and there to pull themselves up and avoid slipping on the washed-out trail.

"Ms. Behr?" Grandad called as they neared the house. "Is anyone here?"

They reached a fork in the trail that led around the house in two directions.

"You take the low road and I'll take the high road," Grandad said, pointing and whistling a tune that Macy had heard, but couldn't place as he walked away.

Macy followed the path, keeping her eyes on the house as she did. The place didn't look quite as bad up close, but it still appeared as though whoever lived there had long since fallen behind on any kind of exterior upkeep. Dead leaves were piled beside the house at least a few feet deep, the wraparound decking was cluttered with pine needles, leaves, and other woodland debris, and one of the exterior windows had been broken by a fallen limb. She reached a gravel driveway that stretched off into the forest. The gravel extended into a two-car parking area under the house that was vacant except for a few old gardening tools.

"See anything?"

Macy turned to see Grandad as he reached the edge of the driveway. "Nada."

"Are the marshals' visits like surprise inspections or what because it doesn't look like anyone's been here in months at least."

Macy shrugged. "The dates in the file are all pretty random except for being once a quarter. There's got to some kind of schedule or advance notice, though, otherwise, they could show up when she's out shopping or something." She noticed a set of steps along the inside rear wall of the parking area. She frowned and made her way to them, looking up to see a single entry door at the top.

"Hold up."

She turned to look at Grandad. He pulled a set of nitrile gloves from his pocket and handed them over.

"We don't want any fingerprints or anything that can prove we were here if we're trying to make a case for the Marshals to follow."

The rubbery material squeaked as Macy pulled on the gloves and started onto the steps.

"No. Let me go first. She knows me."

Macy stood aside as Grandad climbed the steps, pulling on another pair of gloves as he did.

"Ms. Behr? It's Lee Abendt. We knew each other for a while quite a few years ago. I'm not here to hurt you. I'm coming up the steps now."

Macy watched intently. Her gut told her someone who'd required protection from vengeful criminals might not be too happy about two strangers suddenly appearing. But what choice did they have? If they were going to find out who Sara Decker really was and what she was up to they had to start somewhere. The steps creaked beneath Grandad's weight. He reached for the door and to Macy's surprise didn't even need to use the knob. He pushed it open and looked back at her with concern.

She joined him inside a few moments later. As she crested the steps she was struck by the open floor plan and by how surprisingly modern the inside was laid out and decorated. Someone had spent some money in there at some point. But just like the exterior, it hadn't been kept up in awhile. A thick coating of dust hung on every surface and the air had a musty smell from the invasion of moisture through the broken window.

"It's just like I feared," Grandad said. "No one's been here in months."

"Then who's been making the check-ins?"

Grandad shook his head and gave her a look that said he was thinking exactly what she was; that someone had somehow managed to circumvent the Marshals' system.

From their vantage point in the wide-open living area it was obvious there was no one present in the two loft bedrooms, upper and lower bathrooms, or galley kitchen. Macy surveyed the walls, noticing there were no photos or anything of a personal nature, only neutral art pieces like you'd find in a vacation rental. "Looks like a lonely existence. I mean all the way out here without anyone? What are we… an hour away from the nearest town?"

"Something like that. This is the north side of the lake. If you're trying to avoid PSD, which I'm assuming she would, then there really isn't anything significant up here for hundreds of miles." Grandad turned toward the kitchen. "Take a look upstairs for anything useful. I'll start down here."

Macy did as he said and climbed the spiraled, wrought iron staircase to the loft. At the top of the steps were two bedrooms separated by a full bathroom. The first bedroom was just that, a neatly laid out bedroom with a bed that didn't appear to have been slept in at any time in the recent past. She made her way to the second bedroom and stopped dead in the doorway. "I think I found something."

She heard Grandad on the steps as she entered the home office. In one corner was a bank of computer monitors mounted to the wall above a triangular desk that was filled with neatly organized binders.

"What do ya got?" Grandad appeared in the doorway.

Macy studied the labels on the binders and framed certificates on the wall. "Looks like Jennifer Behr is actually Dr. Jennifer Behr. She earned a medical degree and has been working as a remote Pediatric ICU doctor."

"A remote what?"

"A doctor who sees patients over the Internet, Grandad. We studied this kind of thing in a nursing class last year. Doctors and nurses who are specialists in certain fields can log in remotely to help with patients who have critical needs that locals aren't experienced in handling."

"Sounds complicated."

She flashed him a look. "Not really. It sounds like the perfect way for someone hiding out to earn a good living."

"And what do you make of this?"

Macy turned. "Then there's that." She moved closer to the whiteboard on the wall opposite the monitors. It was filled with photos and pins that had colored strings tied between them. "It looks like she was putting together some kind of genealogy project."

"Yeah, but none of these look like her family. They're all different sets of people."

Macy moved to a wooden dresser beneath the board. On it were stacks of manila folders. She opened one, leafed through it, and then selected another. They were all the same type of records, but belonging to different people. "These all belong to sets of twins."

"Hey ho."

Macy turned to see Grandad holding up a leather-bound journal with the initials BJW monogrammed on the front. He flipped it open, scanned the first entry, and whistled.

"I think we just solved this mystery." He handed the book over.

Macy read over the entry dated nearly six years earlier. "She had a twin sister?"

Grandad frowned. "Apparently so. And it seems time and tide got the better of her. She reached out."

Macy flipped through the entries one at a time, reading pieces and parts until she came to an abrupt end. On the last page, as though Barbara had been writing in it at the time, was a few full sentences, then half a word, and a long pen mark as though she'd suddenly been interrupted. She showed Grandad.

"She reached out and they came for her, huh?" He shook his head and looked down at the carpet. "My God. Why'd she do it? She had to have known better."

"She was lonely and she was trying to help. Her sister was born with a list of illnesses and conditions as long as my last research paper. She was hated by their mother and treated like a freak by everyone who worked for her. That's what all of this is," Macy motioned to the whiteboard and the medical files. "She was researching a theory called Polar Twins and trying to find a way to cure her sister of at least some of what was wrong."

Grandad pursed his lips. "Noble cause, but look where it got her. They knew she'd eventually make contact and were waiting when she did."

"No. I don't think so. These entries sound like she was successful. She discovered that Polar Twins can have different fathers and it sounds like she was on her way to unlocking some of the genetic abnormalities caused by… caused by two pregnancies in a short period. Ugh. That means The Alderwoman—"

"Yeah, I know what it means." Grandad frowned and turned away.

Macy flipped through a few more entries. "Barbara reached her sister–Jacqueline–and they were meeting for a few years. It actually sounds like they became friends again. And then this–just over three years ago."

"Three years ago?" Grandad turned around. "Then who the heck has been making the check-ins and visits?"

Macy shrugged. "Do you really think they killed her?"

"Macy these aren't the kind of people who leave well enough alone. If they followed her sister to her they would have exacted some serious revenge. So, yes. I think Barbara Wraith is dead."

"But you said you saw her."

"The sister–are there any photos of her?"

Macy set the journal down and pulled open the dresser. "Tons." Inside were boxes upon boxes of old photos and documents. She plucked a stack from the top box and started flipping through them. "These all look like they're from some kind of private high school and are mostly of Barbara. But look at this one… that's gotta be her there towards the back."

"Holy cow." Grandad studied the photo for a long moment. "That's her. The sickly-looking one is the person I saw outside the city house that night." He touched his abdomen and frowned.

"She looks more like Decker, too, now that I see them close together."

Grandad shook his head. "It's been a lot of years and I assumed the changes in her appearance were just the effects of aging–I mean not everyone can stay as beautiful as me–but now I can see the difference. They look almost exactly alike except for the smallest details. I'll be. We need to get this back to town."

"So, Jacqueline Wraith betrayed and murdered her sister who was trying to help her and has been masquerading as her to the Marshals ever since?"

Grandad shrugged. "That's the best answer I've got. Maybe the sister remained loyal to The Alderwoman for some reason."

"But why?"

"You got me, kiddo. Who knows why people do what they do? But we're going to have to find out because convincing the feds that their system has been fooled isn't going to be easy. We're going to need a lot more than a journal and some old photos. Start getting some pictures with your phone and let's get out of here."

Macy's phone vibrated for the first time in nearly twenty-four hours as they neared the Lafayette Dam in Grandad's truck. For some reason the dam seemed to be the boundary of the cellular service in and around PSD–anywhere north of it you had spotty service at best. Macy thumbed the screen and watched as multiple text messages arrived at once. One from a number she didn't recognize brought a smile to her face.

> *Wow. I'm such a genius that I forgot to get your number. It took me 45 minutes of texting people, but I finally found someone who had Keri's. Anyways, she says you're out of town for a bit with your grandfather, but text me back when you get this. If you want to. Oh, this is Patrick by the way.*

Macy clicked the number and selected the new contact option from the menu that appeared. She typed in Patrick's name and added a big smiley emoji after it, thinking back over their conversation on her front porch as she did. They really had forgotten to exchange numbers, hadn't they? She blushed even though Grandad was the only one around to see. She thumbed the screen again and looked at the other messages. Most were photos from Keri that weren't downloading yet as the signal was still too weak and there was one from the school automated message service. *Boring.* She went back to Patrick's.

> *Hey. :) Just rolling back into town. What's up?*

She watched the screen for a response, but nothing happened. Maybe he wasn't near his phone.

"You look like you're having a good time over there. Anyone I should know about?"

Macy blushed again. "Patrick."

"Ohhh ho." Grandad chuckled. "*The* Patrick?"

Macy gave him a look.

"I'll take that as a yes." He looked at her and winked. "You know… that's how this whole thing got started, right? Maybe when we hand this over to the Marshals you can go back to the original intent."

She raised an eyebrow. "You mean tell him I'm Stellar?"

"Sure. Why not? Once this thing is handed over to the feds you can hang up the hood forever. They'll be on this like white on rice and Zmija or Jacqueline Wraith or whatever she's calling herself this week will be thrown into Ocran Holm where she belongs."

"Huh." Macy shrugged. She'd already wished she could tell Patrick as they were talking on the porch. Maybe Grandad was on to something. "Do you think we'll have to testify or anything?"

"Maybe. I'm sure they'll want to know how all this came about at some point."

"So, the world's going to find out about Stellar eventually anyways?"

"I'd say that's a likely assumption."

"Huh." The idea was intriguing to Macy. If the world was going to have to find out then why shouldn't Patrick be the first to know? He'd created Stellar and she'd dressed up as her to impress him. But would he be impressed? Stellar was so personal to him that she could imagine him being upset. She had done it innocently enough but felt as though she'd kind of overstepped some invisible line. But impressed or angry he deserved to know the truth before the rest of the world.

"But we've got to get to that point first."

"Okay. So, any idea what we need to do next?"

Grandad drummed his fingers on the steering wheel for a moment. "Not exactly. How much do you know about your principal?"

"Not much. She walks around the school at least once a day with a small entourage of vice-principals and assistants and both students and teachers scatter like mice at the slightest hint of her presence. She wears turtlenecks even when it's hot out and I'd say she's about as in touch with the average student as an owl is with a mouse."

"Sounds like Congress."

"When Keri and I tried searching for information on her there was nothing. Only the one article I already told you about. She doesn't have any social media accounts and we couldn't find any addresses listed, which makes sense, I guess, if Sara Decker isn't her real name."

"Sure does. So, basically what you're telling me is there's no easy approach outside of the school."

Macy shrugged. "Yeah, I guess not. She's got to live somewhere, though. What are the chances of her living under her real name?"

"I'd say slim to none, but just in case I'm wrong see what you can find on your little magic screen thing there."

Macy brought up the web browser on her phone and typed in Jacqueline Wraith. The search engine was cached, but the websites beyond wouldn't load. "The magic screen needs to be a little closer to civilization first."

"Well, drat."

Macy's phone buzzed.

Hey! Not much. We just launched the Stellar website and Josh is testing things out. Wanna see?

Macy thumbed out a response.

Awesome! Link me. Service is still too weak here, but I'll check it out as soon as I get home.

Patrick replied with a link and an idea hit Macy like a bug on a windshield.

Have you posted your message for Stellar yet?

She mulled the idea more as she waited for a response.

Not yet. I'm going to post it in my introduction to the site tonight. We're re-launching the library video. I hope she sees it before Monday.

What happens Monday?

We're going to launch the new video of her in the school atrium and about the lab underneath Monday at noon and hit social media hard once it's live. That should draw in some serious traffic and get everyone talking.

Why Monday at noon? Wouldn't more people see it on the weekend and give it time to generate buzz?

Maybe, but we want to cause a spike in attendance at the community meeting Monday night so the administration has to answer some really hard questions without being able to prepare in advance.

What commun–

Macy deleted the response and thumbed back to the automated message from the school.

A community meeting will be held this Monday evening in the Alum Ridge High School gymnasium at 7pm to discuss the immediate future of the property and to answer public questions.

Macy grinned. This dovetailed perfectly with her idea.

Genius! I'm sure she'll see it in time. The administration will have a hard time lying their way out of that video.

She looked at Grandad. "So, I have an idea."

"Shoot."

"I think Stellar should handle confronting Decker and I think I know just where and when to do it."

Grandad pursed his lips.

"I mean follow me through this. Decker–or Wraith–or whoever–thinks you're dead, right?"

Grandad nodded.

"So, why ruin that by rolling up on her yourself? She has to know who you are or else she wouldn't have attacked you. She could come at you again and if she knows you it wouldn't be a stretch for her to find mom and dad and me. We'd all be in danger."

"Okay."

"So, I'll confront her as Stellar. She has no clue who Stellar is thanks to Luminesa or Bright Flash Barbie or whoever it was and that will protect everyone."

"How is that any less dangerous considering what happened last time you faced her… assuming she's this Zmija."

"The timing and the location is what makes it less dangerous. There's a community meeting Monday night about the future of the school. Decker will be there for sure and there's no way she'll have an army of thugs with her at such a public event."

Grandad smiled. "I like it, kiddo. I like it a lot."

Macy made a fist. "When the meeting's done Decker will be leaving alone and she and Stellar can have a nice, safe, recorded chat."

Macy pressed the doorbell and a set of sing-song chimes sounded throughout the spacious house. She placed her hands in the pockets of her jeans and stood patiently under the covered porch.

Ardmore House, as it was known throughout Greater Avendale, wasn't a mansion by most definitions, but looked so in comparison to the homes around it. Its central location, surrounding brick knee wall, multi-acre yard, solid brick facade, and three white-columned porches dwarfed anything else nearby.

"Hello?" Keri said over the modern doorbell system.

"Hey. It's me."

"Oh, good. Get up here."

Macy turned and waved to her mom who was parked in the driveway. The reverse lights lit up on the Ford Freestyle and Macy turned back, opened the door, and stepped into the house.

Inside, she moved through the long foyer and past the granite-accented kitchen to a doorway she knew led to the three-car garage. Like the outside of Ardmore House, the inside was a cut above other area homes with its high-arched ceilings, intricately-carved crown and chair moldings, and French oak floors. She entered the garage and climbed a set of stairs along the back wall that led to a second-floor Keri had turned into a fashion studio. Before she could knock on the door at the top, Keri opened it, grabbed her by the hand, and tugged her into the room beyond.

"Wow. You'd think you were working on something you didn't want anyone to see."

Keri gave her a look.

The studio, or as Macy had jokingly named it after they'd started taking French, La Maison de Keri le Magnifique, was a wide-open space with high-arched ceilings, track lighting, and enough shelves filled with different fabrics to make Ralph Lauren jealous. In the center of the room stood multiple workstations and mannequins in various states of dress.

Macy placed her hands in her pockets and stood waiting as Keri moved to the back of the room where a tall curtain hid the space beyond. Macy had seen the space before and knew it housed a small, circular stage surrounded by different kinds of lighting equipment that Keri used when she photographed her designs.

Keri gripped one side of the curtain. "Are you ready?"

Macy lifted an eyebrow. "Should I close my eyes and act surprised?"

Keri rolled her eyes and pushed the curtain.

The floor-to-ceiling length piece of canvas made a metallic rolling sound as it glided across the room and a set of track lights illuminated the stage.

Macy's eyes went wide. She had been kidding about being surprised, but now she actually was. Standing on a mannequin in the center of the stage was the brand new Stellar costume.

"Holy cow, Keri." Macy stared, her eyes wide. This wasn't a costume. This was a suit.

Keri beamed.

Macy circled the stage, taking in every detail of the suit. Gone were the metal-lined sports pads with glued fabric and the printed spandex. She tapped on the armor with a knuckle and it made a solid sound like a tree trunk. She flattened her hand and ran it over the covering fabric. It was far more rigid and textured than the previous version and had sewn-in grooves instead of a printed design.

Keri touched it. "The armor's an ultra-lightweight, state of the art poly para-aramid combo called DecTac developed in Israel for soldiers on the front lines. It's heat and friction resistant and in testing stood up to a DJ391R blade and a high velocity round from a CMG 583 automatic rifle. Whatever those are."

Macy opened her mouth and shook her head, but no words came out. Once again Keri had outdone herself—something she just hadn't thought possible. "But… how… how did you do all of this in less than a week?"

Keri shrugged. "I started working on it weeks ago. And you haven't seen the best parts yet." She reached up and pulled back the hood. Instead of the adjustable mask, there was now a helmet complete with a chin strap. But unlike most helmets, this one wasn't big and bulky like a motorcycle helmet. It was thin and closely followed the contours of the human head and face making it no different in appearance from the mask when the hood was up. "DecTac will protect your noggin, too. And check this out." Keri pulled the hood back up and it fell into place automatically. "Magnets. Bye, bye barrettes."

Macy shook her head again. "You've created an actual battle suit. And weeks ago?"

Keri shrugged again. "I knew when you decided to carry on after fighting Zeke and his gang you would eventually need something more than that cosplay outfit. It might have looked good, but functional wasn't what I'd had in mind when I made it."

"But this must have cost—"

"Thousands. Thankfully my mom compensates for her workaholic nature and lack of time spent with me in the form of a fat credit line on an American Express."

Macy nodded. "Right."

"There's one last thing." Keri smiled as she picked up a roll of something. Her smile broadened as she let it unravel, slung it around the waist of the suit, and fastened it together in the center with a metallic snap.

Macy stood back and took in the sight of the perfectly matched utility belt, her mouth stretching into a grin as her eyes fell on the Stellar symbol buckle.

Keri moved to stand beside her. "So, ready to try it on?"

"I just can't anymore." Keri pushed the swivel chair back from the computer and held up her hands in surrender. "I've read at least a dozen articles on secret codes and none of it makes any sense.

Whatever he's done just isn't… it's just not for normal people."

Macy glanced at the computer screen as she continued to stretch and twist, breaking in the new suit. She'd gotten used to moving in the old suit, but couldn't believe the difference in breathability and maneuverability. She could feel the breeze from the ceiling fan and had stretched out into a full-twisting split with zero loss of flexibility. She threw a series of slow kicks at a nearby mannequin and dropped back into a defensive stance. *This thing is awesome.* She almost wished Decker would show up to the community meeting with a throng of goons at her side.

She stood upright and looked more fully at the computer on one of Keri's workstations. "I don't know." She shrugged. "He said it would be something only Stellar would understand so–"

"So, you're Stellar and you don't understand. It looks like The Secret Decoder Ring Gang has stumped us both. I've read every message and watched each video on this site at least three times. If there's any kind of code here it's way too subtle."

Macy took a seat and scrolled through the few posts on the page. The site Patrick and Josh had built was gorgeous. Patrick's hand-drawn images against a light background with faint hints of city buildings just popped as soon as it loaded. Set up like a blog with different entries, the current crowning features of the site were the original video Striker had taken in the library and an interactive map of PSD showing the locations where Stellar had been seen. Right now the map was pretty boring as only the location of Alum Ridge High School was illuminated, but maybe if she could figure out whatever code he'd hidden here about meeting Stellar she'd tell him about the tunnels and the basement full of passageways to help fill things out a bit–or maybe she wouldn't since she didn't have any idea where those places were other than somewhere under the ground.

"The only thing I see that looks anything like a code is the very first post," Keri said as she wheeled herself back over to the computer as Macy scrolled down to the bottom of the page. "It's that Latin Lorem Ipsum stuff, though, and I checked online for translations. Some reporter had some professor do one, but it was basically gibberish."

Macy looked at the text. Keri was right. It was the space filler text that populated on a lot of programs before the user had entered any of their own text. But something about it struck her as odd. Why would someone leave space filler text in a post on a website that was otherwise so beautifully done? "That's got to be it." She turned to Keri and explained her reasoning.

Keri shrugged. "I guess so, but how do we figure out what it says? The Latin professor dude in that one article did that and I didn't see anything useful in it."

"I don't know." Macy turned back to the computer. "Show me what the professor guy came up with."

Keri took the mouse and clicked a tab near the top of the screen. "There."

Macy scanned the page. Keri was right again. Someone had translated the Latin text into something approaching English, but it didn't make any more sense than the original. There were English words and some of them were in a readable order, but not enough for the paragraph to have any kind of meaning. She clicked back to the Stellar website and moved the mouse over the placeholder text, studying it as she thought about what to do next. She was certain they were looking at Patrick's code, but what was the key to unlocking it?

"Why don't you just text him and ask him what it is? You could play like you're curious and see if he'll reveal it to you." Keri's mouth stretched into a grin. "You two are 'talking' now."

Macy pursed her lips. It wasn't a terrible idea.

"Or–I got it–you could text him about the placeholder text and act like you think it's a mistake and that you're looking out for him by alerting him. Maybe that will get a conversation about it rolling and you can work your way into asking him what it means."

Again, not a terrible idea. But Macy wasn't sure if she wanted to go that route yet. What she really wanted was to figure it out and to prove to herself more than to anyone else that she was every bit the detective Patrick had created Stellar to be. She clicked back to the newspaper article and ran the mouse over the words there. An idea hit her. "Wait. Look at this." She copied and pasted the text onto a new document and repeated the process on the Stellar site. Now the two paragraphs of placeholder text were beside each other. "Do you see the differences?"

Keri leaned forward and studied the text. "Yeah. I do."

"So, that's gotta be it, right?"

"They're different, but they're still just random Latin words." Keri shrugged. "How do you know his computer just doesn't do placeholders differently than some others?"

Macy looked back at the screen. "I don't know. Are there different versions? Why would there be different versions?"

Keri didn't answer. Instead, she was pointing at the screen and counting something. "I think you're right actually. It's every fifth word that's different. That had to be done on purpose."

Macy smiled.

"Copy the different words out and paste them together. Let's see what we end up with."

Macy did so. She lifted an eyebrow as she read the result aloud. "Terra wertul tu turom fasar dahi potid ug dase edun dahi…" She stopped reading and shook her head. "Ugh. Just the sound of that is giving me a headache."

"Sounds like the gibberish version of Santa's reindeer or something."

"I know, right?"

"So it's a code within a code? Why do I feel like that guy on that show…" Keri made her voice sound manly. "It's a clue that leads to another clue and another clue!"

Macy lifted an eyebrow. "I don't think I've seen it, but yeah. It looks like a code within a code."

"Here. Let me."

Macy scooted out of the way and let Keri take over at the computer.

"I'm telling you I read at least a dozen articles on this. We just have to figure out which cipher method he used and then we should be able to—there! It's this one."

Macy looked at the screen. "A keyboard cipher?"

"Yeah, it's got to be. Look." Keri studied the words closely. "Each word can be spelled using only one line on a keyboard except for one letter–in this case, the last letter of each word."

"And that one letter, when combined with the others, spells out a message."

"Exactly."

"Genius." Macy spun around in her swivel chair. "You're a genius."

Keri smiled. "Girl, they're going to be calling me your sidekick."

"Team Stellar." Macy made a tough guy face and gave a thumbs up like the last scene of an old action movie. So it wasn't one hundred percent her detective skills that solved their problem, but yay Team Stellar, right? She watched as Keri wrote out the letters.

A L U M R I D G E

C O N S T R U C T I O N

N I N E P M S U N D A Y

Macy grinned as she read the message. "I'll be there."

CHAPTER 21

Macy stepped to the edge of the roof and looked down over the gathered construction equipment, orange cones, and piles of rubble. Patrick stood in the center of the site. She took a deep breath, made eye contact, and fell into a front flip, landing on the tin roof of the loading dock and then swinging down onto the pavement. She stood slowly.

Patrick looked floored. "…"

Macy kept her face neutral, but inside she was all grins. It was a cool entrance if she did say so herself and was just what she'd been aiming for. Stellar couldn't disappoint her creator after all.

"I… I was worried you wouldn't see my message."

Macy could feel the nervous energy coming from him.

"I thought maybe I'd hidden it too well. I almost changed it a dozen times."

"You did fine." She kept her distance, choosing to stand in the shadow of a hulking piece of equipment. "The question is why did you leave it?" She knew of course, but couldn't say so. She had to let him explain it or else she'd risk revealing too much.

Patrick's eyes darted around and settled on the ground in front of him. "I... uhh... we took a video of the way down to that lab and of your fight in the atrium the night we followed you into the school. I have some theories about what's going on and I think you know the truth."

He made eye contact and quickly looked away again. He was waiting for a response, but Macy stayed silent.

"We're uploading it to the site tomorrow. We want the administration to answer for the lab because I think they knew it was there. I think they've been covering it up for a long time."

"They did and they are—or were."

"They threatened my dad. I'm sure of it. That's why he's been so frustrated and distant. He wants to do something about it, but he doesn't know what and he's afraid they'll hurt the people he cares about."

"They could. They've hurt a lot of others." Macy glanced at the ground. "There are bodies buried beneath this site right now—lab workers they smuggled in from somewhere and abandoned once the place was discovered. This 'collapse' was them trying to destroy the evidence."

Patrick scanned the site, his face haunted. "I knew it." His face grew more determined. "I want us to work together. It's the community's responsibility to fight this kind of thing—not just one person's."

Macy considered him for a moment. He didn't know anything about The Alderwoman or about the true past of PSD being hidden from young people for decades. How did she begin to tell him? Should she tell him? "Not everyone can do what I can."

"No, they can't. But we all have talents we could put into the cause. Even if it isn't hand to hand combat. You can't do this alone… whoever you are."

He was right. Grandad had said it was a ragtag group of shop owners, restaurateurs, and other civilians who had joined Luminesa in her quest and who had provided the numbers needed to battle the criminals. But was this really a quest? Had it risen to that level? If she could stop Jacqueline Wraith here and now, The Alderwoman would be a memory again. And that was the idea she had come to talk to him about. She did need his help.

"Say you're right. What do you propose to do?"

Patrick took a deep breath. "You need a public voice. You need an outlet for what you find out, a way for the public to know what you've uncovered. We can be that. We have the website, the cameras, and the–"

"No." The thought of working with Josh Friddle and Striker Austreicher or whatever his actual name was made her queasy.

"But–"

"I'll work with you. Only you. And it won't be a long term thing. After the meeting tomorrow night this gets handed off to the authorities if we get it right."

Patrick nodded. "Okay. What is it we need to get right?"

CHAPTER 22

Macy stood from the back seat of her mom's Ford Freestyle. She opened the door for her mom and together they walked toward the front doors of Alum Ridge in a throng of others as her dad pulled away to find parking in the already crowded lot. Patrick's upload of the atrium video and the afternoon social media campaign had had the desired effect. Macy had seen thread after thread of messages questioning the contents and now the result was visible in the turnout.

Deputy Newell and three of the school's eight security officers stood at the front entrance holding doors and greeting people as they entered. "101 to 102, over?" Newell said into a radio handset as Macy neared.

"102, over."

"We may need more seating. You'd better bring in a few rows of chairs for the front, over."

There was a long silence.

"Uhh 10-4, over."

Newell clicked the mic once in response. "Macy. Mrs. Davis."

"Deputy Newell," Macy said, standing aside and letting her mother enter first. She followed closely, the warmth of the atrium blanketing her as she crossed the threshold. The meeting wasn't a particularly formal occasion, but she'd chosen to wear a gray sweater dress, black leggings, and loose-fitting boots. It was about as formal as she got and it all came off a lot quicker than anything else she had in her closet. And that was important as she was anticipating a speedy change of outfits as soon as the meeting ended.

"Don't forget I'm riding home with Keri and her mom tonight."

"I didn't forget."

"You and dad didn't have to come. Keri offered me a ride."

"I hate to embarrass you by being in such close proximity in public, but we're as concerned as anyone about the future of this school, Macy. The next closest school is Wynmere High and you'd be on the bus for at least an hour each way."

Macy wrinkled her nose. Wynmere High was located in the far northeast corner of Greater Avendale and was Alum Ridge's chief rival in everything from football to chess club. Plus, the students there were known for being snobs. Macy stayed a step behind her mom as they followed the crowd around to the auditorium entrance where another security officer stood.

"Okay, folks. Take the furthest seat available so we can keep things moving along and get started on time."

Ugh. There was nothing more annoying than being treated like cattle and schools were the best at it. Macy hadn't missed shuffling from class to class in a building filled with over two thousand people. If only she could talk her parents into letting her be homeschooled from here on out. She caught sight of Keri sitting on the back row just as they had agreed and just as planned she'd managed to save a seat.

"If it's okay I think I'll sit with Keri, too, since it looks kind of crowded. It'll be easier to get out of here when it's done."

Her mom smiled over her shoulder. "Fine then. I'll make sure I shout extra loud so you can hear me in the back."

Macy stuck out her tongue playfully as her mom entered a middle row and she kept climbing. She entered the last row and excused herself past everyone. As she arrived at the seat Keri had saved her eyes fell on the seat next to it and her chest tightened.

"Good evening, Miss Davis," The Spade said, sitting regally and holding onto a small purse with both hands as though Macy might snatch it.

"Hello, Mrs. Spader."

Keri made a face and mouthed an apology. The Spade's presence meant a moratorium on any conversation they may have otherwise managed. Macy took her seat and sat rigidly trying her best to be as far away from The Spade as possible.

"I was very glad to hear that you were alright after being so badly injured."

Macy looked at the older woman. She really hadn't expected her to make conversation and the effort seemed difficult. "Thank you." Macy knew the words sounded tentative, but it was all she'd been able to manage.

"You're welcome. I hope you enjoy the extended Christmas break."

"I'm sure I will. I hope you do as well."

"Thank you."

The exchange felt oddly formal–like the first awkward moments spent with someone you'd just met, but were expected to get to know and form some kind of a relationship with. Although she had been in the woman's science class since the sixth grade, the words passed between them outside of a classroom setting could probably be counted on one hand. She shook the feeling off as the lights in the auditorium dimmed and the doors closed. A moment later Principal Decker's entourage appeared on the stage, taking their seats behind the podium. Decker's assistant, Ms. Pollard, placed a stack of papers and a bottle of water on the podium like a dutiful servant and retreated backstage.

The audience hushed to just above a whisper and Macy scanned the crowd for Patrick. She spotted him seated near the front with a spiral-bound notebook in his hand and a pen behind his ear. He looked like a reporter ready to pounce on a long-awaited headline and she could honestly see him being just that in the years to come.

"I honestly don't know what you see in that boy, Miss Davis. He's skinny, disheveled, and a complete daydreamer."

Macy felt her mouth fall open as she turned to look at The Spade. Had she really just inserted herself so boldly into Macy's love life–if you wanted to call it that? Macy closed her mouth and resisted the urge to lash out.

"When I was your age my father would have set me straight."

Macy leaned in closer than she'd ever wanted to be to the old woman. "When you were my age, dinosaurs probably roamed the earth, men wore loincloths, and attracted women by building the biggest fire." A smile crept onto her face. "On second thought, it's really not all that different from the way men attract women now and that's why I like Patrick. He's quiet. He thinks about what he's going to say before he says it–sometimes a little too much, but he'll grow out of that–and he dares to dream of something other than what everyone else tells him he should. So, mind your own, Mrs. Spader." She turned away as she heard the old woman gasp and stutter for a response. She looked at Keri whose eyes were wide, and smiles inched onto their faces. Macy had been waiting to do that since earlier in the year when The Spade had publicly embarrassed Patrick. She may have just ensured herself a failing grade in any future science classes, but she'd take the punishment with glee.

The auditorium hushed as Principal Decker walked onto the stage and stood behind the podium, placing her hands on both sides of it as she had done in every speech Macy had seen. Macy couldn't ignore the mental image of a bird of prey surveying the fields below for mice. This was the first time she'd seen Decker in person since learning her true identity and her prior intuition about the woman's nature seemed spot on.

Decker cleared her throat. "Good evening. I want to start tonight by taking you through the report that was given to me earlier today by the lead contractor on the repairs to D Wing." She looked down at the stack of papers on the podium and began to read.

Macy listened but wasn't really hearing much of what was being said. She was certain that whoever this contractor was, he or she had been paid or threatened into saying whatever it was Decker wanted people to believe. She wondered if the contractor had children and whether they were now among those being held until the reports and repairs were done as ordered. Surely things were to be completed in a manner that covered up the existence of the old bomb factory and the entrance to it in the far corners of D Wing.

"That concludes the report issued this morning by J. Michael & Associates Engineering & Architecture. Now I want to turn to recent conversations with the school board about the future of Alum Ridge. As you all are undoubtedly aware, the current student body is nearly twenty-five percent above the allowable capacity of these buildings.

This has led to classes being moved into temporary facilities including the basement of the main building, which will now be unavailable due to the construction necessary to repair D Wing. With both the basement and an entire wing of the school off limits until the completion of the repairs we have two options. The school board will be voting in two weeks on which of the two will be undertaken at the start of school in January.

Option number one is to place a temporary hold on construction efforts and have the contractors turn their attention immediately to excavating the east field for the placement of a minimum of ten new trailers on a gravel lot."

The option drew a series of boos and moans from the gathered parents and students. Macy held her reaction.

"Option number two is to move the same number of students that would be housed in the trailers to Valley High beginning in January and to decide on a method in which those students will be chosen."

More boos and groans and this time Macy joined them. Moving students off the Alum Ridge Campus meant she and Keri and even Patrick could end up in different schools and that was a non-starter.

Decker ignored the reactions. "The school board meeting will be held in this room in two weeks and both options are being studied for feasibility." She stood back from the podium and people began to rise from their seats. Was she not going to take any questions? It was clear the audience had plenty as they were shouted over the top of one another. Macy lost sight of Patrick in the melee and for the first time, concern about this not going as they had anticipated descended on her. She made eye contact with Keri who shared the same worried expression.

Decker stepped back to the podium and the audience quieted. She held up her hands and the last of those questioning took their seats. "I realize there are many questions about the future of the school and about a video that was uploaded this afternoon," Decker said dismissively, "but my administration and I will not be the ones to address those concerns. Effective immediately I am tendering my resignation to the Greater Avendale School Board and will not be joining the Alum Ridge student body at the resumption of the school year."

"Oh, no way!" someone shouted as the room again rose to its feet and questions erupted.

Macy sat stunned for a moment and then turned her attention back to Decker. The woman's expression, while technically neutral to anyone not knowing her true identity and intentions, revealed a sort of glee. A smile played at the edges of her mouth. She'd seen the video, had known what was coming and had devised a checkmate after all. Of course, she wouldn't be continuing on as the principal of the school. Her only real reason for ever being so was to cover up the activities going on beneath it and once the evidence of that was erased forever, she could move on safely.

Macy made eye contact with Keri again and reached for the backpack at Keri's feet.

"Wait. What are you doing?"

"Improvising."

Macy pulled up the hood of the Stellar suit and felt it click into place as she ran across the parking lot for the car waiting at the curb. It was a dark-colored four-door sedan that no doubt awaited Dr. Sara Decker. What kind of school principal arranged a limousine service in advance? One who was planning an expedient exit and who was really the offspring of an evil and now incarcerated crime lord. That's who.

Macy bounded onto the sedan, feeling the roof dent under her weight as the front doors of the school flew open and the first of Decker's entourage appeared on the steps. She jumped down onto the sidewalk and stood neutrally. The gathering of vice-principals and assistants stopped in their tracks as their eyes fell on her blocking their exit. Decker appeared a second later, exiting slowly, her eyes fixed on Stellar. A few of the entourage turned back but saw their way blocked by the audience that had exited the auditorium and was now making their way through the atrium to the front entrance.

Decker moved down the steps, her associates cautiously falling in behind her as she took the lead. The first of the audience arrived at the front doors, saw what was happening, and word began to spread quickly back to those still in the atrium. People began to flood through the doors, their eyes on Stellar.

"It's her," people whispered. "It's the masked woman from the videos." They closed in around Decker's entourage who looked trapped and terrified.

"You've lied to this school and the community of Greater Avendale, Dr. Decker," Macy said, trying to make her voice sound deeper, "and if you won't answer to them tonight you will answer to me."

Decker sneered. "Lied? About what exactly?"

"Let's start with the laboratory underneath the school. You remember, right? The one located in the forgotten World War II-era bomb factory. The one used to make the drug known as Spaz until you oversaw its destruction and caused D Wing to 'collapse' in the process."

A shocked murmur passed through the crowd.

Decker's eyes narrowed. She opened her mouth to speak, but no words came out for several seconds. "I don't know what you're talking about. Whoever you are it sounds like you have quite an imagination."

"It's not her imagination."

Macy turned her head to see that Patrick had pushed his way to the front of the crowd.

"It's a fact. I saw it myself. That's why the fight happened in the atrium. My friend and I found the lab and people were chasing us. They were going to kill us, I'm sure of it. She saved us." He turned to the crowd. "You saw it all on the video. That's why you're here. You saw the stairwell and the room beyond. You saw us open the door and then you saw us running. We were running for our lives." He pointed at Macy. "She drew them away from us and to the atrium. She stopped them."

The crowd looked at each other and murmured responses rose and fell again.

"You can't really believe any of this," Decker said, looking around. "This boy is clearly imagining things and in need of more attention at home. He skipped the part about creating this," she motioned to Macy, "this… whatever she is. It's all over the website he's set up. This is nothing but the imagination of bored students trying to make a name for themselves on whatever social media platform is trending this month."

"Don't you talk about my son that way." Deputy Newell appeared from the crowd and stood next to Patrick. "Now I clearly don't know everything about what's going on around here, but I can tell you an investigation is in order. The bullying in this school has been out of control for a long time, but it goes deeper than that. There has been something else going on for a while and people, including me, have been threatened into keeping quiet about it. Earlier this year, someone was sent to attack my son. They failed thanks to," he motioned and turned to Macy, "Stellar, is it?"

A lock of hair fell out of Decker's usual tight bun. She brushed it back, but it fell again. Macy studied her closely. She could see the beginnings of stress on her face and in her movements and there was something else–the lines on her face and at the edges of her eyes seemed to be getting more pronounced.

"Does this have anything to do with the disappearance of Brittany Crumb, Deputy?"

Macy recognized her mom's voice. *Good one, mom.* She was having a hard time keeping a sloppy grin off her face. While she hadn't imagined things going this way, Decker was still getting publicly grilled, and that had been the linchpin of the plan all along.

Deputy Newell stood silent for a moment. "Yes. I believe it does."

Shocked and angry responses arose from the crowd.

"Now I don't have any proof of that," Deputy Newell continued, "but it is my opinion that Brittany Crumb found something she wasn't supposed to and was… she was taken away as a result."

Macy glanced over the crowd. Phones were held overhead and the proceedings were being recorded by far more devices than had been planned. They'd have more proof of what was said here than they could ever need. She turned her attention back to Decker. "Brittany was taken and is being held to keep her father and his company in compliance with the manufacturing of Spaz. They've been using his company's refrigerated trucks to deliver one of the chief compounds required to manufacture the drug and they've been covering it up with the nightly food deliveries. I know because I've seen it happen."

Decker stumbled and was caught by her assistant. "You have no proof of that… of any of this!" Her voice was shrill and her appearance becoming even more haggard. As she stood there being supported by her assistant she breathed in and out steadily as though she were having trouble doing so. Her vice-principals began to step back into the crowd as though they were trying to distance themselves from her and hoping people would forget about their presence. Decker looked back and forth at them. "Cowards!" She drew in a deep breath and straightened up, slyly pressing a button on something located on her wrist beneath her sleeve.

Macy narrowed her eyes as she watched the woman's complexion return to normal and the lines on her face retreat. What kind of devices had Jacqueline Wraith invented to make herself look like a normal, healthy person?

"How's this for proof?"

Macy turned to see Grandad step forward from the crowd, holding the U.S. Marshals file. She felt her eyes widen and her mouth open, but she stopped herself and returned to a neutral reaction. *What is he thinking?* They'd decided on this course of action to avoid revealing he was still alive.

"This woman's name isn't Dr. Sara Decker. It's Jacqueline Wraith and she's the daughter of Adelia Blackville-Wraith–The Alderwoman." A few people in the crowd gasped and Grandad turned the file inside out, holding it up so the picture could be seen. "Some of you aren't old enough to remember who that is, but enough of you are. My name is Esley Abendt and I was the Defense Intelligence Officer who handled the case of one Barbara Wraith– this woman's twin sister who has since gone missing."

"Arghhh!" Decker's face twisted and her eyes narrowed. "Lies!"

"It's not a lie!"

Decker drew in a ragged breath and reached for Ms. Pollard again. Macy narrowed her eyes. Any doubt in her mind about the identity of Zmija had vanished.

Grandad continued. "This woman has been plotting The Alderwoman's return and has been using this Spaz drug to whip the city into a frenzy to keep the attention focused elsewhere. If it wasn't for Stellar none of this would have been made public."

The crowd's attention fell again on Macy as the name Stellar began to pass through the crowd. "Stellar!" someone yelled triumphantly. A chorus began and Macy felt her face go as red as the Stellar suit. She gave a small wave.

"Alright. Alright." Deputy Newell stepped out into the center of the gathering next to Macy waving his hands to quiet the crowd. "That's enough." He regarded her with a worried expression for a moment and then turned back to the crowd. "Now I'm not about to stand here and pretend that I like how any of this came about. As far as I'm concerned, there's no place for vigilantism in a civilized society, but I suppose in rare cases it can be useful." A cheer sounded and Newell frowned again. "Yeah. Yay, Stellar." He looked back at Macy and golf clapped before holding up his hands and turning back to the crowd again. "What we need here is some old-fashioned law and—"

A gunshot sounded and the crowd screamed and ducked. Two more shots sent them scrambling in all directions. Macy turned toward the sound to see the driver of the dark sedan standing with the rear door held open and a pistol pointed high in the air.

Ms. Pollard rushed forward supporting Decker.

"Hey! Wait!" Newell made to stop them, but the sedan driver aimed the pistol at him. He froze.

Standing in a row with Newell and Grandad, Macy watched as Decker and Pollard entered the sedan and the driver closed the door, keeping the pistol aimed as he did.

Macy stepped back. Decker was escaping, but that was okay. She'd never planned to hold her, only to get recorded evidence and they had plenty of that. If anything, the nature of the escape helped their case. This was the perfect time to disappear.

CHAPTER 23

Macy checked her look in the mirror again. She was determined not to be embarrassed again like she was on the porch in her pajamas.

"Mace, you've got it." Keri stood from the bed and straightened the collar on the denim jacket Macy was wearing. "You're good."

"Are you sure denim is back in?"

Keri raised an eyebrow. "It is if I say it is. Trust me."

"Ugh." Macy held out her hand to show it trembling. "I'm such a wreck."

"It's going to be okay. You're friends now."

Macy frowned. "I know. But that sort of makes it worse. I want to hang out with him and get to know him, but then part of me still feels like–like I don't know."

"Just relax. What'd you do when he first walked up the other day?"

"Have a mental freak out like I'm doing right now."

Keri gave her a look. "That's not what I mean."

"I just sat down and we started talking–mostly about Stellar."

"So, that's what you're going to do tonight, right?"

"Yeah."

"Then just relax and let it happen naturally."

Macy took a deep breath and willed herself to calm down. She knew Keri was right and honestly couldn't zero in on a reason why she was so nervous. She did one more turn in front of the mirror, nodded to herself, and moved to the door.

"Wait."

Macy turned back.

Keri looked at the hand-drawn image of Stellar on Macy's mirror. "Are you sure about this?"

"I'm sure." Macy looked at the image. She and Grandad had talked about telling Patrick she was Stellar and the more she had thought about it the more she liked the idea–especially since he'd been so integral in outing Jacqueline Wraith publicly. "He deserves to know."

Macy left the front porch and made her way to the sidewalk in front of her house.

"You sure you don't want me to walk with you?" Keri said, coming out after having said her goodbyes to Macy's parents and grandad.

"I'm sure. I could use the time alone."

"Okay then. I'll take the other way home."

Macy smiled and watched her walk in the opposite direction.

The neighborhoods in Greater Avendale could seem like a

complex set of circular streets and cul-de-sacs, but in reality, were still largely laid out in blocks. Once you got used to navigating them, getting from one place to another wasn't all that hard. She buttoned her coat and moved on along the sidewalk.

Patrick's house was six blocks away and she was meeting him there in half an hour. They really hadn't discussed what they would do. What was there to do in December when neither of you could drive and the adults in your life were unlikely to allow you to take public transportation anywhere? That bit was annoying, to say the least, but she felt like she understood. Part of the blessing and the curse that was being a crimefighter–that's what Stellar was at this point, right?– was that she had seen firsthand the kind of dangers that were out there. Vague parental fears and warnings about such things as abduction and human trafficking took on a whole new meaning when you'd gone fist to fist with the kind of people who carried out such acts. She guessed she and Patrick would just stay home and chat like they had the other day. She was sure he'd have a lot of questions once she got around to revealing she was Stellar.

She had thought about the idea over and over but had yet to come up with a plan as to how exactly to reveal it. His reaction still concerned her, though she felt like he'd made a sort of peace with Stellar that had been evident in their meeting at the school. While he had still been nervous, he hadn't shown any of the emotion he had when she'd confronted him at the school after taking down the goons in the atrium. In the end, she figured it would come down to simply summoning the courage to just say it.

She thought back over the first time she'd been planning to talk to him about Stellar. Getting dressed in the school bathroom, making her way around to the library, being so nervous she could feel her insides vibrating. Hopefully, this time would have a better ending than that attempt.

Maybe afterward he could show her the new Stellar website and how he was planning to create and upload things to it. That might be cool considering she had the inside track on Stellar's point of view. She let that idea bounce around her head as she walked. She really hadn't thought much about what would happen after she told Patrick she was Stellar. In fact, the website hadn't come into her mental equations at all. Would he still need or want the site after he knew the truth? Maybe they could turn it into something they could do together. Since the rest of the world was destined to soon find out about Stellar and the crimes she'd exposed, perhaps they could turn it into a sort of one-stop-shop. After all, Stellar was Patrick's creation, most of the footage that had been captured of her to date was also Patrick's, and with her–his girlfriend, maybe?–being Stellar any access the world wanted had to come through them. Maybe there was even some way they could monetize it. She laughed to herself at the idea as she arrived on Patrick's block.

The houses in this part of Greater Avendale were different from hers. Instead of the two-story, craftsman style homes with large front porches, the homes here were single floor ranches that varied only in the contour of the roofs and the color of the siding. She started down the road, her nerves returning slightly as she drew closer.

The sound of floating paper on the breeze drew her attention. She looked to see a single page moving across the pavement towards her. The paper wrapped around her shin and she retrieved it, scanning the writing on it. "Jacopo Carbonelli." The page was filled with the stats of a character she immediately recognized as the one from Patrick's notebook. More loose pages blew randomly toward her and she followed their trail with her eyes until she landed on an open notebook in the driveway of a house in the center of the cul-de-sac–Patrick's house. Her heart jumped and her eyes widened. The house was brightly illuminated by exterior lighting that had been installed in the flower gardens, the inside lights were on, the front door was open, and a dark-colored SUV sat in the driveway. Something was wrong.

Movement in the well-lit windows of the home caught her eye. She stepped away from the sidewalk closer to the hedges and trees that lined the neighboring yards and made her way toward the house. Maybe Deputy Newell was just preparing to leave for working overtime again at one of the Oaklawn convenience stores that had seen a rise in crime over the last few months–no, that couldn't be it. Her parents had called and made sure there would be an adult in the house with her and Patrick before allowing her to go. But if that wasn't the case, why was Patrick's notebook lying in the driveway like it had been discarded? Were he and his dad fighting about Patrick's actions the night before?

More movement in the windows preceded the appearance of a figure in the opened doorway and then another. Two people moved single file toward the SUV and opened its rear passenger side door, standing aside as others appeared in the doorway and made their way out.

Macy stopped in her tracks at the sight of someone bound and gagged being pushed out of the house to the SUV. It was Deputy Newell and following closely behind—also bound and gagged was Patrick. Her mind raced and she crouched into a fighting stance, preparing to rush to their rescue only to stop as she realized she wasn't there as Stellar. She was there as Macy Davis. The only piece of Stellar she had with her was the part of the shoulder armor that featured the Stellar symbol–proof in case Patrick had trouble believing her.

She stood frozen as the two were pushed into the back of the SUV and the door was closed. The men with them made their way into the other doors of the SUV and lastly, a lone figure stood in the doorway of the house–Zmija. Macy recognized the robe-like coat and circular-rimmed hat. Jacqueline Wraith hadn't fled town as she and Grandad had anticipated. Instead, she'd stuck around for revenge.

Macy's mind continued to race. Did she try to intervene? There were at least half a dozen men present. She'd faced those kinds of odds before and came out on top, but not without the Stellar suit and at least some measure of protection. Could she perform the same in jeans and a T-shirt? Would revealing her identity by attacking in her street clothes place her family in greater danger?

Zmija entered the passenger side of the SUV and the vehicle tore out of the driveway, passing Macy seconds later as the driver sped towards the end of the road and turned the corner. A moment later it was gone and Patrick and his father with it.

"They're gone! They're gone!" Macy said breathlessly into her phone as she ran.

"Who's gone?" There was confusion in Keri's voice. "What are you talking about?"

Macy stopped and concentrated on breathing. She'd run four blocks and her body was about done. "Patrick and his father. Zmija took them. When I got to the house... Zmija was there and she took them."

There was a shocked silence on the other end. "O–okay. Where are you now?"

"On my way back to my house." Macy started walking again, her pace as fast as she could manage while trying to breathe and talk at the same time.

"I'll meet you there." Keri hung up.

Macy turned onto her street as a set of headlights illuminated and a car sped away from a curb up ahead. Was it... it was at her house. She watched as her mom's Ford Freestyle sped past her and turned the corner. She looked after the SUV until it was out of sight and then ran for her house, her purse flopping around behind her. She crossed the street and arrived at the sidewalk, seeing her front door wide open.

"Mom? Dad?" She ran through the door and stopped. Pictures from the walls, shoes from their shoe rack, and random items from a folding desk in the hallway lay strewn about and the banister on the steps had been broken down. "Mom? Oh my god."

She turned this way and that, running a hand through her hair as she desperately tried to figure out what she needed to do. Why had Zmija come here? Did she know who Stellar was? She shook her head. She couldn't possibly know unless… Grandad. A sinking feeling hit her. Had Grandad's presence at the meeting last night exposed them all?

"Grandad? Anyone?"

She ran up the steps two at a time, pushing open her parents' bedroom door. Nothing. The upstairs hallway and bedrooms hadn't been touched, which meant the invaders had found what they were looking for on the ground floor.

She bounded down the steps and made for the kitchen.

"Ugh… Macy?"

"Dad?"

Macy ran to her father who was lying near the back door, his glasses gone and his shirt ripped. Pots and pans had been thrown about and every drawer had been pulled out and turned over.

"Dad? Are you okay?"

William Davis rose gingerly into a sitting position, a cut above his eye bleeding. Macy wiped the blood away with her sleeve, but more appeared just as quick. She choked back tears.

"Where'd Mom go? And Grandad?"

Her dad looked confused and shook his head. "I… I don't know."

"Oh no." Macy fought back a sob. "No."

"We were here in the kitchen… your mom and I… and… and there was a knock at the door and then… then a loud snap. Your grandfather yelled in the den and then… then there were just these… these people everywhere." He placed his head in his hands. A moment later he looked up again. "Becky?"

Macy stood and moved around the kitchen, looking into the dining room and hallway again for any sign of Grandad. "She left, dad. I saw her drive away."

"Drive away? When?"

Macy moved into the den. The television and the armoire it sat in had been pulled over and things from their bookshelf had been thrown about or smashed. But there was no sign of anyone. Grandad's favorite lounge chair sat askew as though he had exited it in a hurry, shoving it into the table that it sat beside and knocking the table over. She stood in the center of the room, a feeling of hopelessness descending on her. Jacqueline Wraith had come for Grandad, at least, and possibly all of them. Had her mom tried to chase them? Why else would she have driven away so fast? Had it even been her driving?

"Macy?" Keri ran up the steps and appeared at the front door. "Macy?" She entered the living room and stopped, dropping a backpack as she looked about. "Oh my God."

Macy stood looking at Keri, tears streaming down her face.

"At Patrick's, too?"

Macy managed a nod.

"Oh my God."

Macy took a deep breath and shook her head.

Her dad appeared from the kitchen, a dish towel pressed to his head.

"Dad… did they say anything?"

He shook his head. "They just yelled and yelled–'get it! yeah!

smash it!'–and started knocking over things and throwing things." He looked around. "I've got to… got to call the police and find your mom." He looked around again. "We've been… we've had a home invasion." He walked back towards the kitchen, a stunned look on his face.

Macy looked at Keri, glanced at the backpack at her feet, and then held her gaze for a long moment. They both knew this was anything but a random home invasion.

Red and blue lights danced along the walls from the squad cars in the driveway and along the street. Macy sat with Keri at the top of the steps, listening as deputies talked with her father and EMTs saw to his head.

"We've put out an APB on your wife's Ford Freestyle, Mr. Davis. If she and your father-in-law did try to chase the crooks, they should be pretty easy to spot."

"Thank you. That's… that's the only place I can think of that they'd have gone."

Macy frowned. She wasn't at all certain that it had been her mother or grandfather who had passed her on the street. The windows of the SUV had been tinted by whoever had owned it previously and her mom hadn't changed it, which meant seeing into the vehicle at night was difficult at best. Her mom liked it that way because she thought it deterred thieves since they couldn't see what valuables if any might be inside. But why would Zmija and her thugs have taken her mom's car? Maybe they'd arrived in the same SUV that had been at Patrick's. Maybe they'd been dropped off and had taken her mom's car to get away. But then where were her mom and Grandad? Had they taken both of them the way they had taken Patrick and his father? If so, why leave her dad? Macy felt like her head was going to explode.

"There seems to be a crew of home invaders working this area tonight," one of the deputies said. "We had another report over on Azalea Circle just a few minutes ago."

Macy looked at Keri. Patrick's house. His neighbors must have finally noticed something wasn't right and grown suspicious.

"If the same crew hit Azalea," the deputy continued, "then maybe your wife and father-in-law called it in. I'm waiting now for word from the dispatcher."

"Thank you."

A pair of EMTs moved a gurney up the steps and through the front door.

"I told you I didn't need an ambulance."

"I'm afraid we have to insist on you being seen by a doctor, Mr. Davis," one of the EMTs said. "Anytime there's a head injury we have to do that."

Macy heard her father sigh in disgust.

"But my daughter… she's upstairs."

"She can stay with us tonight, Mr. Davis," Keri said.

"Your daughter's friend is right, Mr. Davis," one of the deputies said. "You should go and get yourself checked out. Those head injuries can be serious even if they don't seem like it."

Macy didn't hear any further protests from her father. He wasn't as strong-headed as her mother or grandfather. He'd give in when presented with a reasonable course of action and going to the hospital after being hit in the head with whatever he'd been hit with was reasonable in anyone's book.

"We'll finish gathering whatever evidence we can find here and make sure your daughter and her friend get settled," the deputy continued. "We'll be in touch as soon as we find your wife and father-in-law."

A while later Macy followed Keri as they climbed the steps to Keri's studio above the three-car garage at Ardmore House. Keri closed the door behind them, gave a huge shrug, and widened her eyes. "Okay… what in the…?"

Macy knew what Keri was feeling. The last hour or so had felt like an eternity as they hadn't been able to talk about anything that had actually happened in the presence of the deputies.

Macy let out a long breath. "I don't know." She held her arms up. "I don't have any idea." She was past the initial freakout, but now her body was saying it was time for the second wind freakout as her stomach began to feel like butterflies again.

"I mean… what are they going to do to Patrick and his dad?" Keri paced. "And do you think they took your mom and Grandad, too, or did he and your mom really try to chase them?"

Macy shook her head for what felt like the umpteenth time. "I really don't have any idea." She fell into the swivel chair at Keri's desk.

"I mean… are they… are they going to kill them?"

Macy stared at the multicolored flecks in the carpeting. "I'm sure they will eventually."

"Eventually?"

"They'll hurt them first… torture them for Stellar's identity."

Keri deflated into the other swivel chair. "So they can come back and do the same to you."

Macy nodded. "No doubt."

"Then we have to save them."

"How?" Macy shrugged. "Where? If you have a map to where she'd take them and some way to get there I'm game, but otherwise I don't have a clue where to even start."

Keri frowned. "I don't have a clue either, but I think I might know someone who does."

Macy looked up. "…"

Keri tossed the backpack containing the Stellar suit to her. "Luke Bartlett."

Luke Bartlett's house was as close to Oaklawn as you could get without being in it. Sometimes. His parents were divorced so he split his time between two homes, though he was usually with his mom on the weekdays because of school or so Keri had learned in a rapid series of texts with Taylor and Emma.

Macy crouched down inside a grove of trees at the edge of a postage stamp-sized yard belonging to a small-ish brick ranch. She'd really expected more in terms of housing for a Bartlett—even if his mom was a former Bartlett. Luke's father was the mayor of PSD after all and while Macy had no idea what that job paid she was sure it was more than what her parents—a real estate broker and a robotics scientist—made combined.

She pulled up the Stellar hood and it clicked into place as she surveyed the side of the house. The lights were on and she could see movement inside, but she had no idea what Luke drove and with school being out it was impossible to tell where he'd be. This idea was a roll of the dice at best.

"Yeah? Well, at dad's house I can get texts and calls anytime I want."

"This isn't your dad's house, Luke, and he doesn't have to get up at 5am."

"I don't care what time you have to get up, *Terry*. I'm sick of this dump. I'm going back to dad's."

"Hey now! You owe your mother more respect than that. We may not have much, but we work hard for every bit of it. But you know what… go. I've had it with your attitude."

"Well, then why don't you do something about it?"

"That answers that question," Macy said to herself as she heard a door slam inside the house. Apparently, Luke Bartlett was here and was being every bit the gentleman to his mother and to whoever Terry was as he usually was to his classmates and teachers. *Shocker.*

The side door of the house flew open and Luke hobbled through. In the excitement of the evening so far, Macy had nearly forgotten about the crutches and physical difficulties Luke was experiencing in the wake of his Spaz overdose. *Click. Click. Click.* Luke made his way towards a pickup truck with expensive rims parked last in line on the single lane driveway.

She waited until he'd passed her position and then ran for the truck, vaulting over a rock knee wall and landing in front of him just before he reached the driver's door.

"Hey!"

She stood slowly, making eye contact. Alook of recognition crossed his face followed quickly by a flash of fear. Stellar had kicked his butt once already and he clearly knew she could do it again.

"You."

"Me," Macy smirked.

Luke's eyes darted between her and the truck door. "What do you want?" He took a step back as though he was expecting an attack.

"Not to hurt you. It looks as though someone else has already done a fine job of that."

Luke scoffed.

"I want to know where Jacqueline Wraith calls home."

"Who?"

"I guess you're more familiar with her darkly-clad alter ego… the hat… the robes… the voice that sounds like she gargled broken glass."

Luke made a face like that of someone preparing to vomit. "I don't know anything about—"

"Cut the crap, big boy. I've seen you with her twice now. Once at the school and again when she dosed you with Spaz," Macy motioned to the crutches, "and caused your current condition."

Luke adjusted the crutches and frowned.

"If she'll do that to someone loyal to her imagine what she'll do to someone who's not."

"That witch cost me everything. My senior year in football. Any chance I had at a college scholarship."

"So, here's your chance to get a bit of comeuppance. You tell me what you know and I'll open up a can on her... all nice and professional-like."

Luke scoffed. "Alright. You've heard of Blackville House?"

Macy nodded.

"Apparently she's got some major 'mommy didn't love me' issues so she hangs out at an abandoned Renaissance Fair she found as a kid. I've never been there, but I've been told it's located next to the river and adjacent to the Blackville House property where she grew up."

Macy smiled devilishly. "Thanks."

"You've gotta see this," Keri said as Macy climbed into the backseat of the Uber they had used to get to Luke's.

Macy set the backpack containing the Stellar suit on the floor between them and took the phone Keri was holding out. She clicked the on button on the phone as the SUV pulled away from the curb and started back toward Ardmore House. The screen lit up with the whited-out cityscape background of the Stellar website and a moment later the red and blue-outlined logo Patrick had designed for Stellar appeared. At the top of the site was a new video entry time-stamped for only minutes earlier.

Macy clicked the play button and waited for it to load. Her eyes narrowed as Zmija appeared on the screen holding a gagged and kneeling Patrick up by his hair. Macy studied the background quickly but found nothing of use–only a weathered brick wall that could be located anywhere. Patrick struggled, but Zmija jerked his head back where she wanted it.

"Hmph… this message is for you Stellar. As you can see, I have your friend here. Also in my possession are the sons and daughters of the city council, the district attorney, and the police chief as well as a bumbling school resource officer and the spy monger who aided my dear sweet sister in betraying our mother all those years ago. Thanks to your interference and the reemergence of our old enemy Luminesa you've moved my timeline up considerably. Hmph… you will both show yourselves tomorrow night at Fallon Park where you will surrender to being unmasked. If you do not the old man, the rent-a-cop, and all of the children will be given a concentrated dose of Spaz and set loose in Yardley Square." Zmija jabbed a syringe filled with neon green liquid into Patrick's neck and pointed at the screen threateningly. "8pm at the Fallon Fountain. Come alone. I am prepared to do whatever it takes. Are you?" The video went black.

Macy closed her eyes and took a deep breath. *Spy monger?* She knew where Grandad was now, but what about her mom? Had anyone heard from her yet? And surely unmasking wasn't all Zmija had planned. She'd murder both Stellar and Luminesa and then spaz up the hostages anyway. What did she have to lose? Her secret was out and her plans were exposed. Something needed to be done and it needed to be done much sooner than tomorrow night.

"Sounds like this Stellar's in real trouble now," said the Uber driver, glancing into the rearview mirror. "But I remember Luminesa. She'll find a way out of it for everyone. She always did."

Macy forced a smile. It would be something if the driver was right, but how did anyone know for sure that the Luminesa who would undoubtedly see the message was the same Luminesa who had played such an integral role in the first defeat of The Alderwoman? That person, whoever she was, would have to be in her forties or fifties at least by now, which made it far more likely that whoever had rescued Macy was someone new. Maybe this someone new wouldn't have the same luck. Maybe getting the drop on a basement full of distracted bad guys beating on a teenager was the best she had. Maybe…

Macy stopped and stared at the back of the seat in front of her. Maybe her mom was Luminesa. *No way.* She tried to dismiss the thought, but doing so didn't feel right. Her parents had lied to her in her bedroom and she'd known it. But if her mom was Luminesa and her dad was in on it… did that mean Grandad had lied to her, too? He'd claimed to not know who Luminesa was, but how could he not know his own daughter was the crime fighter who'd helped take down The Alderwoman when he had been so involved in doing so?

She blinked at her own stupidity as anger rose from her stomach into her chest. How could she have been so dense? She thought back over recent events. Whoever had rescued her had known her well enough to take her back to Alum Ridge or to at least craft that as a story and she'd known the list of people who could have done that was small, but maybe not as small as she'd thought. Maybe her mom belonged on that list along with Grandad and Keri. Maybe both her parents did.

"What hospital would they have taken my dad to?"

Keri furrowed her brow. "Community I'm sure."

"Can we go there? I need to see him."

"You got it. Change of plans, miss. Do you mind? I have cash." Keri held up a few twenties so the driver could see it in the rear view mirror.

The driver nodded. "Not at all."

Macy frowned. "Sorry. I just… he's alone. And I need to find out if he's heard anything from my mom."

"Wait. I'm coming with you," Keri said at the curb of the hospital as Macy slid out, pulling the backpack out of the SUV after her.

"No. Not this time." Macy gave her a knowing look. "This is a Davis family affair."

Keri frowned but gave a small nod. "Okay."

Macy closed the door and watched as the Uber pulled away. *What now, Macy?* She followed the SUV out of the lot with her eyes and then stood looking at the hospital entrance, the weight of the world bearing down on her. Whatever her dad could could say she wasn't interested in hearing right now. She wanted to talk to her mom and she was certain she wasn't here. If Stellar had figured out where Zmija was Luminesa would, too. She held up a hand and let out a loud whistle, signaling a nearby taxi.

CHAPTER 24

"You sure you want to go out here, miss?"

The taxi driver's words repeated in Macy's head as she looked over a rusted gate that briefly interrupted a stone wall. One side of the gate was hanging from a single hinge and the property beyond was covered in leafy green vines. After an eighty dollar cab ride to the crest of the Panorama Heights and at least a mile hike up an ill-maintained private road, she was finally looking at Blackville House–or at least what remained of it.

Was she sure she wanted to be here? No. But she was and she couldn't think of anywhere else she needed to be more. Somewhere adjacent to this property her mother was either fighting or getting ready to fight Zmija she was sure of it. The more she had rolled the idea around the more it had seemed like a sure thing. Topping the pile of evidence was the way her mom had taken off so fast after their home had been broken into and Grandad abducted. What other explanation could there be? Who else would have been driving and where else could she have gone other than to figure out where they'd taken her father and to get him back?

Macy latched Stellar's utility belt around her waist and brought the hood up, the magnets finding their match inside her helmet with a *click* and securing it in place. She took out the tactical flashlight in one of the compartments on the belt and clicked it on, illuminating a wrought iron crown insignia placed ominously in the center of the formally ornate gate. She pulled a twisted vine loose from the gate and kicked at the rusted hinge until it broke loose and the gate fell inward with a rusty screech.

Starting out in a jog, she jumped potholes and puddles like an American Ninja Warrior contestant until she stood at the center of a circular driveway belonging to a three-story chateau-like house with high arched windows and a gothic perpendicular roof. She shined the light along the walls. It was just as Grandad had said; a ruin. Windows had been smashed in and vandals had covered the walls with expletives and crude drawings.

But she wasn't here for the house. She only needed it to orient herself to the location of the abandoned Renaissance Fair Luke had talked about. She'd tried searching online and had only found a few references, but no location. Apparently, it had opened and closed long before the internet was a thing and existed now only for abandoned building enthusiasts to find and photograph.

Wherever the fair was it had to be close enough that a child could run to it. A horn sounded in the distance and Macy turned the light to the far side of the house. She recognized the sound as that of the increasing water level warning on Lafayette Dam. The spillways were preparing to open and release excess water from Lake Wasena into the Ocran River. She moved toward the sound. If the abandoned fair was located along the river as Luke had said, the dam was a good indicator of the direction she needed to go.

She plowed through waist-high grass into a grown over forest as the first of the ninety-second warnings faded. Breaking off branches and stepping over fallen trees, she made her way towards the sound until she spotted a clearing ahead. The tree cover broke just enough for a long-forsaken road to cut through the forest. The road stretched into the distance. She swept the light along the route and stopped on a set of deep trenches in the road—tire tracks. Judging by the clear presence of the tread pattern, Macy was sure the tracks had been made recently and belonged to a heavy vehicle like an SUV.

She followed the tracks, eventually coming to a single lane wooden bridge covered with rotting leaves. Just beyond the bridge a weathered sign with an arrow read *Carriage Parking $3. Geez. No wonder this place failed commercially and was abandoned.* It was located so far off the beaten path only someone who'd set out to find it ever would. And who really ever cared about Renaissance Parks except for history aficionados and the tabletop gaming crowd? Surely those weren't a large enough segment of the population to support a badly located theme park.

Macy kept the light low to hide her presence and crossed the bridge, feeling the surface beneath her boots harden as the trees cleared completely and two staggered rectangular lots led to a caved-in hut with signage that read *Ye Olde Ticket Booth*. Nature had long since retaken the parking area as weeds had grown through cracks in the pavement and tree roots had created tall bulges.

The second of the dam warnings sounded as Macy surveyed the scene. From her position at the top of the parking area, she could see down into the fair all the way to the river. Lights blinked on the dam in the distance and the spired roofs of castle replicas stuck out above more overgrown trees. Had Luke been wrong? Had she come here for nothing? There were no signs of a fight and the place looked as abandoned as ever. But it would be the perfect hideout and the tire tracks told her someone had been here in recent days.

She lifted the light and swept it over the areas below. The beam glinted off of something in the trees and she swept it back toward the source, revealing the dark-colored metal of an SUV tailgate. She clicked the light off and made her way down, passing the ticket booth. Tucked into a perfectly-sized notch in the tree cover was the SUV she'd seen leaving Patrick's house. A winding path led away from the booth and the vehicle toward the grounds of the park. Had the fight not yet begun… or was it already over?

She followed the winding path, taking her steps more cautiously and staying close to the treeline to hide her approach. She reached a drawbridge and realized the park was surrounded by a wall and a moat that was now more of a swamp. Up close, the place looked even more abandoned than it had from above.

She stepped onto the drawbridge and made for the arched gateway. There were enough shadows cast by the walls to hide her as she snuck around the inside of the park. Keeping her eyes moving for any signs of activity inside, she crossed through the gateway. A faint *click* preceded a hollow *thunk* and a spotlight lit up her position. A portcullis fell across the gateway behind her with the rattle of retreating chains and a powerful slam.

Macy turned this way and that, her eyes wide and her heartbeat accelerating as outdoor fog lights lit up the park one by one. From somewhere above, gloved hands clapped slowly. Macy looked to a darkened doorway atop a stone staircase leading into a castle.

"Hmph… welcome, Stellar." Zmija appeared in the opening. "I congratulate you. You've proven your resourcefulness a few times now, so your presence here tonight was expected."

Macy deflated inside. She'd walked right into a trap. Her confidence vanished and was replaced by welling up fear as thugs appeared from other openings in the castle and doorways of the half-timber buildings located further into the park. Rattling chains sounded from a nearby opening and preceded the appearance of Patrick, an emaciated Brittany Crumb, and a chain gang of other teens all shackled with medieval irons. Deputy Newell and Grandad shuffled out last, Grandad's eyes falling on Macy and his expression communicating the kind of dread that was making her insides shrink. She'd never faced numbers like this before and the result surely wouldn't be in her favor.

"Hmph… now the city can see what happens to people who want to play hero." Zmija made her way down the steps withdrawing a vial filled with neon green liquid and a syringe gun from her coat. "You've shown remarkable skill in… hmph… martial arts and hand-to-hand combat, Stellar. When the police have to unload a hundred rounds into you tomorrow morning to prevent you from using those skills on pedestrians… hmph… in the banking district the people will be much more apt to listen when next I make demands."

Macy's teeth were clenched tight, but she managed to steel herself just enough to avoid her voice trembling. "Then the meeting in Fallon Park was a ruse."

"Correct. By this time… hmph… tomorrow there won't be any need for a meeting. The city will have seen firsthand what happens when someone's on my little special blend here and city council will have no choice but to bow to my wishes."

"But this is America. You can't think other cities and states or the feds are just going to stand by while you take over PSD and rule it like your own fiefdom. That kind of stuff might work when you're operating in dark alleys and smokey rooms, but not if people actually know what's happening."

"A minor setback… hmph… and a small change in my timetable, true, but The Alderwoman will return to rule this city and the fortunes of the Blackville-Wraiths will be restored… hmph… and they'll all have me to thank for it."

Macy scoffed. "Is that what this is to you? Mommy looks at me I'm a big kid now? What makes you think she'll respect you anymore now than she ever did? What makes you think someone like your mother's love was ever based on ability and not just pretty faces? Because I've seen your face, Jacqueline, and I'm sure time hasn't done you any favors since those photos were taken."

"Faces?" Zmija loaded the vial into the syringe gun. "Hmph… you want to talk about faces?"

Macy dropped into a defensive position. "You don't really think you're going to jab that in my neck without a fight, do you?"

"What makes you think I'd start with you?" Zmija cocked the syringe gun and turned, firing the vial like a dart.

"No!"

Three loud whistles sounded and Macy grimaced, holding her eyes tightly shut as explosions of light happened around her. She knew the sound–Luminesa was here. More whistles sounded like incoming mortars in a war movie. Macy felt the shock waves, but she opened her eyes, keeping her vision focused on the ground in front of her as she launched into a front kick directed at Zmija. The attack connected and she heard Zmija cry out as she was driven to the ground, the syringe gun clattering away over the cobblestones.

"Argh! Get her!"

Macy turned and began to make her way towards the hostages. Maybe she could get them to safety while Luminesa's distraction was still effective. The group of them had hit the deck as the chaos had erupted and lay groping in different directions for safety. "This way."

Macy made for the end of the row where she spotted Grandad. She took his hands and helped him up. "C'mon!"

"Ahh… I… uhh…"

Macy looked back. "No!"

Zmija's dart had found its target in Grandad's chest and he stood trying to bring his hands up to knock the vial loose, but his restraints prevented him from reaching it. His face twisted into a grimace as the green liquid emptied. He blinked rapidly.

"Oh no." Macy knocked the syringe away, but more than half the liquid was already gone. "C'mon. We've gotta get out of here." She pulled him in the direction of the doorway the hostages had come from. She wasn't sure what was inside, but whatever it was would offer at least some protection from the fight.

"Yah!" a thug jumped into their path and raised his fists.

Macy let go of Grandad. "Keep going." She blocked a punch and then another, launching her foot into the thug's groin as he made to protect his face. The man collapsed. The hostages' chains rattled as they continued to shuffle into the doorway, finally disappearing into the darkness. More explosions sounded and more shock waves passed over the area threatening to throw Macy off her balance, but she steeled herself.

"Get the keys!" a deep, but feminine voice yelled.

Macy turned back, shielding her eyes, but catching a glimpse of Luminesa as she let loose another volley of explosives with a powerful, but smooth wave of her arm. The hero wore a light blue and silver suit but vanished into a flash of light as one of her bombs exploded and Macy had to look away.

"Get the keys!" she repeated from somewhere up ahead.

Macy focused on the ground again, scanning until she saw the edge of a black robe–Zmija. She moved to the downed villain, staying low as light bombs whistled and exploded and thugs fell around her.

She pulled at the robes, searching for a pocket or belt that might contain a set of keys.

"No!" Zmija growled, sitting up and grabbing Macy's arms.

Macy closed her eyes and drove her head forward, pushing past the rim of Zmija's hat and connecting with her brow.

"Argh!"

The villain lost her grip as Macy felt a set of glasses break beneath the force of her headbutt. She felt the impact through her helmet, but no pain. She opened her eyes to see Zmija fall away, her hat missing, and a set of dark, medical-like sunglasses broken in half on her pale face. The villain brought her hands up, knocking away the glasses as she gripped her forehead.

Macy tore back into the black robes, pushing them aside until she reached the body underneath. The villain writhed and screamed and tried swatting her hands away, but Macy kept at it, her suit and helmet easily blocking the weak strikes.

"Argh!"

The villain sat up again and Macy threw a punch, connecting with her face and knocking her out cold.

"There. That's more like it." She reached around her body until she felt a set of keys hanging from her belt. She undid the belt and pulled it loose, causing the keys to fall free.

"Got 'em!" she yelled, turning to look for Luminesa, but the battle had moved on. Explosions of light and painful shouts now came from the inner areas of the castle. How did Luminesa move so fast? An explosion would come from one window or door and then another, followed by falling or fleeing thugs. Macy took a deep breath and refocused. Her questions about Luminesa could be answered after the hostages were freed.

She stood, facing off with a thug as he rushed at her, but then thought better of it and retreated in the opposite direction. She moved toward the doorway where she'd left the hostages, jumping over unconscious bodies as she went.

"Here!" She entered the doorway, leafing through the keys. Most were normal-sized keys you would find on any keychain, but one stuck out. It was a long iron-looking key with a circular bow and a flag-like pin that made it look medieval.

"Ughhh!" Grandad writhed, holding his chest.

"He's hurting. He's not going to make it," Deputy Newell yelled.

"Arghhhh!" Grandad sat up, his face twisted in anger as he pulled at his shirt trying to free it from his chest.

Macy knocked his hands away, gripped his shoulders, and looked him in the eye. "No! You've got to fight it!"

"I'm… trying!" The veins in his neck bulged and his face reddened.

Macy's heart sank. She remembered what Zmija had said about Luke's heart after a Spaz overdose. If a teen football player was in danger of a major heart attack from the drug, what chance did a seventy-something-year-old man have? She choked back a sob and fumbled with the key, trying to unlock his restraints. Finally, she was able to insert the key and turn it, feeling the mechanics in the lock *click* just before the restraints fell loose. She kicked the restraints toward Newell. "I've got to get him out of here."

"Go!" Newell yelled. "I've got them."

Macy nodded. "Whatever you do, stay together!"

"Go!"

Macy turned and placed an arm around Grandad's back, doing her best to support him. She had to get him someplace secure before the Spaz could take complete control. He tensed and yelled out before nearly collapsing onto her. She held him up and pulled him toward the opening. "We've got to get you someplace safe. C'mon."

They started out the door, Grandad assisting as much as he could between powerful spasms. She could feel the heat radiating from beneath his clothes. "The dam," she said to herself. "The river." Maybe water would cool him down and slow the effect of the drug until medics could arrive. Surely the police had to be en route by now, right? But this place was so far away from anything. Could anyone see anything that was happening or were they on their own?

She glanced around for any sign of Luminesa. A few brief pops and flashes came from inside the castle. The fight was winding down. The majority of Zmija's thugs had been defeated or had fled. She moved toward the river, passing the mock peasant homes and shops that made up the rest of the faux-medieval village.

"I remember you!"

Macy looked to see Zeke Pennington standing at the door of a half-timber house.

Trevor Wright stood behind him, pulling at his buddy's sleeve. "Let's go, Zeke!"

"No! She's not getting the better of us again."

"I don't have time for this!"

"Too bad, babe." Zeke ran at her.

Macy lowered Grandad to the ground. "I remember you, too. I remember kicking your butt outside the school library. Are you sure you want a Round Two?"

Zeke reared his fist back, launching into the air in a move Macy recognized as a superman punch. *Is he crazy?* She spun, swinging her leg around and thrusting it forward, easily connecting with his abdomen before his fist was anywhere near her. His eyes went wide as his momentum was stopped instantly. The air exploded from his lungs and his body folded around her foot. He fell like a dizzy kid from a seesaw, gasping for air.

Trevor arrived, his hands up in surrender as he bent down beside Zeke.

Macy returned to a neutral stance. "Congratulations on the 0-2 season, big boy. Your participation trophy's in the mail."

Trevor took hold of his fallen friend's clothes and dragged him away.

Macy returned to Grandad, struggling to stand him up and get him moving. "C'mon. You've got to help me. You're too heavy for me to carry." She tugged at him as another powerful spasm tensed his body. "C'mon, soldier!"

"Argh!" Grandad hurled himself forward and they were moving again.

Macy had no idea how long Spaz took to do its worst, but if it was anything like the drugs she'd studied in eighth-grade nursing it could be anywhere from a few minutes to a few hours. The last time she had seen anyone on a dose was when Luke had been unloaded from a truck and she had no idea how long he'd been there.

The medieval village ended abruptly and they were surrounded by trees again, a narrow path leading into the darkness beyond. Macy looked to see the blinking lights of the dam to one side. They were still heading toward the river.

A few dozen yards later a white and red sign stood at the end of the path. *DANGER! DAM & HAZARDOUS CURRENTS AHEAD.* Macy frowned but tugged Grandad past it. Hopefully, the water was calm enough on the surface to get some handfuls at least. They arrived at the river edge and Macy looked down, her heart sinking. The edge of the water was at least six feet below the bank. There was no way she could get to it without falling in.

The third and last of the high water warnings sounded and Macy looked to the dam. In the darkness, it seemed like an enormous gray submarine ominously floating just offshore. The water leaped and sloshed inches from the top. The dam was the only surface nearby that was close to the water. She pulled Grandad along the river edge, down a rusted staircase, and onto the crest of the dam. She felt her boots slide on the slick concrete as a fine, blowing mist hit her, the icy chill of the water evident on the exposed part of her face. She lowered herself to her knees and helped Grandad down beside her. Cupping her hands, she splashed water onto him, the temperature having an instant effect.

"Ahh! That's…" he breathed deeply, "that's cold."

She smiled and splashed him again. He drew himself up in a tense shiver as the water dripped from his head down his back.

"Breath," she said, splashing again. "Keep breathing."

He made to take a deep breath, but his face twisted as another spasm came.

"Fight it! Please! C'mon!" She splashed him again, but his body stayed rigid and he brought his arms into his chest, curling up. "No! Don't give up. Fight it!"

"Argh!" Grandad threw his head back and opened his arms wide, nearly knocking her down. "Pfft! Argh! Pfft!" Spittle flew from his mouth and his eyes bulged.

"No! Fight it! Please!"

Macy reached down and cupped her hands again.

A gunshot sounded and she felt the displaced air as a bullet passed her narrowly. She snapped her head toward Grandad as a piece of concrete was torn loose from the dam. The shot had missed. She slid sideways, lifting her head to the staircase as she positioned herself in front of Grandad, her arms open as if she could stop the next round.

"There is no fighting it!" Zmija stood aiming a snub-nosed revolver, her black robe-like coat blowing to one side like a cape. 'Hmph… this is the only way you stop the Spazzed."

Macy could see a wicked smile in the woman's eyes, but her mouth and nose were covered with something that looked like a black oxygen mask. But for the first time, Macy was looking at the woman's face–her real face. There were faint hints of Sara Decker and Barbara

Wraith still there, but it looked as if each were three days dead. Whatever devices and methods Zmija used to disguise herself were gone. Dark circles sat beneath her eyes and her skin was a sickly white like it had been in the high school photo. Dark, but thinning hair spilled over her shoulders and blew across her face. Macy couldn't tell how much of her look was the result of the headbutt and punch and how much was the genetic sickness that ravaged her body.

Macy opened her mouth to speak, but the words caught in her throat. What could she possibly say that would change anything this woman wanted to do? Nothing. She couldn't say anything that would change Jacqueline Wraith's outlook on the world. But she could do something to stop her. Maybe. She stood to her full height but stayed in front of Grandad.

"You have two choices, Stellar. Hmph… either he kills you while I watch or I kill him and enjoy killing you myself. Your decision."

Macy thought about Grandad's number one rule for fighting; create distance. But rules were meant to be broken, especially when done to good effect and right now she needed the opposite of distance. She needed to be closer. She needed to take that gun out of play.

"Do you really think any of this is going to change anything with your mother?" she said, inching forward. "Even if you do kill me and manage to free her from Ocran Holm do you really think she'll ever accept you as her child and heir? I've only spoken to her once, but I don't get the impression that Priori Iustitia applies to the mentally and physically infirm."

Zmija's eyes narrowed and she reached up to her face, tearing loose the black mask and exposing a mouth full of crooked teeth. "Me? Mentally infirm?" she hissed, her voice now a shrill whisper. "You know nothing. Nothing!"

"I know you killed the one person who loved you for certain–your sister, Barbara."

Zmija laughed. "Oh, yes. My perfect older sister. Older by only a few minutes, but ahead by miles in my parents' eyes. Do you know what it's like to be treated as though you're beneath the servants hired to wait on your every whim? Do you know what it's like to be superior in every invisible way," she pointed at her head, "but still looked at like you're some kind of a mutant? Perfect grades in high school, but I was passed over for valedictorian for someone prettier. Three bachelor's degrees in psychology, biology, and chemistry before most students had one. Through medical school in less than half the time it normally takes and with a specialty in medical genetics," her chest was rising and falling wildly and her voice was getting higher, "but still not good enough. But oh, don't worry… my perfect older sister with her night school medical degree and a critical care pediatrics specialization was going to save me. Oh, yes. She was going to unlock all the mysteries."

"Maybe if you could have seen past your hatred long enough to actually look at what she'd done you'd have realized she was close. I read her journal. You know… the one she was writing in when you bashed her in the head."

"Bashed her in the head?" Zmija laughed again. "Do you really think I went to all the trouble of meeting with her and working with her just to take a blunt instrument to the back of her head? No. I had other plans for dear sweet Barbara I assure you."

Macy scoffed, the distance between them slowly closing. "So, you're quite the little sneak, huh? Well, congratulations. You got the drop on the one person who accepted you as you are."

"'Sneak'? You're close. The men who worked for my mother and father had a name for me and it was close to 'sneak.' In their native tongue, they called me Zmija… snake! Do you know what it's like for a little girl to be called a snake?"

Macy shook her head. "Nope. Two folks and a grandparent who

love me, a cat who tolerates me, and some goldfish who seemed pretty happy until they were eaten by the cat." Macy smirked. "I don't have a clue what your life's been like and after everything you've done, I couldn't care less about getting one. You can blame whoever you want, but ultimately you're the one responsible for your own actions."

"Ahhh!" Zmija lowered the revolver and reached into her coat. "Eventually I began to show them just how snake-like I could be!" She produced a vial of orange Spaz from inside her coat. "Venom anyone?"

"No thanks." Macy lowered her shoulders and dug in as best she could against the slick concrete. *It's now or never.* She pushed off and Zmija flinched, her eyes widening as she raised the revolver.

"Nooooargh!"

Grandad knocked Macy aside, her boots slipping against the concrete and causing her to fall. A gunshot sounded and then another. Macy slipped and landed on the concrete, her momentum carrying her forward and the movement happening so fast she couldn't remember falling. She flipped herself over and looked, her eyes going wide as she didn't see Grandad behind her. "No... no." Had he been shot? Had he fallen over the dam? "No..."

Zmija laughed, the sound high and wheezy. "You... almost... got me."

Macy turned back, locking eyes with the villain. She planted her hands on the concrete and brought her legs up, pushing herself to her feet and jumping into a spin, her movements fueled by a rage so deep her mouth tasted metallic. The world spun with her in slow motion. A gunshot sounded and her rear foot connected with a hook kick to the arm followed by her front foot with a driving kick to the chest. She landed, hearing something heavy as it plunked into the water. Her feet slipped from under her and her momentum carried her to the concrete. The impact took her breath away, but her adrenaline forced her back to her feet. She stood into a defensive stance and looked to see Zmija bent abnormally against the edge of the rusted staircase railing, the arm that had been holding the revolver obviously broken. Pain registered on the woman's face and she fell sideways, disappearing over the edge of the dam.

Macy breathed deeply, watching as the current from the open spillway carried her enemy's body down into a thick, churning mist. She drew herself up to her full height, inhaling cold, refreshing air. She exhaled and looked about. She was alone, the world around her muted by the rushing water in the spillway.

"Grandad," she said, tears beginning to stream.

An audible *clink* sounded above the noise of the water and she turned to see Luminesa on the metal staircase, her light blue and silver suit stained with dirt. Luminesa looked to each side of the dam and then back again. Macy held her gaze as tears continued to fall.

The hero lowered her head and frowned. "I'm sorry, Macy."

Macy's breath came in short gasps. She tried to choke them back, feeling like a child needing someone to hold her. She needed the tough, lasting embrace only a mother could give, but as she stood there seeing Luminesa fully for the first time she knew her mother wasn't there. Though the hero's face was covered with a blue helmet, blonde hair flowed out of it in a high ponytail and the face beneath was narrow and angular. Luminesa wasn't Becky Davis. Macy didn't know who she was. Her eyes settled on the hero's belt. There in the center of it was a polished buckle she recognized as her own. Macy stared, the blinking lights of the dam reflecting off the Stellar symbol on Luminesa's belt.

"We have to go," Luminesa said. "The police are here and it won't take them long to find us."

Macy shook her head. "I… I can't. I can't just… just leave him."

Luminesa stepped forward and grabbed her by the shoulders, making eye contact inches from her face. "You've chosen the life of a costumed hero, Macy. This is the cost of that life. We have to go." She stepped off and made for the staircase, turning back momentarily. "Now."

Macy closed her eyes and put one foot in front of the other. Before she knew it, she was moving up the stairs, the metal sounding under her boots and then the thudding of the earth at the edge of the river. She was running away–running for her life after a blue and silver phantom that seemed to grow further away the faster she ran.

CHAPTER 25

The priest held up his hands, his palms open and his eyes cast downward onto the plain aluminum box before him. "O God, whose mercies cannot be numbered, accept our prayers on behalf of thy servant, Lee—our father, grandfather, and friend—and grant him entrance into the land of light and joy, in the fellowship of thy saints, through Jesus Christ thy Son our Lord, who liveth and reigneth with thee in the unity of the Holy Spirit, one God, now and forever. Amen."

Macy stood stiffly beside her parents, fighting back tears and a growing sob as the small crowd gathered in the walled courtyard of St. Dominic's Independent Catholic Church crossed themselves and repeated, "Amen." Deacons from the church picked up the aluminum box and reverently moved it out of the courtyard.

"It's okay, Macy." Her mom placed her arms around her gently. "Let it out."

But it wasn't okay, and Macy didn't want to let anything out. Letting it out would be like her seal of approval on a chain of events she knew to be a complete sham. Her parents had decided to hold this funeral–if that's what you wanted to call having a priest bless a government-issued aluminum box full of uniforms, medals, and other belongings and then storing it for a later date–as a way of helping everyone move on.

But move on from what? Yes, the search of the grounds at the Wasena Renaissance Faire had been concluded and the authorities had found no sign of Grandad, the only hostage still unaccounted for, but that meant nothing. Brittany Crumb had been missing for months, written off as dead by most everyone, and yet she was alive and well today. The same could be true for Grandad. No one had dredged the river below the Lafayette Dam and no body meant no death as far as Macy was concerned.

She shrugged her mother's arms away and left the courtyard through a wrought iron gate, entering a cobblestone alleyway next to the 19th-century church and choosing to stand there alone rather than be around anyone. She leaned against the cold stone walls and tears fell. If they could store a blessed box until some unspecified 'later date' why couldn't they just wait, period?

Somewhere deep down inside she knew she wasn't being fair. The police had been handed a mess of differing eyewitness accounts, conflicting statements, crudely shot videos, and half-truths that would take months to straighten out into any kind of a sensible narrative and her parents, like everyone else in the city, were simply acting on the best information they had–information that in reality wasn't ever going to be complete since the two chief witnesses who could tie it all together were masked vigilantes unable and unwilling to come forward. But she didn't care about being fair. She wanted to wait and see what happened. Maybe the combination of cold water, adrenaline, and Spaz had made it possible to survive gunshots, powerful currents, and a fall that had to be hundreds of feet at least.

The sob that had been building burst free. Who was she kidding? Water leaked from her eyes and nose and her face twisted involuntarily into a grimace as she collapsed against the church wall, sliding down to a sitting position and placing her head in her hands.

The hinges of the wrought iron gate sounded and someone rushed out. "Macy, honey!" Becky Davis hit her knees next to her teenage daughter and pulled her into a tight hug. "It's going to be okay."

"He… can't… be… dead."

"Oh, honey." Her mom rubbed the back of her head and held her. "I'm so sorry."

Macy pulled away. "You… you lied to me!" She slapped her mother's hands away. "Why did you lie to me?"

Her mother looked crestfallen. "Lied to you? Honey, about what?"

Macy heard the gate hinges sound again and other footsteps nearby. Her complete emotional breakdown was on primetime for everyone to see. *Wonderful.* She sucked in as much of the water from her face as she could, wiping at her eyes and trying to put herself back together. She looked up to see her father staring down at them, his glasses off, and blinking away tears of his own. Keri stood a few feet behind him, her face clear, but her expression informed and sympathetic. Macy looked away and concentrated on breathing. In the last handful of seconds, it was as if she had allowed a giant void to open inside her and she had no idea how to fill it again. She was lashing out–asking questions she wanted answers to and throwing caution to the wind.

"You both lied to me in my room," she choked back more tears, "why did you lie to me?"

Her mom looked over her shoulder at her dad and back again. "Honey," she shook her head, "we've never lied to you. We just didn't know what you'd be able to handle when you'd first awoken. The doctor warned us about upsetting you." She smiled. "But I think you're tougher than he was giving you credit for."

"But… where did you go when he was taken? Why weren't you there?"

"I tried to chase them," her mother looked down and shook her head again. "I didn't know what else to do. I lost them on the highway."

Macy blinked away tears and wiped her face again. Had she been wrong about her parents lying? She'd been wrong about Luminesa. Her face twisted up again and more tears came.

"It's okay," her mom said again, cupping Macy's chin and making eye contact as she reached up and took William Davis's hand. "We're going to get through this as a family."

Macy stared back at her mom, analyzing the contours of her face and the color of her hair. It was her face plus a decade or two that looked back at her. It wasn't a hero's face or at least not the hero she had thought, but–her train of thought was interrupted by another and for a long moment she sat just looking–just studying and remembering.

She closed her eyes but stayed focused on the face in front of her. Luminesa had vanished into the forests surrounding Lake Wasena not long after they'd taken off from the dam. She'd stuck around just long enough to make sure Macy was clear of being discovered by the police and then it was as if she'd never been there at all. But Macy knew she had been. Her mother's face morphed in her mind into the narrow, angular face she remembered under the mask. The contours of the face, the flowing blonde hair, the deep and authoritative voice–she remembered them all–but the clearest picture in her mind was of the belt buckle with Stellar's symbol–her symbol.

She opened her eyes. Her mother was right. She was going to get through this because she had to get through this–because there was work to be done. And work, like Grandad had said not long ago, was the best way to get better. She was going to make sure The Alderwoman never returned, she was going to protect the innocent people in PSD, she was going to find out who Luminesa was, and she was going to find out why they wore the same symbol. Stellar was going back to work.

The brick face, multiple stories, and Supreme Court-like columns of Alum Ridge High School seemed to loom further above than they had in the past as the bus pulled along the front curb and stopped with a sharp hiss of air. Macy stood from her seat and filed out onto the sidewalk.

"And so it begins," Keri said, stepping off the bus behind Macy. "Again."

"Yup." Macy nodded. It felt like it had been ages since they'd last entered this building together and in the intervening weeks so much had changed that not even arriving at school could be entirely normal. The line of buses that usually came to rest along the side of the school now lined up like fallen dominos in front of the main entrance, their usual place occupied by a newly excavated lot, more sidewalks, and at least a dozen new trailers.

"I guess this year didn't turn out quite like we'd expected, huh?" Keri clearly sensed the heaviness of the moment. "But you're closer to going out with Patrick. That's something, right?"

"Yeah. That's something."

Macy shouldered her backpack and they made their way toward the front entrance in a mass of teenagers all coming together like the end of a pine needle as they left the dozens of lined-up buses.

"Macy! Wait up."

Macy turned to see Patrick jogging up the sidewalk, a brown leather messenger bag bobbing beside him as he dodged his way through the crowd in their direction.

"Hey," he said, out of breath, as he arrived at their position. "I–uhh–I thought we could walk in together."

"Uh-oh.." A grin spread across Keri's face. "They're all gonna be shippin' it now."

Patrick blushed.

Macy smiled. "Okay."

"Hey. Real quick." Patrick opened his bag and took out his notebook. "I made something for you." He shrugged. "Again."

"Oh, great" Striker said, arriving behind Patrick and putting an arm around him. "Here we go."

Macy raised her eyebrows and stared at the blond hulk as Josh Friddle arrived.

"You cheated back there, cuz." Friddle slapped Striker on the back.

"Nuh-uh."

The two of them moved on to a bench up ahead, continuing to argue about something. Macy followed them with her eyes, doing a mental facepalm. Turning back, she looked at the page Patrick had flipped to. It was the first page in a new notebook and at the top Stellar was written in red and blue letters. Below the title, in a comic book panel, was a hand-drawn picture of a smiling, dark-haired girl sitting on the front porch steps of a house. "Name… age…" A smile stretched across Macy's face. "Birthplace—"

"She's you." Patrick interrupted.

Keri's eyes widened and she gave a quick frown that turned just as quickly into a silent laugh.

"I mean… I created Stellar the hero to honor my mom, but I decided her secret identity should honor someone else. Someone who's been there for me recently," he shrugged, "and someone who's lost a loved one recently just like I have."

Macy stared at the picture–incredulous at the detail– and scanned the point by point description of Stellar's secret identity. Hair. Eyes. He'd skipped weight–he really was a gentleman. She blushed and opened her mouth to speak. "I–uhh–I love it." She looked up at him and grinned, shaking her head in amazement.

A smile slowly stretched onto Patrick's reddening face. He shrugged and moved away toward the bench.

Keri leaned in close. "I can live with this ending."

"Ending?" Macy raised an eyebrow. "Listen to you talking like this is over." She made eye contact. "Stellar's only just getting started."

ALUM RIDGE
THE END... FOR NOW

BE THE FIRST TO FIND OUT THE LATEST STELLAR NEWS, SPECIAL OFFERS, AND TO STAY IN TOUCH WITH TEAM STELLAR AS WE WORK TO BRING YOU MORE STELLAR NOVELS BY SIGNING UP FOR STELLAR FAN MAIL TODAY! WHEN YOU SIGN UP YOU WILL RECEIVE A FREE STELLAR MINI-COMIC, CHARACTER DOSSIERS, AND A MAP OF PORT SAINT DOMINIC – ALL EXCLUSIVELY FOR FAN MAIL SUBSCRIBERS!